ADVANCE PRAISE FOR *COME MIDNIGHT*

"Summoning all readers. Veronica Sattler delivers danger, redemption, and a great love story. What else do you need?"

—*New York Times'* best-selling author
Kasey Michaels

"No one writes the Regency period better than Veronica Sattler. A devilishly good read! Anyone who reads this book is going to be blown away, is going to love it!"

—Maggie Osborne, author of
I Do, I Do, I Do and *Band of Gold*

"Veronica Sattler weaves a tapestry of epic proportions with COME MIDNIGHT. This powerful and poignant tale is historical fantasy at its very best!"

—Deb Stover, award-winning author of
No Place for a Lady

MORE RAVES!

"Ms. Sattler's unique style of bringing her characters to life while accurately depicting the era is what turns ordinary storytelling into unforgettable reading."

—*Romantic Times* on A TRUE PRINCE,
a Top Pick for December 2000

"With ONCE A PRINCESS, Veronica Sattler delivers an exciting, tender and more than satisfying fairy-tale-like romance."

—*Romantic Times* on ONCE A PRINCESS,
a Top Pick for August 2001

BOOK YOUR PLACE ON OUR WEBSITE AND MAKE THE READING CONNECTION!

We've created a customized website just for our very special readers, where you can get the inside scoop on everything that's going on with Zebra, Pinnacle and Kensington books.

When you come online, you'll have the exciting opportunity to:

- View covers of upcoming books
- Read sample chapters
- Learn about our future publishing schedule (listed by publication month *and author*)
- Find out when your favorite authors will be visiting a city near you
- Search for and order backlist books from our online catalog
- Check out author bios and background information
- Send e-mail to your favorite authors
- Meet the Kensington staff online
- Join us in weekly chats with authors, readers and other guests
- Get writing guidelines
- AND MUCH MORE!

Visit our website at
http://www.kensingtonbooks.com

COME MIDNIGHT

Veronica Sattler

ZEBRA BOOKS
KENSINGTON PUBLISHING CORP.
http://www.kensingtonbooks.com

ZEBRA BOOKS are published by

Kensington Publishing Corp.
850 Third Avenue
New York, NY 10022

All Kensington titles, imprints and distributed lines are available at special quantity discounts for bulk purchases for sales promotion, premiums, fund-raising, educational or institutional use.

Special book excerpts or customized printings can also be created to fit specific needs. For details, write or phone the office of the Kensington Special Sales Manager: Kensington Publishing Corp., 850 Third Avenue, New York, NY 10022. Attn. Special Sales Department. Phone: 1-800-221-2647.

Zebra and the Z logo Reg. U.S. Pat. & TM Off.

First Printing: February 2002
10 9 8 7 6 5 4 3 2 1

Printed in the United States of America

For Sara

Author's Note

In the mid-eighties, having two published romances under my belt, I first tried my hand at writing a romance set in Regency England. I called the book *The Bargain*, and the rest, as they say, is "history." Not only did *The Bargain* become my first national best-seller; it won me critical acclaim that included a Gold Certificate from *Affaire de Coeur* magazine, and a place among the "100 All-time Favorite Books" chosen by the reviewers of *Romantic Times* magazine to celebrate its 200th issue. Moreover, it seemed readers weren't content with a single helping of Ashleigh and Brett's love story; when *The Bargain* was reissued in the nineties, it became a national best-seller all over again!

But its "history" didn't end there. For years, I thought of writing a sequel. Indeed, the mail I received from readers asked and pleaded for one. But to be a sequel worthy of what has arguably become a classic of the genre, the story had to be special. A germ of an idea arose, spent several years perking and brewing in my imagination, and finally emerged as the novel you have here. I feel *Come Midnight* is, in every way, a worthy sequel to *The Bargain*. I hope you agree.

Foreword

Romance has a long history. Long before the term applied to the genre comprising the lion's share of today's popular fiction, romance occupied a place in the consciousness of Western man. From the chansons de geste of the troubadours in the Middle Ages, to the art of the Romantic Movement in early nineteenth century Europe, to the stuff of countless stories, films and songs of the past century, romance has snagged our collective imagination and stubbornly refused to let go.

It is an idealized form, to be sure, its trappings belonging more often to the world of the imagination than that reflected by the six-o'-clock news. Romance embodies lofty themes and distant or exotic settings, larger-than-life heroes and darker-than-dark foes. Yet for all its departure from reality, the best romance speaks to us of universal truths in the human condition: of quintessential conflicts, like the struggle between good and evil; of themes like sacrifice for honor's sake and the quest for undying love. The tale you are about to read here is no exception.

Some say it is an English tale, born in Kent, among the gently rolling hills south of London, country the English call the downs. Some insist it is Irish, or at least that it began in Ireland, moving on to London before it ended in Kent, but Irish all the same. Most agree it has elements of both, and there are Americans who swear they've heard it told for generations on their side of the Atlantic. It is a tale told in great houses and small, often before a cozy fire in the dead of winter, though a campfire on a soft summer night will do.

Whatever its origins, this is a cautionary tale, and not for the faint of heart. It is a story of an unforgettable woman and the extraordinary man who became her destiny. It is a romance in every sense of the word: the story of a great love, certainly, of high ideals and noble acts, but of darker things as well. Did it really happen? Who can say? I am but the storyteller, the vehicle by which the events, as I first heard them, are recorded in written form. Nearly two centuries have passed since those events unfolded. Who can say how many more years will pass before they are lost in the mists of time? Read on, then, before they are lost forever.

Prologue

County Cork, Ireland, 1815

Crionna was dying. Caitlin had known, of course. Long before she'd planted herself at the old woman's bedside and begun her vigil. She'd had the dream more than a fortnight ago, and the dreams never lied. Caitlin wished to God they did. And not just because of Crionna.

Caitlin O'Brien's dreams weren't like the dreams of ordinary people. When others awoke, they could happily dismiss the things they'd seen in sleep. "Wasn't that a lovely dream?" they could say. Or even, "Oh, what a terrible dream!" And that would be an end to it. It was only a dream, after all. But not with Caitlin. When Caitlin awoke, she was frightened.

And then there were the visions. They were even more frightening. Ordinary people never had visions at all. Portents that suddenly filled the mind, even when wide awake. Aye, frightening.

The Sight, Crionna called it. Caitlin called it a curse. Not that she'd ever done so to Crionna's face. Crionna was a *bhean uasal*, after all ... an "honored woman," in the Gaelic still spoken in the village. Once Caitlin had heard one of the Sassenachs who lived on the big estate call her "the wise woman." But no matter what the language, Caitlin had reasons aplenty to honor the old woman. Crionna was the only mother she'd ever known. Crionna loved her.

A soft moan drew Caitlin's attention to the shrunken figure on the bed. "Crionna? Are ye ... Can ye hear me?"

"I can, *macushla*." The old woman's voice was thready, weak. "How ... long have I slept?"

Their tiny cottage on the outskirts of the village boasted no clocks, but Caitlin was used to judging time by other means. "A few hours," she replied, noting the length of the shadows outside the open doorway. It was late afternoon, and because the day was unseasonably warm for October, she had left the door ajar ....

'Twas not the true reason you left it open, she chided herself. *Admit it,* colleen. *You wanted the comfort of sunlight about you. You're frightened, and the shadows—*

"Too long!" Crionna's voice rose, distress in its papery rasp. "Ye ought t' have wakened me, lass. I've ... things t' tell ye ... not much time—"

"Crionna, please don't—"

"Hush, lass. 'Tis not long fer this world I am, and we both know it. Pretendin' itherwise is foolish, and I've niver been a fool." The old woman's eyes, still a keen, piercing blue in the wizened face, drilled into Caitlin's. "Nor did I raise one."

No, she'd not been raised a fool. Crionna meant "wise" in the Gaelic, and Caitlin knew her foster mother had lived up to her name. There were those in the village, though, who'd thought Crionna the fool for taking in another woman's child. Especially when times were hard. When everyone, let alone a solitary old woman, had all they could do to feed and clothe themselves.

But it was just that that had led Pegeen O'Brien, newly widowed and left with a brood of hungry children, to give away her newborn. " 'Tis not that yer ma didn't love ye," Crionna had reminded Caitlin over the years. " 'Tis that she loved ye enough t' give ye up. She'd not see ye starve."

Caitlin had accepted this. Yet she often wondered what it might have been like to know her true mother. To have brothers and sisters she could speak with . . . laugh with . . . aye, even cry with. But Pegeen had left the village mere days after surrendering her youngest to the *bhean uasal*. Caitlin had never known her.

" 'Twas the only way, lass," Crionna had once explained. "Yer ma couldn't live nearby. The poor woman would always be reminded o' the babe she'd given up. 'Twould have made it all the harder." It made sense. Nevertheless, Caitlin couldn't help—

"Yer ma loved ye, lass. Niver doubt it."

Caitlin's wide green eyes flew to the old woman's face. It wasn't the first time Crionna had seemed to read her mind. Yet she couldn't help being startled. Too much of exactly that sort of thing had been happening lately. Her nerves were stretched to the breaking point.

"Don't fash yerself, *macushla*," Crionna murmured. "We two have iver been close"—she gave a dry rasp that might have been a chuckle—"and yer lovely face niver could hide a thing. 'Tis an open book ye are, Caitlin O'Brien."

Caitlin nodded. Still, she felt there was more to it than Crionna was admitting. The *bhean uasal*, while not possessed of the Sight herself, certainly had skills that ordinary folk didn't. Father O'Malley, the priest in the village, called Crionna a heathen and a heretic. And while Caitlin thought that was going too far, she knew in her heart that Crionna was only nominally Christian. That the *bhean uasal's* true faith had its roots in the Old Ways. The beliefs and customs of the ancient Celts. She also suspected mind reading was the least of the skills her foster mother had from the Old Ways.

No one knew how old Crionna was. Or where she'd come from, who'd raised her. She'd seemed old even when Caitlin was a child. People in the village said the *bhean uasal* had always been here. Her wee cottage hidden in the wood, with its racks of dried herbs and—

"As I was sayin', lass," Crionna went on, "yer ma loved ye. But 'tis time ye knew what else drove her t' part with ye."

"What . . . else?" This was the first Caitlin had heard of anything new in the matter. That Crionna had waited nineteen years to mention it, whatever it was, had her eyeing the old woman warily.

Crionna ran her tongue over lips that were dry and cracked. Caitlin quickly poured her a cup of the herbal tea she'd brewed while the old woman slept. Slipping her hand behind the *bhean uasal's* head, she carefully propped her up and held the cup to her lips while she took a few swallows.

Crionna nodded and motioned the cup away. She met Caitlin's eyes. "Yer ma was frightened, colleen, just as ye're frightened now."

The green eyes widened. "Frightened? What are ye—"

"I'll not lie t' ye, lass. 'Twasn't in me head t' take ye home with me at first. I was the village midwife in those days. I was there . . . merely t' see t' yer birthin'. And as I sometimes did when a new life came into the world, I told the mother what I saw.''

''What ye *saw?*'' What was Crionna saying? That she had the Sight, after all? ''But ye've always told me ye don't—''

''I don't. Not in the way o' yer own gift, lass. I've niver had visions . . . or the dreams. But sometimes—not very often, mind ye, but occasionally, when helpin' t' birth a child I . . . sensed things. And niver more strongly than that night.''

Caitlin felt oddly apprehensive . . . uneasy. Why was Crionna telling her these things only now? ''Ye *sensed* it about me . . . from the very start? That I'd have—''

''The Sight, aye. As strong as I've iver felt it.''

Caitlin heaved a weary sigh. ''And when ye told me ma . . . Ach, Crionna! Small wonder she was—''

''I had t' tell her, lass. Ye see, Pegeen sensed somethin' herself. 'What peculiar eyes she has!' she said t' me. 'Green as moss. Not the deep blue of a newborn's, and I've seen enough t' know. They frighten me, Crionna. They look like divil's eyes!' ''

Caitlin gasped and couldn't quell a shudder. *Devil's eyes! Holy Mother—*

''Stop it, lass!'' Crionna's gnarled, age-spotted hand reached out from the bedclothes. Her grip on Caitlin's arm was surprisingly strong. ''There's not a grain o' truth in what Pegeen said. And I told her so . . . just as I'm tellin' ye now. As I've told ye countless times before. Yer gift, like yer lovely eyes, has nothin' evil about it!''

''But if me own ma—''

''People fear what they don't understand, *macushla.*'' Crionna's voice was growing weaker, and she motioned the girl close. There was so little time. It was important she not miss anything.

''Ignorance . . .'' The old woman spoke slowly, as if

measuring out words against the strength she had left. " 'Tis at the root of all ... superstition. When I explained, I ... think Pegeen finally accepted ... believed yer gift wasn't evil. Yet she was still frightened. And who could blame her? 'Tis a grave responsibility ... rearin' a babe has the Sight. The gift holds no evil, just as I said. Yet one who has it must be taught ... if 'tis t' be used fer good. Impossible t' do it ... if the one who raises the child ... doesn't understand."

Caitlin nodded pensively. Father O'Malley thought the thing was evil. Was he ignorant? But a priest was a learned man. Father O'Malley educated the parish children, and Caitlin herself had been one of his stellar pupils. How could an educated man of God be accounted superstitious?

Again, it was as if Crionna had read her thoughts. "Father O'Malley understood the least!" she spat. "I niver regretted takin' ye and rearin' ye as me own, lass. But sendin' ye t' the priest fer schoolin' was a mistake! I wish—"

A fit of coughing seized her. Caitlin bit her lip as spasms wracked the old woman. She hurriedly raised the pillow beneath the narrow shoulders—when had Crionna grown so spare?—so she could breathe better. It seemed to help. The *bhean uasal* closed her eyes and sank back against the mattress, finally quiet. Too quiet.

Mother of God, is she ... ? Caitlin placed a hand atop the faded quilt covering the old woman's chest. She let out a breath she hadn't known she'd been holding. A barely detectable rise and fall, but it was there. *Just asleep, then.*

She began to settle back to resume her vigil. Then a glance at the lengthening shadows in the room had her rising quickly. She checked the level of water in the kettle hanging from a crane at the hearth. Swinging it back over the fire, she measured out some herbs for more tea. Grabbing a spill from the mantel, she lit it from the fire. Only when she'd lit every lamp and candlestick in the room did she return to watch at the bed.

Crionna hadn't moved at all. Caitlin found herself checking her breathing again. Shallow . . . the same as before. She ran troubled eyes over the *bhean uasal*, noting the myriad wrinkles in the beloved face, the sparse white hair lying lank on the pillow. With a sigh, she sat back in her chair, letting her mind drift.

Crionna had been after her all her life to accept the Sight . . . her gift, as she called it. To see the good it could do, and not deny it. But it had been hard. Father O'Malley had been present at one of her earliest visions . . . .

They'd been at lessons. Caitlin had seen a hazy light around little Kevin McCarthy. Suddenly a great white bandage had appeared on his head. It had completely covered his hair, which was even redder than Caitlin's. She'd cried out, stammering to the whole class what she saw.

Father O'Malley had been extremely overset . . . and angry, she thought. And a week later, hadn't young Kevin gone and fallen from that tree where he'd been pilfering apples? Hadn't he cracked his foolish skull open, requiring the very sort of bandage she'd seen?

Father O'Malley had gone straightaway to Crionna when he heard. They'd had angry words over it. Caitlin had been sent outside and couldn't hear what they said exactly; but the anger in their raised voices had been plain enough.

There'd been other visions over the years . . . and dreams. None in front of the priest, thank the Blessed Virgin, but Father O'Malley still knew. Ballacairag was a small village, and people talked. After a time, the priest began to pray for Caitlin's soul. Not to mention those long "talks" he had with her after mass on Sundays. Telling her she must pray to be forgiven the sins that had brought this evil upon her.

When she grew older, she read about the saints who had experienced miraculous visions in their time. She had dared to question the priest about them. About the possibility hers might be akin to those. And hadn't that brought the good father's wrath!

" 'Tis wicked ye be, Caitlin O'Brien, t' be placin' yerself with the blessed saints!" he'd cried. "Can ye tell me one holy thing that's come of all yer black dreams and such—can ye?" And of course she couldn't. There'd never been anything discernibly religious in what she saw.

Far from it, she told herself with a shiver. *And certainly not in this latest . . . .*

Without wanting to, she found herself remembering the reason she was especially afraid lately. The dream. The first that had ever repeated itself. Three times, she'd had it now. It terrified her. For one thing, 'twas the only dream she'd ever had with herself in it. And what was *in* the dream . . . .

She was seated at a table in an unfamiliar room. A grand chamber, with velvet draped at the windows and candles burning in heavy silver holders on a huge mantelpiece. There was a game on a board before her. She'd seen pictures of chess pieces in a book, so she knew what it was. She also knew she'd never learned this game. Yet she played.

Off to the side stood a man. A tall, starkly masculine figure. He was standing in shadow, but she could still make out his features. He was dark haired and . . . beautiful. Beautiful, but for one thing: an angry scar slashed across one of his high, perfectly molded cheekbones.

Across the table from her sat a figure from a nightmare. An enormous winged creature with demonic features she avoided looking upon. Indeed, she'd glanced at it but once, then had to look away. It had been enough. She'd seen the clawed hands . . . the horned protrusions set forward in the skull . . . the soulless eyes that froze her blood: Satan. *She was playing chess with the Lord of Hell himself.*

Caitlin shuddered. She'd not told Crionna about the dream at first. She'd been too frightened even to think about it, and Crionna hadn't been well. But the old woman had heard her cry out in her sleep the second time, and she'd asked about it. By then Caitlin had been frantic and grateful for the chance to unburden herself. So she'd told the *bhean uasal . . .* all of it.

Crionna's reaction had been passing odd. True, she had cautioned Caitlin not to assume 'twas evil, just as she always had. But then she'd said she needed time to "think what to do." She had also said Caitlin was to tell her if the dream came again.

That had been over a fortnight ago, and in the meantime she'd had the dream of Crionna dying. They'd spoken no more words about the other. The third occurrence had come only last night, and what with Crionna's state, Caitlin hadn't mentioned it.

But Caitlin had had plenty of time to think the matter through. And try as she might, she couldn't help feeling the dream was a portent of evil, if not evil in itself. She'd spent a great deal of time praying, as Father O'Malley had urged so long ago. Indeed, after last night's recurrence, she'd spent the hours till dawn on her knees. 'Twas what she longed to do now as well.

With a brief glance at Crionna, Caitlin made the sign of the cross. "Hail, Mary, full of grace," she whispered . . . .

A gust of wind slammed the cottage door shut. Caitlin gave an involuntary cry. All the lamps and candles had been snuffed, throwing the room into darkness. The only light came from the embers on the hearth.

Quelling a shudder, Caitlin made herself rise and quickly set about relighting the lamps. She was building up the fire when a moan drew her to the bed.

"Are . . . are ye there, child?" Crionna's voice was weaker than before, a faded whisper. "I must—"

"Save yer strength, Crionna. Here . . . I'll brew us some fresh tea."

The old woman waved her back as she rose to fetch the kettle. "No time . . . must . . . prepare ye."

Caitlin started to argue. A look from the *bhean uasal* stopped her cold.

"Ye've . . . had the dream again . . . haven't ye, lass." It was a statement, not a question.

Caitlin nodded. "Only last night, though."

"Good . . . means we've . . . some time."

"Time? Time t' do wh—"

"Listen t' me, lass!" There was no brooking the command, thin and raspy though it was. Crionna had been formidable and impossible to thwart in her time; Caitlin heard the power of her will even now.

"Three times . . . ," the old woman went on, "means a warnin' . . . a warnin' ye . . . cannot ignore. Ye must heed this dream, Caitlin! T' do itherwise . . . 'twill mean the difference 'twixt joy and misery in yer life, *macushla*. Perhaps even . . . life or death. Ach, I might as well say it. 'Tis yer very soul's at risk, lass! Yer own . . . and that of anither."

Her *soul*. Sweet Mary, Mother of God! Then, Father O'Malley was right! Only, Crionna wanted her to—

"I know what ye're thinkin', child, but ye *mustn't*. The priest . . . the priest sees only his side of it. He—"

Crionna fell into a paroxysm of coughing that shook the bed. Quickly, Caitlin did what she could. Again, she

elevated the pillow, but to no avail. She offered water
. . . the healing tea she'd learned to brew from Crionna
herself. Useless. She'd been trained by the *bhean uasal*
in the use of herbs and simples to heal the sick; yet
Crionna's affliction was beyond remedy, and she knew
it. In the end she was forced to stand by helplessly and
watch. Tears were streaming down her face when it was
over.

The old woman's eyes peered out of sockets that were
sunken hollows in a bloodless face. She trained them
on Caitlin's, forced herself to go on. "Time . . . time
fer but . . . one thing, lass. 'Tis a protection ye'll . . .
ye'll need. A charm . . . and 'tis in the auld tongue, so
. . . listen carefully. And . . . and ye must repeat it . . .
after me . . . with yer eyes open, d'ye hear? Open!
There's . . . good reason fer this. 'Tis necessary because . . ."

In halting phrases, the old woman told Caitlin about
the protective chant. Told her that to work, it must be
spoken with the eyes closed. That it was so powerful, it
should be used only twice at the most. Crionna wasn't
certain—she'd never heard of it being done—but she
suspected a third time would kill the user.

"This I promise ye . . . Caitlin," the *bhean uasal*
finished in a voice growing weaker by the second.
"The words . . . they . . . they'll be needed . . . when
the time . . . o' the dream . . . is at hand. Now, repeat
after me . . ."

"But—"

"Do it!" There was a ferocity to Crionna's command
that had Caitlin nodding, despite the tears still coursing
down her cheeks.

"*A Mháthair Mór,*" the *bhean uasal* chanted, "*go maire
tú i bhfad! Nár lige . . .*"

Concentrating on the Gaelic words, Caitlin made herself remember them the very first time. Saying them even once seemed to be costing Crionna the last of her strength; Caitlin would not make her repeat them.

The *bhean uasal's* eyes closed as the girl gave them back to her. Caitlin's were so blurred by tears, she could barely see the old woman's face. Next, she promised to use the chant when the need was upon her. They both knew she did this reluctantly, and solely for the *bhean uasal.* She was helpless not to, for she was granting a dying wish.

As she breathed her last, Crionna could only hope it would be enough.

Chapter 1

London, Spring 1816

"I shall never forgive you for this, m'lord—never!"

Lord Adam Lightfoot, fifth marquis of Ravenskeep, ran a bored gaze over his wife. Not for the first time in their seven-year marriage, he wondered what had possessed him to wed her. He supposed Lucinda had been pretty in a bland sort of way. Once. Now he couldn't get past the sour lines of dissatisfaction about her mouth, the irritating whine in her voice.

"Save your histrionics for the rustic set, m'dear," he drawled. "I fear I find them rather . . . tedious."

Lucinda shrieked, and lunged at him, her fingers curved like talons. Adam didn't doubt she'd have clawed his face if he let her. He caught her wrists an instant before her nails raked his skin.

"My souvenir from the French will suffice, Lucinda.

I hardly require others to keep it company." Irritation mingled with disgust as he thrust her from him.

The marchioness eyed the line of newly healed flesh on his face; the work of a French saber, it ran from the top of his high, sculpted cheekbone to the edge of his perfectly chiseled lips. "What?" she sneered. "Afraid Vanessa Marley won't be able to abide you in her bed, m'lord?"

Adam wondered briefly where she'd learned about Vanessa; he'd hardly had time to break in his latest mistress. This only served to inform him Lucinda had already been in town too long to suit him. *Ton* gossip invariably found its way to willing ears. It was why he'd determined to keep his wife neatly tucked away on his country estate when he came up for the Season.

But Lucinda had tried to thwart those plans. She'd followed him up to London without his leave, which was bad enough; that she'd dragged their young son with her was reprehensible. He'd be damned if he'd let her use Andrew as a weapon to achieve her selfish ends!

"Well?" Lucinda carped bitterly. "It's true, isn't it? Vanessa Marley's the reason you're sending me back to Kent. You don't want the inconvenience of a wife complicating your disgusting—"

"Spare me your petty jealousies, Lucinda." Adam pinched the bridge of his nose with thumb and forefinger. Damnation, how he hated these scenes! "It isn't as if my lifestyle's a secret. I made it clear from the start, I'd no intention of giving it up. Or were you too busy congratulating yourself on snaring a rich title to pay attention?"

"You bastard! I did my duty. You had your precious heir—in less than a year's time! Why shouldn't I enjoy the Season in town? Other wives—"

"Your *duty*," he spat. "That's all it ever was to you,

wasn't it, Lucinda? Bloody hell! It's a wonder Andrew exists at all, given the ice between your thighs!"

Ignoring her gasp, Adam closed the distance between them. He caught her arm when she raised it to strike him. A tight smile spread across his face, but it didn't reach his eyes. With his free hand, he cupped one of the breasts that filled the muslin bodice of her high-waisted gown. Lightly abrading its center with his thumb, he awaited the reaction he anticipated, and wasn't disappointed: Revulsion filled her face.

Adam made a sound of disgust and released her. The eyes that met hers were hard. Blue-white diamonds in a face that had been called indecently handsome despite the saber scar. "Did it never occur to you, Lucinda," he asked in a voice that held weary resignation, "there might be a reason I seek other beds? Fact is, my less-than-dear wife, a man courts *frostbite* in yours."

"Oh, very good, m'lord—place all the blame on me! Only, I know *better.*"

Lucinda stalked to the door connecting their chambers. Reaching it, she whirled to face him. "Everyone in England knows you for a rake, Adam Lightfoot. It's said you run through women as readily as Brummel changes his linens. Well, let me tell you something, m'lord Rut! You can bury me in the country, but you can't still my tongue. With every mile that takes me from London, I'll curse you with it, d'you hear? You'll rue the day you did this to me—I swear it!"

As she slammed the door behind her, Adam considered what she'd said. It was true, of course. He'd lost count of the mistresses he'd kept since he inherited at seventeen. Yet he honestly hadn't expected those appetites to extend into his maturity. Tucked in the back of his mind was a hazy yearning he vaguely recalled from years ago . . . for a wife to love . . . adore, even . . . a brood of laughing children . . . .

Bloody hell, had he ever been that young? That naive? Had he actually expected to find a woman who'd be those things to him? Who'd make him want to retire contentedly to the country estate he now avoided like the plague?

He'd be thirty-four in July. When had it all gone sour? The war had done its part, of course. He'd seen enough carnage to harden a saint. Yet to be honest, he'd begun to grow world-weary well before he purchased his commission. He'd joined the regiment in '09. The year after he'd married. He'd already begun to grow tired of life. Pity he'd survived to . . . .

His gaze fell upon a framed miniature on his bed stand, throttling the thought. A child's shyly smiling face looked back at him with eyes the exact color of his own. His son . . . the one thing in the world he gave a damn about. As long as he had Andrew, he'd something to live for.

He threw an irritated glance at the connecting door. Lucinda was well aware of his love for the boy. It was what had allowed her to think she could manipulate him with the child. The ploy had nearly worked. If he weren't convinced London was an unsavory place for the lad—

A self-deprecating snort truncated the thought. *At least be honest with yourself, old man! It's unsavory because of the life you lead here. Even now, you await not only your wife's departure, but your son's. So that you'll be free for another night's debauchery!*

Another glance at the miniature had him swearing under his breath. Only this morning Andrew had begged to be allowed to stay. The pleading in the child's eyes said it wasn't merely because his mother had put him up to it. Yet Adam had steadfastly refused him, though he'd longed to give in. The hardest part had been his inability to tell the child why. He could still feel the shame twisting his gut when Andrew had asked. He hadn't been able to meet his son's eyes.

How did a man explain to a six-year-old? That what had once been a careless option had become a necessity. That, since Salamanca and Vitoria, he needed the nights of dissipation to forget. To endure.

No, he could hardly tell a child about the bloodletting. The slaughter. The screams of dying men and horses . . . limbs and torsos torn apart by cannon, littering the ground.

Since returning from the Peninsula he'd found his mind haunted by agonized pleas from dying men. Young men, pouring out their lifeblood, asking for their mothers. Men hardly more than boys, whom he'd sent to their deaths in the name of duty. *Duty*. The word made him sick!

The memories gave him screaming nightmares.

So he kept the nightmares at bay . . . sometimes. If he was drunk enough . . . if the whore was clever enough . . . if . . . .

With a disgusted snarl, Adam tore his gaze from the miniature and rang for his valet. From outside on the drive came the sound of carriage wheels turning on the cobbles. His own carriage, by the sound of it. *Finally departing, thank—*

Adam's bitter laughter obliterated the word he couldn't utter, even in his mind. The Deity had no place in his thoughts . . . or in his life. Salamanca and Vitoria had left him believing in nothing and no one. Not even himself.

Better to think on the night ahead. Yet the forgetting had become harder. Even debauchery had begun to pall. He was all too aware he was fighting boredom along with the emptiness in his soul. If he had a soul. More likely, it had been devoured by the same beast that brought the nightmares.

Well, for now there was always Vanessa. An accommodating Cyprian with a voluptuous body and the practiced tricks of a whore.

And he mustn't forget m'lord Appleby. Though he'd met this latest among his reckless cohorts only a fortnight ago, Appleby showed promise. Of a certainty, he was one of the most intriguing and imaginative roués Adam had ever encountered. Appleby had an inventiveness in the gaming hells that rivaled Vanessa's in the bedchamber. Surely, between the two, he'd be safe from the beast . . . at least for a time . . . wouldn't he?

A tapping at the door brought welcome relief from his thoughts. Calling permission to enter, Adam surrendered to the ministrations of his valet. Heretofore, he'd never bothered with a personal manservant, priding himself on a self-sufficiency at odds with the ways of the *ton*. But he'd won the highly touted Parks from Alvanley in a game of whist. Bored by the usual round of wagering one evening at Brooks', he'd wagered a prime piece of horseflesh, purchased at Tatt's only that morning. Wagered it against "the incomparable Parks," as Alvanley's envious cronies had called the servant. Poor Alvanley—the look on his jaded face when he lost! It had brought a measure of satisfaction, however fleeting; he might as well avail himself of the valet's expertise.

"I thought the striped might serve this evening, your lordship," Parks murmured a good two hours later. He held a waistcoat of subdued blue and gray stripes for the marquis's inspection.

"Yes, yes—whatever!" His irritation obvious, Adam allowed the manservant to settle the garment onto his shoulders. The tall-case clock on the landing had just struck nine. Not late by the *ton's* standards, but he'd had about all he could stomach of the valet's fussing. Blood and ashes, his cravat alone had taken six attempts before Parks was satisfied!

Unruffled by his employer's scowl, the valet helped him into a superbly tailored coat of deep blue superfine. Parks stepped back with a look of admiration. It had begun to rain earlier, and he raised his voice over a peal of distant thunder. "If I may say so, your lordship, we have achieved an image of the perfect Corinth—"

A frantic pounding resounded from the door. *Bloody hell—now what?* Adam wondered as he barked admittance. A glance at the mantel clock told him he was due to meet Appleby in less than—

A middle-aged woman rushed into the chamber: Mrs. Hodgkins, his housekeeper. "Begging your pardon, your lordship, but there's been—your lordship, forgive me, but I've terrible news!"

Adam eyed the normally unflappable servant sharply. The damned woman was *crying*. "Spit it out, Hodgkins." His tone was the same he'd used toward nervous junior officers. "What the devil's happened?"

The housekeeper made an attempt at speaking past the tears coursing down her homely face; her voice nonetheless cracked as she delivered her news. "There's been a-a carriage—oh, your lordship! Your carriage overturned, killing her ladyship and—"

"My son!" Adam's face was bloodless as he speared the woman with his eyes. "What of *my son?*"

"Alive, but badly injured, your lordship. He's—" She got no further. The marquis tore through the door, the sound of his rapid footsteps blending with urgent voices from the entry foyer below.

Adam flew down the stairs, trying desperately not to listen to the voice that jeered in his head. *You sent them away in that carriage!* You *did this to him! You!*

Jepson, his butler of many years, met him at the base of the stairs. The servant's lined face was tightly composed, if unusually pale. Then he saw the look on the marquis's face. The old retainer's eyes widened in alarm.

"Where is he, man?" No need for Adam to mention Andrew by name; they all knew how he felt about the child.

"Just arriving outside, your lordship. A passerby was kind enough to lend his carriage to—"

The front door banged open, snaring their attention. The blood drained from Adam's face as several liveried servants pushed through. Rain slanted through the open doorway, and their dripping attire puddled the floor. They bore a makeshift stretcher of some kind. A harsh cry died in Adam's throat as his gaze went to the small figure lying on it. Lying so horribly still.

It was nearly midnight when the marquis at last found himself alone with his son. The storm was reaching its peak. Thunder crashed overhead. Blue-white flashes of light flickered eerily at the windows. At Adam's feet, beside the bedside chair where he slouched, stood a half-consumed bottle of brandy; an empty snifter dangled from his hand. He eyed it absently for a moment, then shut his eyes in abject resignation. Half a bottle, and still no effect. But then, he doubted anything could provide the oblivion he sought.

His own chambers being closest, they'd brought the child here. Andrew lay in the middle of his father's huge tester bed. Adam's face twisted in anguish as he ran his eyes over the boy; he looked so awfully small and fragile against the great expanse of sheets.

A bandage covering a severe wound to the head obscured Andrew's curly dark locks. The bedclothes hid the splints and heavy gauze that bandaged a crushed leg; yet in his mind's eye, Adam could see them as clearly as the crimson-stained gauze wound about his son's head.

The physician, as well as a highly regarded surgeon they'd summoned, had left over an hour ago. Andrew still hadn't regained consciousness. Best to realize, they'd told the distraught father, he likely never would.

His son was dying.

Hissing an obscenity, Adam grabbed the bottle and poured himself a hefty measure. He raised the glass to his lips, tossed down its contents. The liquid burned a trail to his stomach. He wished to hell it could burn away his thoughts.

Guilt, terrible and unforgiving, ate into his mind. Like a cancer. A living thing that devoured from within. *You sent them away. The wife you took . . . used, but never loved. Dead, because of you. The son you've loved all too well . . . the son who,* because *of you, will soon—*

"N-o-o-o!" The snifter splintered against the far wall as Adam's howl rose over the storm. Wrenching himself from the chair with a violence that knocked it over, he bent over the bed. Arms rigid, he drove his fists into the mattress and made himself look at the small, ashen face of his son. "You *can't* die. I won't let you! I—"

Adam dropped his chin and shut his eyes. The ges-

ture, made by another, would have signaled prayer. But
Adam Lightfoot didn't pray. Hadn't, for years. Couldn't.
Not to a Deity who clearly condoned the things he'd
seen. Who gazed impassively from a heaven that over-
looked the filth that was war. A God who would allow
this to happen to an innocent child, when it was the
father who'd—

"I'm the one!'' he raged. The clock on the landing
had begun to chime the hour, but Adam's cry overrode
the sound. "I'm the one to blame—not the child! Take
me, and let the boy live—damn it! I'd barter my soul
for it—I swear I would!''

At that exact moment, there came a sharp rapping
at the door. Thunder rumbled overhead, but didn't
obscure the sound. Nor the final strike of the clock on
the landing, which had reached twelve.

Outraged that anyone would have the temerity to
disturb him at such a time, Adam snarled an obscenity
and stalked to the door. By Judas's balls, he'd have the
bastard's head! Giving the doorknob a vicious twist, he
thrust the door wide. "What the . . . ?''

He'd expected one of the staff, prepared to sack the
feckless creature on the spot. But this was no servant.
Before him was a man who wore the unmistakable hau-
teur of an aristocrat. Slender as a serpent, of average
height, he wore the sartorially splendid garb of a dandy:
A high, heavily starched cravat which had been tied just
so. Tasseled Hessians, buffed and polished to a fare-
thee-well. Held at a fashionable angle was an ebony
walking stick, its silver head carved in the likeness of
some animal Adam couldn't make out.

The aging face bore unmistakable traces of dissipation; it was heavily maquillaged, the cheeks and lips
rouged. A quizzing glass poised in one elegantly gloved
hand completed the picture.

"Appleby . . ." Adam scowled. "What the devil are *you* doing here?"

"Why, my dear fellow," said his visitor, sauntering carelessly into the room. "How very apt!"

Chapter 2

"Apt?" Adam scowled all the more. "What, exactly, is that supposed to mean?" As Appleby clearly meant to stay, he shut the door after him, wondering briefly where the servants were. More to the point, how Appleby had gotten past the keenly vigilant Jepson.

Ignoring his query, Appleby slanted a glance at the bed. "Heard about the mishap, Ravenskeep. Pity ... understand the lad's barely out of leading strings."

Raising his quizzing glass, Appleby approached the bed. Suddenly Adam found himself moving to place himself in the way. He couldn't say why, but there was something about the man that urged him to put a barrier between the visitor and his son.

Noting this, Appleby arched a thinly plucked brow and chuckled. "Come, dear boy! You can scarcely object to my presence when you've summoned me yourself."

"Summoned ... I did no such thing! I scarcely know you."

"On the contrary, my dear Ravenskeep. Fact is, you've been flirting with my acquaintance for some time now." Appleby helped himself to a chair, a distance from the bed. Setting the walking stick across his knees, he regarded his host with assessing black eyes that seemed mocking and sly at the same time. "You and I go back a deal of years."

"Rubbish!" With Appleby safely seated, Adam breathed a bit easier, but didn't move from before the bed. Taking the bedside chair, he turned it and sat, facing his guest. "I recollect we were introduced but a fortnight ago."

"By my present mode of address, yes." Appleby withdrew a silver snuffbox from his waistcoat pocket, flicked it open with his thumb. "But, my dear fellow, I've a deal of other names, d'you see . . ." He paused, a pinch of snuff held artfully between thumb and forefinger, eyeing the marquis archly. "Happy to enumerate them for you, but . . . ah, perhaps you'd care to pour yourself another brandy first?"

"Just get on with it," Adam growled. He felt almost as if Appleby were . . . toying with him somehow. Like a cat with a mouse.

His visitor deposited the snuff on the back of his hand. Raising it to his nostrils, he inhaled, then sneezed delicately into a lace-edged handkerchief. "Ahh, just the thing," he sighed. "Now, b'lieve *I'll* have a brandy, if you don't mind."

Adam blinked, then stared at him. He in no way recalled pouring the man a brandy. How the devil had Appleby come by that snifter in his hand? Giving his head a shake, he decided the liquor he'd consumed had more of an effect on him than he'd realized. Odd, though. He didn't *feel* foxed.

"Certain you won't have another, old boy?" Appleby

prodded, indicating the bottle at his host's feet. "No? Very well, then," he added cheerfully, "but never say I didn't warn you."

The smile he bestowed on his host, displaying sharp, catlike teeth, had the effect of raising the hairs on the back of Adam's neck. Yet the marquis was hard put to say why. *Foxed, of a certainty.*

"I've many names," Appleby went on, "some of them ancient, others more recent. Came with the peoples who used 'em, d'you see. Now, Lucifer is the oldest, but it was quickly followed by Beelzebub. Then we have the more folksy sort . . . Old Nick . . . Old Harry . . . Old Scratch . . . You take my meaning. The most universal, or well known perhaps, is Satan. I own, I'm rather fond of that one myself. Never did like being called the Antichrist, though. I mean, how'd *He* like being called the *Antidevil*, eh? But you get my drift, I'm sure."

Appleby raised his brandy for a toast. "Cheers, old boy." He took a swallow, while the marquis stared at him as if he'd acquired two heads.

"Your name is Appleby," Adam murmured warily, wondering if he were entertaining an escaped lunatic. "Lord Appleby!"

"Well, that, too," his guest told him merrily. "Fact is, Appleby's my all-time favorite. Comes from an association with the fruit, d'you see. Of course, it wasn't really an apple. But the incident involved, my dear Ravenskeep"—he winked conspiratorially at his host—"represents my most successful transaction, ever!"

Adam scowled. Definitely a refugee from Bedlam! Where the devil was Jepson? Wondering if he ought to chance ringing for the butler, he quickly thought better of the idea. Madmen could be dangerous; if he humored him, perhaps Appleby would leave on his own.

Yet Adam was unable to hide his irritation. His son

was dying, damn it! The last thing he wanted was to entertain this lunatic. It was all he could do to brace himself for what lay ahead: the plunge into an abyss of unbearable pain and loss. Blood and ashes, it hardly bore thinking on! "Why've you come?" he demanded.

"Tut-tut, dear fellow! Thought I'd explained all that. I'm here at your summoning."

"Summoning?"

Appleby heaved a sigh, throwing him a look one might send an errant child. "Did you, or did you not, *swear* you'd *barter your soul* for your son's life?"

"How the devil could you . . . ? I said that when I was alone with my—"

"But you *did* say it." For some reason Appleby seemed intent on establishing the point. He propped his walking stick before him; one hand capped the other atop its head, and he leaned forward, spearing the marquis with his gaze.

Back to humoring him, Adam shrugged. "I said it."

Appleby relaxed. "Then, there was a summoning, Ravenskeep, and no mistake."

"Summoning?" Adam questioned a second time.

"Indeed," said Appleby, producing an apple from his pocket, polishing it on his sleeve. "When any mortal offers to barter his soul"—he smiled, and Adam felt a chill run down his spine, though he couldn't say why— "he summons *me.*"

"You're mad," Adam whispered, not sure he even believed any of this was happening. Perhaps he'd fallen asleep, and it was all a bad dream. Or the brandy he'd consumed. He'd heard of drunkards having tremors accompanied by hellish hallucinations. But there were no tremors, just . . . . "Madder than a March hare," he added emphatically.

Appleby took a bite out of the apple and shook his

head. Yet he smiled, not at all put out by the accusation. "Sane as a bishop, as the saying goes. I am who I've said I am, Ravenskeep. Make no mistake about it."

Adam snorted. "My only mistake was to admit you." When Appleby didn't respond, he leaned forward, meeting his gaze with narrowed eyes. "Why should I believe you?"

Appleby flicked a glance at the bed. "I should think that would be obvious. Because you can save your son's life by doing what you've already offered."

"And that is . . . ?"

"Consigning your soul, old boy"—Appleby's fingers caressed the head of the walking stick, and Adam suddenly noted its shape: a serpent's head—"into *my* keeping."

"Damn it, Appleby, what kind of a gudgeon d'you take me for? My son's dying! *Dying*, d'you hear? And—"

"And *I* have the power to reverse it."

The words were simply spoken. Not bombastically. Not as a braggart might utter them. And by their very lack of ornamentation, they had the ring of truth. Adam's eyes went to the bed. If, by some chance . . . .

"Prove it!" he snapped. "If you are . . . who you say you are, then you ought to be able to offer me proof."

Appleby's grin was sly, and a smugness glinted in the eyes he ran over his host. He knew he had him now. "Very well," he said, gesturing with his walking stick toward the hearth. "Observe carefully, if you will."

Adam followed the gesture, his gaze falling on the fire, which had died to mere embers. "I don't see— bloody hell!"

Adam leapt out of his chair. With a roar, a blaze as big as a bonfire had exploded from the embers. A fire so bright, he threw his arm before his eyes to shield them. "Blood and ashes, man!" he cried. "Are you trying to burn the house down?"

"Hardly," Appleby chuckled, and waved his walking stick at the conflagration. It went out.

There was utter silence in the room as Adam slowly lowered his arm. He stared at Appleby. "How . . . ," he began in a choked whisper. "How did you—"

"Afraid the 'how' would be quite beyond you, old boy, but does it really matter? What you saw—"

"Was a trick of some kind . . . a sleight of hand." His initial shock past, Adam grew more determined to show Appleby up for the fraud he was, and get rid of him. "A clever one, I'll own, but I've seen stage magicians—"

"You have another scar on your body," Appleby cut in. "Beyond the one on your face, that is. It's on the inside of your left knee and shaped like the letter Y. Came by it when you were seven. A fall from your pony. His name was Mudge, and you'd taken a jump you'd been told by your father you weren't to attempt—over a stone wall dividing the south pasture from . . ."

Appleby's words trailed off as Adam slowly shook his head at him. "Still not convinced? Hmm, let me see . . . Ah, I have it! You were quite the idealist in your youth . . . especially regarding matters of . . . the heart, shall we say? Your parents had an unusual marriage for their class. A love match. Lasted till the day they died—tragically, at sea, when you were seventee—"

"All facts anyone could have ascertained!"

"True, but the rest isn't at all common knowledge."

"The rest?"

Appleby's smile was sly and knowing. "Seems their wedded bliss led you to believe you could have the same . . . a woman you adored, who loved you deeply . . . children you both—"

"Tricks!" Adam insisted, yet he was far from sure.

He'd never told a living soul about those embarrassing yearnings. Indeed, he'd buried them in the back of his own mind. When it became clear he'd never have those things . . . that he'd been a fool to even imagine them. "Clever parlor tricks," he told Appleby, "and nothing more!"

"Tsk, tsk." Appleby sighed again, shaking his head. "Recollect your file saying you're stubborn, old fellow, but I'd no idea . . ."

"My file!" Adam sneered. "Any dossier you put together ought to have advised you can't fob me off so easily! Before that happens, m'lord, it'll be a cold day in he—"

As Adam stopped himself, Appleby broke into a wild giggle. "Never have 'em, Ravenskeep—rest assured!" He gave a loud guffaw, slapping his knee. "Not even a chilly one, old boy, I do assure you!"

"Appleby," Adam growled, beyond irritation now. An anxious glance at Andrew told him nothing had changed, but he was impatient to be alone with his child. It was time he got rid of this rouged fop! He started to say so.

The look on Appleby's face stopped him.

"The hour grows late, m'lord, and I'm done with wasting time!" his midnight visitor snapped. "You require irrefutable proof? So be it!"

A sudden clap of thunder boomed overhead. Every light in the chamber went out. Yet an odd kind of pale, flickering luminescence washed the room. Though its source was unidentifiable, it allowed the marquis to see what was happening. He noted a vaguely familiar smell, sharp and pungent, as of something burning, but was too stunned to ascribe a name to it.

Appleby seemed to rise from his chair. It took Adam a second to realize he wasn't really rising. He was . . .

growing. Growing and—*blood and ashes!* With a hoarse cry, Adam leapt from his chair, knocking it over. Appleby was—

Changing. All at once, a creature of gargantuan proportions filled the space where his visitor had sat. Reaching to the very top of the high ceiling, dwarfing everything in the chamber. The breath left Adam's lungs. He wanted to cry out, but couldn't. The very blood seemed to freeze in his veins. He gaped, mindless with dread, at the thing that hovered over him in Appleby's place.

"Now do you believe, mortal?" The inflection was the dandy's, but with voice greatly enhanced ... embellished ten times over. Booming. Echoing, as if from a vast chamber. Adam jammed his hands over his ears, trying to shut it out.

The beast moved. A great pair of appendages spread outward, as if it were trying to measure the breadth of the chamber with those vast, membranous wings. Its hands were—not hands! Scaled claws, with razor-sharp talons!

Adam felt his own weight upon him ... a mountain of dread, and he dropped to his knees under it. His gaze fell on the creature's feet. Which were not feet at all, but *cloven hooves.* Blood and ashes! All the stories ... the legends and myths—they were all *true!*

"Mortal!" The creature—fiend, whatever it was— seemed suddenly impatient. As if it were done toying with him. It loomed closer ... as if it would rather rend him to pieces on the spot.

Adam whipped his gaze to the bed. Andrew! He must not let it near his son! He staggered to his feet, just as the creature flapped those enormous wings. A howling wind struck him in the face.

"Your answer, mortal—now!"

Adam flung himself against the bed, never taking his eyes off the spectacle. "Yes, *yes! Anything*—only, take it away! *Away,* I say!"

There was a pleased echo in the terrible laughter that boomed in his ears before it faded. Just as the monster itself disappeared. Yet an unmistakable scent lingered in the air; he could identify it now: brimstone.

And then it was gone. The lamps in the room resumed burning. Everything seemed back to normal. Even Appleby, sitting in the chair, calmly munching his apple.

"I do really dislike coming it so dramatic, old boy," the dandy said around a bite of the fruit. "But the time's growing short, and I've other calls to make. Are you ready to deal?"

Casting a fleeting glance at the bed, Adam picked up his chair and lowered himself into it on shaking limbs. He reached for the brandy, poured an entire snifter of the liquid with hands that were none too steady. It wasn't until he'd downed it that he met the visitor's gaze. "I'll deal," he said tersely.

"Excellent!" The apple vanished from Appleby's hand. In its place appeared a sheet of foolscap, which he thrust at his host. "Now, if you'll just sign—"

"What the devil is it?" Adam stared at the paper as if it might attack him. Every nerve in his body was ajangle, his muscles taut as bowstrings.

"Why, a contract, of course. This is a business arrangement, my friend, and we want no questions regarding what it entails."

Eyeing him warily, Adam took the paper and began to read. It took him only seconds. He looked up from it with a frown. "This is hardly a proper contract. It's merely the bare bones of what we discussed: my soul in exchange for my son's life. What of the details?"

"Details?" Appleby clearly didn't care for this question. "The simpler, the better, I should think! No chance for misunderstanding, that way."

But Adam was recalling a name for the devil that Appleby hadn't included among those he'd given earlier: the Father of Lies. No chance for misunderstanding? He wouldn't wager on it. Certainly not if Appleby had his way. And any misunderstanding would be at the human's expense! He must be awake upon every suit.

"Afraid I'll need to know more," he told the dandy. "How many years, for example. Exactly how many years of life will my son have, Appleby, from *the sale of my immortal soul?*"

Appleby looked nonplussed for the first time since his arrival. "I say, old boy, that's something that's never—"

"How many?" Adam demanded.

Appleby sighed and withdrew a small black notebook from his waistcoat pocket. "Highly irregular, y'know," he grumbled as he leafed through it. "Lightfoot . . . Lightfoot, Adam . . . no—ah, here we are—*Andrew.*" His finger came to rest on a page, and he looked up at his host.

"Well . . . ?"

"See for yourself," said Appleby somewhat sourly. He gestured at the contract.

Adam's brows rose as he spied an addition that had suddenly appeared upon the foolscap in his hand. ". . . a lifespan of eighty-one years," he read aloud. He shot Appleby a glance. "Acceptable, I suppose, but—"

"Acceptable! It's downright *generous,*" Appleby cried. "Now, if you'll just sign—"

"Sorry, but it's not enough."

"Not enough!" the dandy sputtered. "It's a damned sight more than you've a right to expect!" His hand shot out and seemed to pull something out of the air. A small knife.

Adam glowered at it. "What in hell's that for?"

"Nothing dastardly, I assure you," said Appleby. "It's merely to prick your finger." He gestured at the contract. "The bargain must be signed in your own blood, of course."

"Of course," Adam said dryly. "But I'm not quite ready to do that yet."

"And why not?" Appleby snapped.

"Because," said Adam, "I also wish to know how may years this buys *me.*" Appleby sputtered and muttered something about impertinence, but his host ignored him. "After all," Adam went on, "what good is saving my child's life if he's to become an orphan? The boy has just lost his mother—"

"Who barely had contact with him," Appleby pointed out. "The child was left almost entirely in the care of a nursemaid, and then a governess."

"I'm aware of that," Adam said darkly. "All the more reason *I* should be here for him, from now on. I want to ... nurture my son, Appleby. See him properly launched into manhood. I insist upon it."

"Insist! *Insist?* That's quite the outside of enough, Ravenskeep!" the dandy cried. "All these demands!" He leapt from his chair. "What arrogant effrontery! And in a mere *human* ... Why, I've never seen the like!"

The walking stick was back in his hand, and he thrust it in Adam's face. "I suggest you recall whom you're dealing with, m'lord," he said in a menacing tone. "I suggest it strongly!"

Adam's gaze remained steady, the blue eyes wintry and unblinking. "And I suggest," he said coolly, "you recall the *price* you're exacting for meeting my demands. I require what amounts to a matter of mere years,

Appleby. You, on the other hand, can expect *all of eternity* to savor *your* end of the bargain."

There was a moment of silence as Appleby took his measure. He'd hoped to have this particular soul in a year's time; Ravenskeep was a war hero, and therefore quite the prize. Still, having him signed and sealed, even if it was for later . . . . He supposed it would have to do. A deal better than not having him at all. There'd always been some doubt about Lightfoot's damnation. Best not risk it.

He resumed sitting. "Very well," he said sullenly, taking out the notebook again. "Tell me how much time you require, and I'll see what I can do. But I warn you, m'lord. You're not likely to get all you want. There are limits to how far I can be pushed!"

Adam glanced at his son. Andrew hadn't moved; the translucent skin beneath the bandage looked paler than ever. *Ah, my son! I can't bear to see you this way. Yet if this thing is truly possible . . . if I can truly manage to . . . .*

Adam's eyes moved to a small table at the far side of the chamber. On it lay a marble and onyx chess set. An excellent player, Adam had been teaching Andrew how to play. It suddenly gave him an idea.

"Appleby," he said as his gaze found the dandy's, "I've a proposal. I suggest we play a game of chess. Five years added to my current age, for every piece of yours I capture." He shrugged. "Of course, if I fail to capture any . . ."

"Done." Appleby smiled. Better than he'd expected. Hadn't the marquis heard? The devil was an expert gamesman!

Adam didn't like the looks of that smile. Or that he'd won this concession so readily. But most on his mind at the moment was what he liked least of all: Appleby even remotely near his son.

"Very well, then," he said, rising from his seat. "But I prefer to play in the library, if you don't mind."

"Not at all, dear boy." Appleby rose, too, as his host cast a worried look at his son.

Again, the easy concession. Adam swore softly under his breath as he grabbed a taper to light the way. The little bastard was too bloody accommodating! He met Appleby's gaze. "I require your promise nothing will happen to Andrew until our match is over, and our bargain concluded."

"The lad will be completely safe," the dandy replied cheerfully.

Too damned cheerfully, Adam thought as he nodded and they made their way to the library down the hall. *He's up to something, but damned if I—*

Smothering the grim irony in this thought, Adam lit a branch from the taper as they entered the library. He led Appleby to a table near the hearth, where another chess set waited in readiness. They began to play.

Chapter 3

Caitlin trudged wearily up the stairs. The worn and splintered steps creaked when she set her slight weight upon them. Her lodgings were far from grand, but they were all she could afford. She grimaced with the thought. Her rent was due tomorrow, and she hadn't the coin to meet it.

Worry about that in the morning, she told herself as she reached her door. Fumbling amid the sodden folds of her cloak, she found her key. She'd been caught in a devilish downpour while making her way back to the shabby chamber. Now it was past midnight, and she was soaked nearly to the skin and bone-weary.

Yet it was a satisfying exhaustion, she thought, setting a worn leather bag down, just inside the door. Crossing the tiny chamber in the dark, she groped for the tinder-box beside the bed and lit a candle. She took a deep breath, let it out slowly, and felt herself relax.

Aye, satisfying. Up at dawn, she'd seen over a dozen

of London's poor before the sun read noon. And she'd left most of them better off than when she came.

A wee tad better, she amended as she stripped off the dripping cloak. Their worst affliction was something no herbs and simples could heal: a grinding poverty that frequently led to an early grave. Yet Caitlin did what she could. Using the knowledge she'd gained under Crionna's roof, she'd become an itinerant healer. She supported herself, albeit none too grandly, as she traveled the countryside, asking for those in need.

More often than not, they had no money to pay, and she accepted other things instead: a loaf of bread, a few eggs, some roots and greens from a humble garden. *Even clothing,* she thought, removing the wet half boots she had from a poor country vicar's wife she'd seen through a fever.

She'd left Ireland more than six months ago. Buried her foster mother, mourned her, then set out at once for England. She couldn't say why, exactly, but she'd needed to get away. Sometimes, like tonight, when she was especially tired, an inner voice told her she was running away. She ignored it. The dreams hadn't come since she put her native soil behind her. That was the important thing.

She refused to examine the strange compulsion that had drawn her to London in early April. Heretofore, she'd traveled strictly in the countryside, for she was country-bred. But it didn't matter where she plied her skills. There were poor everywhere, and . . . .

The thought faded as she dropped onto the room's narrow cot with a groan. She'd spent the last six hours delivering the ragman's wife of a set of twins. Healthy babes, if a bit on the scrawny side. She smiled ruefully. Her concern for the wee mites was why she hadn't the

rent; she'd told the ragman to take those farthings and
buy his nursing wife some nourish—

A rapping on her door had her eyeing it sharply.
Who'd be after calling at this hour? She'd no friends
to speak of, having been in the city but a fortnight,
and—

The rapping came again, sounding urgent. Someone
in need? She dragged herself off the cot and moved to
the door. She may not have made any friends, but she
knew word had already spread about her work. "The
Irish Angel," they'd begun to call her, though she saw
nothing angelic in what she did. Anyone with a few
healing skills and a bit of compassion could have done
the same.

"Aye?" she called through the door, not yet ready to
open it. The East End was rife with footpads, cutthroats
and worse; she wasn't a fool. "Who is it ye seek?"

"I was told the Irish Angel lives here," said a woman's
voice. "Oh, please, miss! If you're the one they told me
about, I-I'm *begging* your help."

The desperation in the voice had Caitlin swiftly opening the door. "Come in, then," she said to the middle-
aged woman who looked at her with imploring eyes.

"Are . . . are you really the Irish Angel?" the woman
asked uncertainly. The slender creature facing her
looked so young! A mere slip of a girl, with a sprinkling
of freckles across her nose. Very pretty, though.

Caitlin gave her a tired smile. "Some call me that,
aye. But me name's Caitlin . . . Caitlin O'Brien. And
ye're . . . ?"

"I'm Mrs. Hodgkins . . . Sally Hodgkins. You may
recall my sister, for you cured her of a terrible skin rash
when—"

"Ach, the shopkeeper's wife! How's she farin' these
days?"

"Splendidly, thanks to you. But, Miss O'Brien, that's not why I'm here. I've come to you because . . . Well, I know what you did for Jenny, and—and we've nowhere else to turn!"

The woman began to weep softly. Exhausted though she was, Caitlin couldn't ignore her. Her heart went out to the woman. "Here," she said, guiding her to the room's single chair. "Sit down and tell me about it."

Nodding gratefully, Mrs. Hodgkins complied, then mastered her emotions enough to tell of her quest. An errand of mercy, but not for herself. For a six-year-old child. The son of a nobleman in a great household where she was employed as housekeeper. There had been a carriage accident, and the child was badly injured. The physician didn't expect him to live past morning.

"But what leads ye t' think I can help?" Caitlin was shaking her head. "If this lord's own physician doesn't—"

"But you're the Irish Angel!" Mrs. Hodgkins cried. "My sister says a prayer for you each day, blessing you for her cure. You healed her of that rash that came near to driving her mad—for *two years*. Two years, miss! With visits to one physician after another, and none of them able to do a thing for her!"

The woman started to weep again, and Caitlin patted her shoulder soothingly, wondering what to do. She was a healer, not a miracle worker, despite what some said. Yet she was touched by this woman's request. By her compassion. She wept for a child not even her own. "Describe the injuries for me, if ye will," she said at last.

Mrs. Hodgkins dried her eyes and did so. But after hearing of the crushed leg and a severe head wound that had left the child senseless, Caitlin despaired more than ever. It didn't sound good. "Ach, the poor babe," she murmured with genuine sympathy. "And his parents—they must be beside themselves with anguish!"

Stifling a sob, Mrs. Hodgkins shook her head. "But one p-parent now, Miss O'Brien. Little Lord Andrew has only his father left him. The p-poor child's mother was k-killed in that same accident."

Caitlin murmured softly and crossed herself.

"And his lordship's in a terrible state, miss! He's shut himself away in that room for *hours*. Won't talk to anyone . . . won't sleep or take any food. And himself just home from the war, with his own wound barely healed!"

"Ach, the poor man!"

Mrs. Hodgkins nodded. "I'll be honest with you, miss. The marquis has no idea I'm here. For how could he, with him not seeing anyone? But it wouldn't matter, I'm sure, if you were to help his son. And he's a man of great wealth, Lord Ravenskeep is. Not at all the niggardly sort, either. I'm sure he'd pay handsomely for your help." She placed a hand on Caitlin's sleeve. "Oh, won't you at least *try*?"

Caitlin felt buffeted by the pull on her emotions. A wee lad, given up for lost. The mother dead, the father clearly grieving for his wife, in despair over his son. It all sounded so hopeless. What could she, a mere folk healer, do?

Still, she'd never been one to quit before even trying. And there was always the power of prayer. Those she treated didn't know it, but she prayed over them as much as she plied her skills from Crionna.

And, of course, there was the matter of her rent. This lord would pay well, the housekeeper said. With a weary sigh, Caitlin slipped on her half boots, grabbed her wet

cloak and turned to the bag she'd set beside the door.
It held her herbs and simples.

"Take me t' the lad," she said.

Jepson eyed the waiflike creature standing beside
Sally Hodgkins with great misgivings. God knew, he
loved little Lord Andrew as well as the rest of the staff
did. The lad had a way about him. And they'd long felt
sorry for him, what with that cold marchioness for a
mother. Not to mention his lordship being away so
much during the war, and then so brooding and distant
since his return. But Sally was clearly grasping at straws
here. Irish Angel, indeed! The so-called healer was little
more than a child herself.

"What makes you think you can succeed where a
physician and a renowned surgeon have given up?" he
asked Caitlin.

Taking in the stone-faced butler's forbidding
demeanor, Caitlin gathered her courage. "Perhaps
that's just the trouble, sorr."

The butler arched a brow at her. "Explain yourself,
miss."

"They've given up," Caitlin told him. She glanced at
the housekeeper. "But Mrs. Hodgkins here hasn't, and
neither should you, I'm thinkin'. Perhaps too many have
given up on the lad already," she added, recalling the
father who'd apparently abandoned himself to grief.

A reluctant smile tugged at Jepson's lips, though he
kept it in check; he was not a man given to smiles. But
the girl's words hit home. Were, in fact, what he'd been
thinking himself. To hear it from the mouth of this
callow lass, fresh from the Irish countryside . . . . Perhaps
she wasn't as young and inexperienced as she looked.

Jepson sighed, and met the housekeeper's eyes, his

features still unyielding. "I needn't remind you, Hodgkins, his lordship's a difficult man in the best of circumstances. Adding to that, his distress over the child, I hardly think—"

"Is he still in his chambers?" she broke in.

Jepson shook his head to the contrary. "Oddly enough, his lordship repaired to the library sometime during the night. I saw light coming from under the door when I—"

"Well, that's ideal, then!" she cried. "A blessing, in fact. The Angel here can steal in to see the boy without—"

"Beggin' yer pardon, Mrs. Hodgkins," Caitlin put in, "but I'd scarcely feel right, seein' the lad without his da knowin' it. 'Twouldn't be honest, d'ye see, and I'm that, if nothin' else."

Jepson's opinion of the girl rose another notch. Most in her circumstances would jump at the chance to make some easy money, and nothing more. He ran his eyes over her slight form. Though neat and clean, if damp from the storm, her garments were worn; they showed several patches and neatly mended tears. Another of Ireland's poor immigrants, without a doubt. Yet she scrupled to refuse a potentially lucrative engagement, as she feared it would be dishonest! Intrigued, he found himself pondering how he might persuade her to accept.

"Miss O'Brien," he said carefully, "I understand your principles entirely. And normally I would agree with you. But you must know this is not a normal situation. I collect Mrs. Hodgkins has told you of his lordship's . . . ah, retreat, in the wake of what's occurred?"

"She has, sorr."

"Then, you will understand why it is impossible to secure his lordship's permission any time soon."

"And *time* is the very thing we don't have!" the house-keeper cried, picking up the thread. "If we wait until his lordship is approachable, Lord Andrew could . . . could be—" She broke off on a sob.

Caitlin glanced from one to the other, seeing the strain on their plain, no-nonsense faces. They clearly doted on the lad. They were even willing to risk their employer's displeasure to save him. How could she, a healer, do less?

She sighed, and touched the housekeeper's sleeve. "I'm not promisin' anythin', understand, but . . . If ye'll be showin' me the way, I'll do me best."

Her reward was a fresh bout of weeping from the housekeeper, who hugged her. And a glimmer of a smile from the butler she'd have sworn never smiled at all.

A quick check revealed the marquis was still shut up in the library. But before they let Caitlin in to see the child, they urged her to prepare for the possibility his lordship might discover her. It took some persuading, but they convinced her to masquerade as a new house-maid they'd taken on. Mrs. Hodgkins even produced a proper costume, borrowed from one of the maid-servants.

A short time later, Caitlin tiptoed into the bed-chamber. The butler had built up the fire, which had nearly gone out, then repaired to another part of the house on some errand. The housekeeper waited outside the partially open door. Likely to keep an eye peeled for the distraught father, though she hadn't said.

On the other hand, Caitlin thought as she moved toward the great canopied bed, Mrs. Hodgkins could very well be keeping an eye on *her*. To make certain she did no harm. In the next instant, she dismissed the thought as uncharitable.

Reaching the bed, she let out a soft sigh as she took in the small figure lying there. A comely lad, to be sure, even with his wee features so slack and pale. *Ach, the little ones are always the worst to see this way! Children should be vibrant and laughing . . . full of life and straining at the bit to embrace it!*

Moving quickly and efficiently, she examined the boy. She felt for a pulse—it was thready and weak—and frowned when she laid her hand on the side of his neck: feverish. She began to lift the bandages . . . .

And suppressed a groan. The mangled leg was bad, very bad. But someone had done a fair job of stitching torn flesh and setting broken bones. Perhaps he wouldn't lose it, though he'd surely lose the use of it. The wound to the head was another matter. This was, indeed, grave . . . and likely mortal.

Yet as she'd indicated to the servants, she didn't believe in giving up. Praying silently to the Blessed Virgin for help and guidance, she withdrew some pouches from her bag. At her request, the butler had brought a kettle of water with them and set it to the boil when he built up the fire. Stirring the powders from her bag into the water, she sat down to watch. And wait.

Minutes passed, the ticking of the clock on the mantel measuring out seconds. Glancing at the bed, Caitlin bit her lip, schooling herself to patience. She must allow the exact time needed for the brew to steep, just as Crionna had shown her. Ach, but it was so hard, what with the lad lying there, still as death! At long last, she heaved a sigh. The brew was finally right. Caitlin withdrew some clean rags from her bag and set about making a poultice . . . .

* * *

Quelling a shudder, Adam watched a disgruntled Appleby take his leave. He'd half expected the creature to disappear in a puff of smoke, but m'lord merely closed the library door behind him. Slammed it, actually.

Adam smiled. He'd always had an affinity for chess. No one at Eton had ever bested him. The worst he'd ever suffered at Oxford was a stalemate, and that was on a night he'd been thoroughly foxed.

Now, at the age of thirty-four, he'd lost more men than he'd ever done in a lifetime of playing. And lost the match. Yet it was the greatest victory he could imagine. Because, before losing, he'd managed to capture no less than eight chessmen from his opponent. From the devil himself.

He looked at the eight white marble pieces piled behind his side of the board. He remembered how chagrined he'd been when Appleby had won the draw for white; since white always went first, it had given Appleby the automatic advantage. Adam had felt sure it was an unlucky portent of how the match would go.

And yet he'd no complaints. Eight men! Giving him another *forty years of life* before the bargain was fulfilled. By the time that bloody fiend came to drag him to perdition, his son would be well launched. Andrew would likely present him with grandchildren before he . . . .

Thoughts of his son had him suddenly rigid with suspicion. Prior to leaving, Appleby had assured him he'd find Andrew alive and improving, yet what did that mean? He ought to have insisted on taking the little bastard back to his chamber and seen for himself. Contract or no, he didn't trust the archfiend. Not one bloody bit!

Pivoting on his heel, Adam raced from the room. On his way to his son, he absently rubbed a finger on his left hand; the tip was sore from where he'd pricked it with Appleby's knife. He dismissed it. The little reminder would soon fade. He'd give the damned business no more thought. He had no regrets. His son was what mattered, not he.

He'd been living in hell for years, anyway.

Caitlin shifted her weight as she knelt beside the huge canopied bed. She was fighting exhaustion, but she wouldn't give in to it. Not while she had strength enough to pray. As she saw it, prayer was the lad's only hope.

She'd done everything she could think of for the wee lord. And yet he'd not shown the slightest sign of regaining his senses. She feared . . . *Ach, no!* That way lay certain failure. She'd not *let* herself fear!

"Hail, Mary, full o' Grace," she murmured for the countless time since kneeling. "The Lord is with Thee. Blessed art Thou among—"

"Mama, my leg hurts!"

A gasp from Mrs. Hodgkins at the doorway echoed in the still chamber. Caitlin's breath caught. Releasing it slowly, she raised her head. And met the clear-eyed gaze of the child on the bed.

"God be praised!" she whispered, but this was drowned out by the housekeeper's cry of wonder.

In a steady voice, the boy complained of thirst. Weeping with joy, Mrs. Hodgkins ran to fetch Jepson. Caitlin said a silent, "Hail, Mary," and helped the child sip from a cup of water she'd left on the bed stand.

"Are you my new governess?" the boy asked as Caitlin

set the cup aside and checked him for fever. He was cool to the touch.

"No," she answered, smiling. He had the loveliest blue eyes. Like the sky on a clear summer's day, they were, and fringed with thick, sooty lashes. "Me name's Caitlin, and I'm . . . a friend."

"My name's Andrew," he told her as she began to check his wounds. It was astounding . . . a miracle, really. Not only that he'd regained his senses, although that was astonishing all by itself. But the head wound! It had healed beyond anything she might have expected. A miracle, sure.

Andrew complained again about the pain in his leg, and she swiftly raised the blanket to check it. Murmuring words of reassurance when he began to whimper with the pain, she frowned. The leg hadn't fared as well as his head; it was still in terrible—

"Who the devil are you!"

Caitlin swung sharply about, saw a tall man charging through the doorway.

"And what the hell are you doing with my *son*?" he demanded in a furious voice, hovering over her with clenched fists.

Caitlin blanched, and hurriedly crossed herself. It was the man with the scar. From her dream.

Chapter 4

Heart slamming against her chest, Caitlin stared mutely at the irate lord. Dark . . . uncommonly handsome, despite the scar . . . imposing, he was the exact image of the man in her dream. The one who watched as she played chess with—

"Answer me, damn it!"

His demand jerked her mind from that chilling image. Caitlin licked lips suddenly gone dry, trying to gather her wits. "I-I'm the new—"

"M'lord, *is it true?*" The butler's excited voice rang from the doorway. "Is his lordship awake?"

Adam tore his eyes from the red-haired girl and darted an irritated glance over his shoulder. Jepson hovered in the doorway, backed by several murmuring servants clad in nightclothes. All were straining for a glimpse of the bed. Swearing softly, Adam swung his gaze to it . . . .

He wanted to sob and shout for joy at the same time.

He'd done it! *He'd saved his son*. Andrew's eyes . . . his own eyes . . . looked back at him from his son's small face, their gentian depths lucid and focused.

"Andrew . . . ," he murmured thickly, "I—" His voice cracked, and he fell silent, trying to master his emotions.

"Papa," the boy whimpered, "it h-hurts! My leg . . ."

A sudden movement beside him drew Adam's attention. The stranger he'd surprised at the bedside was reaching for his son.

"Keep your bloody hands off him!" he snarled, shoving her away.

"Your lordship!" Jepson rushed into the room as Caitlin recoiled from the marquis's angry hands. "Please don't blame the girl, your lordship," the butler implored. "She's the one who worked this miracle. She's—"

"Explain yourself, man." Adam wanted to laugh at the biting irony of Jepson's words. No miracle had brought his son's cure. Far from it! But he worried the red-haired chit was somehow tied to Appleby. Out of the corner of his eye, he saw the creature try to withdraw. He clamped a hand on her shoulder and speared his butler with an angry gaze. "*Now*, Jepson! Or I'll let the magistrate deal with this intruder."

Mrs. Hodgkins hurried forward. "B-begging your pardon, your l-lordship, but she's no intruder. She—she's the Irish Angel, and she—"

"She's *what*?"

Jepson coughed discreetly and set a hand on the housekeeper's arm. "Ahem, actually, your lordship, she's a new housemaid we've hired." He glanced at Hodgkins. "But those who . . . where she was formerly employed, ah, sometimes called her the Irish Angel." The staid butler looked almost comical as he tried to summon an explanation that would satisfy his employer.

"Ah . . . for her extraordinary healing skills, your lord-ship."

"Indeed." Adam offered the word coolly, running his eyes over the trembling girl in the silence that followed. Satisfied Appleby had kept his word regarding Andrew, he considered the odd coincidence of the girl's appearance.

His gaze moved to a poultice applied to his son's brow. That hadn't been there before. Someone had made a clumsy attempt of some kind . . . .

His eyes returned to the girl, and he gazed at her thoughtfully. The servants' claims were all rot, of course. But he all at once saw the advantage in letting them stand. He'd be saved unwelcome speculation about Andrew's otherworldly recovery.

"What's your name, girl?" It was a command, though he tried to soften the tone somewhat. With a growing awareness, he noted the chit was young . . . and inordinately pretty.

"C-Caitlin, sorr—I mean, yer lordship." Caitlin was still dealing with the shock of recognition. And the fact that he still had her pinned by the shoulder wasn't helping her composure. "Caitlin O'Brien," she added, summoning the bravado to raise her chin a notch.

"The Irish Angel?"

Caitlin bristled. The mockery in his voice was subtle, perhaps meant to go over a poor Irish peasant's head, but she hadn't missed it. She forced a nod, not trusting her voice. It wasn't just his tone that angered her; the child was *hurting*, and *he* stood here asking questions!

"Very well, Caitlin." The marquis released her shoulder. "I collect I am obliged to you for my son's . . . miraculous recovery."

Adam's gaze shifted to his two upper servants. "She's to have a rise in wages," he told them, then gestured at the doorway. "Now remove everyone at once. I wish to be alone with my son."

"Oh, but yer lordship!" Caitlin pulled her gaze from the softly fretting child and looked up at him. "I cannot leave the lad yet! He's hurtin', and I've some willow bark in—"

The marquis's quelling look stopped her cold. "Remove *everyone,* Jepson," he said dismissively, and he turned to the bed.

Caitlin opened her mouth to protest, but a look from the butler froze the words in her throat. Mrs. Hodgkins placed a hand on her arm, and the two upper servants led her hurriedly from the chamber.

Livid with anger, Adam paced the bedchamber. Andrew was asleep, finally. But not before his father had spent nearly thirty long, agonizing minutes hearing him cry with pain. The leg wasn't healed at all!

Appleby had *tricked* him. Andrew was alive, yes, but his leg was so badly crushed, even a layman like himself could see he'd never walk again. His son would be a cripple.

Rage, naked and terrible, welled up like lava inside him. "Appleby, you bastard!" he screamed. "Come *back* here. You've unfinished business with me!"

The walls rang with Adam's fury. The child whimpered and stirred restlessly on the bed. Yet nothing else happened.

No one came.

Adam Lightfoot, fifth marquis of Ravenskeep . . . war hero . . . rakehell . . . unbeliever, clenched his fists and howled.

* * *

"Have some honey with your tea, Caitlin," Mrs. Hodgkins urged solicitously. "I've always found peppermint
tea soothing when taken with honey, and you do seem
a bit out of sorts." They were sitting at a heavy oak table
in the servants' hall, just off the kitchens. Having sent
the rest of the staff back to bed, the butler and the
housekeeper had ushered Caitlin here after the
marquis's brusque dismissal.

"Looks as though she could do with some sleep,"
Jepson pointed out as Caitlin stifled a yawn. "Fact is,
we all could," he added, taking a sip of his own tea.
"Been a long night."

"Indeed," Mrs. Hodgkins said cheerfully. "And
who'd have imagined it would turn out so different from
the way it began?" She beamed at Caitlin. "Thanks
entirely to the Irish Angel here."

Caitlin shook her head tiredly. "I truly didn't do all
that much." She kept seeing the vastly improved head
wound in her mind. Only the Almighty could have done
that. She reminded herself never, ever, to underestimate
the power of prayer. "But I do worry for the lad's leg,
sorr," she added, frowning. "It needs further tendin',
and—and . . ." Thoughts of the marquis's abrupt dismissal had her biting her lip.

"There, there, child." Mrs. Hodgkins patted her
hand. "His lordship isn't a cold man, despite how he
seemed. He's just been under a terrible strain, what
with all that's happened. I'm sure he'll be more . . .
approachable in the morning."

"Exactly," said Jepson. He gave Caitlin a level look.
"There's no question but that you'll remain, of course."

Remain? In the very house belonging to—

"To oversee Lord Andrew's recovery, if nothing else," said the butler, noting her frown.

"Oh, but I—"

"Indeed, my dear," Mrs. Hodgkins put in quickly. "You've already won a rise in wages, and Jepson and I can see your duties are manageable, so never fret. The important thing is Lord Andr—"

An agonized howl resounded from the upper quarters of the town house. The marquis's quarters.

"Good heavens!" the housekeeper cried. "What—"

It came again. Raw . . . chilling in its intensity. Frozen, the three looked at one another, worry vying with fear in their eyes.

It was Jepson who broke the tableau. "Perhaps something's happened to . . ." He couldn't say the thing they all feared. He leapt instead from the table and made for the stairs. The two women quickly followed, Caitlin's pulse hammering in her throat. Had the lad been taken, after all? Was it the wail of a father's grief they'd heard?

Signaling the women to wait down the hallway, Jepson gingerly approached the marquis's bedchamber. As he raised his hand to knock, something crashed against the door. He hesitated. The sound of splintering wood reverberated through the oak panels. Alarmed, he mastered his apprehension and knocked.

There was a moment of silence before the door swung wide. *"I'll wring your stinking—*bloody hell! Jepson, I thought I told you to go to bed!" The marquis's face was thunderous, his eyes crackling with rage.

"Beg pardon, your lordship." Jepson backed carefully away. "I-I was just—I'm on my way, your lordship. At once, your—"

"No, wait!"

The butler stood absolutely still. He'd never seen his employer like this, and he'd served the household many years. The man looked crazed. Had events unhinged him? A soft whimpering from the bed told him the child was alive, thank heaven, but—

"My son . . ." Adam made a helpless gesture toward the bed. "It's his leg. He's—"

"I understand, your lordship." Jepson's face sagged with relief: Lord Andrew's suffering had brought on this terrible anger. He took in the broken vase on the carpet, the splintered chair. *Understandable . . . entirely understandable.* "Shall I fetch someone to tend him, your lordship?"

"Yes . . . do that," Adam said tightly. He reached for the coat he'd slung over a chair sometime during the night. Rage still seethed inside him. He'd all he could do to keep it in check, yet he knew he must. Anger sapped the ability to think clearly, and he was having difficulty doing that right now; his emotions were bubbling over. It was why he couldn't go near Andrew. The child's pain threatened to tear him apart.

But overriding all was the burning need to get hold of Appleby. To find that demonic piece of slime and crush him under his boot heel like the vermin he was! "Have my curricle brought round," he told the butler. He'd an idea, and the sooner he moved on it, the better.

"At once, your lordship." Jepson paused, glanced down the hallway where the two women waited. "Ah, shall I fetch the young miss to attend his lordship? The young Irishwoman, that is, your lordship. I mean, since she's already—"

"Yes, yes," Adam replied absently, drawing on his driving gloves and moving toward the door. His thoughts were already on his club. It was where he'd met Appleby. Someone at Brooks' ought to be able to direct him to the bastard's lodgings. *Some other damned fool.*

* * *

"I've never heard anyone who talks like you, Caitlin,"
Andrew told her shyly. "It's quite different, d'you know
. . . all lovely and—and a little like singing."

The child's smile displayed deep dimples. They made
Caitlin wonder if he resembled his father in that respect
as well as others. But then, she couldn't imagine that
dark lord smiling, no matter how hard she tried.

"Is it, now?" she returned with an exaggerated look
of surprise. "Ach! And here I was thinkin' I'd mastered
tyin' me tongue in knots and soundin' just like a proper
Englishwoman!"

The sound of Andrew's laughter was a joy. Such a far
cry from the pitiful whimpering that tore at her heart
when she'd first come to try to ease his pain. But the
willow bark tea had done its work, and perhaps the fresh
poultices she'd applied to the leg as well.

"How's the leg, lad?" she asked with as little concern
as she could muster. No sense frightening the child.
"And none o' that stiff upper lip blather, me boyo!"
she added, wagging a finger at him.

He'd suffered through her ministrations so bravely,
she'd wanted to cry herself. There'd been tears in his
eyes, and his small square chin had trembled, but not
a sound out of him. The lad was brave as they come.
Not to mention sweet-tempered, and bright as a brand-
new penny. Her heart had gone out to him at once.

"It hardly hurts at all," he said, then slid a glance to
the plate standing beside a glass of milk on the bed
stand. "But perhaps . . . ," he added, eyeing her carefully, "if I had another biscuit, I'd feel even better."

"Hmm . . . ," she replied, making a great show of
giving this due consideration. "D'ye really think so?"

"Oh, yes! Cook makes the most delic—uh, the most helpful biscuits."

Sharp as a tack, and no mistake. Caitlin handed him one of the sugared treats Mrs. Hodgkins had brought up from the kitchens. She, Jepson and Caitlin were, none of them, getting any sleep this night; yet they were so buoyed by the lad's recovery, they seemed to have tapped into a store of energy they hadn't known was there. "But," she said to Andrew, "ye must drink up yer milk with it, lad. Milk's what's wanted for mendin' broken bones, and ye've yer share o' those."

Andrew dutifully took the glass she handed him. "You know lots of things," he said around a yawn.

Caitlin nodded to herself. The sleeping draught she'd given him was working. And high time, too. 'Twas a couple of hours before dawn. "Do I, now?" she said.

Andrew nodded sleepily, swallowed the last of his milk. "Like milk for mending bones. Who told them to you?"

Caitlin saw Crionna's beloved face in her mind's eye, and suddenly she found herself fighting a wave of grief. It was stronger than anything she'd experienced in months. She wondered why she should be so affected now.

The reason wasn't that hard to piece out. She'd been alone for so long, throwing herself into her work. It had kept her busy . . . kept the darkness at bay. But now, suddenly, she was in the midst of a large household. A household with people she'd already come to know in a way she never knew those she encountered in her far-ranging travels. People she'd come to know, aye . . . and care about.

And the caring awoke kindred feelings . . . memories of the woman she'd loved. *Ach, Crionna! I miss ye so.*

*How I long for your wisdom and strength. Especially now I've
blundered into the dream's terrible—*

"Caitlin . . . ?" Andrew's prompting pulled her back
to the moment. Reminding her he'd asked her a question.

"Who taught me?" she said with a smile. "A wonderful auld wise woman, lad. She told me such things . . .
taught me all I know. All that's important, that is."

"Was she your governess?"

Caitlin laughed. "In a manner o' speakin', she was.
But she was also somethin' more."

"But she wasn't your mother, was she." It was not a
question. Andrew stared intently at his lap. "Mothers
don't have time to tell you things."

Caitlin felt a stab of pity. So, his mother hadn't had
"time" to tell him things, had she? Was that a clue why
the lad hadn't asked for her? She'd been thinking them
lucky. She and the two upper servants had discussed
the marchioness's death, and how it might affect him.
They'd decided it wasn't their place to tell him, but
they'd worried what to say it if he asked for his mother.
Now it seemed there might be reasons why he hadn't.
And Caitlin didn't like what she was hearing.

"I think 'tis time ye were asleep, lad," she said. She
eased him down and began to tuck the covers around
him. "But I'll sing t' ye, t' help the sleep along, if ye
like."

Andrew's eyes went wide. "Oh, yes, awfully! Nurse
used to sing to me." He frowned. "But that was a long
time ago. I have a governess now"—he yawned sleepily—"instead of Nurse. And my governess . . . says"—
another yawn—"I'm too old . . . for a lulla—a lulla—"

"A lullaby?"

He nodded.

"Well, that may be because she doesn't know any—

but *I* do!'' Caitlin winked at him, and when he grinned back at her, she began to sing . . . .

Dawn was lighting the eastern sky above the rooftops as Adam returned home. Telling the sleepy-eyed footman on duty to find his bed, he made for the stairs. His mood was foul. No one could tell him where Appleby might be found. Fact was, the more he asked about the mysterious stranger who'd appeared in their midst in April, the less he could be sure anyone knew.

Some said they believed he hailed from the south, but they couldn't say where, exactly. Others swore he was a northerner. Still others maintained he'd come from the Continent. Only one thing was certain: Appleby had vanished without a trace.

Disheartened by the whole affair, Adam decided to let it rest until he caught some sleep. He was dead tired and sick with worry over Andrew. Guilt gnawed at him as he approached his chambers. He'd been so caught up in his frenzy to find Appleby, he'd left while his son was distressed and in pain. What in hell was the matter with him?

A grim smile twisted his lips. What in *hell,* indeed.

He entered his bedchamber, closing the door softly behind him. Light from a few candles guttering in a branch near the bed allowed him to see it clearly. He paused. The scene that met his gaze was reassuring . . . and oddly touching.

The little Irish maid sat in a bedside chair beside his son, who'd edged to the side of the bed closest to her. The girl's head rested on her forearm, which lay on the mattress near Andrew's head. She was sleeping as soundly as his son. Her free hand was on the mattress, too, where Andrew clutched it, even in sleep. There was a soft smile on the child's face.

Adam must have made some sound as he approached the bed. The girl came awake with a start. Her head swung toward him, and she gasped.

"Sorry if I gave you a fright," he said, keeping his voice low. He glanced at Andrew; the child hadn't awakened.

"Oh, no, sorr—Ach! Yer lordship, I mean." Caitlin glanced down and carefully extricated her hand from the boy's. " 'Tis I should be apologizin', milord. I-I didn't mean t' fall asleep here, d'ye see, but I was singin' the lad this lullaby, and—"

"Miss . . . Caitlin, isn't it?" As she nodded, Adam ran his gaze over her. He recalled thinking her pretty. Now he realized that had been well short of the mark.

She was exquisite.

Coppery hair, burnished with fiery highlights, fell over her arms and shoulders in a wealth of shining curls. Her eyes, huge in her face, were the most incredible shade of green, not the gray he'd thought them earlier. Soft and deep, they reminded him of mossy banks along a hidden stream in summer.

Her features were soft, too, and delicate. Blinking up at him, still muzzy from sleep, she looked like a sleepy-eyed angel . . . .

He hid a smile. "Caitlin . . . the Irish Angel?" He thought he saw her blush, but the lighting made it impossible to be sure.

"Well, Caitlin," he said, allowing the smile to form at last, "there's no need to apologize. It's clear you've been a great help to my son. I'm grateful for it."

Caitlin nodded, too mesmerized to speak. His smile! It

thoroughly transformed the man. Utterly, she thought, noting the answer to the thing she'd wondered about earlier. The adult version of Andrew's dimples were deep grooves bracketing his father's mouth when he smiled. The marquis was so handsome, she could scarcely look at him. Beautiful, in a dark sort of way, despite the scar on his . . . .

Thoughts of the scar plunged her into the old fear. She tore her eyes from him and quickly stood, searching for something to say. Anything, as long as it banished the thing hovering at the edges of her mind.

"I made some willow bark tea for the lad," she said, gesturing at a cup on the bed stand. "If he should awaken in discomfort, ye might offer him some more.

" 'Twill ease the pain, d'ye see," she added when he didn't respond. "And the leg—well, I won't lie t' ye, milord—'tis in a bad way. But I've been applyin' poultices to it"—*and prayin' somethin' fierce*—"which is what I did for that wound t' his head . . ."

"What is it?" Adam asked, seeing her frown.

Caitlin met his eyes and nearly looked away. They were beautiful eyes, now he was no longer scowling. A deep, vibrant blue and fringed with thick black lashes, just like Andrew's.

She cleared her throat, swallowed. "Odd thing, that head wound, milord. 'Twas healed remarkably at the time ye left, earlier this evenin', but . . ."

"Go on," he said. Her voice had a low, husky quality to it that was at odds with her diminutive size. And then there was that lilting brogue. He thought he could listen to her speak all night and never tire of it.

"Well," said Caitlin, " 'tis healed even further now, milord. Beyond what I found earlier, I mean. Greatly beyond. There's naught but a slight reddenin' o' the skin! Lord Lightfoot, I've presided over the healin' of a great many injuries in me time, young as I am, but . . ." She shook her head. "I've niver seen the like!"

Caitlin was at a loss to explain the marquis's bitter laugh as he abruptly told her to go to bed.

Chapter 5

"Jepson, his lordship wants you!" Sally Hodgkins paused to catch her breath as she reached the servants' hall. "And he's in a temper!"

Jepson set down his dish of tea and made at once for the stairs. In a temper? In a rage, more likely! Rage seemed the only way to describe his lordship's state of mind lately. The marquis had not been an easy man to work for since his return from the Peninsula. Since the events of two nights ago, he'd become downright difficult.

They were all overset about the child's leg, of course. But his lordship was taking it especially hard. Yesterday he'd had no less than three additional doctors in to examine the lad. Not to mention the Prince Regent's personal physician. After each left, sadly shaking his head, Lord Lightfoot had become further enraged. If that were even possible.

Jepson didn't understand it. The child was *alive.* Alive,

when he'd been given up for dead! One would think a parent might be grateful for such a miracle. But Lord Andrew's miraculous reprieve had only served to drive his father into the worst sort of . . . melancholy.

Yes, melancholy, Jepson decided as he reached the top of the stairs. He'd served the man a long time. He recognized the sad, haunted look behind the anger. A look that had first appeared after his lordship's marriage. Deep melancholy, for a certainty, though the outward show was rage.

Jepson sighed as he approached the lord's chambers. He wondered what had set him off this time.

His employer was furiously pacing the length of the Aubusson carpet when he bade the butler enter. Jepson wisely remained just inside the door; he'd wait to be told what was amiss. Doing otherwise would only earn him a measure of that wrath heaped upon his own head.

The marquis reached the edge of the carpet, pivoted, and speared Jepson with his eyes. "Are you aware of the identity of a woman named Murch?" He ground this out between clenched teeth.

"Yes, your lordship. Miss Murch is the governess her ladyship recently engaged for—"

"And were you aware she brought the creature up with her from Kent?"

Jepson hesitated, then gave a nod. He'd totally forgotten Murch. The marchioness had given the woman leave to visit a sick relative in the city, just after they arrived; he'd barely taken notice of her. He explained this to his irate employer, wondering how the governess had had the misfortune to run afoul of his lordship's temper. Not that it was a difficult thing to do these days.

"I see," said the marquis in a voice that had grown dangerously soft. "And were you aware that Miss Murch had returned this morning?"

Jepson opened his mouth to answer, but the marquis leaned forward and cut him off. "Or that," he said tightly, "having read about my wife's demise in the *Post*, she took it upon herself to resume her duties, first thing—*by telling my son he's motherless?*"

"Good heavens!" Jepson was appalled. He hadn't known of her return, yet even if he had, he couldn't imagine needing to counsel the woman as to the delicacy of the situation. He hadn't hired her, but governesses were supposed to know what they were about. "The woman must be a heartless incompetent," he added without thinking, for it wasn't his place to comment.

Adam gave him a stiff nod, trying to control his anger. He hadn't liked the last woman Lucinda had engaged. He'd found her cold and rigid, and told his wife to sack her. That she'd replaced the creature with this equally worthless bitch made his blood boil.

He'd entered his son's chambers this morning to find the child sobbing. Murch was there, and the stupid twit blithely explained what she'd done. "Lady Lightfoot said I mustn't mollycoddle him," she'd informed him!

"I-I humbly beg your lordship's forgiveness," Jepson stammered. "I ought to have been aware Miss Murch had returned. Your lordship, I take full responsibil—"

"Never mind! I've just turned her off—without a character."

The butler nodded, schooling his features to show neither approval nor the relief he felt at his own reprieve. But what of the poor child? He ventured a query. "How is Lord Andrew faring, your lordship? Does he require someone to—"

"He already has her."

"Your lordship?"

With mixed feelings, Adam thought about the first

serious conversation he'd ever had with his son. He liked children, always had, and he loved his son. Yet he'd been away for a deal of the time the boy was growing past his infancy. How did one talk to a six-year-old? he'd wondered.

Somehow, he'd managed to dry Andrew's tears and get through the deuced difficult business of explaining the nature of death. He'd tried to be gentle, but because of his simmering wrath, he still wasn't sure he'd succeeded. He only knew he'd been grateful for getting through the entire business without once referring to heaven. Fortunately, Andrew hadn't asked if that was where his mother was. *He* certainly hadn't volunteered it!

The boy had seemed satisfied with what he'd told him, and Adam had been vastly relieved. Relieved, and then astonished. His tears forgotten, Andrew had promptly asked for that little Irish baggage to keep him company!

Glancing up, Adam saw the butler patiently waiting for a response. "Lord Andrew has requested that the new Irish maid attend him," he informed him.

Jepson's features rarely showed emotion, but Adam thought he detected an interested gleam in the old retainer's eyes.

"She's with him now," he added, then frowned. He didn't want to think about the warm smile Andrew had for the chit when she'd arrived. And that he himself had been unable to coax even the smallest one out of his son.

"She's to have an appropriate rise in wages," he told the butler crisply. Grabbing his hat and gloves, he strode toward the door.

Jepson looked completely at sea. "Er . . . appropriate, your lordship?"

Adam glanced at him before heading for the drive where his curricle waited. "Appropriate," he repeated. "I've just elevated her to governess."

"Caitlin, is Mama in heaven now?" Andrew looked at his new governess with worried eyes. He knew about heaven. The vicar at Ravenskeep's village church was to be his tutor one day, and he'd spoken of it. And about the Bad Place. Andrew had wanted to ask his father the question he now put to Caitlin, but he hadn't. Something in Papa's eyes had told him not to.

Caitlin gave him that smile that made him feel all warm and safe inside. Andrew felt himself relax a little. Caitlin was even easier to talk to than his best friend, Jeremy.

Though she smiled, Caitlin considered carefully how she should answer him. Privately, she had her doubts about heaven for a woman who'd had no time for her son. Yet she'd cut out her tongue before voicing them to the child. Andrew needed comforting, and, by all the saints, that's what he'd have! Still, she wouldn't lie outright to the lad . . . .

"And where else would she be?" she replied, careful to maintain her smile.

Andrew bit his lip, pondering for a moment, then met her eyes. "Jeremy Wells said a lot of people go to the Bad Place when they die."

"Did he, now?"

Andrew nodded solemnly, looking ill at ease.

"And who is Jeremy Wells, if I might be askin'?"

"He's the vicar's son, and he's *eight*."

Caitlin nodded thoughtfully. "Well, now, bein' a vicar's son is nothin' t' sneeze at, o' course. And as for his bein' eight"—she gave Andrew a look that said she was properly impressed—"I suppose we must regard what Jeremy says very carefully."

Another solemn nod.

"And what else does Master Jeremy say . . . about the bad place, I mean?"

"He says it's where the *wicked* go—straightaway!"

"Ach!" Caitlin exclaimed, pretending not to see the worried look on the boy's face. "There we have it, then!"

"We . . . we do?"

"We do, indeed." The two had been sitting side by side on a window seat in the schoolroom, with Andrew's injured leg propped on a chair amid some pillows. Now Caitlin scooted off the seat and knelt before the child. She took his small hand in hers.

"Andrew," she said, meeting his anxious eyes, "ye cannot think yer mother was a wicked person, now, can ye?" She held her breath, suddenly wondering if the question were wise.

She also hoped Andrew didn't notice her let it out in relief when he shook his head and smiled at her. Smiled with his whole face. The blue eyes crinkled at the corners, and his dimples deepened, just like his—

She cut off the thought; his father was already in her thoughts more than she liked. No sense inviting the devil—*Ach! The man has me worried, and no mistake! If it weren't for the lad—*

Again, Caitlin throttled her thoughts. "Have we answered yer question, then?" she asked Andrew softly.

"Yes, thank you, Caitlin." Andrew looked thoughtful as she rejoined him on the window seat. "Caitlin . . . ?"

"Aye, lad?"

"Why is it all right to call you 'Caitlin'? Mama said I must call my other governess 'Miss Murch.' She said it wasn't"—Andrew paused, his brow furrowed in thought—"wasn't proper to call a governess by her Christian name."

Caitlin smiled. She was hardly a "proper" governess. Not that that had mattered to Lord Lightfoot. He'd asked if she could read and cipher. When she told him she could, he'd pronounced her the lad's new governess—just like that! Ach, he was a strange one, he was.

Aye, strange . . . and he frightens me out of my wits!

The child's tug on her sleeve pulled Caitlin back to the present. "Well, ye see, lad," she said, "there are all sorts o' people in the world. Some are . . . Christian-name people . . . d'ye know, like yer friend Jeremy . . ."

"He's my *onliest* bestest friend," Andrew put in.

She nodded. "And ithers who are family-name people . . ."

"Like Miss Murch?"

"Aye, like Miss Murch . . . and the bishop when he comes t' call." She wasn't certain Anglican bishops did this, but it seemed a safe bet, given the importance of Andrew's family. "Now, meself," she went on, "I'm a Christian-name sort . . . most o' the time, at least. That means, lad, that if I heard ye Miss O'Brienin' me, I'd likely faint dead away!"

She looked at him wide-eyed, clutching his shoulders in an exaggerated show of seeking reassurance. "And we couldn't have that, now, could we?"

He shook his head, a grin tugging at the corners of his mouth.

"I mean," she went on with a straight face, "there I'd be, laid out on the carpet"—she gestured broadly at the floor with a sweep of her arm—"as if someone had popped me a facer!"

Andrew covered his mouth as the giggle emerged.

"And ye'd be callin' for a footman t' fetch the vinai-grette and hartshorn, all the day long! Well, we simply cannot have it. So 'tis Caitlin, me boyo.'' She winked at him and grinned. "Caitlin, the live-long day!''

"Oh, Caitlin,'' Andrew told her between giggles, "Jeremy isn't my onliest bestest friend anymore. Now *you're* my bestest friend, too!''

Adam returned early from his club, no further along in his search for clues to Appleby's whereabouts. He'd had a throbbing headache since rising that morning. A legacy from the night before, when he'd polished off a bottle of brandy. Not that it had done any good. The confirming opinions of four highly recommended physicians, including Prinny's own, hadn't been changed by getting foxed. Andrew would never walk again, and no amount of liquor could blot that truth from his mind.

Hoping to banish his despairing mood, he headed straight for the schoolroom. The time spent with his son that morning had been the singular bright spot in his day. It had also reminded him how little he knew his only child. He vowed to remedy that—starting now.

As he drew near the room on the third floor, he heard . . . *giggles*. A child's giggles . . . and a female's.

The schoolroom door was partially ajar. As the sounds of merriment spilled into the hallway, Adam slowed and stood just outside the door. The lilting syllables of an Irish brogue rippled on the air.

"Ach, go on with ye! Six! The poor man had *six fingers*—all on one hand? And what o' his ither hand, then?''

Andrew's giggles didn't abate. "Just five—but he's not a poor man, Caitlin. Jeremy says he's nasty. And rich as Cro—Cro—''

"Croesus?''

"Yes, and . . . Caitlin, what's Croesus?"

"Not *what,* but *who,* lad. Croesus was a very rich king who lived a long time ago, as I recall hearin' somewhere. But back t' Jeremy's rich uncle o' the six fingers, boyo."

A smothered giggle. "His rich, *nasty* uncle, Caitlin!"

"Aye, that one. If the poor—er, not very poor man has the normal five fingers on one hand, but six on the ither, can ye tell me how many fingers he has alt'gither, Andrew?"

Adam's brows lifted as he caught the drift of what she was doing. The little minx was actually conducting a lesson! But had ciphering ever been taught this painlessly? He recollected his own sessions with tutors. Each with a book in one hand—and a birch rod in the other.

But did the chit's method work? All well and good to spare the rod, but—

"Eleven!" Andrew's triumphant voice rang out, and his father grinned.

"Right ye are, boyo!" Caitlin announced, giving Andrew a hug. "Ach, ye're a clever one, ye are, and that's no blarney! Why, most six-year-olds can't even *count* to eleven, Andrew, yet here ye are—"

"Ah, but we Lightfoots have a history of producing precocious children, Miss O'Brien." Adam saw the girl's eyes widen as he strolled into the schoolroom. So did his son's, but there was a difference: Andrew merely seemed surprised, while . . . . *Bloody hell. The chit's afraid of me!*

Andrew's giggle pulled Adam from this disturbing thought. "You're going to make her faint, Papa!" the child exclaimed.

Caitlin tore her gaze from the handsome face with its ominous scar as the child tugged on her sleeve. "What is it, lad?"

"Papa just *Miss O'Briened* you!" Andrew chortled. "Shall we ring for the vinai—vinai—"

"Vinaigrette, t' be sure!" Caitlin exclaimed, thrusting her fears aside for the moment. She slapped her hand comically on her chest. "Ach, I'm feelin' faint already!"

Despite his ugly mood of minutes before, Adam felt oddly buoyant. His headache was gone. Laughter welled up inside him, drawn by his son's infectious giggles. "Would someone"—he chuckled, looking from his son's delighted face to the diminutive, grinning redhead—"please tell me what's going on?"

Andrew explained about "Miss O'Briening," and when Adam promised to call the governess only Caitlin from then on, they all laughed.

At length, the marquis grew serious. "Andrew . . ." His eyes moved to a table bearing a chess set, and he strode over to it and carried it to the window seat. "While I have a chat with Miss, uh, with Caitlin, would you set up the men as I showed you, son?"

The boy grinned, complying at once, while Adam drew Caitlin aside. "How's his leg?" he murmured. "Any pain?"

"Look at him, milord," she whispered. "Does he look as if it hurts him?"

Adam looked, and heard his son humming as he carefully set up the chessmen. He shook his head. "No, of course not. But . . . it's just that the physicians said—"

"Physicians don't know everythin', milord," Caitlin sniffed. The one who'd attended the Prince Regent was the most arrogant man she'd ever met. He'd taken one look at her poultices and pronounced them quackery, she later learned. That was after the numbskull sought her out and told her to go back to her Irish bogs!

"I'm aware," said Adam, "of the rudeness of His

Highness's physician toward you, and I'm sorry for it, Caitlin."

Still speaking in a low voice, he had to bend to reach her ear, because of her diminutive stature, and Caitlin felt herself flush. It wasn't so much because of the incident he cited as it was the man's nearness. He was so close, she could distinguish the tiny white lines fanning his eyes, where the sun hadn't bronzed his skin. And the scent of him. He smelled . . . masculine, she supposed it was, but in the nicest sort of way. Of horses, and leather, and a faintly spicy scent that might have come from the soap he used.

Then he smiled at her, and her breath caught. It was only a smile, but bestowed on her this close, it—*Sweet Holy Mary!* Her reaction went clear to her toes.

"Suffice it to say, Caitlin," he went on, "my son requested the restoration of your poultices the moment the man left."

As she stepped back a pace and nodded, Adam noted a charming blush stealing over her face, and the light sprinkling of freckles dusting her pert little nose. With those wide green eyes, she was all innocence, and purity itself. He'd forgotten there were such females in the world.

The thought made him frown. If she knew what was good for her, the innocent Miss Caitlin O'Brien would run from this place. From *him*—and never look back! Blood and ashes, he felt filthy just looking at her.

"Take an hour for yourself, Caitlin," he said curtly. "I require some time alone with my son. You'll be summoned when his chess lesson is over."

Adam watched hurt and confusion cross her face at his tone, and he wondered at the stab of regret he felt. *Silly chit!* he admonished silently as she curtsied and scurried out. *You should be thanking your stars I've any charity left in me.*

He made a mental note to see Vanessa that evening. The clever Cyprian was just what he needed. Just the thing, in fact: a damned whore for his damned soul!

Chapter 6

Caitlin stood in the schoolroom. Across the chamber from her, Andrew sat at a table, playing chess with his father. The child laughed at something the marquis said, and moved a white piece on the board. His father nodded approvingly and moved a black one. Caitlin's eyes went from father to son as each took his turn, several times. At length, the marquis moved the tallest black piece on the board. Once again, Caitlin's gaze moved back to the child. But as she did this, Andrew disappeared. In his place sat the monstrous satanic figure she recalled from another time. The Beast. With a taloned claw, it moved a white piece on the board. She saw the marquis reach for one of the black pieces. No! She knew he must not play with the black piece. She tried to tell him, but the words stuck in her throat. The marquis's hand drew nearer to the piece. Still, the words wouldn't come. Yet she had to warn him! She—

Caitlin awoke with a scream clogging her throat. A nameless terror nailed her to the bed. She kept her eyes shut, afraid of what she might see. Perspiration trickled down her back, soaking her bed gown. She was shaking so hard, she thought she might shatter into countless brittle pieces. Jaws clenched, she made herself open her eyes and look around . . . .

Moonlight filtered into the small bedchamber they'd given her in the servants' wing. It limned the plain white curtains at the window and silvered the room's few pieces of simple furniture. There was enough light to tell her she was alone.

She let out a harsh breath, forced herself to relax tautly drawn muscles. Sucking in air, she let out another. Slowly, she felt the terror recede. Not completely, but to a plane where she could examine it. Consider its ramifications without succumbing to the scream that still pushed at her throat.

So the dreams had followed her. She had to own, she'd been expecting it. Lord Lightfoot was the man with the scar, after all. But tonight's dream was different. In the earlier version, *she'd* been the one playing chess with . . . .

She shuddered, and thrust the image from her mind, concentrating on the marquis. Something about him had changed as well. And not just in the dream. He no longer frightened her as he had at first. Instead, she felt . . . what? Pity? Perhaps, yet there was more to it than that. She feared for him, though she couldn't say why. And something else . . . .

Something continued to draw her to this man. She still wasn't certain what it was, but there was that . . . darkness about him. Yet she knew it hadn't always been there. And not just because she'd overheard Mrs. Hodgkins grumble that the war had scarred him in more ways than one. Caitlin herself had caught glimpses of another sort of man. Another man entirely, hidden inside the tortured soul he presented to the world.

She recalled his laughter when he'd played with his son. His obvious love for the lad seemed to bring out the . . . light inside him. Or what was left of it beneath the darkness . . . .

The darkness he isn't meant to have!

Caitlin gasped as the revelation struck. And it was a revelation, sure as she was Irish! She felt the truth of it, deep in her bones. The man wasn't meant for the evil she sensed hovering over his head. He was meant for the *Light*.

Was that why she was here? Why she'd had the dreams? But . . . what could she do? A poor Irish lass with no power at all? Merely thinking of those dreams had her quaking with fear.

Yet she couldn't shake the sense Lord Lightfoot desperately needed help. Hers? Ach, she wished Crionna were here! Wished she knew herself what it all meant.

A sense of desperation wound its way through these questions, and with it, the return of her fear. Closing her eyes, Caitlin did what she'd always done in the wake of her dreams and visions.

She began to pray.

Vanessa Marley trailed a perfectly manicured fingernail down the marquis of Ravenskeep's chest. "Ah, m'lord," she purred, her golden eyes following the trail as it crossed his hard, flat abdomen, "you are, indeed, a glorious specimen. I fear you've ruined me for anyone else."

Adam arched a brow, catching its reflection in the mirror cleverly concealed within the canopy over his mistress's bed. "Considering what you've cost me in clothes and trinkets, m'dear," he drawled, not moving his head from one of her satin pillows, "there had better be no one else." He played idly with a lock of her honey gold hair. "I'm known to be generous," he added in the same lazy tone, "but only when I'm assured exclusivity. If there's someone else . . ." His words trailed off suggestively.

Vanessa's finger paused, and she raised her head, smiling at him. Looking every inch the statuesque golden cat her beauty suggested. "And if there were, m'lord?" Her voice was seductive, teasing, but the golden eyes watched him carefully. "What would you do?"

Adam's hand caressed her perfumed shoulder, then toyed with the pouting nipple of a generous breast. He smiled back at her. "Why, I'd send your bills to him directly, of course," he replied, the smile not reaching his eyes, ". . . and your charming self as well."

Vanessa's lush mouth formed a moue. "It is really too bad of you, Adam, to tease me so callously. You know I've eyes for no one else."

She leaned forward, dangling her breasts just over his chest. Her breasts, she knew, were her best feature. On a body that had been praised by male members of the *haut ton* from Pall Mall to Piccadilly. The Prince Regent himself had remarked on them.

"Besides," she murmured, reaching for that part of his anatomy which had driven her to ecstasy only minutes before, "no one else has ever satisfied me as you have." She surrounded his shaft with her long, clever fingers. "Why, the size of you alone is proof of your singularity among men! But there's also your excellent knowledge of what to do with such magnificence, and—"

She gasped as he hardened in her hand. "You see, m'lord? Ready again in minutes! I vow, you are insatiable!"

Adam swallowed a bitter laugh as she slid over him and clamped her thighs around his erection like a vise. Little did she know how true her words were. Insatiable, indeed. Because he was never wholly satisfied in the first place. Not with her, not with any of the women he'd bedded in the dozens.

True, he thought as Vanessa managed a tricky little maneuver and began to undulate against him, he went through the motions readily enough. With a cunning bit of muslin like Vanessa practicing her wiles, he'd need to be dead not to respond physically. Just as he was now.

And in a few more moments he'd turn the tables and have her moaning and clawing at him for release. Then he'd drive into her till she screamed her pleasure and finally find his own physical release.

Yes, he went through all the motions. But finished hungrier than before. And he knew, if he spent his seed a dozen times of an evening, it would remain the same. *He* would remain the same. Empty. Bored with surfeit and condemned to remain so. *Blood and ashes, is this all there is?*

With a sound somewhere between a sob and a snarl, Adam twisted and pushed his mistress into the mattress. He caught the excitement in her eyes as she looked up at him, sensing the suppressed violence. He never hurt her, but she knew he was deliciously deft at making her beg.

Vanessa hissed, again reminding him of a cat, as he began to make good on the promise in his eyes. Plying the skills he'd honed on dozens of women like her, Adam gave himself over to the pleasures of the flesh.

Maybe, he told himself, maybe this time it would be enough.

* * *

It was nearly dawn when the marquis left the comfortably appointed, secluded town house he'd leased for his mistress. His curricle passed other fashionable conveyances as he tooled through the thoroughfares of London's West End. The *ton* partied and played late, with many a reveler finding his way home in the brief hours before dawn. Most would sleep the rest of the morning hours away, not rising from their silken covers until noon, or even later.

Adam's hands were steady on the ribbons despite the great deal of liquor he'd consumed. He'd instructed Vanessa to keep a liberal supply of his favorite brandy on hand when he set her up, and he hadn't stinted on making use of it tonight. He supposed he was foxed. Too bad it wasn't sufficient. Foxed . . . when he needed oblivion.

Reaching his Kensington town house, he handed over the curricle and team to a groom. Taking a branch from the yawning footman who let him in, he sent the man to bed. As he ascended the stairs, he stumbled halfway up, caught himself, and managed to negotiate the rest without mishap. He was weaving his way toward his chambers when he paused. A thin ribbon of light shone beneath the library doors.

Odd. The library was his inner sanctum. He knew of no one who'd appropriate it without his leave. Least of all at half five in the morning.

Caitlin whirled about and flattened herself against the books at her back when the door opened suddenly. "M-milord!" she exclaimed. A slim volume dangled from her nerveless fingers as she took in the disheveled figure of her employer. "Ach, but ye gave me a turn!"

"So . . . it's the little Irish Angel . . ." Adam stopped just inside the double doors, raking his eyes over her small, slender figure. She was clad in a simple white bed gown. A thick copper braid hung over one shoulder, its woven length burnished by light from a chamberstick resting on one of the shelves. She was barefoot. He wanted to smile at the toes peeking out from beneath her hem. But there wasn't a smile left in him tonight.

He scowled instead. "Who the devil gave you leave to prowl my library?"

"I-I . . . n-no one, milord." Caitlin wanted to run from him, from the anger in his voice and his threatening stance, but there was no way she could. He was clearly not himself . . . whatever that was, she found herself thinking. His fancy clothes were rumpled . . . neckcloth half undone . . . coat hooked on a finger and slung over his shoulder . . . midnight hair falling over his handsome brow.

"Well . . . ?" he prompted. Still scowling, Adam took a few steps toward her. He wasn't certain why he'd suddenly latched on to anger. Perhaps it was the way she looked. Pure and unsullied. Innocent as a child, while he himself reeked of dissipation and debauchery. Of far too much brandy and rutting in the bed of a high-priced whore.

Frightened, Caitlin shrank against the bookshelves as he drew near. But it was fear of the darkness she sensed more than a fear of the man himself. He looked angry, aye, but . . . .

She gathered her courage and met his gaze . . . and felt her breathing still. *His eyes.* Someone had said the eyes were windows to the soul. And if that were so, Lord Lightfoot was a soul in torment. Sweet Mary, she'd never seen such *pain*. Faith, and what on God's good green earth had put it there?

Licking lips suddenly gone dry, Caitlin stiffened her spine and raised her chin. Swallowing past her fear, she forced herself to retain his gaze and take a step toward him. More than ever, she sensed a need to help this man, and she would. God help her, if she could find a way, she *would*.

"I . . . I couldn't sleep, milord," she said with a calm she reached for and found, though she couldn't say how. "And I came here for somethin' t' read. 'Tis sorry I am t' be intrudin' where I oughtn't."

She paused, gave a small shrug. " 'Tis just that I"— she didn't know why she was telling him, but the words tumbled out, almost of their own accord—"I have disturbin' dreams sometimes. 'Tis often difficult t' return t' sleep."

"Disturbing dreams . . . ," Adam murmured. He knew about such things. Nightmares filled with maimed bodies and the screams of dying men . . . the stench of death everywhere. And blood, so much blood, all the rivers of the world couldn't begin to wash it away.

And then, of course, there was that other nightmare. The one that had come at the stroke of twelve on a night when he'd bartered his—

He yanked his thoughts back to the girl. What could *she* know to disturb her rest? She was an innocent, barely more than a child. Perhaps that was it. Perhaps her dreams were merely the stuff of childish fears. Like one he recollected Andrew having when he was three or four and a thunderstorm had frightened him. Yes, that had to be the case . . . a child's nightmares, nothing more.

Yet when he looked into those huge green eyes, as now, what he saw wasn't childlike. She was young, yes, but the eyes that met his gaze were strangely calm, and somehow . . . reassuring.

Adam gave himself a mental shake, wondering if the brandy had him hallucinating. But as he continued to probe, he knew he wasn't. There was enormous strength in that green-eyed gaze; it was filled with a resolve no child would have.

Slowly, half afraid she'd disappear if he moved too quickly, Adam cupped her face with his palm. "Who are you, Caitlin O'Brien?" he whispered. "Why are you here?"

Caitlin's pulse took a leap as his hand met her cheek. His touch was gentle, yet she burned with it. Not in a way that was painful, but—dear God! 'Twas like a current passing straight through her!

Swallowing past a thickness in her throat, she concentrated on what he'd asked . . . on the plea of desperation in his words. "I . . . I am a healer, milord. Just . . . a healer."

The blue eyes shone hard and brittle as glass in the candlelight. "And do you think you can heal me, Caitlin O'Brien? Do you really think you can do such a thing?"

"I . . . I can try, milord . . . if ye'll tell me what's hurtin'."

Adam gave a harsh laugh and dropped his hand. "Don't be so ready to accept such a burden, little Caitlin," he said bitterly. "You might find you'd bitten off far more than you can chew!"

"I . . . don't understand, milord." Yet Caitlin all at once thought perhaps she did. 'Twas the darkness, and he didn't want to speak of it. He didn't think she could bear it.

Perhaps I can't, she thought as an image of cloven hooves and great, hovering wings seized her. *Perhaps I'm mad even to try.*

"Excellent," Adam said, reaching for her chamberstick and placing it in her hand. "I suggest you find your bed before I decide to enlighten you."

"But—"

"Go to bed, Caitlin." Adam turned his back to her, a gesture of dismissal. "And be glad it's only dreams disturb your rest."

"Good mornin', Andrew," Caitlin chirped as she briskly entered the schoolroom. She'd had precious little sleep, what with the dream and her encounter with the marquis in the library; still, she was determined not to let it affect her mood. There was the child to think of.

"G'morning, Caitlin," came Andrew's barely audible response.

Caitlin stopped just inside the door, noting his frown. "Sure and there must be a reason ye're lookin' so glum, Andrew Lightfoot," she said, eyeing him carefully.

Was he in pain again? The leg had been coming along nicely, considering the damage that had been done to flesh and bone. It shouldn't be troubling him, but one could never be certain with a limb so badly mangled. She still marveled he hadn't lost it.

The six-year-old heaved a sigh and gestured morosely at the windows. "It's raining, Caitlin," he complained, "and today's the day we were to have our lessons *outside!*"

So that was it. His young lordship was growing restless after a fortnight of bedrest and confinement indoors. A good sign, for it showed he was well on the road to recovery.

As she crossed to where he sat, Caitlin tried not to dwell on how limited that recovery would be. Or on the effect this was bound to have on an energetic child who

was used to being active. "Ach, lad," she said sympatheti-
cally, "I know ye're disappointed, but the rain won't
last forever. Why, it might even clear by afternoon."

Andrew gave her a dubious look. "Jepson said it's a
good and steady, soaking rain that makes things grow."

Sitting beside him on the window seat, Caitlin took
his hand, smiled at him. "And so it will, Andrew. The
trees, the grass and shrubs, they all need rain. Especially
in the spring. 'Tis God's plan, d'ye see, the very thing
makes them green again after the long winter."

Andrew nodded reluctantly, casting another mourn-
ful look at the rain-streaked windows. "Caitlin . . . ?"
he asked as she reached for their ciphering slate. "Is it
truly God's plan? The rain, I mean."

"I've niver doubted it, lad. O' course, it calls for
sunshine as well. But without the rain, we'd niver have
all the lovely flowers, and that would be a shame."

The boy grew thoughtful for a moment, then slanted
a glance at the windows. "Well," he said grumpily, "if
that's so, why couldn't He make it rain only at night? I
shouldn't mind staying indoors *at night.*"

Ach! Why, indeed? Caitlin recalled asking Crionna the
same thing once. She also recalled Crionna's answer.
"Perhaps 'tis t' teach us patience, lad. And that we
cannot have everythin' we wish for, exactly when we
want it."

He nodded, but still looked glum. She doubted they'd
get very far with his lesson at this rate. "Very well, boyo,"
she said briskly, "since we can't be goin' t' the garden,
perhaps ye can think o' somethin' else that's . . . interestin'. T' make the time pass swiftly?"

She watched him ponder a second, then suddenly
brighten. "And no nonsense, ye understand!" she
added, wary of the look in his eye.

"It wouldn't be nonsense, Caitlin—honest!"

"All right, then, what is it?" She smiled at his excitement.

"I could teach you to play chess!"

God in heaven! Of all the things he might have suggested . . . Caitlin shivered, feeling as if something was closing in on her . . . something she couldn't prevent.

She made herself speak, but with great difficulty; her heart was beating like a giant drum. "Ah . . . Andrew . . ."

Wound up with enthusiasm, the child didn't notice the raw whisper of her voice. "Papa says it's bene—bene-fish-all to the mind, you know," he told her. "That means it's not at all nonsense! And I'll be fair, I promise. I'll even let you choose white. White always goes first, d'you see, and . . ."

At last noting her silence, her frozen posture, Andrew's face began to fall. "Caitlin . . . ?" he questioned plaintively. "What's the matter? Don't you want to? Oh, Caitlin—please say you'll try!"

She looked at him then. Looked at the crestfallen edges eating away the enthusiasm of seconds before. How could she disappoint him? This child who'd already been dealt more than one severe blow by fate. His mother dead . . . himself crippled, never to walk again.

But she was frightened. Scared to death of coming to fulfill the prophecy of the dreams. Dreams in which she played chess with the devil himself. But if she didn't know *how* to play . . . .

"Caitlin . . . ?" Andrew's lower lip quivered, and her heart went straight out to him. God save her, she already loved this child like her own! How could she possibly dash his hopes? She'd be no better than that Miss Murch.

She summoned a shaky smile. "I'll fetch the board," she told him.

* * *

A fortnight after Caitlin began learning the rudiments of chess, her employer came home one evening, totally dispirited. Someone at Watier's had mentioned that afternoon that he thought Appleby was a friend of Lord Byron's. Adam had immediately seized upon the notion. It made perfect sense.

Byron, already the subject of much talk for his affair with the outrageous Lady Caroline Lamb, had awakened one morning to find his wife had left him. The former Lady Annabella Milbanke had separated from her famous husband in January. Under scandalous circumstances. *Ton* gossip was rife with rumors the author of *Childe Harold* had been intimate with his own half sister, Augusta. Word was, he'd sired a child born to her the previous April! Byron had become a social pariah with the same *ton* that had lionized him a few years before.

What better candidate for a liaison with Appleby? The poet was a classic case of a man in thrall to the devil. Owned by him, and forever damned.

Just like Adam Lightfoot.

As Adam thought about it, it made more and more sense. Even the man's poetry—which the marquis admired no end—was fraught with allusions to a self-inflicted damnation: "I have been cunning in mine overthrow, / The careful pilot of my proper woe."

Adam grew so convinced, he'd set out at once for Byron's London residence. He'd been near certain the poet could help him locate Appleby. He was to be grievously disappointed.

George Gordon, Lord Byron, finding himself ostracized by the very people who'd once adored him, had left England, forever an exile. He'd departed for the Continent on April twenty-fifth. Today, the day the marquis of Ravenskeep had gone to look for him, was the twenty-sixth.

Adam wanted desperately not to dwell on it. It was almost as if he were being tantalized, fulfillment of his desires dangled before him, tempting him, but always out of reach. As if someone were toying with him. The way a heartless feline would torment a helpless mouse.

He didn't like to dwell on who that someone was, either. So after Jepson let him in this evening, he did the only thing he could think of to turn his mind to something more pleasant. He asked for his son.

"Ah, I believe it is past his lordship's bedtime," Jepson replied, "but your lordship just might be able to catch him if you hurry. Miss O'Brien's been with him, and . . ."

The butler's words trailed off as his employer dashed up the stairs. *Hope he finds the lad awake,* the old servant thought as he watched the marquis take the stairs two at a time. *He needs time with the child. Needs it more, even, than the child does. It's the only time the poor man seems alive.*

Chapter 7

Adam's steps slowed as he neared the bedchamber they'd given Andrew once he began to recover. Unlike the child's former quarters in the nursery, this was across the hall from Adam's own chambers. The door was ajar, spilling light into the hallway. Still, that didn't necessarily mean Andrew was awake.

Since the accident, Andrew slept poorly unless a lamp was left burning. Caitlin had suggested Andrew's door be left open as well, that his father might better hear him if he called. Adam had happily agreed. He, too, slept better knowing his son was within easy call.

Better, perhaps, but not well, Adam thought sardonically. All the lamps, all the wide-open doors in the world, couldn't prevent the night terrors that stalked his own sleep. Nightmares, alive with demons. Hellish fiends with cloven hooves and membranous wings, who laughed with menace when he tried to evade their talons.

"Check, Caitlin." His son's voice from inside the chamber dispelled these morose thoughts. Andrew sounded confident, but in no way triumphant. Adam nodded approvingly as he drew closer. Andrew had told him he was teaching Caitlin to play. His father had approved, while reminding him to behave courteously. "A gentleman accepts his losses with good grace and never crows over his wins," he'd told him. It remained to see if Andrew remembered this instruction, should his check lead to a checkmate.

"Ach!" Caitlin's voice. "Ye're far too deft at this game, boyo, and—wait a minute. There, now. What d'ye say t' that, lad?"

His son groaned, but he sounded good-humored. "Dash it, Caitlin, you just made the bestest move you could to save yourself! See? Now *both* kings are trapped. It's a stalemate."

"It *is*? D'ye mean t' say ye've not beaten me for once?"

"Papa!" Andrew exclaimed as his father came through the door. "Caitlin's coming it frightfully clever at chess. Course, she hasn't won yet, but she's not been at it very long. And this time—look! We're *stalemated.*"

Caitlin blushed, darting a glance at her employer. Discovering his eyes on her, she quickly lowered her gaze to the board.

"So you are," Adam said, charmed by that blush. "And you've been playing together . . . what? Less than a week?" He grinned as the blush deepened. Caitlin's fair complexion was a dead giveaway. Her milky, translucent skin fell easy prey to the telltale rosy glow. He saw it climb even to the tips of her ears, for her shiny auburn hair was drawn up and wound into a loose knot upon her head. Tiny wisps and tendrils had escaped its confines to grace her heart-shaped face. And that, too, he found charming.

"Six days," Caitlin managed to reply, not an easy thing with the marquis flashing that devilish grin. She avoided his eyes, which seemed to be studying her with uncommon interest, and focused on the child. "What amazes me, Andrew, is that ye knew 'twas a stalemate the instant I moved me knight."

"That's 'cause a good player thinks ahead and antici—antic—what's that word, Papa?"

"Anticipates," Adam said with a smile. "Well done, both of you." He scrutinized the board. "A lively game, I collect."

"Aye, and a long one," said Caitlin, glancing at the mantel clock. " 'Tis past yer bedtime, lad."

"I know," the child replied around a yawn. Darting a glance at his father, he gave her a sleepy grin. "But this way I got to see Papa 'fore I fell asleep."

Point taken, son. Adam resolved, then and there, to amend his habits. He wasn't gammoning Appleby when he said he wished to nurture his son. And that meant *being* there for him, for all the times a child found meaningful. All the times he hadn't been, before. "Andrew . . . ," he said carefully, feeling his way over unfamiliar terrain, "suppose that, in future, I endeavor to come by in time for us to say our good nights before you fall asleep. Would you like that?"

"Oh, yes, Papa—ever so much!"

"Then, so I shall." He bent and kissed the child's brow. "Good night, son."

"G'night, Papa."

Caitlin began to tuck the child in, and Adam took it upon himself to put away the game. The array of fallen pieces as well as the positions of those remaining on the board told his experienced eye the two were closely matched. He eyed Caitlin appraisingly. Andrew played well for his age, but the little governess was learning fast. She showed excellent promise, in fact, and—

"Have ye said yer prayers, lad?" Caitlin asked, and Adam froze.

His son sighed, and murmured he'd forgotten.

Without even being aware how he'd come there, Adam found himself outside in the hallway. Through the open doorway came his son's sleepy murmur: "God bless Papa, God bless Caitlin, God bless . . ."

Sweat beaded Adam's brow. Guilt and anger battered at heart and mind. Guilt, because he counted himself fortunate he'd escaped before Andrew asked him to join in. Anger, because . . . . *Damn it, I ought to be glad she's performing that function so critical to a child's rearing! It's* me *should be in there, hearing my son's prayers!* But even as he ruthlessly chided himself for his cowardice, Adam knew it was all hollow: A damned soul had precious little right to hear the prayers of the innocent. And none at all to pray himself.

"Fast asleep," Caitlin informed the marquis as she tiptoed out of the room. Noting his look of distraction, she eyed him quizzically. What, she wondered, could have caused him to leave so precipitously?

For a moment he failed to comment, then seemed to collect himself. "And well on his way to pleasant dreams, I make no doubt," he told her, not quite managing a smile.

"Aye." She knew she ought to repair to her own quarters, yet something suggested she linger. He seemed to her somehow . . . lost. Lonely, even. And wasn't *that* ridiculous. The man must have friends in the dozens. Didn't he take himself off every evening, after that valet fellow spent hours seeing him all rigged out in his finery? "The lad does seem t' sleep better these days," she offered, uncertain what else to say.

"All thanks to you, Caitlin O'Brien," he said. "You've a deal of experience with children, I collect, to know so well how to soothe their fears."

"Ach, I've truly had very little," she said wistfully.

"Indeed? I thought all you Irish had . . . uh, that is . . ."

"Children in the dozens?" she supplied with a wry smile. " 'Tis no harm in sayin' it, milord. Most Irish do have lots o' children, though not always enough food t' feed those they're blessed with. But as for me . . ." She sighed. "I was reared a lone orphan, milord."

"An orphan," he echoed. He was stunned to realize how little he knew of this woman he'd willy-nilly installed as his son's governess. Yet as he looked at her, he realized he knew she had all the qualities that mattered. Her kindness and compassion toward his son were evident in every word and gesture. Andrew smiled often now, and the laughter they shared had become a familiar sound. In a house that hadn't known laughter in years. Not since he himself was a child, and his parents were alive. And he still marveled at Caitlin's unique ability to use a child's natural love of play to teach—without the pain the Miss Murches of the world felt it necessary to bring to the schoolroom. How did such a young woman—she seemed barely more than a child herself—come by so much wisdom? And an orphan, at that!

"Do they . . . have orphanages in Ireland?" he asked, half dreading the answer. He knew something of orphanages, in England at least. Dreary, forbidding places, where they existed at all. The mere thought of Caitlin the child shut up in such a cheerless place distressed him.

She shrugged. "I'm not aware of any, milord. But sure and the Church does what it can. I was lucky,

however, for I'd a carin' foster mother. Thanks t' Crionna, I niver lacked for love and kindness.''

Relief made him smile. "And where is Crionna now?''

"I buried her in the autumn, milord.''

He caught the sadness in her voice. He'd wondered
about the plain frocks of unrelieved black she always
wore. Why hadn't he realized she was in mourning?
"I'm sorry for your loss, then.''

Caitlin nodded. " 'Twas Crionna's time, though. She
was passin' ancient. Not that it keeps me from missin'
her, but I've accepted the loss. Far easier t' bear the
passin' of an auld woman than a young—ach, forgive
me! I-I know ye must be grievin', milord. For—for
Andrew's mother,'' she added when he simply stared
at her. "And here I am, remindin' ye—''

"Forgiveness isn't necessary,'' Adam snapped, instantly regretting his tone at the look on her face.

"Mi-milord?''

Adam sighed. "While I regret her death, there was
no love lost between Lady Lightfoot and me,'' he found
himself explaining. And wondered why he did so; none
of his set would deign to explain such to a hired servant.
But there was something about this fresh-faced lass that
urged him to set the usual class distinctions aside,
though he was hard put to say what. She was bright and
competent, of course, but so was Jepson. Then again,
she was far lovelier to look at than his dour-faced butler . . . .

Uncomfortable with the thought, he sought a change
of subject, grasping at the first thing that came to mind.
"Would you care to join me in a game of chess?''

Caitlin sucked in her breath. The net was drawing
tighter. And she was helpless as ever to prevent it. Learning the game for the child's sake was one thing; pursuing
it with the man in her dark dream was quite another.

Yet hadn't she committed herself to helping this troubled lord? This man she knew, knew with a power beyond reason, was meant for the Light?

Taking her discomfort for a natural reluctance to mingle socially with her betters, Adam sought to allay her misgivings. "It's early yet," he said with a casual shrug, "and I find myself disinclined to seek amusement abroad tonight. Thought I might pass the evening by teaching you some finer points of the game. A more challenging opponent can only sharpen Andrew's skills."

This was true enough, as far as it went. No doubt Vanessa would receive him eagerly this evening. Yet he suddenly found himself loath to seek her bed. *Blood and ashes, but two months my mistress, and the creature's already begun to pall! How Appleby must be laughing! Forty more years so hopelessly jaded? That's living with one foot already in hell!*

Caitlin tried to tell herself it was the bitter, haunted look in his eyes that convinced her. That she could hardly help him if she avoided his company. But she knew, even as she tried to rationalize, there were other reasons as well. Adam Lightfoot was a fine figure of a man. Darkly beautiful, in a way that made her intensely aware of him . . . *as* a man.

She frowned. This had never happened to her before. She'd spent time among the lads at home while growing up, but Father O'Malley discouraged such mingling once the village children reached adolescence. Indeed, only a few—the brightest lads, those meant for the priesthood—continued their schooling at all; their female counterparts, never. In the last years before Crionna's death, Caitlin had spent almost no time in the company of males. Her life with the wise woman allowed for none, save in healing the sick, and such encounters were brief and impersonal.

No, she'd little experience of men. But the plain fact was, *this* man could make her pulse race, as it had tonight, when he entered Andrew's room unannounced. Made it race even now, when she thought of spending time exclusively in his company. Appalling that she could have such thoughts, but there it was. If he knew, Father O'Malley would berate her good and proper. *'Tis shameless you are, Caitlin O'Brien, and that's a fact!*

"And where shall we play, milord?" she asked. Despite all her misgivings, only hoping he didn't catch the breathlessness in her voice.

"The library, I should think." Adam reached for the chamberstick she'd carried from Andrew's room. He threw her an arch grin as they walked toward the library. "No doubt you recollect I've a board set up there?"

"Aye," she replied, swallowing thickly as she recalled that strange encounter in the library. Sure and he'd been a dark and brooding soul that night. And hadn't she been three times a fool, to be roaming the lord's library at such an hour? "His lordship's *sanctus sanctum*," she later heard Jepson call it. She counted herself lucky she'd not been turned off on the spot.

Reaching the library, Adam lighted a branch and set it upon a shelf above the table where his favorite chess set rested. An old one, with men of carved ivory and ebony worn to a fine patina. Inherited from his father, who'd taught him how to play. Not the set he'd employed with a certain midnight visitor, no. That bitter reminder had been relegated to the fire in a fit of rage.

"Here, allow me." He drew a chair back from the table, from the side bearing the ivory pieces, and gestured for Caitlin to sit. "You're the beginner," he said at her questioning look. "I think it only fair you play white."

Caitlin nodded without speaking, too aware of his nearness, of his sheer physical presence as he seated her. On impulse, she closed her eyes, confirming what she already knew: She could identify him by smell alone. She was instantly aware of scents she'd come to recognize as belonging to him, and no other: a faint drift of spice from the soap he used . . . of leather from a pair of driving gloves tucked carelessly into a coat pocket . . . of starch from the immaculate stock tied at his throat . . . and the fresh, clean scent of his hair, which shone with health and was blessedly free of the pomade some gentlemen used.

Adam was no less immune to her. As he tucked in her chair, a hint of some long-forgotten fragrance— wildflowers, perhaps—drifted up to tease his senses. Coming around the table to take his seat, he noted how the candlelight bathed her skin in a soft luminescence; it drew the eye and pronounced what it saw as flawless. Yet those same flames drew fire from her hair. An abundant mass of molten copper, it glinted with fiery highlights: living flame that danced along the shining silken strands. He found himself imagining how her hair might appear loosened from its modest confinement, spread out upon a pillow—*no!*

You've no business sullying this innocent with such imaginings, you sorry, thrice-damned fool. Yes, thrice damned— doomed by your profligate ways, condemned by your heedless tongue, and consigned to hell by your own hand!

"Is-is something amiss, milord?" The candlelight made it difficult to be certain, but Caitlin thought he grimaced, as if in pain. Jepson and Mrs. Hodgkins spoke of injuries he'd taken in the war. Were they troubling him? "Are yer wounds—are you in pain, milord? I-I've a draught I can . . ." Her words faded as he shook his head no. Yet everything from the tormented look in his eyes to the grim set of his mouth belied the denial.

"White moves first," he said tautly, indicating the ivory pieces.

"Aye, milord."

They began to play. And Caitlin began losing men at every turn. She realized it was only a matter of minutes till she'd find herself checkmated. Still, she hardly minded, for his mood had lightened considerably once into the game. On the other hand, she knew this was but a temporary reprieve, and that wouldn't do. She'd not risked the certain danger she knew was tied somehow to this game merely to secure him a brief respite. There had to be a way to draw him out as they played, to learn whatever it was that troubled—

"You're playing badly."

His words, uttered so baldly in the midst of these thoughts, had her sitting bolt upright in her chair. "I-I niver pretended t' be an expert player, milord!" she protested, stung.

Adam cursed himself for his thoughtless words. "Forgive me," he said, and smiled gently in apology. "What I ought to have said is that you're not concentrating. I never expected you to trounce me—after all, I've been playing for decades. But it's clear you've not been giving your moves the forethought essential to mastering the game. You seem . . . distracted."

She nodded, hoping he didn't see her flush. Of course she'd been distracted—puzzling how to help him! Yet he'd surely deem this presumptuous of a mere governess, so she couldn't tell him so. She was a healer by training, a governess by accident, but he seemed to see her only as the latter. The rest of the household believed she had healed Andrew, and perhaps she had, with God's help. Yet she sensed the marquis was disinclined to believe it. What he did hold responsible for his son's recovery, she'd no idea. Sure and he didn't seem at all a man of faith.

"Any distracted player plays badly," Adam said kindly, "no matter what his level of expertise." Then, noting her silence: "Caitlin, is there something I can do to help . . . clear your mind, that is?"

Aye, help me clear yours of what's weighing it down! But with this silent plea came the realization this could be the entrée she sought. "Truth t' tell, milord," she fibbed, "I kept thinkin' about all yer years of experience with the game. Decades, did ye say? Sure and ye started playin' in the cradle."

He chuckled. "Not quite, but my father taught me on this very board, when I was younger than Andrew. Of course, I was a deal older before I bested him. And after that, only rarely."

She noted how his face softened when he mentioned his father. How he fingered the bishop in his hand as he did so, almost . . . caressing it, aye, that was the word. He had long, capable-looking fingers, strong and well shaped, yet at the same time gentle as they moved over the smooth, age-mellowed ivory. She all at once had an image—not one of her visions, no, but every bit as clear—of those fingers caressing a woman's skin. *Her* skin?

Heat invaded every inch of that skin. She ducked her head, certain he must see. Holy Mother, what was wrong with her? She was after healing his troubled mind—his poor, tortured soul. Such carnal images had no place in it!

Appalled at her wanton thoughts, she forced her mind back to the matter at hand. That insight into his feelings about his father . . . it seemed important. Heretofore, the only thing she'd seen evoke such a tenderness of expression was Andrew. But the father was no longer alive. Jepson had referred to his lordship's inheriting the title; that didn't happen unless the old lord had passed on.

"Yer da . . . ," she ventured carefully, not wanting to blunder as she had about his feelings for his dead wife. "Playin' upon this lovely auld board must bring back memories."

Adam stared silently at the ivory bishop. At the tiny marks where, decades ago, a new puppy had scored it with its teeth. Because he'd been careless, forgetting to put the pieces away—always his task after a game. He remembered his distress when he'd found it and had to confess to his father. And Tom Lightfoot's gentle reply: "We all make mistakes, son. The only harm's in not learning from them. I've every confidence you'll never make this one again." He never had.

Strange, but he hadn't thought of that in years. The contrast between his present life and those early years, so secure in the love and warmth radiating from his parents' marriage, was just too painful. Yet now . . . it wasn't pain he felt. Just a deep, bittersweet yearning . . . for something he also hadn't dared dwell upon in years.

He glanced at the small slip of a girl sitting patiently across the table. She had a calm serenity that reminded him of his mother. They looked nothing alike, but Catherine Lightfoot had often sat like that, patiently looking on, while he and his father played. Odd. He hadn't thought nostalgically about either of his parents in recent memory. And here, in the space of a few seconds, Caitlin had evoked memories—sweet, warm memories—of both.

"Yes, it does," he replied softly. "Fond memories. I sat where you are now, my father across from me. In that chair"—smiling in reminiscence, he indicated an armchair by the hearth—"my mother used to sit. She always brought her needlework." He shook his head in wonder. "There she sat, managing all those tiny, perfect stitches—while somehow knowing *exactly* whose move it was."

"There's no mystery in such mastery o' the womanly arts," Caitlin said with a smile. "In the village back home, we'd an auld blind woman could stitch circles round the younger lasses."

Adam nodded, then chuckled. "I remember thinking my mother used magic . . . that she'd an ability to see with a second set of eyes. I've heard you Irish even have a name for such a thing . . . the Sight. Isn't that what you call it?"

Caitlin gasped, and covered it by pretending a fit of coughing. "Not . . . not to worry, milord," she managed, holding up her hand to stay him when he leapt from his chair, concerned.

Adam frowned at her. She'd turned white as parchment, her pallor evident even in the dim candlelight. "Here," he said, reaching for a decanter on the sideboard. He poured a measure of brandy, came around the table and placed it in her hand. "Sip it slowly, now."

She did, grimacing at the fiery taste of the liquid. Then began to cough in earnest as it went down. "Saints alive!" she cried when she could speak. "Is that what's meant by 'fightin' fire with fire'? Sure and 'tis a case o' the cure bein' worse'n what ails ye!"

Adam's lips quirked, but the smile faded as he ran his eyes over her. Her color had come back, but . . . . "Caitlin . . . are you ill?" She didn't appear consumptive, but the disease was all too common, especially among the poor.

Catching his meaning, she quickly shook her head no. "Milord, if I'd the consumption, I'd not be here.

I'd niver risk Andrew's health . . . or yer own," she added at his questioning look. "There's disagreement on it bein' catchin'. But I've seen folk who were in prolonged contact with consumptives. Too many succumb t' the wastin' disease themselves, t' make me doubt it.

" 'Twas just a case o' . . . a tickle in me throat," she added, wondering if fibbing to him was destined to become a habit. "And then yer cure, o' course," she added wryly, handing him the brandy glass.

His fingers brushed hers as he took it from her, sending a ripple of sensation across her skin. Sparks flared and burned, like chain lightning, across her nerve endings.

Adam felt it, too. He tried to tell himself it was a variation on that old game they'd played at school: rub your feet across the carpet, sneak up upon an unsuspecting fellow, and send an unpleasant shock through him. But he knew better.

What he'd just felt was a prelude to pleasure. Pleasure whose dimensions he well understood, though he doubted Caitlin did. He was suddenly alert to it in every pore. Alive with it as he took in her innocent look of surprise and wonder. Oh, yes, he understood it only too well. He'd chased its allure across London and back again. He understood its sudden power, its ability to hold him in thrall—at least for a while, if he were lucky—and its name was lust.

What he didn't understand, not nearly, was its unsuspected source. Caitlin? She was a total innocent. As far removed from the likes of Vanessa Marley and her ilk as silk from sackcloth. How could such as she spark the desire surging hot and heavy through his loins?

And yet, he thought, turning to the sideboard—as much to hide the evidence of his lust as to put away the brandy glass—perhaps it made an absurd kind of sense.

Caitlin affected him in more than one way that was totally unexpected: Wasn't he sitting at home, playing chess with her this evening, instead of pursuing his obsessive debauchery? Preferring her company to Vanessa's? And in that innocent company, he'd felt free to reminisce about hopes and dreams long buried. No one else—no one—had been able to do that. She was a breath of fresh air in a stale room. The stale room that had been his life for longer than he cared to remember.

Caitlin wrestled her feelings under control, at last noting his silence as he stood rigidly facing the sideboard. "Milord? Are ye feelin' all right?" she asked for the second time that night. And when he didn't reply: "Are ye ill, or in pain, milord?"

His reaction mastered, Adam turned and gave her a brilliant smile. "Not at all. Fact is, my dear Caitlin, I've never felt better."

His smile was . . . wonderful. He didn't smile nearly enough, but when he did, the darkness receded. If only she could find a way to rid him of it forever. If only she could convince him to let her *try*. "Ach, I'm so glad," she said, meaning it with all her heart. Realizing this man had become important to her in ways she didn't understand. What she did understand—unlike before, when he'd been but the frightening figure in her dream, not this flesh-and-blood man with a terrible need inside him—was that she'd been brought here to answer that need. And that she must not fail him.

The fierce honesty in her eyes hit Adam like a fist in the gut. She *meant* it. She honestly gave a damn. Not about what he could give her, not about his vaunted title, his wealth and position, and certainly not about his prowess in bed. About *him* . . . as a human being who might, or might not, be in pain. And for the first

time since that hellish night in early April, for this brief
moment at least, the pain was gone.

Taking a step toward her, Adam searched her face
for several long seconds. "What is it about you, Caitlin
O'Brien," he said at last, "that seems to banish ills?"

Her trill of laughter rippled over his tortured soul
like sunlight on a stormy sea. "Milord, I thought ye
knew," she replied. "I'm a *healer.*"

Adam met her green, green eyes and slowly nodded.
"Perhaps you are," he murmured softly. "Perhaps you
are, at that."

Chapter 8

Caitlin and Adam played chess every night that week. True to his word, he would arrive in time to visit with his son before Andrew fell asleep. He always contrived to avoid the bedtime prayers, however, and if Caitlin or Andrew noticed, they didn't comment. Afterward, it seemed a natural thing to progress with Caitlin to the library and continue her instruction at chess. Yet chess was the least of the lessons learned there. Foremost were the things they learned of each other.

For Caitlin, it was like seeing several new faces beneath a familiar mask. His lordship could still be sardonic and brooding, yes; but he also had a quiet, thoughtful side. And a fine sense of humor. He was given to lively story-telling—amusing accounts of his childhood, of boyish pranks and hijinks—a side of him she'd never suspected. She learned he had a childhood friend named Robert, son of a neighboring squire. The mischief they got into! Daredevil antics that were both hair-raising and hilarious, when he described them.

"Robert sounds a right scamp, but a wonderful friend," she remarked at one point. "Where is he now, milord?"

At once his face went shuttered and drawn. "Dead," he replied, not a hint of inflection in his voice. "Slain at Salamanca." The bleakness in his response warned her not to pursue it. "Your move," he said, gesturing at the board.

In the matter of chess, he was patience itself: quietly pointing out where she might make a better move; calling her to task only when she forgot to concentrate on her game. The latter, however, happened more often than Caitlin wished.

Alone with him in the library, for hours at a stretch, she couldn't help being distracted from time to time. His low rumble of laughter could easily pull her thoughts away as could the elegant arch of his brow as she made an incautious move; and a simple gesture from those strong, capable fingers could send her thoughts skittering, far, far from opening gambits and endgame strategies. Though he never again brushed those fingers against hers, never touched her at all, she was aware of him from the moment they sat down to play. When that awareness slipped under her guard, chess was the last thing on her mind.

What Adam learned of Caitlin was equally engaging, and therefore precarious. The better he knew her, the more he felt drawn to her: mentally, which was fine; but he was also drawn to her physically—which was not. Because of his determination not to soil her innocence, the nightly sessions became a tormenting exercise in self-restraint. More than once he went to his empty bed with a curse—and with desire clawing at his loins. In the morning he'd resolve to end the lessons forthwith. Yet when evening came, he found himself inviting her yet again.

She was all things young and lovely, pure and untarnished. A woman who was blessedly free of the *ton's* jaded sophistication and untouched by the ugliness of the world at large. How long had it been since he'd encountered such innocence, such simple goodness and generosity? The filth and brutality of war and its aftermath had stripped such things from his ken. He'd forgotten they even existed—apart from his son and children like him.

And Caitlin, for all her youth, was no child. This was never more apparent than when she described her life in the year after her foster mother died. He found it hard to credit that she'd left her home and all she knew, with little more than the clothes on her back. Traveled the open road, in a strange land, seeking out the sick— for the dubious reward of tending those who'd no coin to pay. It boggled the mind.

Moreover, it was dangerous. "Didn't you ever fear for your own safety?" he asked when she had described a particular incident: A drunken father had threatened to kill her if she failed to cure his son—it seemed the lad was needed for the spring plowing.

"Aye," she replied, gazing soberly at him with those wide green eyes, "but I feared for the child and his fever more."

They returned to this subject one evening toward the end of the week. A dog barking in the distance reminded Caitlin of a time she'd evaded a farmer's dogs by hastily climbing a tree. "They weren't vicious dogs, milord," she explained when he scowled. "Just doin' their job, really. How were they t' know I'd heard their master's wife was ailin'? Still"—she laughed—" 'twas the better part of an hour before the farmer came out to investigate and let me in t' see the poor woman.''

"Not vicious," he muttered, clearly disbelieving.

" 'Tis the truth," she insisted. "Once I was admitted, the beasties even licked me hand." And then, when he merely glared at her, appalled at her naivete: "I took no harm, milord."

He heaved a sigh. "Fate watches over children and fools, I've heard."

"Then, ye've heard it wrong, milord," she said gently.

"Hmm?" he murmured absently, studying the board.

"*Heaven* watches over children and fools . . . That's as I've heard it said, milord."

His head lifted, and he sent her a scowl fiercer than any she'd yet seen. "Then, it's a fool said it!"

"Mi-milord?" she stammered. The darkness was on him now. She saw that at once, but she was at a loss to explain its sudden appearance.

"Heaven has little to do with watching over children," he spat. "One look at London's poor ought to have told you that."

And when she didn't respond: "The East End is teeming with pitiful young beggars. Children who will die before they can raise a beard or take on a woman's healthy curves. Emaciated babes with running sores. Climbing boys coughing their lives away, covered with burns from the hot chimneys they're forced to enter."

He leaned over the board, the blue of his eyes burning into hers. "And where is your fool's heaven then, Caitlin?" he asked in a voice grown low and dangerous.

" 'Tis"—she swallowed past a fearful lump in her throat, confused by his sudden anger—" 'tis merely a thing some say, milord. I'm sure they mean no—"

"But you've seen those wretched beggars, haven't

you?" It was a demand, not a question. "Those children without a shred of hope . . . without a future?"

"Aye . . . I've seen them," she replied gravely. " 'Tis why I've tried t' . . . t' do what I could . . . t' help them in some small measure."

"Yet now you're here." He searched her face for a reaction. "Engaged to teach a rich man's child his letters. And playing chess with that rich man . . . with a titled lord."

"There are all kinds o' need, milord," she said quietly. "And I go where . . . I'm needed."

Adam caught the slight hesitation. He wondered if there were some deeper meaning hidden beneath the surface of her reply. He thought he might have glimpsed something significant—an unspoken message, perhaps, in her eyes—then dismissed it as his imagination.

"And if you weren't engaged here as governess?" he questioned, bent on discovering what she was made of. She intrigued and fascinated him. More than any woman he'd ever met, and he needed to know why. "The Irish Angel would still be out there"—he gestured toward the world beyond the windows, with their snugly drawn draperies—"plying her skills, wouldn't she?" Again, it was not a question.

Caitlin flushed and ducked her head. "She . . . she still is . . . occasionally, milord."

"What!"

"I-I do it only on me own time!" Color stained Caitlin's cheeks as she raised her head to look at him. "And—and not too often. 'Tis just that . . . Well, the people remember me, d'ye see. And if I've the time, whilst Andrew's abed, or havin' his bath, or—"

"Do you mean to tell me you go out at night, all alone? To the East End? Good grief, woman! Where the devil's your *sense?*"

"I-I—"

"You will tell Jepson exactly where you are going from now on," he said, his tone brooking no argument. "Henceforth he will know to have my carriage brought round, with a pair of stout grooms for your protection. You are to travel nowhere without them, Caitlin—is that clear?"

"A-aye . . . thank ye, milord."

With a nod of satisfaction, he turned his attention to the board and abruptly moved his queen. "Checkmate."

"Ach—the divil, ye say!"

Sardonic amusement—she couldn't begin to imagine its source—flared in his eyes. "Be that as it may . . . ," he murmured dryly.

In her shock, she had knocked a captured knight to the floor. Pushing back her chair, she bent to retrieve it.

"Here, I'll do that."

Caitlin froze. His voice, so near that she felt his breath on her nape, sent a shiver along her spine. And not an unpleasant shiver. When had he moved? How had he come so close? More to the point, could he hear her foolish heart thumping as he stayed her with a hand on her arm?

Adam regretted touching her the moment it happened. He jerked his hand away. She twisted aside at the same moment. His fingers grazed the pliant softness of a surprisingly full breast. A potent curse rose to his lips. He throttled it, and backed away to give her room.

"Never mind the chessmen," he said tightly. He willed himself not to conjecture the shape and color of the breast beneath the modest gown. "I shall put them away."

"I . . ." Caitlin was too mortified with embarrassment

to finish. Her breast burned from that accidental touch. *She* burned—and shivered—gone hot and cold all over. What was happening to her? Then a new sensation . . . one she understood:

The vision struck with unusual force. It was more powerful than any thrust upon her in the past: She saw herself, sprawled upon silken monogrammed sheets, her unbound hair in disarray. And Adam Lightfoot, lamplight gleaming on his bare shoulders, smiling down at her—his hand upon her naked breast!

"Lesson's over." His words, unnaturally loud in the still room, covered her gasp. She managed to look at him, saw him bow, much as if she were a fine lady. "Good night, Caitlin," he said curtly.

Unable to speak, shaking from the raw force of the vision, Caitlin stumbled blindly from the room.

Two nights later—two nights in which he did not ask Caitlin to play chess—Adam visited his mistress. And came home early—staggering with drink. With the effects of Vanessa's fine French brandy. And with Vanessa's words, hurled at his departing back, still ringing in his ears: "Who is she, Adam? Who's the bitch has replaced me in your bed!"

The irony of those words provoked a gust of bitter laughter as he surrendered his curricle to a waiting groom. "Poor V'nessha," he mumbled, lurching drunkenly to his door. Natural for her to assume he was bedding someone else, he supposed through his brandy-induced fog, when he hadn't performed in hers. "Couldn' rishe t' th' occasion—*hic*—sho t' shpeak—*hic*." The hiccup gave way to a drunken laugh.

Vanessa's assumption had him shaking his head—a

mistake: he slumped against the door, waiting for the
wave of dizziness to pass. Fact was, he had bedded no
one in weeks, and that included his jealous mistress.
"Not," he muttered as he fumbled with the latch, "that
y' haven' *imagined* beddin' shom—*hic*—shomeone, ol
boy."

A footman let him in, face impassive as he took in
his lordship's disheveled appearance, the reek of spirits
permeating the front hall. Clumsily doffing his coat and
gloves, Adam handed them over, his words slurred as
he ordered the man to bed. A glance at the marble
staircase rising gracefully to the second floor produced
two sets of stairs; he shut one eye, squinting at the double
image until it resolved into one.

Tottering before it, he grabbed the newel post to
keep his feet, and blinked. Another image interposed,
swimming in the brandy haze, then coming clearer:
Caitlin, as she'd appeared that morning. At the top of
those stairs, an uncertain smile on her face when she
saw him. Just before he'd beaten a hasty retreat to his
club. *We missed ye last night, milord, the lad and I. Are ye
feelin' better now? I've a powder works wonders for the headache,
should ye need it, milord.*

Shame washed over him, permeating the alcoholic
haze. Shame for the lie he'd sent, rather than face that
innocent pair. Rather than risk them seeing the unholy
truth in his eyes. Of the lust that had ridden him mercilessly all night. He had never lied to Andrew before—
not outright. And to lie in the face of a promise! He'd
given his word he would visit the child each night before
he fell asleep. And because of his lust for a captivating
little Irish baggage, he had broken it—two nights running.

The clock on the landing began to chime, breaking
into his unwelcome thoughts, and he set about negotiat-

ing the stairs. Squinting at the clock's engraved face, he thought it read midnight, but he couldn't be sure; he'd lost count of the chimes. On drawing near, he saw that both hands were pointing straight up. As the last chime fell away, a wild giggle echoed in the pit of his mind.

With a savage curse, he whirled on the landing, and nearly fell as his gaze swept the shadows below. He gripped the banister with white-knuckled fists, squinting through the gloom. There was no one there.

Growling an obscenity, he resumed climbing. His pace slowed by the laborious, painstaking movements of an inebriate, it was a good deal of time before he found himself upstairs. More indicative of his sodden state was a total inability to recall how he came to be facing a door not his own. This was nowhere near his chambers, but in the servants' quarters . . . and then he knew: He was standing outside Caitlin's bedchamber.

There was a faint ribbon of light under her door.

Muttering a curse, he shoved a hand haphazardly through his hair, trying to focus his mind. This cost him his balance, and he groped at a console table set against the opposite wall. He managed to steady himself, just barely. Muddled thoughts seeped through the alcoholic fog as he stared at the door: *Lovely Caitlin . . . so sweet . . . no . . . move . . . shouldn't . . . must have . . . shred of decency . . . somewhere.*

Somehow the shred of decency he hoped to summon from the depths of his damned soul won out. With a final curse, he lurched away from the table—and sent it crashing to the floor.

Caitlin finished brushing her hair and was about to braid it when she heard the crash. "Mother o' God—

what on *earth* . . . ?" Grabbing her night candle, she hurried to the door, then hesitated. Muttered imprecations competed with the sound of something heavy being knocked about, just outside the door. Then silence.

Undoing the latch, she inched the door open. The servants' hallway wasn't well lit; a single candle burned in the wall sconce at the far end, over the stairs. Yet she had no trouble making out the console table lying on its side. And moving beyond it, a tall, dark figure that could only be . . . . *His lordship? But what's he doing here? Good God, he's weaving in his tracks! Is he ill?*

Closing the door behind her, she shielded her candle and padded after him on bare feet. She took care not to startle him. A man in the village back home walked in his sleep, and Crionna had warned his wife not to wake him, saying the shock could be harmful. If the marquis was a sleepwalker. . . .

The reek of spirits disabused her of the thought.

Holy Mother and all the saints, he's foxed! Caitlin's lips tightened as she watched her employer stagger toward the stairs. Light from the sconce shone on rumpled clothes, a cravat undone and hanging about his neck, hair that looked as if he'd just climbed out of the covers. *Aye, foxed. What's more, he's not likely to thank you for spying on him in that condition. If you know what's good for you, my girl, you'll turn around and go straight to bed.*

She was about to heed her own advice when he stumbled and lurched precariously toward the head of the stairs. Caitlin's hand flew to her mouth as his feet went out from under him. Only when he managed to hook his arm about the newel post, narrowly missing a headlong tumble, did she resume breathing.

Heaven might, or might not, watch over children and fools, she thought irritably, recalling their exchange in the library; but one thing was clear: *She* must watch over *this* fool before he broke his lordly neck!

Heaving a sigh, she followed in his reeling wake.

She trailed him all the way to his door, not even trying to remain inconspicuous. Someone that pickled, she thought with increasing irritation, wouldn't notice if a cadre of foot soldiers dogged his heels! She'd little patience with drunks. The village had had its share of men who were too fond of the poteen. And their wives and children suffered for it. Not that she believed his lordship was a habitual drunk, but—

"Damn it!" His curse rang out as he fumbled with the latch. The door appeared stuck, and he shoved at it with his shoulder, putting all his weight behind it. Suddenly it gave, and his lordship careened forward, unable to—

"Bloody hell!"

"Milord!" Caitlin entered, and quickly shut the door as he crashed into a bookcase; she could only hope the noise hadn't wakened anyone—especially Andrew. She watched in horror as heavy tomes tumbled over the marquis and onto the carpet. Milord followed them to the floor. Night braid flying, she rushed forward, snuffing her candle as she dropped to her knees beside him. "Milord, are ye hurt?"

With a groan, Adam opened his eyes and blinked. He squeezed them shut and tried again. She was still there. Caitlin, sweet nemesis of his sensual imaginings. Not just the tantalizing image that disturbed his sleep. The innocent *provocateur* of his wet dreams—a nightly phenomenon lately, which he'd not suffered since he was a green boy—stood before him in the flesh. Warm, living flesh that still carried the scent of wildflowers. . . .

"Caitl'n . . ." Not trusting his befuddled brain, he reached up to touch her, to be sure she wasn't a dream.

His hand cupped her small chin and closed on silken skin, solid and real yet softer than his dreams. A sweet, delicate chin that ... trembled? "Caitl'n, don' be 'fraid," he mumbled. "Won' hurt you."

"Milord," Caitlin asked, "did—did ye harm yerself?" She knew she was trembling. Whether from fear or something more subtle—and equally potent—she wasn't certain. That unnerving vision of two nights past was something she didn't want to think about. Not that she'd any choice: Unless deeply immersed in her duties, she thought about little else! How could she avoid it, when every such vision had come true?

But this one—it seemed so *impossible*. Not to mention outright wicked! Perhaps it hadn't been one of *those* visions after all. Perhaps it was simply a foolish girl's imagination. Only now, with Adam Lightfoot's hand firm and warm against her skin, his touch exquisitely gentle ....

"Shall—shall I help you up, milord?" she stammered as he began to thread his fingers through her hair.

"Li'l Caitl'n ... sho lovely." Adam's fingers slid to her nape, and Caitlin found herself leaning into the warm caress. "Sho del'cate 'n' shoft," he murmured with a lazy smile.

All at once his slurred speech and brandy breath brought Caitlin back to the reality of her predicament. This was no time to indulge his drunken fancies—or her own wicked imaginings! She must somehow get him to bed—and hope, come morning, he'd not recall how he got there (not at all a vain hope, given his state). Pulling out of reach, she scrambled to her feet, bent to seize him by the hand. "Let's get you up, milord. Come along now, easy does it."

It was not a happy prospect. He outweighed her by at least seven stone. His slack-muscled state made all of it feel like dead weight. Still, by pulling, shoving, and what only by the wildest stretch of imagination passed for cooperation on his part, Caitlin somehow managed to heave him upright.

Then the trouble began.

She'd no sooner propped him against the bookcase, his arm over her shoulder, than he stopped being passive. His other arm curled around her waist. Before she could draw breath, he pulled her hard against him. Protest formed, then flew out of her brain as his mouth swooped down and covered hers.

Adam couldn't believe his luck. The minx had actually pulled his arm about her! As she'd done so, out of the brandy haze rose an image of Vanessa doing something similar, her invitation unmistakable. Caitlin had to be of the same mind, and he was happy to oblige her.

Stunned and rigid with shock, Caitlin couldn't have moved if she tried. For a man who, seconds ago, was barely able to point his limbs in the right direction, his arms were amazingly capable—and strong. He held her firmly against him. She could feel, beneath the thin flannel of her bed gown, every nuance of his clothing pressing into her flesh. The folds of his lapels against her breasts . . . the buttons on his waistcoat pushing into the soft plane of her stomach . . . the muscular thighs beneath his breeches hard against her belly and thighs.

And he'd certainly no trouble directing his mouth! Hard and demanding, it plundered and took without restraint, feasting on her like a bird of prey. Gone was the gentle touch of moments before, and she knew its loss with a curious pang of regret. Here was the figure of impending danger from her dark dream. She had to get away!

Her chance came when he broke the kiss, inhaling a great breath of air. As if his very life depended on it,

and wasn't *that* a daft notion. But hers might, she'd
remember thinking later, when she could think at all.
Which was just as daft: He was out of his mind with
drink, but hardly bent on murder.

Yet she was frightened. They were alone in his rooms,
the rest of the household asleep. And he didn't seem
to know his own strength. At the very least, her chastity
was threatened. But what she feared most was a loss of
the fragile bridge they'd begun to build between them.
If she couldn't stop him, it would never survive—and
it *must*. He needed her help, even if he didn't know it.

"Lord Lightfoot—stop!" she cried when he tore his
lips free. It was as if he hadn't heard. Murmuring something unintelligible, he slid his mouth along the curve
of her neck. Laved the sensitive skin with his tongue.
Advanced, openmouthed, to her collarbone . . . .

"Milord, don't do this!" she begged, twisting her
head, the only part of her not held immobile.

The arm about her shoulder slid away. She thought
he might have heard after all, that he was about to free
her. Instead, she felt his hand close about her breast.

"No!" she cried as he began to squeeze and fondle it.
"Milord, ye don't want t' do this! I know ye don't—"

His mouth cut off her plea. This kiss was softer than
the first, but just as resolute. She couldn't speak,
couldn't sway him. Frantic, she clawed at the hand on
her breast, to no avail. He suddenly scooped her up
in his arms, and panic set in. Reeling drunkenly, he
managed to carry her forward two paces without stum-
bling over the wreckage. Then he turned abruptly, staggered forward again, and advanced with her through
an inner door. The door to his bedchamber.

Before she knew it, Caitlin found herself dropped
upon his bed. The largest, grandest bed she'd ever seen.
Sprawled on its vast expanse of silken coverlet, she felt

twice as small and vulnerable. He smiled drunkenly, looming over her, swaying as he reached for—merciful God, he was undoing his *breeches*. His lordship was bent on rape.

It came to Caitlin suddenly, she'd but one way to save herself. Frightened and trembling, she squeezed her eyes shut: *"A Mháthair Mór . . ."*

She'd no way of knowing if Crionna's charm would work. With her eyes shut, she couldn't check to see what was happening. Fraught with panic and fear, she could only hope it deterred him. Tears were sliding down her cheeks, she realized, and she was filled with a huge sadness. As the last of the Gaelic words fell from her lips, she hoped with all her heart they wouldn't harm him.

There was utter silence in the room. Taking a deep breath, Caitlin opened her eyes. Adam Lightfoot stood just where she'd last seen him, frozen in place. He'd an aspect of mild confusion, nothing worse. Until she looked into his eyes and saw the shadows deep within.

Shaking, sobbing uncontrollably now, she slid from the bed and fled the chamber without looking back. Not stopping till she reached the safety of her room and threw the latch.

And then she cried herself to sleep.

Chapter 9

The charm's effect ended when Caitlin fell asleep. Abruptly freed from the binding, Adam stumbled forward, barely avoiding a fall on his face. He blinked owlishly and looked about in bewilderment. Where the devil was Caitlin? Had he imagined her? Staggering to the door, he halted, swaying on his feet. In the antechamber, a chamberstick he recognized as hers lay on the carpet, beside a jumble of books. No, he hadn't imagined it. She'd been here, in his rooms. He didn't think he'd imagined kissing her, either. Or the feel of a sweetly rounded breast. But . . . something devilish queer had happened. That little Irish minx . . . .

He yawned, trying to follow the thought. Hours of imbibing at last caught up with him, and it faded. With a dismissive shrug, he staggered back into the bedchamber and fell into bed without further ado.

* * *

When Adam awoke, however—well past noon, his head pounding like the devil—he wasn't inclined to be as dismissive—or charitable. He rang for a footman, his thoughts black while he waited for the servant to fetch him coffee. Seeing his lordship's scowl, the poor man nearly dropped the tray before he hurriedly withdrew.

Little by little, the events of the previous night fell into place as Adam sipped the strong brew. Summoning his valet, he endured the man's fussing as long as he was able, at length dismissing him with a growl. The coffee and a long soak in his bath made him feel slightly more human but hadn't improved his mood one jot.

There was no dodging it. He'd behaved egregiously. Toward Caitlin, the last person in the world he wished to offend. Save one, he amended, thanking his stars Andrew hadn't seen him last night. Caitlin should have been spared his odious presence as well. Instead, he'd gone to the servants' wing and . . . .

Try as he might, he couldn't recall how she'd come to be in his chambers. That part was all a blank. Yet she'd been here, and what had followed . . . . Guilt stabbed him. He couldn't even call it a seduction, which would have been bad enough, given who she was . . . who and what *he* was. But the scratches on his hand said it had been something much uglier: he had tried to rape her. He, who'd had men in his regiment flogged for rape! Who'd never in his life taken an unwilling woman to bed.

He sank into a chair and dropped his head into his hands. He'd have to face her . . . somehow make it right with her. But how did one ever rectify something so cowardly and despicable? Hell and damnation, if she hadn't managed to elude him . . . . An image arose in his mind: Caitlin, sprawled across his bed, staring up at him in shock. And then she'd—

He *hadn't* imagined it. She'd mumbled some gibberish at him—and *that* had stopped him—stopped him cold. What the devil had she done?

Erupting from the chair, he sprang for the bellpull. The footman who appeared moments later was whitefaced and out of breath. "Inform Miss O'Brien I wish to see her in the library," his lordship barked, "at once!"

Adam paced the length of the library and back yet again, scowling at the clock on the mantel. He'd sent for Caitlin twenty minutes ago. She wasn't coming. Had she fled? Not that he'd blame her, but—

A scratching at the door had him stalking across the carpet and yanking it ajar. The solid oak panels vibrated in their frame. "Well . . . ?" he growled at the hapless footman.

"M-Miss O'Brien d-doesn't answer her door, y-your lordship."

"Doesn't—or *won't?*"

"I-I cannot s-say, your lord—" The servant flattened himself against the door as his lordship thrust past him and raced down the hallway.

Minutes later, Adam stood at Caitlin's door. He raised his fist to knock, then thought better of it. In his present mood, he'd pound the door into oblivion. "Caitlin," he called, "are you in there?"

No answer.

"Caitlin, I realize it may be difficult for you, but we need to talk."

Again, no response. Then he thought he detected movement within. What if she was in difficulty, unable to respond? He wasn't entirely clear on all of his actions last night. He had a horrifying thought that hadn't occurred till now: *If I hurt her . . . injured her . . . .*

"Caitlin!" Anxiety rang in his voice. "If you're in there, I beg you will say something. Let me know you're all right!"

Alarmed by the continuing silence, he tried the door, surprised when it gave no resistance. Without further thought, he flung it wide—and froze in his tracks.

She stood facing him across the small room. Wearing one of her ubiquitous mourning gowns. The unrelieved black as well as the red of her hair contrasted starkly with the deathlike pallor of her face. As did her eyes, when he dared to meet them. He took a faltering step back.

The fear in her eyes sickened him.

Without another word, Adam turned and left. Furious with himself for his loss of control, for what he'd done, for things he couldn't yet put a name to. He was in a towering rage by the time he reached the hall and sent for Jepson. "Prepare for the household's removal to Ravenskeep Hall," he told the butler. "Inform Hodgkins, and set the staff packing without delay."

"Yes, your lordship. And when shall I inform her you expect to—"

"Tomorrow."

"Tomorrow, m'lord?" Even the impassive face of Jepson couldn't contain his shock. The removal of a great household from the city to a family's country estate normally took days of preparation.

"You heard me, man," Adam snapped. "I don't give a damn if the packing takes all night. By this time tomorrow, I expect to be on the road to Kent!"

Caitlin learned of the marquis's decision without having to ask. The sounds of scurrying feet drew her into the hallway. Maids hurried past with piles of Holland covers in their arms; footmen lugged portmanteaus and trunks hastily hauled from the attics. Their muttered complaints made clear what they thought of their task. His lordship's insistence on leaving by tomorrow was crack-brained, it was! Who ever heard of packing up a household on such short notice? Fine for *him* to say. Wasn't *him* had to do the work, was it? Everything from stripping the beds to taking down the knocker from the door. Aye, his lordship paid good wages, but when he was in one of his tempers, a body could be worked something cruel.

Caitlin listened with but half an ear. Her mind was on what she had to do. Her own few belongings were packed. It only remained for her to say her good-byes, and she could leave. *Only?* questioned an inner voice, and she swallowed past a surge of emotion. Taking leave of friends she'd made among the staff, especially Jepson and Mrs. Hodgkins, would be hard enough. Saying good-bye to Andrew—

She sucked in a breath and released it, forcing back tears. Saying farewell to the lad would be past hard. But there was no help for it. She could no longer function as she had done, not after last night. Andrew would miss her, but he no longer needed her healing skills; he was recovering nicely from his wounds. Not so, his father. From whatever wounds he carried deep inside. And she hadn't even learned what they were. Instead of helping him, she seemed to have made matters worse. Before she botched things completely, she must leave. Take her healing skills back on the road, perhaps even to Ireland. What she'd feared hadn't been there, but here.

You're running away again, the inner voice taunted. She shook her head to dispel it. She'd wrestled with that voice all morning. Andrew had gone for a fitting with the tailor; she'd had time on her hands to contemplate her options.

She'd had her mind half made up when she awoke this morning. What had decided matters was what she had seen on his lordship's face when he fled her chamber. No one should have to endure that much anguish. Sure and he'd been a troubled soul before she came. But after last night, he seemed more tormented than ever.

All because of her.

Don't be daft, said the voice. *You didn't pour those spirits down his throat!*

No, she hadn't. She'd done something far more imprudent. She very much feared she'd fallen in love with him. With Lord Adam Lightfoot, a man as far above her as the moon. There, she'd admitted it. She'd fallen in love with the man, and no good could come of it. Best to leave now, before she was no good to anyone.

Turning back to her chamber, she went to collect her things.

"Never say you mean to leave for *good?*" Sally Hodgkins placed an imploring hand on Caitlin's sleeve as they stood beside the green baize door in the dining hall. Around them, servants hurried to and fro, tending to chores in frantic haste. She waved away a chambermaid who approached with a torn Holland cover. "Not now, Letty! Can't you see I'm busy?"

"I've no choice but t' leave, Mrs. Hodgkins," Caitlin said as the maid scurried off. "With countless souls ailin' and desperate, how can I not? How can I ignore their plight when I've been blessed with the means"—she indicated the worn satchel at her feet—"t' help them?"

"But—but what of Lord Andrew?" the older woman

stammered. "Doesn't he need you? The child will be sorely grieved to lose—"

"His patched-t'gither governess?" Caitlin smiled wryly and shook her head. "I'm a healer, Mrs. Hodgkins, not a—"

"You've become much more than that to him, Caitlin, and well you know it. He regards you as his friend."

Jeremy isn't my onliest bestest friend anymore. Now you're my bestest friend, too! Caitlin winced as she recalled the child's own words.

"And the boy isn't the only one thinks of you that way." Having noted Caitlin's reaction, the housekeeper pressed her advantage. "Why, Jepson and I were saying just the other day—ah, there you are, Jepson!" she exclaimed, spying the butler entering the room. "Perhaps you can convince her."

"Perhaps I can," said Jepson, depositing an armload of polished silver on the sideboard and turning to face her. "If you will be so good as to inform me—"

"Miss O'Brien's set on leaving us!" the housekeeper cried.

The redoubtable butler's sangfroid didn't desert him, but his brows lifted. "Indeed?" he said, turning to Caitlin. "Do I take it you've given his lordship notice?"

Caitlin shifted uncomfortably. His lordship was the *last* person she wished to see. "Er . . . I was hopin' ye'd carry word t' him for me, sorr."

The butler contained a smile. *Then, there's time to change her mind.* "I fear that's not possible," he said gently.

"It . . . it isn't?" Apprehension showed clearly on Caitlin's face. *If I have to face him . . . .*

"Perhaps I'd better explain how it's done," Jepson said. He glanced at the housekeeper. "Mrs. Hodgkins, Lord Andrew's just returned from Bond Street. Be so

good as to see if he's in need of help with his packing."
He sent her an arch look over Caitlin's head. "And
then, as we could all do with a respite, I suggest you
join us in the servants' hall for a dish of tea."

Hodgkins gave him a comprehending nod and hurried off. The pair had worked together for years and
understood each other perfectly. Jepson had no doubt
there'd be a fourth for tea, even if the venue weren't
his usual. He drew Caitlin gently by the arm. "Come
along, my dear. There's a proper protocol for giving
notice, do you see, and . . ."

Twenty minutes later, Caitlin knew she was in difficulty. The chat with Jepson supplied her first clue she
might not be able to leave. At least, not at once. Even
the lower servants, he told her, were expected to give
at least a week's notice. Upper servants—a governess was
loosely grouped with these—normally gave a fortnight's
warning, or more. Indeed, a governess or tutor usually
stayed on until a suitable replacement was found. Bar-
ring emergencies such as illness or death, there was no
departing from these strictures. None that was honorable, he said.

She was trying desperately to devise a means of calling
her situation an emergency when Andrew entered the
servants' hall: her second clue she was in difficulty. Pro-
pelled forward in his new Bath chair by Hodgkins, he
spied her at once. "Caitlin!" he cried. "We're all going
to Kent—did you know? Kent's where Jeremy lives, and
I shall introduce you to him straightaway, and then we
can all be friends, and . . ." His words faltered as he
noticed the dismay on her face. "What—what's wrong?"

When she didn't answer, the boy glanced at Jepson.

"What is it?" he asked, his lower lip beginning to tremble. "Oh, please—tell me!"

The butler cleared his throat. "Ah . . . Miss O'Brien was thinking of giving notice, I'm afraid."

"Giving . . . notice? D'you mean *leaving?*"

Before Jepson could reply, Andrew's head whipped toward Caitlin. "It's not true, is it?" Tears welled in his eyes as he gazed at her distraught face in abject misery. "Oh, *please* say it's not true. I shan't be able to bear it if you leave, Caitlin—I shan't!"

Caitlin couldn't bear it either. She stayed.

The next afternoon the marquis's entourage lumbered along the post road to Kent. A frazzled but pleased Mrs. Hodgkins as well as the perennially unruffled Jepson remained behind, for their domain was the London residence. They had their counterparts in Kent, who saw to the running of Ravenskeep Hall. Congratulating themselves on "keeping the Irish Angel in the family," the pair settled back for a well-earned rest.

Except for a skeleton staff left in London to assist them, the rest of the servants were not so fortunate. Ravenskeep was a vast holding. When the master came to reside at the Hall, those who went with him could expect to work as hard at settling him in as they had with his removal. And in the present circumstances, perhaps harder, since the marquis hadn't resided there since he went to war. True, some of them had served his marchioness in Kent before she stuck her spoon in the wall, but his lordship was another kettle of fish. No telling what *he'd* require settling in.

Caitlin gleaned all of this, as well as a host of interesting details about the marquis's country estate, from the servants. Tired and overworked from the peremptory removal on such short notice, they grumbled prodigiously over their grievances; Caitlin couldn't help overhearing them when the entourage stopped to rest or water the horses. And what she didn't learn from the servants, she learned from Andrew.

The child was her sole companion in the carriage. His lordship rode ahead in his phaeton. They had not spoken since that disquieting encounter the morning before, and while Caitlin knew it couldn't last, she was grateful for the reprieve. Meanwhile, the lad knew a remarkable amount of the Hall's history for someone his age, and he was eager to share it.

Ravenskeep Hall was the centuries old family seat of the Lightfoots. Built in the time of Queen Elizabeth, who had stayed there during several of her many "progresses," the house had been laid out in the shape of an *E* to honor the Tudor monarch. Constructed entirely of native stone, it boasted over a hundred and twenty rooms. A quarter of these had been modernized by Andrew's grandfather. "But Papa added the indoor necessaries after I was born," Andrew told her.

She also learned that Capability Brown had designed the Hall's surrounding grounds. The deer park, which included a large manmade lake, covered over a hundred acres; the home farm, twelve thousand. All of the outbuildings, from the stables to the hunting lodge in the wood, were built of matching stone.

Needless to say, all this splendor had to be maintained. The permanent staff numbered one hundred and thirty, its ranks swollen by the additional twenty who now traveled with them from London. Andrew knew a great many of the servants by name, he told Caitlin proudly, and he was determined to learn the rest before long.

"Mama didn't think it was necessary to know their

names," he confided, " 'cept for the upper servants, I mean, like Doris, her lady's maid, and Mrs. Needham—she's the housekeeper. But Papa told me that *his* papa thought it was the lord's duty to know the name of everyone who worked for him. 'Course, Papa's been away in the war, so he hasn't had the chance to do that himself—well, not yet, but I'll bet he will, now we're going to live at the Hall. And I shall be the marquis someday, so I've been practicing—doing what Grandfather did, I mean." He paused, eyeing Caitlin askance. "Er . . . don't you think that's a good idea?"

Caitlin pondered this for a moment, sensing his uncertainty. As his mother had held with a different practice, perhaps he needed to be reassured that making the decision to follow in the grandfather's footsteps didn't make him disloyal to his dead mother. "I think 'tis a fine idea," she answered at length. "Mind ye, there are many who'd disagree—and that's their right, lad—but I think servants are people with feelin's, just like everyone else. Wouldn't it hurt yer own feelin's, Andrew, if ye were loyal and worked hard, every day, for someone who didn't even know who ye were—or at the very least, what yer name was?"

"Oh, it *would,*" he replied, looking vastly relieved. "And I *like* knowing who people are." After this exchange, they rode in silence for a while. Then, as their carriage followed his father's equipage up a long drive, Andrew grew excited. The drive would soon deposit them at the Hall, he informed her. "I can't wait to see how you like it, and I just know you're going to like our Townsend," he added with a grin.

"What's a Townsend?" she asked, pulling her gaze from the window. She'd been observing a herd of deer grazing in a landscape so lushly green, it reminded her of Ireland. "And why shall I like it?"

Andrew giggled. "Townsend's not an *it*. He's our major domo—that's like a butler. He's a very proper gentleman and every bit as nice as Jepson, only he smiles more. 'Course, Jepson smiles more than some people think." He gave her a look that said he had a secret. "I can tell."

"Does he, now?" Caitlin asked, recognizing the look and playing along. "And how is that?"

Andrew grinned. " 'Cause he smiles with his eyes." He cocked his head and gave her a considering look. "Just like you're doing now."

"Ach, ye found me out!" Caitlin cried, her mouth mimicking her eyes. She reached over to give him a hug, and they both laughed.

Up ahead, Adam heard their laughter with mixed feelings. He was profoundly relieved that Caitlin was still able to laugh. And grateful that she generously shared that laughter with his son. He doubted she would ever again share her generous spirit with *him*, however. His reasons for removing to the Hall had included a faint hope that having more space would help clear the air between them. Now, as he reflected, the hope grew fainter. In all likelihood, she would use that space to put more distance between them. It was what he would do in her place. Fact was, if he were in her place, he'd be long gone. He counted himself fortunate that she hadn't bolted. The laughter coming from the carriage told him he had only her bond with his son to thank for that.

With a pang of bitter regret, Adam urged his team to a faster pace.

After a perfunctory introduction of the new governess to his majordomo and the housekeeper, Adam left them to settle her in. He lingered only long enough to accept their condolences on the death of Lady Lightfoot. Then he went to confer with his estate manager. Silas White had managed Ravenskeep for two decades, and he had sent his employer detailed reports with unflagging regularity. But it was past time Adam observed things first-hand. It also gave him an excellent excuse to absent himself from the immediate vicinity of the Hall—and from Caitlin. This conveniently consumed the bulk of his time in the month that followed.

Caitlin saw little of him in that month, and never in private. He visited Andrew at bedtime, but stayed only long enough to bid him good night, explaining that he had estate business to attend to. On each occasion Caitlin merited merely a polite nod, and then he was gone. At other times she would see him riding off on a huge black beast that looked as if it breathed fire. "A stallion," Andrew informed her. "Papa bought him at Tatt's when he came home from the war. Jepson told me. It was the day I saw the stablemen taking him off to Kent. Jepson said he's s'posed to sire some racing stock, but Papa rides him as well. His name's Attila, but I heard one of the grooms in London say that Papa calls him the Hun."

His lordship dined at the Hall only twice in that time, taking most of his meals away. Where away was, Caitlin had no idea, except that it involved his daily sojourns on estate business. Her own days revolved entirely around the child. Andrew was a joy to teach and a delight to be with. The bond they shared deepened, and for that alone, she was glad she'd been persuaded not to leave. There was one thing that troubled her, however.

All that remained of Andrew's wounds was the damage to his leg. Yet no one had said a word to him about it being irreparable. Soon the child would begin asking questions, for he was far too bright not to notice. Someone should prepare him for the fact he wouldn't walk again, before he figured it out for himself. And while she'd have done so, despite the enormous emotional toll it would take on both of them, she felt it wasn't her place. The only one who could rightfully assume that responsibility was his father. And his father was not doing so. Was he too distracted to see the problem? Worse yet, was he avoiding it? In any event, his lordship was hardly ever in evidence long enough to address it.

The first time Caitlin saw him for more than an instant, a heavy downpour had kept him from riding out. Word arrived, the marquis would dine at home. Mrs. Needham informed Caitlin his lordship wished his son and the governess to join him at dinner. No need to change the child's schedule—his lordship observed country hours. Andrew was ecstatic; Caitlin, apprehensive.

It was so dark and stormy at four o'clock, the servants had lighted all the wall sconces in the dining hall, and three branches on the table as well. Fortunately, vases of spring flowers and a fire burning cheerily in the grate kept the vast formal chamber from being entirely oppressive. The three of them sat clumped about one end of the long table. Andrew remained in his Bath chair, elevated by several pillows.

Aside from a brief word of greeting to Caitlin, throughout the meal the marquis conversed almost entirely with his son. "Andrew," he began as the soup was served, "I regret that estate matters have kept me from seeing as much of you as I'd like. Tell me, how are you going on, now we're at the Hall?"

"Well, Papa, it's been awfully nice seeing everyone again ... the staff, I mean." The child's brow knitted in a frown. "But I do wish those dashed mumps weren't keeping Jeremy at home. I've told Caitlin all about him, do you see. I was so looking forward to making them known to each other."

His father's glance flicked briefly to Caitlin before it returned to the boy. "Yes, well, I'm sure Jeremy's confinement can't last too much longer. I'll have my secretary send a note to the vicarage, shall I? Asking after Jeremy's health and when it might be possible for him to accept an invitation to visit?"

"Oh, yes—thank you, Papa!"

"That's settled, then. Now, tell me what else has been going on. I trust you've been keeping up with your lessons. What is it you are studying at present?"

A footman came to remove the soup plates, and another served the next course. While this went on, Caitlin took the opportunity to observe her employer. The question about lessons might have been directed at her, she thought. After all, she was the child's governess. Yet his lordship had pointedly avoided her gaze, making it clear this discourse was meant to engage Andrew alone.

She told herself she should be glad. In light of how they'd left things back in London, she'd dreaded any discourse between them. The dread was still there, yet oddly enough, she also found herself miffed, though she wasn't certain she cared to examine her reasons. Yet miffed she was. *Here we are, sharing a meal, and he's scarcely looked my way. Why on earth did he bother to include me, then? 'Tis as if I were invisible. Or worse . . . as if I were nothing more than—than a stick of furniture or one of his dinner plates!*

Between polite bites of turbot, Andrew recounted the morning's lessons. First, he'd done his ciphering, he told his father, which was fun and not hard at all. Then he'd learned a deal about the gods and goddesses of ancient Greece. "I know all of their names now, Papa, and I know what each of them stood for as well," he announced proudly. "And Caitlin says that tomorrow we shall go on to their Roman coun—count—what's that word, Caitlin?"

"Counterparts," she supplied with a smile. Again, she saw his lordship's eyes dart her way: a bare flicker, no more.

"That's it," said Andrew, returning her smile. "It means they have the same things, but with different names," he told his father. And, again, quite proudly: "I already know 'bout one count-counterpart, Papa! The Greeks called their goddess of wisdom Athena, but the Romans called her Minerva. Cook's cat is named Minerva, do you see, and when I told Caitlin, she explained where the name came from.

"And, Papa," he went on excitedly, "Cook's Minerva has had kittens!"

"Indeed?"

"Yes, four of them, and . . . Papa, may I please have one to keep for my very own? Cook said he'd be pleased to let me have one, but that I must first ask you. 'Course, it couldn't happen till after they're weaned, but I should so like to have a kitten!"

"I don't see why not," his father replied with a smile. "But only if you promise to take very good care of it."

"Oh, I *will*—thank you, Papa!" Andrew grinned at both his tablemates. "There's a little calico puss that's awfully pretty. Cook says the calicoes are always girl cats. He says this one's awfully clever 'cause she's always the first one to find her dinner." He studied his plate thoughtfully for a second, then looked up at Caitlin. "Would that make her a wise kitten, do you think?"

She pondered this for a moment, then nodded. " 'Tis

a wise creature knows where its next meal is comin' from, sure.''

Andrew's grin widened. "Then, I shall call her Athena!''

"An excellent choice," said his lordship.

"A fine choice," said Caitlin at the same time.

There was a moment of awkward silence before Andrew—unwittingly or not, Caitlin never learned—rescued them. "Papa, the Greeks said that Athena—er, the goddess, I mean—wasn't really borned at all . . . well, not properly borned, anyway. They believed she just popped out of her father's forehead!''

"Did they, now?" his father asked with an indulgent smile.

"They did! And her father's name was Zeus. He was the *king* of their gods, do you see. So Athena didn't have a mama, just Zeus. And when he wanted a wise daughter, out she came—all growed up and everything! Isn't that famous?''

His lordship agreed that it was, and they went on to the next course. By the time they came to the sweet—a lemon tart, and Andrew's favorite—however, he found it impossible to avoid talking to Caitlin altogether. She suspected this was largely because the child kept including her in the conversation. His lordship limited these exchanges to small talk. Even so, in the end they proved more than Caitlin might have bargained for.

The only questions he put to her directly had to do with the adequacy of supplies in the schoolroom and whether she found her rooms agreeable. Yet when he asked them, when Caitlin found that striking blue-eyed gaze turned her way, she felt her foolish heart thump maddeningly against her rib cage. Sure and it pounded so loud, he must hear it. If he did, however, he gave no indication, and for that she was passing grateful. When at last the meal drew to an end, she breathed a silent prayer of thanks to the Virgin that she'd come through the ordeal without making an entire cake of herself. With a sigh of relief, she escorted Andrew back to the schoolroom.

But there came a second time the three of them dined together—a fortnight later, during a thunderstorm— and this proceeded much the same as the first. Andrew reported on the progress of his kitten. He was glad he'd named her Athena, he told them, " 'cause she's truly a wise and clever little puss. She already knows her name!"

There followed another exchange about the gods of classical antiquity. Caitlin had found a copy of Chapman's *Homer* in the schoolroom and was reading it to Andrew. Next, the child waxed enthusiastic over Jeremy's forthcoming visit. They were finishing another lemon tart when a loud peal of thunder brought speculation on the nature of thunderstorms.

The marquis recounted something he'd read, years before, about the American colonist Benjamin Franklin and his experiments with a kite and a key.

"That sounds ever so exciting!" Andrew exclaimed. "May we try his 'speriment, Papa?"

His father shook his head no. "I'm sorry, Andrew, but lightning can be extremely dangerous. It's true, Mr. Franklin wasn't hurt during his experiment, but the man studied natural philosophy for years and knew what he was about. I want you to promise me you'll never try to duplicate what he did."

"I promise, Papa."

The child hung his head, greatly subdued, and Caitlin's heart went out to him. She scrambled in her mind for some discreet way to soften the rejection—it wouldn't do to offend his father—when the marquis made this unnecessary.

"You do understand, don't you, son?" he asked gently. Smiling, he reached across the table to stroke the child's cheek. "You are far, far too precious to risk."

Andrew's smile was like sunshine breaking through clouds. Seeing it, Caitlin's opinion of the marquis of Ravenskeep rose several notches. Indeed, by the time this meal was over, she realized she'd lost her dread of facing the man, though she was still far from comfortable in his presence. The child proved to be an excellent buffer between them. But she lived in constant dread of one day running into his lordship without Andrew's ameliorating influence.

At best, she decided, what existed between them was a wary truce. Since coming to Ravenskeep Hall, they had never once alluded to what had occurred in London. Indeed, they never touched on personal matters at all.

And if, alone at night in her tidy bed, Caitlin dreamed of monogrammed satin sheets and a very different bed where she was not at all alone, in the morning she thrust the memory swiftly aside. The child was why she had remained, she reminded herself. Andrew, the sweet motherless lad she had come to love as her own. He was what mattered, and she would stay as long as he needed her. She refused to think a day beyond that.

Still, the problem of his damaged leg gnawed at her. He didn't fret about it, now he had the Bath chair to provide some mobility, but she dreaded the day he'd ask her about walking. She even debated gathering her courage and going to his father about it. But with the man so often away, there never seemed an opportunity. Meanwhile, she felt frustrated and helpless.

Then one day she recalled the "mortal" wound to Andrew's head. Great physicians had given up on it, but

she hadn't, had she? She had plied every skill she knew,
had spent hours praying for his recovery—and see what
that had accomplished! Chiding herself for losing sight
of what faith and tenacity could do, Caitlin at once set
about changing direction.

She had been massaging Andrew's leg occasionally,
to relieve cramping. Now she massaged it even more
often. And she prayed over it every chance she got—
but only in the privacy of her room. She wasn't certain
why, but she thought it might be best if his lordship
didn't learn of it. The man seemed oddly ill at ease,
sure, whenever there was praying to be done. No sense
discommoding him. At least she needn't be secretive
about the massaging. It merely wanted being a tad clever
about why she suddenly did it so frequently.

" 'Tis t' prevent the cramps instead o' waitin' till they
trouble ye," she told Andrew when he asked. Which
was the truth, if not all of it. For good measure, she
pulled a face and thumped herself on the forehead.
"Ach, 'tis a dunce I am, not t' have thought of it
sooner!"

Andrew's giggling protest had her grinning. "Caitlin," he said, "you could *never* be a dunce. I bet you're
wiser than Zeus's Athena!"

She added exercises to strengthen the leg. She had
him lift it with books tied on with strips of cloth, first
small ones, then larger, to gradually increase the weight.
Until the day Townsend happened upon them—and
sent at once to the blacksmith. "To fashion gradual
weights that are less cumbersome, Miss Caitlin," he said
with a smile. (Andrew had warned him about Miss
O'Briening her, but the very proper majordomo
couldn't bring himself to do away with form entirely.)

As the days wore on, the leg grew stronger, the cramping a thing of the past. And it was again the majordomo

who suggested another addition to the child's regimen. Townsend introduced Caitlin to Fergus, the estate carpenter, and the next day all three of them introduced Andrew to a pair of carved wooden sticks called crutches.

It was the crutches that changed everything.

Thanking Silas White for the long hours he'd worked the past two months, Adam waved away the man's stuttering gratitude and watched him ride off. The estate manager had a handsome bonus in his pocket, every bit of it earned. Ravenskeep was in excellent shape. He'd given Silas a fortnight's leave as well, suggesting he take Mrs. White on holiday.

Heaving a sigh, Adam surrendered the Hun to a groom and headed for the house. Suggesting how White spend time suddenly in the offing was simple. How to spend his own time now was anything but. Fact was, he'd run out of valid reasons to absent himself from the Hall. And he needed to spend time with his son. To put Andrew off any longer was unthinkable.

Not that he wished to put him off. He loved the child beyond telling, and he would somehow learn to live with the pain of seeing him forever confined to that Bath chair. At times he wanted to howl with rage, knowing that he would never leave it, never walk upright again.

There had been moments in the Peninsula when he thought he might go mad. He had kept himself sane by picturing his son, never in London but here at Ravenskeep, running toward him on sturdy little legs, laughing and carefree. Now that would never happen. Still, the child seemed to have accepted it, and he must do the same.

In any event, the difficulty lay not in being with

Andrew. Time spent with him, however, would surely mean seeing a deal of Caitlin. He couldn't justify putting her off any longer, either. She was past due an apology, at the very least.

The thought of facing her with it scared him to death. He'd ruminated over doing so for untold hours. Pictured himself biting the bullet, going to her, hat in hand—on his knees, even—and all of it had come out wrong. Always, always, the terrible image of her standing there that day intruded. Caitlin . . . shrinking from him with fear in her eyes. Even now, he broke into a cold sweat thinking about it. He tried to tell himself he was being a fool. They had dined together, after all. Twice. And she hadn't looked frightened then, had she? Wary, perhaps, but things had come off fairly well . . . .

Rubbish! cried an inner voice demanding he be honest with himself. *She very likely pasted on a calm face for Andrew's sake, and well you know it. That hardly lets you off the hook, old boy.*

Trouble was, he didn't understand it. What in hell was he afraid of? She was only a woman. A very young one—and a servant, at that. With the exception of his mother, women had always been objects for him to manipulate. To use for mutually advantageous ends, and then move on. How the devil had one little Irish chit got under his skin?

True, he desired her in the face of knowing she was not for the taking. But that was nothing new. He'd been tempted by others who were off limits. He'd refused several of his officers' wives; to dally with the wife of a man he might send to his death was something even he couldn't bring himself to do. And none of them had remotely driven him to this extreme. But Caitlin was more than forbidden fruit. She was . . . an enigma. Try as he might, he couldn't fathom how she fit into—

"Look—it's Papa!" Andrew's piping tones cut across his thoughts. Adam suddenly realized he'd reached the house. He had hoped to enter unobserved, by a little used door to the rose garden, but his son's excited voice put paid to that. "Papa, come and see our surprise! *Look* at me!"

Adam looked, and all at once went very still. Coming toward him on the brick path, flanked by hundreds of roses of every imaginable hue, was his son. Andrew, grinning from ear to ear, propelling himself steadily forward on a stout pair of . . . *crutches? Where the devil did he . . . ?*

He couldn't complete the thought. Andrew's image had suddenly blurred. Without taking his eyes off the precious figure of his son—the *upright* figure of his son—Adam swiped at them with his hand, vaguely aware it came away wet.

"Are you surprised, Papa?" The child drew nearer, laughing. "Caitlin said maybe we should tell you, but I wanted it to be a surprise. Look at me, Papa—I don't need that silly Bath chair anymore!"

"No, son . . . you don't." His voice choked with emotion, Adam took an unsteady step toward him.

"Stay there, Papa! 'Cause I can come to *you* now. See? It's not hard at all, and when I get there—would you like a hug, Papa?"

Not trusting his voice, Adam dropped to his knees and held out his arms. Aching with love for the child he'd believed hopelessly confined to the silly Bath chair. "I'd like that above all else," he managed finally, blinking back fresh tears.

Andrew came. Wielding the crutches as though he'd been born knowing how to use them. Reaching his father, laughing, he let them drop and flung himself into Adam's arms. "See, Caitlin?" he cried. "Papa knows how to catch me!"

"Sure and he does, boyo! And he knows how t' hug ye, too, I'm thinkin'!"

Adam heard the lilting brogue, heard the wealth of love and laughter in her voice. He was able to gather his thoughts for the first time since the sight of his son had moved him to tears. Holding the child to him in a fierce embrace, he lifted his gaze to the woman who'd arranged this wonder.

She stood on the path, framed by myriad roses, their heady scent lacing the soft spring air. She didn't move: a cameo caught in a pool of sunlight. It glinted like copper pennies on her hair, on the tears brimming in her eyes.

In an instant everything fell into place: He knew exactly where the enigma fit, he realized with a mix of relief and sheer terror.

He loved her.

Chapter 10

"You can put me down now, Papa." Andrew wriggled in Adam's grasp, oblivious to the stunning truth that had just struck his father like a blow.

Caught up in the shattering realization, Adam didn't respond. *Caitlin . . . why didn't I see it? She's the dream I once pursued. The forever love I abandoned hope of ever having. And must still abandon: Even if, by some strange twist of fate, she came to love me in return, it's too late! Appleby, you bastard—I smell your hand in this! Who else would damn me to this living hell? This teasing glimpse of a soul mate when I no longer have a soul to share!*

"Papa?" Andrew was still squirming to be set free. "I need to get down so I can practice my turns. Will you help me get my crutches?"

"Crutches . . . ?" He realized the child was speaking to him. "Yes . . . yes, of course." Setting him down, he supported him about the waist, reaching for a crutch; but Caitlin was already there.

"Here, lad." She handed it to Andrew. "Weight on the good leg, now, just as ye did when we practiced."

Andrew nodded, wobbling as he shifted his weight. His father quickly steadied the injured leg with his free hand while the boy tucked the crutch under the opposite arm.

"What the devil . . . ?" Adam ran his hand over the injured leg as Caitlin handed the child the other crutch. "But . . . this is amazing!" he cried. "This leg feels . . . *well muscled.*" His incredulous gaze went to each of them, then to the limb he was testing. "It feels *twice* as sturdy!"

Andrew giggled and threw Caitlin a conspiratorial glance. "That's 'cause Caitlin 'saged it! She rubbed goop into it, too—it's made from leaves and things, and it smells odd, Papa, but it's not *too* bad. An' we did exercises! 'Course, the smith's weights made them ever so much easier than those clumsy books, didn't they, Caitlin?"

"Books?" It was becoming too much to digest. Adam felt battered by an emotional storm. First, Andrew on the crutches; then the bittersweet discovery of his love for Caitlin; now this.

With a laugh, Caitlin explained about the weights.

Was there ever such music as her voice when it's laced with laughter? Adam wondered. "Caitlin . . . ," he began when she'd finished. In the wake of his newly identified feelings, just saying her name tapped a wellspring of emotion he could barely contain. He had to swallow, begin again. "Caitlin, I . . . I don't know where to start. Or how to thank you . . . except to say I'm grateful . . . most humbly grateful."

Suddenly tongue-tied, Caitlin flushed. Would she ever really understand this man? She'd hardly recovered from seeing him moved to tears; this touching gratitude threatened to undo her completely. Both spoke of his love for the child, and she loved the man all the more for it. " 'Twas—'twas what any healer would have done, milord," she stammered.

Andrew paused during one of his "turns" and nodded. "Mrs. Hodgkins says she's the Irish Angel," he told his father, " 'cause she helps people get better. She helps me lots, but I still call her Caitlin." He eyed the two adults with a pensive frown. "D'you know what I wish, Papa?"

"I will, if you tell me," Adam said with an indulgent smile. "Perhaps, as a reward for all your hard work with these"—he indicated the crutches—"we might arrange it."

"I wish . . . ," Andrew began shyly, "I wish Caitlin could be my new mama."

Adam choked, hid it by pretending to cough. Caitlin turned beet red and ducked her head.

A footman rushed from the house, saving them from comment. "Begging your pardon, your lordship," he said. "I'm to inform you callers have arrived."

Adam glanced at the first of a pair of cards the servant proffered and nodded. Andrew would be over the moon. He read the name on the second card and arched a brow. *Ravensford? What the devil's he doing in Kent at the height of the Season—and with the vicar, no less?* "Did they arrive together?" he asked the footman.

"Yes, your lordship, and Master Jeremy as well."

"Jeremy!" In his excitement, Andrew lost control of a crutch, tripping Caitlin in the process. "Oh, Caitlin, I'm *sorry!*"

Adam grabbed her arm to steady her. The first he'd touched her in months. He couldn't avoid it; she'd have fallen if he hadn't. He heard her gasp, braced himself for her reproval—or worse. Her eyes flew to his, and their gazes locked. He felt her trembling. But it wasn't fear or reproval he read in her eyes. His heart began to hammer in his chest. Caitlin's feelings had always been as plain as the freckles on her open face. Could he doubt what he saw? Yet he could swear—*swear* it was there in her clear green eyes: all the love he thought he would never have.

Caitlin thought she murmured assurances to Andrew he wasn't to blame, but couldn't be certain. She felt dizzy, light-headed. His father's touch ran like living fire up her arm. The look blazing in his eyes had her paralyzed with uncertainty. She *had* to be imagining—

"Papa, do let's hurry!" Andrew was beside himself with excitement. "We need to introduce Caitlin to Jeremy . . . er, and the vicar."

Adam gave himself a mental shake, reluctantly releasing Caitlin's gaze. If he got through this day emotionally in one piece, he'd call it a victory past anything he'd done in the Peninsula. "Yes, of course," he said, "and I'll introduce you both to another who's come with them."

He glanced at the footman. "Inform Townsend we'll be there directly. He'll know how the vicar takes his tea. But you'd best alert him His Grace may prefer something stronger."

"His—His *Grace?*" Caitlin gaped at him as the footman bowed and withdrew. "Sure and ye're not after takin' me t' meet a . . ." Unable to complete the thought, she glanced at the house in panic, then back at him.

She looked so adorably flustered, Adam ached to hug her. "Afraid there's no help for it," he said with a smile of sympathy. "You're about meet a duke."

*   *   *

"Past time you showed your face in Kent, Ravens-keep." Brett Westmont, ninth duke of Ravensford, grinned as Adam handed him a brandy. The two had a private moment while Caitlin and Andrew conversed with the vicar and his son. Adam and Brett had been neighbors all their lives, but knew each other largely from London. As young rakehells, they'd scandalized the *ton*. Brett, with his startling turquoise eyes and chest-nut curls, was as outrageously handsome as Adam. It was said prudent mamas hid their daughters when either was in evidence.

"Huh," Adam muttered, keeping his voice low to avoid discomfiting the vicar. "The pot calling the kettle black isn't in it. Since when have you forgone the delights of the Season? Or begun making tame country calls with vicars, for that matter?"

"Since coming to my senses," Brett replied. "Haven't you heard? I'm married."

"Married—*you?*" Westmont had always distrusted women in the extreme. Some said his grandfather, the eighth duke, had raised him to despise them. More than once, Adam had heard him vow to escape the parson's mousetrap, dukedom or no. "I confess, Ravensford, I'm shocked. I collect, like me, you caved to the inevitability of doing one's duty?"

"Duty had nothing to do with it. I've set up my nurs-ery, yes, but only because of the lady involved. If you knew my duchess, you'd see why. She's . . ." With a look in his eyes Adam could have sworn was fatuous, Brett smiled fondly and shook his head. "Ashleigh's like no other woman in the world."

Bloody hell, he's besotted! "Ashleigh . . . have I met this paragon?"

Westmont chuckled. "No, and I'm inclined to keep it that way, but my wife has other ideas."

Adam arched a brow at him.

"Come, Ravenskeep, we both know your appetites. Only a fool would trust you anywhere near his wife ... especially if she's a beauty, and mine is past beautiful, I do assure you. It's because I trust *Ashleigh* and want her happy, I'm making an exception."

"Exception?"

The duke sighed. "Fact is, she's set on having you for a visit. Nothing elaborate—she knows you're in black gloves. When the vicar called this morning and explained about ... your lad, she hatched this idea— well, it's complicated, and I'll explain if you'll find us a spot of privacy before I leave. But she hopes to include your son in the invitation. Will that suit?"

Adam's gaze went to Andrew, who was showing Jeremy one of his crutches. The vicar's son was a bright child who must have had questions about all that had happened. Adam was thankful he was too well bred to voice them. "I don't know, Brett ..." He heaved a sigh. "Needless to say, Andrew hasn't been up to socializing lately. Young Jeremy's his bosom friend, yet this is the first—"

"Ashleigh means to include the vicar's family. Fact is, when she learned Wells was on his way here, she sent me—my dear Ravenskeep, spare me that supercilious look! You cannot credit how ... agreeable I find, uh, *pleasing* my wife. In any event, old man, I'm to inquire when you'll be free to spend the day. If you agree, that is, and invitations will arrive forthwith."

An hour later, Adam paced the drawing room while Caitlin looked on. Andrew was napping, and he'd sent for her the moment she was free. Before the guests left, he and Ravensford had adjourned here, where Brett

Take A Trip Into A Timeless World of Passion and Adventure with Kensington Choice Historical Romances!
—Absolutely FREE!

Let your spirits fly away and enjoy the passion and adventure of another time. Kensington Choice Historical Romances are the finest novels of their kind, written by today's best selling romance authors. Each Kensington Choice Historical Romance transports you to distant lands in a bygone age. Experience the adventure and share the delight as proud men and spirited women discover the wonder and passion of true love.

4 BOOKS WORTH UP TO $23.96— *Absolutely FREE!*

Take **4 FREE** Books!

We created our convenient Home Subscription Service so you'll be sure to have the hottest new romances delivered each month right to your doorstep — usually before they are available in book stores. Just to show you how convenient Zebra Home Subscription Service is, we would like to send you 4 Kensington Choice Historical Romances as a FREE gift. You receive a gift worth up to $23.96 — absolutely FREE. There's no extra charge for shipping and handling. There's no obligation to buy anything - ever!

Save Up To 30% On Home Delivery!

Accept your FREE gift and each month we'll deliver 4 brand new titles as soon as they are published. They'll be yours to examine FREE for 10 days. Then if you decide to keep the books, you'll pay the preferred subscriber's price. That's all 4 books for a savings of up to 30% off the cover price! Just add the cost of shipping and handling. Remember, you are under no obligation to buy any of these books at any time! If you are not delighted with them, simply return then and owe nothing. But if you enjoy Kensington Choice Historical Romances as much as we think you will, pay the special preferred subscriber rate and save over $7.00 off the bookstore price!

We have 4 FREE BOOKS for you as your introduction to
KENSINGTON CHOICE!

To get your FREE BOOKS,
worth up to $23.96, mail the card below
or call TOLL-FREE 1-800-770-1963
Visit our website at www.kensingtonbooks.com.

Take 4 Kensington Choice Historical Romances FREE!

YES! Please send me my 4 FREE KENSINGTON CHOICE HISTORICAL ROMANCES (without obligation to purchase other books). Unless you hear from me after I receive my 4 FREE BOOKS, you may send me 4 new novels – as soon as they are published – to preview each month FREE for 10 days. If I am not satisfied, I may return them and owe nothing. Otherwise, I will pay the money-saving preferred subscriber's price plus shipping and handling. That's a savings of over $7.00 each month. I may return any shipment within 10 days and owe nothing, and I may cancel any time I wish. In any case the 4 FREE books will be mine to keep.

KN022A

Name _____

Address _____ Apt No _____

City _____ State _____ Zip _____

Telephone ( ) _____ Signature _____

(If under 18, parent or guardian must sign)

KENSINGTON CHOICE
Zebra Home Subscription Service, Inc.
P.O. Box 5214
Clifton NJ 07015-5214

PLACE
STAMP
HERE

revealed his duchess's particular reasons for hoping Andrew might visit. Adam had postponed his reply, saying he needed a day to consider it.

Truth was, he wanted Caitlin's opinion. And hungered for her company. But after what had dawned on him earlier, he didn't dare see her privately without a practical matter to ground him. To anchor him to an unemotional plane, for his emotions were something he didn't entirely trust at present. He only knew he must protect Caitlin from himself. And that meant never letting her suspect his feelings. *And hoping to hell I merely imagined* hers!

Heaving a sigh, he dropped into the chair opposite Caitlin's. "It's the damnedest hare-brained scheme I ever heard of," he told her. "Problem is, every time I'm about to send Her Grace my regrets, I begin to wonder if it doesn't make sense. What's your take on it?"

Caitlin smiled to herself. Her take on it? 'Twas daft to be asking a poor colleen to judge the plans of a duchess. Still, she'd been apprehensive when first summoned here; there'd been that moment in the garden when she feared she'd given herself away. Talk of things daft! She could well imagine his lordship's "take" on the poor colleen losing her heart to him! By comparison, the duchess's plans were child's play. "Let's see if I have it right, milord. The duke and duchess have taken in a score o' children orphaned by the war in Europe, aye?"

"Adopted them, yes. His Grace's mother started the project, but Brett says it's become an endeavor dear to his wife's heart. She loves these children"—recalling the rake he once knew, Adam gave his head a disbelieving shake—"and so does he, apparently."

"And these wee orphans are all . . . incapacitated in some way?"

He nodded grimly. "Some are blind . . . others crippled . . . either from birth or maimed in the war."

"Poor things. Yet lucky, too, t' have been rescued by such as Her Grace." Caitlin had been surprised to learn not all Sassenachs were as heartless as many back home believed. The handsome duke had been a surprise, too. She'd been needlessly intimidated by his title; he'd proved charming, kind, and not at all toplofty. "His Grace and his wife must be good people, milord. Sure and they've added deeper meanin' and enrichment t' their lives by savin' these unfortunate babes."

"I suppose they have," Adam murmured, shaking his head again at the transformation in Brett Westmont. *Was it his marriage made the difference? Appears that way, yet I can hardly credit it. Ravensford, head over heels for a woman!*

"Now, about this invitation, milord," Caitlin said. "I take it, when the duchess heard about Andrew from the vicar—"

"Or the gossips," he said sourly. "Even in the country, news travels fast—especially bad news. You may depend on it."

She ignored his cynicism. "And when Her Grace heard about Andrew, she thought perhaps he might benefit from playin' with ither children who are impaired?"

"Exactly. She feels it can help him overcome a sense of being . . . different. Not to mention feeling"—he grimaced—"ostracized. Brett said they saw this happen with their own lot."

Suddenly frowning, Adam leaned forward. "Caitlin . . . how much does Andrew understand of his condition? Does he comprehend he'll never . . . ." *Blood and ashes, I can't even say it!*

"Walk again? But he *is* walkin', milord . . . thanks t' a fine pair o' cr—"

"Devil take it—you know what I mean!" Instantly regretting his temper, he shoved a hand through his hair and sighed. "Forgive me. Never think I mean to devalue what you've accomplished with those crutches. It's nothing short of astounding. But, Caitlin, does my son know he's not expected to walk again—unaided?"

Ah! Caitlin studied the hands folded in her lap. "I'm not certain what he knows, milord. I've not discussed it with him, d'ye see. 'Tis not me place."

"I collect you mean it's not your place, but mine."

She met his eyes. "Aye."

Under the strength of her gaze, Adam's own skittered away. He was at once conscious of the paradox that lay at the root of what Caitlin was: The steadfast wisdom in those green eyes was utterly incongruous with a face so sweetly callow; yet the contradiction made her wisdom all the more apparent. "You're right, of course," he said at length, then heaved a sigh. "I'll need some time to . . . think how to approach it. Deuced difficult, telling your child . . ."

"Aye," she said softly. *Andrew's not the only one needs help here. Perhaps two can benefit from Her Grace's scheme.* "In the meantime, milord, 'twould do Andrew a world o' good t' be with ither children. Whether they're . . . different or no. I think ye'd do well t' take him."

"Very well," he said after a moment. He met her eyes at last. "But *you,* my lass, are coming with us."

"These biscuits are delicious, Yer Grace." Caitlin smiled at her hostess as they sat on the ducal terrace having tea. The two were alone at the moment, Brett and Adam having gone to the stables. His Grace was showing his guest a pair of high steppers he'd purchased at Tatt's. Her Grace, many months pregnant with their second child, had elected to stay and chat with Caitlin.

"I shall tell Anna you said so." The duchess waved a slender hand at a Sevres plate piled high with biscuits. "The child made them herself. She remembered her mama making them, do you see. So when she expressed a longing to taste *biscotti* again, we turned her loose in the kitchens and—*voilà!*"

Caitlin laughed. "Sure and Yer Grace's cook must be an understandin' sort. His lordship's cook has made it known, whoever trespasses in his domain does so at his peril."

Her Grace chuckled. "Ah, but he hasn't met our Anna! The child has a smile could charm the proverbial birds from the trees."

The duchess was a petite woman, very close to Caitlin in stature. Caitlin thought her the most beautiful creature she'd ever seen. She had huge sapphire blue eyes that dominated a delicate, fine-boned face. The tiny mole high on her cheek was a natural beauty mark, calling attention to her creamy complexion. Complementing all was a luxuriant mass of shiny black curls. Caught simply at her nape by a narrow ribbon, they trailed down her back like a young girl's. Indeed, when she smiled, Caitlin was hard put to recall this was not some country lass from the village. Like her husband, she was not at all toplofty. Her next words furthered this impression:

"My dear Caitlin, I beg you will dispense with all these 'Your Graces'! After all, with your young charge insisting we call you by your Christian name, how can I do less? Do please call me Ashleigh."

Caitlin blushed, recalling Andrew's words when his father suggested he introduce Caitlin to the Westmonts. The little slyboots! *If it please Your Graces, this is my governess, and her name's Caitlin. We must all call her by her Christian name, do you see, or she faints—dead away!* "A-aye, Yer Grace," she stammered. "Ach, I mean, Ashleigh!"

"Well, that's settled, then," said Ashleigh, her reply nearly lost amid the shouts of several children. Below, on a stretch of spacious, well-manicured lawn, a dozen youngsters played an unusual version of Blind Man's Bluff. Because two of the Westmonts' adopted children were truly blind, the other participants wore blindfolds—to even the playing field. Andrew had been invited to join them, but for now he'd prudently chosen to watch. *Once I see how it's done, I'll know if I can do it on crutches.* Caitlin was glad to see he wasn't alone. She had worried when Jeremy hadn't come, owing to a death in the family. Joining Andrew on the sidelines was a tall boy who stroked the shaggy head of an enormous black wolfhound; the boy was also on crutches, because of a leg that had been amputated at the knee.

" 'Tis a grand lookin' Irish hound ye have there," Caitlin remarked.

"Ah, so you recognize the breed! Not many do. Sadly, they're close to extinction. My Finn's among the last of his kind."

Caitlin nodded. "Unfortunately, we Irish became too poor t' keep the great hounds. Tell me, the lad with him . . . is he bein' cautious . . . because o' the crutches?" She noticed other children on crutches were playing the game and doing well at it, despite the blindfolds.

Ashleigh smiled. "Enrico's played the game dozens of times. I suspect he's chosen to join Andrew to make him feel less . . . singular. He's always been sensitive to others' feelings."

"Ach, the darlin'! He must make ye proud."

"Mm," Ashleigh replied absently. She was eyeing her guest, a pensive look on her face. "Forgive me for staring, Caitlin, but do you know . . . that is, you remind me of someone. At first I thought it was the brogue. But the longer I look . . . tell me, my dear, have you family in Ireland?"

Caitlin said she was an orphan and left it at that; no sense boring Ashleigh with all the details.

"I see." Ashleigh was still regarding her thoughtfully. "And yet, the closer I look . . . well, I suppose it could be the similar coloring." She gave her head a shake and laughed. "You really do resemble someone I know. A person I'm very fond of . . . someone I adore, actually."

"I do hope you're referring to me, pet," said her husband as he and Adam strolled onto the terrace. Swooping down on his wife, Brett planted a kiss on her nape. "Or I shall be extremely jealous!" Oblivious to their audience, he growled playfully, nuzzling Ashleigh's ear as he fondly rubbed her belly.

"Brett," she cried, laughing, "behave yourself! I adore you above all, but in this instance I was referring to Megan." She glanced from him to Caitlin and back again. "Don't you think Caitlin looks a great deal like her?"

"I'm no judge." Grinning, Brett kissed the top of her head. "I've eyes only for my wife."

"Oh, do be serious!" She was still laughing, but Adam saw how she looked at her husband: Ashleigh truly did adore him—and Brett, the lucky, unpredictable bastard, adored her.

"I suggest you ask Megan herself," the duke told his wife. "Not ten minutes ago, Ravensford and I spied your brother's carriage coming up the drive."

"What!" Ashleigh rose quickly from her chair. "But I thought Megan and Patrick were in London."

"Not anymore, thank the Virgin and all the saints!" A tall, stunning redhead swept onto the terrace in a swirl of green silk. "Ashleigh," she added, removing her bonnet and tossing it at a footman, "if I iver again set foot in Bond Street this time o' year, mark me ripe fer Bedlam!"

"And she means it, too," said the huge man who followed in her wake. "My wife's the only woman in the world who despises the Season, hates to shop, and dares own up to such irreverent thinking! I fear the good ladies of the *ton* may never forgive her."

Laughing, Ashleigh exchanged hugs with the redhead—obviously the Megan recently under discussion. The image this presented was almost comical: Megan was six feet tall and towered over the tiny duchess. Next, Ashleigh found herself lifted off her feet and soundly kissed on both cheeks by Megan's giant of a husband. "Patrick, you wretch!" she scolded. "Why didn't you warn us you were coming?"

"Pay no attention to her," said Brett, welcoming Megan with brotherly peck. "Ashleigh's mad for surprises. Craves 'em more than any child on that lawn." Grinning at his wife as she pulled a face, he caught her hand and gave it a courtly kiss. .

"But come," he said, drawing the couple forward, "and I'll make you known to our guests." He gestured first toward Caitlin at the table. "My dear, allow me to present the St. Clares—the lovely Lady St. Clare and Her Grace's brother, Sir Patrick. Megan, Patrick, this is Miss Caitlin ..." A frown etched the duke's brow as he realized Andrew's unorthodox introduction had left him woefully ignorant of her surname. "Forgive me, my dear, but I fear you have me at a disadv—"

"O'Brien," Caitlin supplied, dropping her gaze and flushing with embarrassment.

"*O'Brien!*" It was Megan who interrupted, staring at Caitlin, thunderstruck. "Niver say ye're—but O'Brien's me *maiden* name! And what's more—" She turned white as parchment and clutched her husband's arm. "Mither o' God, Patrick, 'tis like lookin' in a mirror!"

Ashleigh took one look at her face and signaled the footman hovering near the door. "Fenton, fetch the vinaigrette—hurry!"

Caitlin gaped at the tall redhead, dumbstruck. She was looking into a pair of Irish eyes the exact shape and color of her own. Russet curls the very shade and texture of her own. A *face* that could be her own. *O'Brien's me maiden name* . . . . Her heart began to thud against her ribs like a trapped bird. She was unable to move, only vaguely aware Sir Patrick helped his wife to the chair opposite hers amid what seemed like a babble of voices:

"I *knew* there was a resemblance!" exclaimed the duchess.

"Faces like two peas in a pod," His Grace pronounced in amazement.

"Like twins, but for the difference in size," Adam Lightfoot marveled.

It was chaos on the terrace for a length of time. Drawn by the stir, the children as well as the enormous hound gathered curiously about the adults. The vinaigrette arrived along with several servants. One bore hartshorn; another, a glass of water; a third, a burnt feather she waved under Lady St. Clare's nose. The redhead waved it away, insisting she had never fainted in her life and wasn't about to start now.

Fortunately, she was right. A sense of calm gradually prevailed, restoring order to the terrace. And finally the connection between Megan, Lady St. Clare, and Caitlin

O'Brien, erstwhile orphan . . . itinerant healer . . . governess, came to light.

It turned out Megan was the oldest child of Pegeen O'Brien; Caitlin, the youngest: The two were *sisters*. And yet they'd never met. When her father died, Megan had left Ireland for England, determined to find work and send money home when she could; widowhood had left Pegeen destitute, with too many mouths to feed. But Megan had left before her mother knew she was pregnant . . . with Caitlin. And Pegeen, ashamed of having given away her infant daughter to the wise woman, Crionna, had waited years before she told her oldest daughter of Caitlin's existence. Waited, in fact, till she knew she was dying; sending for Megan, she confessed it to her and the priest on her deathbed.

"Ach, wee *sorcha*," Megan murmured, tears streaming down her face, "it broke me heart, it did. I'm certain our ma loved ye, colleen—niver doubt it. But she couldn't get past her fear o' ye, d'ye see?"

"Fear . . . of an infant?" It was Adam who asked. And not just because Megan's use of the word seemed strange. His eyes had focused on no one but Caitlin through the entire sorting out. And Caitlin had just given a violent start.

"Aye, m'lord," said Megan, stroking her sister's tear-stained cheek. "Odd as it sounds, our ma was deathly afraid o' her own babe. Because even in the cradle 'twas apparent, d'ye see—wee Caitlin has the Sight."

Chapter 11

Caitlin worried her lower lip with her teeth as she left Andrew's chamber. Not because his lordship had slipped out when the lad said his prayers; 'twas his habit, and she'd grown used to it. But on leaving, he had asked her to meet him in the library before she retired. And at the Hall that was *not* his habit. *He's after learning the truth behind Megan's words this afternoon, and no mistake!* Bracing herself for trouble, she stopped at the library's double doors, which stood ajar. "Ye wished t' see me, milord?"

"Yes . . . come in, Caitlin." He'd been standing near the doors. Now he closed them behind her and gestured toward a pair of armchairs by the fire. "Have a seat, please."

She'd not been inside Ravenskeep's library before, perhaps because it was oddly located. According to Townsend, an earlier marquis was an insomniac who'd converted rooms adjoining his bedchamber into a

172 *Veronica Sattler*

library, that he might easily find reading material in the middle of the night. Larger than the library in London, it was as richly appointed, but with furnishings of an earlier age. A masculine room, she thought, noting the time-mellowed oak paneling, the fine Flemish tapestries, the thick, jewel-toned Turkey carpets underfoot. Yet another handsome chessboard sat on a Jacobean oak table near the fireplace. But she knew this was not to be about chess.

Stifling a sigh, Caitlin took her seat. She'd tried to make light of her sister's—dear God, it seemed strange even to think of it—her *sister's* words about her having the Sight. Pegeen's fear, Caitlin had hastened to tell them, was mere superstitious nonsense. *May the Lord and my dead mother both forgive me for the lie. And Crionna! Yet better the lie, surely, than the Pandora's box the truth would unlock.*

She'd no idea if anyone believed the lie; Megan had sent her an odd look and immediately clammed up . . . out of politeness? Family loyalty? The duke and duchess had simply changed the subject, calling for a magnum of champagne from the cellars to celebrate the sisters' reunion. Which was all very well; indeed, she was grateful for it. Unfortunately, the pensive looks his lordship sent her through the remainder of the visit had intimated he was having none of it.

Adam, too, was feeling ill at ease. He was painfully aware of the long overdue apology he owed Caitlin. And just as painfully aware of the difficulty in another matter he couldn't ignore: her denial of her sister's words that afternoon. He didn't believe her. One look at Caitlin's transparent face had convinced him; her denial was what Andrew would call a clanker. Yet to question it was to impugn her honesty. And he'd already offended her past all civility in London. *She can't think worse of you than she does now, so just get on with it!*

"I won't beat about the bush, Caitlin," he said, deciding directness was the best approach. "I behaved abominably toward you in London—no, let me finish ... please. I owe you the deepest apology for my behavior that night. And another for taking so long to address it—for you will agree it has been far too long in coming."

She simply stared at him, as if taken aback, and Adam frowned. Was it so impossible for her to believe a lord would apologize to someone of her station? All the more reason to let her know he meant it, he decided, and plunged ahead. "I humbly beg you will accept my abject apologies, Caitlin, even if you cannot forgive me." He shoved a hand through his hair and shook his head. "What I did was unforgivable."

Ach, not about the Sight, then! Greatly relieved, Caitlin smiled at him. "But, milord, it *is*. Ye weren't in yer right, er, senses. Indeed, if ye'll forgive me sayin' so, 'twas the brandy talkin'."

It was Adam's turn to stare. "The brandy talking ..." he repeated grimly. "And what of the *doing*, Caitlin? It wasn't just my words offended you that night, and we both know it. If you hadn't stopped me with that, that gibberish—"

She suddenly went pale and looked away, avoiding his eyes.

He felt a jolt of recognition. *That's just how she reacted to her sister's words this afternoon!* "Caitlin," he said, leaning forward in his chair, "what the devil *was* that gibberish you spoke that night?"

Reluctantly, Caitlin raised her head, swallowing hard as she met the blue intensity of his gaze. " 'Twasn't

. . . 'twasn't gibberish, milord. 'Twas merely the Gaelic tongue I spoke.''

"Merely? It stopped me in my tracks!"

"A-aye, milord," she murmured, dropping her gaze.

He stared at her bowed head with incredulity. "What the devil *was* it?"

"An auld Irish . . . charm, milord."

"A *charm*—a charm for what, in the name of all sanity! Caitlin, look at me," he pleaded. Cupping her chin, he raised it and met her anguished gaze. "A charm to do what?"

"T' protect me," she whispered, tears brimming in her eyes.

"From me," he said with self-disgust as she began to sob softly. "From the unconscionable rape I'd have perpetrated in my drunken stupidity! And you deem that *forgivable?*

"Ah, sweetheart, I beg of you, don't cry." It was unbearable that he should cause her pain—yet again. Without thinking, he rose, pulled her gently to her feet, and wrapped his arms about her. "I'm not worth it," he murmured against her hair. "Not a single one of your tears, darling Caitlin, not one."

Caitlin was too distraught and miserable to absorb the tender fervency of his words. It was all unraveling, and she was helpless as ever to stop it. He'd know her for the dangerous creature she was now, and a liar to boot. Cursed with powers she'd neither asked for nor wanted. He'd send her away for sure. When all she'd ever wanted was to help him! " 'Twas m-merely an Irish ch-chant Crionna t-taught me," she stammered between hiccuping sobs. "I niver m-meant t' use it, milord!"

"Adam," he found himself saying. Without knowing why, but feeling the rightness of it with an intensity he couldn't explain. There could be no more class barriers here. Not with defenses tumbling down . . . and perhaps, if they were lucky, only the naked truth between them. "I beg you will call me Adam . . . no, I insist on it."

There was a pause as she sniffled. All at once, she drew back to gape at him. "Milord, I couldn't poss—"

"Adam," he repeated, stilling her lips with his thumb. "If what I suspect is true, I am about to intrude upon some deeply guarded . . . secrets. Secrets I wouldn't dream of demanding you reveal to me . . . as one of your so-called betters. But as an equal—and dare I hope, a friend?—perhaps you'll grant me the right to ask. And I swear to you, what you say will never go beyond this room."

Caitlin's head swam. *Call me Adam . . . as an equal . . . a friend.* Words so far beyond what she had ever dared hope, she feared she was dreaming. Any moment now, she'd awaken and find her arms wrapped about her pillow. Aye, her sterile pillow, and not his lean, hard waist; for he'd yet to release her. Not that she was about to protest—no, never. The dream might end and plunge her into the loneliness of her solitary bed; till then, for this brief moment in time, he was hers. With a soft sigh, she leaned her head against his chest. "Ask, then . . . Adam."

The sound of his name on her lips nearly undid him. A shudder passed through him, and with it, a stab of longing so great, he shook with it. A hopeless longing, for a love denied and steeped in futile, gut-wrenching desire. With a strength he wasn't aware he possessed, Adam willed it away.

"Caitlin, the thing your sister mentioned . . ." He stroked her hair, intent on assuring her this wasn't meant to be threatening. "The Sight. I collect it's tied up somehow with—with that protective chant. And none of it is superstitious nonsense, is it?"

With a sniffle, she shook her head no.

The feel of her hair gliding under his palm like living silk brought another surge of longing. Gritting his teeth, Adam again thrust it away. "Your foster mother," he said, keeping his voice neutral. "She gave you these, uh, supernatural powers?" It struck him how absurd he'd once have deemed such a question. A night in early April had made him damned careful, however, what he called absurd.

Still unwilling to lose the comfort of his arms, Caitlin raised her head just enough to look at him. "I had the chant from Crionna, aye, but not the Sight. 'Twas merely that she, bein' what we call a wisewoman, recognized it for what it was. And she niver referred to it as a . . . a power. A *gift*, she called it. Ye may be interested t' know *I* called it a curse."

Smiling down at her earnest face, Adam was greatly tempted to kiss away the tiny frown between her brows. "Would you care to explain why?" he asked gently.

With a sigh, Caitlin nodded. She gave him a brief history of her troubles with the gift. Including her difficulties with Father O'Malley. Including her fear of it. She went on to describe the nature of Crionna's charm, how she'd memorized it to grant the wish of a dying woman, never dreaming she would use it. She was careful to explain the part of Crionna's legacy she valued, however: the healing skills she had taken with her when her fear of the dreams and visions drove her out of Ireland. She held back one thing only, because she was afraid to speak of it: She couldn't bring herself to mention the terrible vision with him in it.

"A thing like the Sight is frightenin'," she finished at length, "unless ye're Irish and at home with the auld ways. I'm not proud of it, but 'tis why I didn't tell the truth this afternoon. Yet I regret . . . Adam, ye don't think too ill o' me ... for lyin'?" she asked, looking worriedly up at him.

"Think ill of you?" *I couldn't love you more than I do right now.* The temptation was too great. He cupped her face with his hands and kissed the tiny frown. "My silly darling, I think you're the bravest, finest, most splendid woman alive!"

"But I'm not ..." She almost said "your darling," then decided she couldn't have heard him right. Or else this *was* a dream, and it was about to explode in her face: the rude awakening she'd feared all along. "A-Adam, would ye repeat what y-ye just said?"

He stood there transfixed, caught by the wonder of her gaze as she searched his face. She was everything to him in that moment, everything he'd ever longed for and thought couldn't possibly exist. "What? Oh ... I said I think you're—"

"N-no, before that."

"I ..." He groaned, at last realizing what he'd blurted out in his zeal to reassure her: *My silly darling? You damned fool! Why not blow it all to perdition and confess you love her in the bargain?* "Forgive me." His eyes shuttered, and he dropped his hands from her face as if they burned him. "I'd no right to—I-I must have been delusional or—I beg you will forget what you heard."

The rejection hurt, and she swallowed a sob. And her pride. She'd gone too far now and had to know, even if she was cruelly mistaken. "Yet ye did say it, didn't ye, milord? I didn't just imagine—"

"Never call me that again!" With an anguished cry, he pulled her into his arms and buried his face in her hair. "It's Adam, do you hear? Blood and ashes, Caitlin, can't you at least give me that?"

Caitlin felt his arms close about her like a benediction. "Adam," she murmured through her tears. "Adam,

Adam and again, Adam! Aye, Adam—who is *my* silly darlin', even if he won't allow me t' be h-his.''

Adam raised his head. Stared at her honest, tear-streaked face as if she were his last hope. And yet, of course, he had no right to hope . . . no right at all. "Caitlin, you don't understand. I cannot—''

"Then, I must brave it alone," she whispered, tracing his anguished face with trembling fingers. "I've f-foolishly lost me heart t' ye, Adam Lightfoot. I love ye.''

"Caitlin," he groaned, "you mustn't—''

Her fingers covered his lips. "Mind, I say foolishly not because I'm ashamed of it. But naught that's g-good can come of a poor colleen lovin' a lord with a grand t-title. I mean, 'tis all very well t' say I mustn't 'milord' ye, but—''

"Don't!" He caught the fingers at his lips and pressed a fervent kiss into her palm. "Don't *ever* think this is about class," he said fiercely. "That you're somehow not good enough for me. It's *I* who am not good enough for *you*, Caitlin. Not good enough—not *worthy*.''

"Ach, now ye truly are bein' foolish! Not worthy? What, because of a single instance when ye let the drink steal yer wits and forgot yerself?''

"No, Caitlin! It's far worse than that. It's about . . .'' He shook his head in defeat. "It's about things I cannot—things I *dare not* explain to you.''

"Dare not explain t' me? Secrets, Adam? After *I've* just confessed t' havin' the Sight itself?''

"Trust me," he said with a weary sigh, "this makes the Sight seem like child's play.''

"I do trust ye. Yet it appears ye don't trust *me*," she said sadly. "Ye think I'm not t' be trusted with yer great secret, is that it?''

"You still don't understand! Caitlin, this secret could

harm you. Making you privy to it could put you in danger you cannot begin to imagine.''

Caitlin's breath stilled, for she finally understood. 'Twas the thing of darkness in him. He feared it, and rightly so: 'Twas at the root of the pain and torment she'd sensed in him from the start. The pain she believed with all her heart she was here to heal. But how to do that when he meant to protect *her* from it? From all knowledge of it, even. Indeed, till now, he hadn't even alluded to it. It came out only because other barriers had been breached, because of the intimacy they'd—

The intimacy they'd begun to share!

The solution struck with such clarity, she was amazed she hadn't seen it sooner. The dreams and visions had been pointing to it all along. Crionna had told her to trust them, but she hadn't listened. Because they were so daunting. They were still daunting. Did she have the strength to heed them? Aye, she did. Yet 'twould be far easier if she knew but one thing. Pausing to gather her courage, she met Adam's tormented eyes. "Do ye love me, Adam?''

Absorbed in constructing arguments to dissuade her, Adam was caught off guard; the simple directness of her question disarmed him. Even as he grasped for an evasion she might accept, the truth blazed in his eyes. Releasing his breath on a long, shuddering sigh, he nodded helplessly. "I love you. Beyond hope, beyond life itself, my foolish, foolish darling.''

A sob caught in her throat, on a surge of incredulous joy. With a small cry, she launched herself at him. Flung her arms about his neck, and covered his face with kisses: eyes, nose, temples, chin, lips. He loved her, *loved* her! Her giddy heart grew wings and soared on the heady currents of hope: They loved, and because they loved, all things were possible.

Every instinct told Adam to resist. He was a lost soul, his doom sealed by his own blood. He had nothing to offer her, less than nothing. He could only save her from himself, send her away, far away, before it was too late. All this he knew, and even at the moment he confessed his love, he reached for the strength to see it through. What he hadn't counted on, however, was the strength of Caitlin's will. Of her determination to pull him from the dark and into the light. Of her love.

The moment she flung herself into his arms, his resistance crumbled. A groan broke from his throat, and his arms closed about her. Catching her to him like a precious gift, he closed his eyes and savored the sweetness of her innocent, untutored kisses. When her mouth found his, when she kissed him fully on it, he tasted the salt of her tears with the honey of her lips. At once the blood beat heavy in his veins. A roaring in his ears eclipsed the last vestiges of impending doom, and he was lost, lost to her honest passion.

He claimed her with a kiss like no other he'd ever given a woman. For he'd not loved before, and now, impossible as it seemed, love was here. Caitlin, his first love and his last. His forever love, whose memory he'd take with him into the fires of hell itself, and none would say him nay!

It was a savagely tender kiss, fierce in its communication of all that lay in his heart and mind, in his bartered soul. Caitlin kissed him back in kind, and it was all he could do not to take her there, on the jewel-toned rug before the fire. "Caitlin," he groaned against her mouth, "I want you desperately, love, and you're making me lose control. I—"

"Control, is it?" she asked on a gust of breathless

laughter. "Sure and ye're not *serious*. Control, Adam, when I want ye so much I could die of it?"

For a heartbeat, Adam went utterly still. Holding his raging passions carefully in check, he released her and set her down before him. "You're sure?" he asked in a ragged whisper.

"I've niver been as sure of somethin' in me life," she replied solemnly. "I-I had a vision, d'ye see, while we were still in London—aye, 'twas the Sight. I saw the two of us, upon a great bed. We . . . we—ach, we lay there in naked abandon! I-I think we'd just made love—or were about t' begin, perhaps. 'Tis still a mystery t' me how . . . how 'tis done, ye understand. But there's no mystery in what the vision portended."

And when he simply stared, as if he didn't dare believe her: "Tell, me, Adam, does yon chamber"—she pointed across the room to a door she was suddenly certain connected to the master bedchamber Townsend had mentioned—"boast a grand bed with a lovely sky blue canopy? And silken sheets embroidered with the letter *L*?"

Adam's head reeled as the full import of her words settled in his brain. Without preamble, he swept her up in his arms and carried her to his bed; the bed with a canopy his father had ordered to match Catherine Lightfoot's sky blue eyes; the bed with the sheets she'd lovingly embroidered with the letter *L* while he and his father played chess; the bed where he'd been conceived in love.

He stopped before it and set Caitlin gently on her feet. Gazing into her eyes, he began to remove the pins from her hair, one by one. He did this without haste, and with a sensual, slowly curving smile that made her breath hitch. He was making love to her with that smile, Caitlin realized with a delicate shiver as each pin dropped to the carpet. And with his heavy-lidded, knowing eyes that promised delicious secrets. A knot of anticipation unfurled in the pit of her belly as she felt the weight of her coppery curls slowly unwinding. Sliding like silk along her neck and onto her shoulders.

"Your hair," Adam murmured, pausing to lift a heavy skein of burnished silk and finger it with awe, "is glorious." Another pin fell, and his eyes continued to caress her with lazy, loving intent. "I can tell you now, my love," he said, "that I've lain sleepless and endlessly tossing in that bed." An indolent grin emerged, wickedly teasing, as he freed another coppery curl. "Because I kept imagining how it would look . . . how *you* would look . . . and feel"—the last pin dropped soundlessly to the carpet—"while I made love to you . . .

"Like this . . . ," he breathed. Lifting the heavy, yard-long curls away from her nape, he slowly released them, letting them sift through his hands to tumble down her back. Lacing his fingers through the hair at the sides of his head, he captured her wondering face and tilted it up for his kiss. A slow, drugging kiss that was entirely new, entirely different from what had gone before. A kiss that made Caitlin wonder if she had truly been kissed at all till now. And she hadn't . . . not like this.

Adam's mouth moved over hers without haste, yet with a thoroughness as delicious in what it promised as in what it gave. He was determined to take his time with her, to make it perfect for her. Despite the white-hot talons of desire clawing at his loins. Slowly, slowly, he savored the pliant sweetness of her lips, molding and shaping them with consummate skill. They were warm and trusting. Innocent and waiting, unaware, for delights he knew she scarcely imagined.

The first overt hint of pleasure came with the sensual glide of his tongue along her lower lip. Then, ever so gently, he sank his teeth into the sensitized flesh, and Caitlin moaned, deep in her throat. When he traced the shape of her upper lip, pausing midway to suck gently at the bow-shaped arch of bee-stung flesh, he felt her shiver. Sliding his tongue leisurely along the sensitive seam between, then back again, he paused to delve into a corner with the very tip. And smiled against her mouth when her lips parted for the sweet, sensual invasion to come.

His hands slid along her neck, doing devastating things to her nerve endings as they stroked the sensitive skin. Pausing to caress her shoulders, then her arms, he eased his hands about her waist and drew her near. While his tongue slipped inside the warm cave of her mouth.

Caitlin made an inarticulate sound, and her own tongue shyly ventured forth to meet his. When Adam grazed it lightly with his teeth, she shuddered. Rising urgently on tiptoe, she wound her arms about his neck and pressed herself closer.

Again, Adam found himself tested to the limits of his control. Her mouth was succulent and sweet beyond telling, her small body trembling with eagerness. Summoning the strength to resist the insistent need throbbing inside his loins, he held them to the same unhurried pace. Now came the lazy exploration, the slow, sensual exchange of taste and texture. Her curious probing delighted him. He felt her surprise, her own delight in discovery upon discovery, for she was an apt pupil. Soon her tentative advances grew bolder, and the exchange became a heady tangling of tongues.

When at last they broke for air, both were breathless and trembling. "Softly, love," Adam murmured unsteadily against her hair as he held her close. "We've a world of time this night, and no need for haste."

"But—"

"Shh." He stroked the lustrous hair cascading down her back, soothing her. At length, taking her gently by the shoulders, he set her slightly apart from him, knowing she needed to cool down as much as he. "We've only just begun," he said, smiling into her eyes. "And I would know a word from you."

"A word?" Her bemused voice was still husky with desire.

"In your lovely Gaelic, darling." He traced the line of her brow and then her jaw, lightly with his finger. "I would know how to say just that . . . how to call you 'darling.' "

She smiled, adoring him with her eyes. "Ye . . . we say *a stór*, Adam . . . or perhaps *macushla*."

"*A stór,*" he whispered, gazing deeply into those wide green eyes. His hands went to the simple sash beneath her breasts. "Black is the color of mourning," he murmured, loosing her high-waisted black cotton gown. "And I respect and honor your wearing of it. But tonight is for love, *macushla*, and mourning must be set aside."

"Cri-Crionna," she stammered as his knuckles grazed the undersides of her breasts, "w-would scarce object, I-I'm thinkin'. She—she l-loved the bright colors o' flowers a-and was niver fond o' black."

"Then, she was truly a wise woman." His smile went wry. "In my dreams, I confess, I've clothed you only in sunny silks and softly hued velvets." With a few deft motions of his hands, the gown fell noiselessly to the floor. "And decked you in emeralds green as your eyes . . ."

Caitlin's breath went shallow as his gaze traveled the length of her. She stood before him clad only in her shift, and she wanted to cover herself. Modesty lay behind this, but so did shame: The homely garment was clean, but greatly darned and worn. Then Adam's gaze returned to hers, and she blushed, yet the shame was gone. The warmth in his eyes was unmistakable. Caitlin knew, with an instinct as old as womankind, he found her pleasing.

Curling his forefinger beneath her chin, Adam tilted her face toward his. He brushed his lips over her brows, then her eyelids when they fluttered closed. Claiming her mouth with another tender kiss, he lingered a moment to savor its sweetness. Now he felt her hands move uncertainly to his chest; the flexing of her fingers as they made contact conveyed a tension he understood. "Curious, *macushla?*" he whispered against her lips, his breath mingling with hers. "Go ahead, then . . . find out . . . learn . . . whatever you wish to know."

He felt her hesitate, then begin to move her hands experimentally over his torso. Shyly at first, then with growing ardor. With a chuckle, he paused to shed his coat and neckcloth. Then his waistcoat, giving her the access she craved.

Caught up in the fascinating exploration of his body, Caitlin forgot her own state of undress. She'd never touched a man before, not like this. He was beautifully made. Wide-shouldered, with a broad, muscular chest tapering to a lean waist and a hard, flat abdomen. His biceps were corded with muscle and sinew, their firm contours the epitome of male strength. And yet she knew how gentle they could be, how safe and protected she felt when she stood in the shelter of his arms.

Adam stood before her unmoving, letting her small hands roam over him at will. But the cost to his control was enormous. All too soon it became impossible to remain passive. Every stroke, every glide of her soft palms over his already heated flesh, set him on fire. Her name broke from his lips in a ragged whisper. He began to move his own hands over her. In a slow, thorough exploration of her semi-clad body.

She was exquisitely proportioned, her graceful limbs suggesting the long-boned elegance of a taller woman; yet they were perfectly attuned to her diminutive size. High, upthrust breasts, lush and full for all her slender stature, gave way to a waist so slight he could span it with his hands. While below, the graceful flare of hip and sweep of thigh robbed him of words to describe what he beheld. The term "Pocket Venus" came briefly to mind before he thrust it aside. Coined by the glib wordsmiths of the day, it didn't begin to describe Caitlin's delicate grace and beauty. She was exquisite ... perfection itself in the shape of woman. She made his throat go dry with longing.

"Caitlin ... so lovely," he murmured, stroking her silken shoulders. He kissed the baby-soft skin where a pulse fluttered at her throat, nuzzled the sensitive place where neck and shoulder joined. His hand swept down her back and came to rest just above the curve of her buttocks. The other found her breast. He cupped it gently so not to alarm her.

"Ohh," Caitlin breathed, ceasing her own exploration as she felt his intimate touch. Then, as his thumb lightly abraded the peak: "Oh!" Pleasure, sudden as it was surprising, shot through her like heat lightning. It leapt from where his thumb teased to the woman's place at her core.

Adam felt her nipple spring to life and furl into a telltale bud. Her reaction threatened to drive him over the edge. Sweet, sweet Caitlin—so responsive, so sensually alive! It was all he could do to remember she was still an untutored innocent. She deserved to be initiated slowly and patiently. He had to disregard the firestorm erupting in his loins. Ah, but it was deuced difficult!

The erection straining his breeches knew nothing of patience.

Biting down on his raging passions, he momentarily stilled his thumb and nuzzled her ear, whispering words of praise and encouragement. At length, he felt her lean into him, her nipple contracting even more. When his fingers gently plucked it, she gasped.

"Easy, my love," he murmured. "It's all right. You're just so very new at this. Listen to your body, sweetheart. Let it teach you. Learn from it while I love you . . . while I give you pleasure."

As he spoke, his other hand moved over the curve of her derriere, caressing her; then lower, to stroke the backs of her silken thighs. His hand slid slowly upward again, bringing the hem of her shift with it; when he cupped her naked buttocks, he heard her moan his name. "Sweet Caitlin," he breathed, and pulled her up against him. As her feet left the floor, the cradle of her hips met the swollen contours of his erection. "Know how I want you," he whispered. "Know the joy that is your birthright as a woman. A woman who is deeply loved, *macushla, a stór.*"

Caitlin lost all sense of time and place after that. Her world narrowed to the two of them and the intense pleasure spiraling through her body. To the love pouring from him in heartfelt words and hot, intimate caresses. Lost in a maelstrom of desire, of pleasure she'd scarcely imagined, she surrendered completely to Adam's knowing hands. Ah, God—his hands!

Without knowing how it happened, she found herself entwined with him on the bed. Her shift had twisted about her waist; her breasts were bared to Adam's relentlessly pleasuring mouth. As he teased and suckled the pouting nipples, she squirmed with pleasure. She wondered if someone could die of such pleasure. She was drowning in sensation. Aware of her body as she'd never been before: of breasts aching with pleasure and begging for more; of the pulsing place below her belly invaded by a sweet, curling sensation she couldn't explain; of trembling thighs that . . . . Mother of God, her naked thighs lay open to his hand, and he was—

"Adam!" she cried, trying to close them to the shocking caress, but she was too late. A moan escaped as his fingers slid along her woman's entrance; then another, even louder, as he slipped one of them inside her. What was happening to her? When had she grown so slippery and slick? Why?

It was as if he'd heard her. "You're wet for me, sweetheart," he explained, smiling into her bewildered eyes. "See?" he whispered, easing a second finger inside her, gently stretching her. "Your body's made you ready . . . for me." He claimed her mouth with a kiss that left her mindless and reeling. And all the while, he stroked her sweetly yielding flesh.

Caitlin began to writhe and twist beneath him on the bed as his fingers worked their magic. Now his thumb found the tiny protrusion nestled in her auburn curls. He stroked the sensitive nub; she moaned in ecstasy. Again, he stroked; her nails dug into his shoulders. The third time, she convulsed under his hand and sobbed his name.

"Shh, love." Adam stopped to hold her tight and soothe her. Sweat beaded his brow as he clung to the last tether of his control. Her artless passion was a siren's call, tempting him to lose patience. He ached to bury himself at once inside her sweetly willing body. But she was untried, and he would die before he hurt her. *Yet for a virgin, some pain is unavoidable,* he thought as he quickly shed his clothes. The only virgin he'd bedded was his late wife, whom all the love play in the world couldn't arouse. He'd finally tried to ease the way with saliva—but that had so repulsed her, he was forced to give it up. In the end, she'd simply lain there like a dead fish, insisting he "get on with it." Her shrieks when he finally gave in had nearly unmanned him.

The distasteful memory cooled his ardor; fortunately, as it happened, for it gave him a chance to reclaim the control Caitlin deserved. When she called his name, he took her in his arms with a smile. "I'm here, love," he murmured, smoothing back the tiny tendrils of hair clinging damply to her brow. He searched her face to gauge her emotional state; meeting her heavy-lidded gaze, he felt his loins quicken anew. Her eyes were pellucid green pools, their centers dark with desire. Yet even as he watched, passion further dilated the pupils; black eclipsed the green. "I'm here," he repeated thickly, "and I want you, *macushla.*"

Caitlin had yet to descend from the pleasurable storm erupting through her body. Myriad feelings, so new she scarcely recognized herself, crowded her thoughts and set them spinning. She only knew she loved this man with every atom of her being. Now, as he held her close and gazed into her eyes, a new realization penetrated the sensual haze: *Adam . . . Holy Mother of God—he's naked!*

As this registered, another element joined the sensual maelstrom: curiosity. She felt firm, warm skin, so different from hers . . . whorls of springy hair on a broad, muscular chest . . . sparser hair along the hard lengths of his thighs. And where they joined, a thicket that covered—"

She swallowed thickly and returned to examining the taut planes of his upper torso. "*Macushla,*" she murmured, her voice a throaty contralto, "ye're iver so b-beautifully made." She ran her hands slowly, wonderingly over his chest, testing the crisp, dark curls. Discovering the flat discs of his nipples, she circled them curiously with her fingertips. And when she felt them tighten: *"Oh!"*

Sucking in his breath, Adam stopped the innocent exploration that nearly undid him, and gave a shaky chuckle. "Any more of that, my lass, and this will be over before it's begun."

"But . . . I don't understand."

"No . . . but you will." His voice had grown thick and husky with desire, yet it held a hint of amusement. Performing the same maneuver on Caitlin's nipples, he saw understanding widen her eyes, even as she shuddered with pleasure.

"A-aye," she managed. And when he continued to fondle and pluck the responsive peaks: "B-but I still don't understand why *I* mustn't d-do it, while *you*—"

"Because a passionate woman . . ." he whispered as his other hand slid between her thighs, "a woman like you, my darling, may reach fulfillment several times in as many minutes. It's different for a man. If I were to let you continue as you were, I'd require long minutes to, uh, recover, before we could bring this loving to its . . . conclusion."

"B-but, Adam," she said, trying to hold on to her thoughts. Not easy with the things he was doing to her body. "That hardly seems fair! I—"

"Just let me love you, *macushla*," he whispered, silencing her with a soul-drugging kiss.

And she did. Surrendering completely to his loving, until she lay taut and trembling beneath him. Open to him, her woman's place aching for him. Every nerve ending vibrating with delicious pleasure and primal need. "P-lease, Adam," she begged, "I want—I want . . ." Her eyes fluttered closed in helpless confusion.

"I know, love," he said thickly, "and so do I. Now look at me, *a stór*. Open your eyes and look at me ... while I take us there." As her eyes met his, their dark pupils entirely eclipsing the green now, he whispered her name with a tender smile. And slid his throbbing shaft slowly, ever so slowly, into her waiting warmth.

Caitlin felt the pressure of him slipping inside her with a surge of elemental joy. "Aye!" she cried, and arched her hips to meet his.

"Caitlin—don't!" Too late, Adam felt the fragile membrane tear, felt her stiffen beneath him. "Hold still, love," he rasped, his body trembling with an effort to do the same. "Hold absolutely still and the pain will pass ... I promise."

"A-aye," she whispered uncertainly. But the pain was already receding. Aware now of how she'd precipitated things, she gave a rueful chuckle. "When—when I was but a wee lass, Crionna was foriver t-tellin' me t' look before I leap. Said I was m-most apt t' forget it when—when I was after f-followin' me heart."

Beads of sweat studding his brow, Adam searched her face with anxious eyes. "And what does your heart say now, *macushla*?"

"That the leap was worth it," she answered with a smile as old as Eve. Gazing deeply into his eyes, she moved her hips—subtly, this time—to tell him her body said the same.

Adam released a quavering breath. He gave her a long, lingering kiss. "Now?" he whispered thickly.

Her reply was a slow rotation of her hips.

"Minx!" he accused with a shaky laugh. Moving his hand to the place where they joined, he found the tiny nub; this, he circled and stroked, and heard her moan something in the Gaelic. Again, and she sobbed it aloud.

On the third pass, she drew her legs about him, begging for completion.

With a groan that was her name, Adam slid deeply home.

Moving on her with care, he felt her melt into him. Now he picked up the pace. Together, they slipped into the age-old rhythm of man and woman. Sweetly rocking, boldly reaching, soaring, soaring to the dreamless stars. Through the magical realm of desire, to the far-flung reaches of the universe itself. Mindless with rapture, they shattered in each other's arms.

And two were one in the name of love.

Chapter 12

Adam lay awake in the bed, Caitlin asleep in his arms. The lovely, satisfied smile she wore sorely tempted him. He'd have liked nothing more than to kiss her awake. And then to kiss her senseless. To take her with him again on that long, sensual glide that swept them, sated and replete, on the dreaming shores of love. But he wouldn't wake her. They'd made love several times through the night, and she had to be exhausted. Mindful of her newly initiated body, he hadn't intended it, but Caitlin had had other ideas. After that first earthshaking joining, she'd slept for a time, then awakened—all sleepy and soft as a kitten—and reached for him with unmistakable intent.

He'd been helpless to resist; the best he could do was to take infinite care with her, and he had. Again and again, throughout the night. She finally fell into a deep slumber about an hour before dawn. Since then, he'd simply held her in his arms. Watching her. Remembering . . . cherishing every moment of their loving—cherishing *her*. But Adam hadn't slept at all.

What kept going round in his head was where they went from here. No matter how he sliced it, he kept returning to one wrenching conclusion: He must send Caitlin away. He made no doubt it would tear him apart. He nonetheless must, *must* somehow find the strength to do it. The very love he bore her put her in deepest peril, and that he would *not* do.

Problem was, he must convince Caitlin this was their only course. As he was learning, she could be fiercely tenacious when it came to loving him. And she did love him, incredible as it seemed. Of that he'd not a single—

"Ye're frownin', *macushla, a stór.*" Warm and muzzy with sleep, Caitlin smiled drowsily up at him. "I don't suppose ye'd be after tellin' me why?"

"A fleabite," Adam lied, quickly summoning a smile. *Not yet. Just a little while longer, and then I'll tell her . . . as I must. But for now . . . ah, it's too soon . . . I can't—not yet.* "Go back to sleep, love," he murmured, pressing his lips tenderly to her brow.

" 'Tis *not* a fleabite," she countered, frowning herself now. "I've come t' read ye too well, Adam Lightfoot, and what I'm seein' in yer eyes speaks o' some great, important matter. I think—" She scrambled to a sitting position, stared at him in disbelief—"ye're after sendin' me away!"

The air left his lungs in a despairing rush: half sigh, half groan. "Caitlin, listen to m—"

"I'll not go."

"Caitlin, I beg you will try to under—"

"We love—*that* is what I understand. 'Tis all I need to understand!" Tears flooded her eyes as she glared at him, immutable resolve in the set of her mouth. "And unless yer own part in that equation has changed—"

"You know it hasn't."

"Then, 'tis simple: Two people who love—who love as *we* love, Adam—are blessed! What right have ye t' throw that away?"

He shoved a hand roughly through his hair and heaved a troubled sigh. "We've been through all this bef—"

"Before, aye—before we knew we loved each ither! Before we made love and . . ." She paled visibly, and her bottom lip trembled. "P-please . . . ," she whispered, "tell me 'tis not what I—what I'm thinkin'. F-Father O'Malley taught us 'tis a sin t' have c-carnal knowledge w-without bein' wed. That"—she swallowed convulsively against the tears clogging her throat—"that a woman who did so was sure t' be c-cast aside—"

"No, Caitlin—*no!*" Privately cursing Father O'Malley and all narrow-minded fools like him, Adam reached for her hands and held them tightly in his. "I cannot believe you'd think me capable—Caitlin, disabuse yourself of such thoughts and *listen* to me. I'm begging you to leave *because* I love you. You are everything to me . . . my life . . . my heart. The heart I'd sooner cut from my body than risk your—no, hear me out!"

There was a wealth of tenderness in his eyes as he smiled at her, but there was sadness in the smile as well. "Never think I intend to abandon you, my darling. Still, you *must* leave me. To stay is fraught with such danger, you cannot imagine it. Sending you away will be the hardest thing I've ever done. I'll die inside when you go, my Caitlin. But listen to me. I mean to *wed* you before we part. You'll have my name and never want for a single—"

"*Wed* me! Ye'd wed me, then send me away?" Tears streaming down her cheeks, she regarded him with an agony of love and pain in her eyes. "Have ye heard the words o' the marriage vows, Adam? Really, truly heard them? I can't believe they're so very different in the English church. 'Till death do us part.' Isn't that what we'll vow before God's holy altar? And what about the part that goes, 'Whom God hath joined, let no man—' "

"This isn't about God, damn it! It's about His very oppos—" Adam clenched his jaws shut, released her hands, and swung off the bed.

Caitlin stared at the rigid back he turned to her, at the hands he held clenched into fists at his sides. "Isn't about God?" she repeated numbly. "About His very . . ."

The blood went to ice in her veins. For a moment she couldn't move. An image out of nightmare loomed in her mind's eye: of evil incarnate, fanning enormous membranous wings, blood and gore dripping from its rapacious jaws. Swept by a wave of nausea, Caitlin brought a fist to her mouth. She bit down hard, till the pain drove it away.

Then she moved, leaping off the bed, careless of her nudity. "Tell me," she demanded, planting herself before him, arms akimbo. Her green eyes blazed fiercely as they met Adam's tormented gaze. "Tell me about God's *opposite* and the hold he has on ye—no, don't even try t' deny it! I've seen the hellish creature, d'ye see—aye, with the Sight! In a nightmare, where I played chess"—she pointed to the handsome chess set resting on a table across the room—"upon that very board. 'Twas while I was yet in Ireland, long before I iver learnt the game! Now, tell me all of it—and when ye've done, niver ask me t' leave you again!"

Thoroughly shaken, Adam stared at her in wordless horror. It sickened him even to think of Caitlin in connection with that monstrous evil. It could only mean she was already somehow mixed up in his fate. Slowly, with haunted eyes, he began to tell her about a visit in early April. About Appleby.

"That pretty well covers it," he finished wearily, long minutes later. They sat together on the edge of the bed, Caitlin clasping his hand as if she'd never let go. Dawn had broken, spearing fingers of pale light between the draperies. The ticking of the mantel clock seemed to punctuate Adam's words as, with a twist of his lips, he recounted: "My unsuspecting vow that summoned Appleby . . . that hellish pact . . . the fiend's treachery in saving Andrew's life without restoring his leg. I'd say that sums it up rather tidily," he added bitterly.

"It explains the darkness I've seen inside ye, Adam, *a stór,*" Caitlin said, suppressing a shudder. The desperation to save Andrew's life, aye, that she could well understand. Didn't she love Adam precisely because he was such a man? An honorable man, one who didn't love easily, but when he loved, gave his all? But the price he'd paid was worse than anything she'd imagined. She felt sickened and terrified by what he'd revealed.

And yet—ach, what did any of it matter? She loved him. She'd travel to the ends of the earth to save him. Aye, to the gates of hell itself!

"Now I understand why the Sight drew me here," she went on, nodding. "I needed t' know, d'ye see. T' learn what it is we must face if I'm t' help ye find the Light."

Adam gaped at her in dread. *"We?* Oh, no—never! Caitlin, what I just described—all the brutal and frightening detail of it—was meant to convince you of one thing, and one thing only. You must flee this evil. Run, Caitlin—as far and as fast as you can!"

Slowly, she shook her head. " 'Tis useless t' run, Adam, as I should know. Aye, I played the coward at first. Only t' discover ye cannot run from what's meant t' be. I ran from it—and the runnin' only led me here.''

"You ran . . . the nightmare?"

She nodded. "Though Crionna warned me I must deal with it. I saw a stranger, a man with a scar." With a tender smile, she reached out to touch the scar on his face. " 'Twas you, only I hadn't yet met ye, didn't know who ye were, then. Ye were just a dark, handsome stranger with a scar . . . who watched me play chess with the divil.''

His face went chalk white. "Caitlin, as you love me— leave before you're further drawn in! He'll—he'll try to use you against me—or worse." *He'll try to win* your *soul as well!*

Again, she shook her head. " 'Tis too late, *macushla,* even if the dreams had niver been. By lovin' ye, d'ye see, I'm already involved. Ach, don't fash yerself, *a stór.* The dreams and visions always have a purpose. They brought me here, I'm thinkin'—no, I'm past certain of it—t' help ye defeat the fiend.''

He gave a bark of mirthless laughter. "Defeat him! I can't even *find* him." Briefly, he described his useless efforts to locate Appleby in London. "For the deceit he practiced with Andrew's leg, I'd like nothing better than to confront the slimy toad. He won't be found, Caitlin, because he doesn't wish to be found. Of a certainty, he'll avoid affording me an opportunity to get round him and that blasted contract! No, I'm hopelessly damned, no matter what I do. And the wretched fiend knows it.''

Caitlin stared pensively at the floor for a moment. "Adam," she said, brightening as she raised her head and met his eyes. "The church teaches that every sinner has a chance t' be saved from perdition. All we need

do is pray for it with a sincere heart! Ye must ask God—
ach, why are ye shakin' yer head?"

"I *can't*, Caitlin." He regarded her with a dull bleakness in his eyes, a look she'd never seen before. "I'm
. . . unable to. Haven't prayed, haven't had the ability
to pray, since . . . the Peninsula. I'm without faith, do
you see—and therefore doubly damned."

Caitlin stared at him, apalled, but also deeply frightened. Of all the things he'd told her, this was the most
troubling. She'd readily seen him as a man willing to
sacrifice himself for his child. As a helpless victim of
the sly archfiend, who'd used that nobility of character
against him. Now he was telling her that at least part of
what had brought him to this pass lay within Adam
himself. Ach, what gross atrocities, what evils, had he
witnessed in those distant battlefields to strip him of his
faith?

She tried to offer him a reassuring smile, failed, and
settled for a simple nod. "Then, ye must work at
regainin' yer faith, *a stór*. I'll not give up on ye, and I
won't leave. I'm committed, d'ye see, no matter what.
And in the meantime, I'll pray *for* ye."

"Ever the Irish Angel," he said, smiling crookedly as
he lightly touched her hair. His eyes blazed with love,
but in his heart of hearts, Adam fought despair.

For Andrew's sake, they went through the motions
of a normal day. Ever sensitive to those around him,
however, the child caught wind of something between
them, sensing an important change in their relation-
ship. He seemed to thrive on it. He was energy itself,
ebullient and laughing, drawing them into various
games he devised.

First, there was a hide-and-seek that allowed him to

"practice on my crutches." Then came an energetic charades, in which the child displayed a repertoire of hand gestures and body language that was nothing short of amazing in one so young. Finally, he introduced them to a game he and Jeremy had invented; it was called "Who Am I?" Here Andrew truly shone, with astonishingly clever imitations of members of the staff. Performances that left Caitlin and Adam doubled with laughter.

"Ach, lad!" Caitlin exclaimed between giggles. "Sure and ye've a future treadin' the boards at the Drury Lane, should ye iver wish it. 'Twas grand mimicry! Wasn't his renderin' o' Cook splendid, milord?" She had gotten Adam to agree to let her "milord" him whenever they were not in private.

"It was priceless—but if Cook ever sees you imitating him," Adam told the boy, trying to look stern while wiping tears of laughter from his eyes, "you'll be in the suds, for sure!"

"Oh, I won't, Papa," Andrew assured him. " 'Cause it might overset him, and I hope I am a gentleman." He turned toward Caitlin, explaining: "Papa says a true gentleman is never unkind toward others, do you see."

"Yer da has the right of it," she said. "After all, *gentle* is the greater part o' that word."

Andrew nodded thoughtfully, then frowned. "I think some gentlemen aren't true gentlemen at all."

"Oh?" Adam thought of the rakes in whose company he'd wasted so much time in London. And wondered if his son could perhaps have gotten wind of such. He'd taken particular care to protect Andrew from knowledge of that lot. *And see where it got you, you damned fool! If you hadn't needed to "protect" him that night, you wouldn't be in the terrible coil you're in now. Then again, you'd never have met Caitlin. Blood and ashes, is life nothing but a big, ironic joke?* "And who, exactly, comes to mind, son?"

"Well, Papa, I heard one of those physicians in London being unkind to Caitlin. Remember? One of them came to see me after she made my head better. When I explained about her being the Irish Angel, he just made a funny noise in his throat. But when he went out, into the hallway, he forgot to close the door. That's when I heard him tell Caitlin she ought to go back to her Irish bog and leave healing to her betters."

He turned toward Caitlin. "Caitlin, what's a bog? I mean, I don't think it could be a very pleasant thing, from the way he said it."

Caitlin smiled at him and shook her head. "A bog's a wet and squishy place, and there are lots o' them in Ireland, t' be sure. They're not bad in themselves, lad. They're full o' peat, which the Irish use for fuel when there's no wood t' be found. Still, I'd not be after dwellin' in one, d'ye see?"

Andrew nodded. "Then, the physician *wasn't* being a true gentleman, was he, Papa? 'Cause he meant that Caitlin *should* dwell in one of those bogs, I could tell!"

"You're right, son. Though a physician is entitled to be addressed as a gentleman in the Polite World, that alone isn't sufficient to make him one. As you've so wisely noted, a man may clothe himself in the trappings of a gentleman without being one." *I hope you're listening, Appleby!* "A valuable lesson, Andrew. And you make me proud, for it's one you've learned all by yourself." Adam affectionately rumpled his son's hair.

Andrew beamed at him, but this was quickly followed by a yawn.

"Ach," said Caitlin, stifling a yawn herself, "sure and ye're fair worn out with all the games we've played t'day, lad. An early bedtime wouldn't go amiss, I'm thinkin'."

Andrew didn't complain when they tucked him in early. He smiled when Caitlin still took the time to massage his overworked muscles, saying she believed his leg might grow stronger yet. Afterward, Adam several times caught Caitlin stifling more of her own yawns. Recalling she'd slept little the night before—and why— he sent her a smile that evoked every nuance of what had passed between them in his bed.

"Find your bed and get a full night's . . . undisturbed sleep," he murmured, bending over her ear. He longed to kiss it, but there were servants about.

Blushing furiously, Caitlin bade him good night and scurried upstairs before one of them noticed.

Long after she'd gone, Adam lay in his own bed, staring at the canopy overhead. He'd been awake for hours, physically tired yet finding it impossible to sleep. Caitlin's refusal to leave him touched him beyond words. And terrified him no end. If there were any way to circumvent her, any way at all, he'd do it in a heart-beat: She was too precious to risk.

As he lay there listening to the mantel clock ticking away the hours, he kept trying to attack the problem from every angle. Caitlin's appearance in his life at this desperate juncture must portend something beyond what they already knew, he reasoned. Her nightmare vision had driven her here. He carefully began to turn over in his mind all the things she'd told him. *The dreams and visions always have a purpose . . . brought me here t' help ye defeat the fiend . . . every sinner has a chance t' be saved from perdition . . . all we need do is pray for it with a sincere heart.*

He even tried heeding that sage prescription for saving one's soul: He tried to pray. Without success. He found it impossible to pray to a deity he'd no wish to believe in. Or, at best, whose goodness and mercy he'd stopped believing in . . . couldn't believe in.

Of course, he hadn't actually told Caitlin he was an apostate, and she hadn't asked. Perhaps she knew. She was wise beyond her years, as he'd long ago discovered. Such wisdom was more than likely to penetrate his long-established habit of silence. The wall he'd erected to shut others out. His reluctance to trust anyone with a knowledge of the things that made him tick.

What still astounded him was Caitlin's trust and faith in *him*. Indeed, her trust and faith, period. Her belief she'd be able to help him find a way out of the hellish hole he'd dug himself greatly humbled him. Wasn't it the very thing had moved him to try praying? But that was the problem, he suspected: He'd done it for Caitlin's sake, not his own. Small wonder her God couldn't be reached. Easier to summon Appleby than—

Adam shot up in bed. Easier to summon Appleby? Not lately, of course, but he suddenly recalled something the fiend had once told him. Appleby had mentioned it right at the start—the night he *had* been successfully summoned: *If any mortal offers to barter his soul, he summons me.*

Of course! Why hadn't he thought of it sooner? He might very well be able to summon the little bastard— by offering to *barter again*. All he had to do was offer to renegotiate the terms of the contract. To make it more attractive to Appleby . . . .

Adam's face went grim as he considered what this would entail. Caitlin might never forgive him, and that was hard. Still, there was no help for it. She and Andrew would be safe, and their safety was paramount. Their safety was everything.

At the moment Adam reached this conclusion, Caitlin

was tiptoeing toward his door. She'd slept soundly for several hours, then abruptly awakened. Troubled by a dream she couldn't recall. Yet it left her with a sense Adam needed her. Moreover, she needed to talk to him. All day, he'd avoided any discussion of their problem. Their past-desperate problem, or its solution. True, they'd had rare moments alone; but at those times, when she'd tried to broach the subject, he'd redirected the conversation. She'd begun to worry he was trying to protect her by shutting her out, and that would never do.

Reaching his door, she tried the latch, gratified to find it unlocked. She took care not to make a sound and slipped through the antechamber to the inner door. If she found Adam sleeping soundly, she'd not awaken him . . . just yet. Warmth flooded her body as she remembered all that had happened there the night before. Now she imagined slipping into the big tester bed, with its lovely sky blue canopy overhead, and stretching out beside him. The warmth escalated, heat scorching her face, as she thought of several delicious ways she might awaken him. And what would follow before they talked!

Ach, 'tis shameless you are, colleen! Focus on what brought you here. Adam might need your help! Immediately sobered, she eased the door ajar. The bedchamber was dark, but for the lone flame of a bedside candle and the feeble glow of some embers in the hearth. Still, she could see the bed was empty. For a moment she thought Adam wasn't there. Then his voice, resounding clearly from the flickering shadows near the hearth, told her he was.

What he said made her blood run cold.

"Appleby, you bastard!" he cried. "For my son's leg to be made whole again, I'll give the remaining forty years of my life!"

There was the unmistakable smell of brimstone. As

Caitlin watched in horror, the satanic figure from her dream appeared. Huge, its enormous membranous wings fanning the air into a great hollow wind that roared overhead. The sound was deafening, and Caitlin covered her ears. Yet the roaring increased. It became an agony inside her head. A whirlwind she felt would suck the marrow from her bones and leave her drained and lifeless on the floor.

Then, just as suddenly as it had come, it was gone.

The hellish beast had abruptly vanished, and in its place stood a slight, foppishly attired gentleman. An overdressed dandy, like the ones she'd spied parading about London's West End. He carried a quizzing glass and held a walking stick tucked jauntily under his arm. His heavily maquillaged face and rouged cheeks compounded with the sly smile he wore to give him a sinister air. This was apparent even before Caitlin collected her shattered thoughts and made the connection: *Appleby*.

Appleby offered Adam a courtly bow. A gesture Caitlin immediately saw was not honest. It was deliberately mocking—and chilling.

"Have off, Appleby!" Adam growled. "I know you for a liar and a cheat, so you needn't play the gentleman here. Save those deceitful niceties for your next victim, you craven slime."

"Tsk, tsk." Appleby seemed unruffled. "Tell me, Ravenskeep," he purred, "how's your little bit of Irish muslin these days, hmm?"

Even in the dim light, Caitlin could see the color drain from Adam's face. "You keep away from her, you gutter scum!" he snarled.

Appleby snickered. "But my dear, sorely smitten marquis," he taunted, "where I come from, an innocent 'Irish Angel' would be quite the prize!"

Caitlin choked back a gasp as Adam lunged at him,

going for his throat. Appleby stopped him cold. With the fiend's tiny hand gesture, a barely discernible flick of the wrist, Adam doubled up and screamed. Caitlin sought wildly in her mind for something to do—dear God, he looked to be in excruciating pain! Then, with another minute gesture, the fiend released him. Hands clenched into fists, Caitlin waited.

"Now you've had a taste of hellish torment, Ravenskeep," Appleby told him briskly, "perhaps you'll keep your hands to yourself. Oh, and a civil tongue in your mouth would be nice. No? Dear me, you *are* a hard case. Most of my clients learn quickly from that little lesson. They comprehend who's master, do you see." He repeated the torture.

Adam screamed in agony and dropped to his knees.

"Do we understand each other?" his tormentor inquired archly.

Teeth clenched in a grimace, Adam jerked his head in a reluctant nod of acquiescence.

"Excellent," Appleby said, and released him. He calmly flicked a speck of lint from his sleeve as his victim struggled to his feet. Only then did it register with Caitlin that Adam was shirtless, dressed only in pantaloons and stockings. She stifled a cry as he straightened: There were burn marks on his back and shoulders.

"Now," said Appleby, sauntering to a chair by the fireplace, "I believe you were about to offer new terms . . . ?"

Adam's eyes smoldered with hatred, his face a study in loathing. "You're aware of what they are, or you wouldn't be here. Where do I sign?"

"Dear boy!" Appleby crowed with delight. A sheet of paper at once materialized in his hand. "Now, that's how I like to do business!" he exclaimed with obvious pleasure as he handed it over. "No hemming and hawing, no beating about the bush. Go ahead, read it. The lad has his leg put right, and you become my permanent guest. Rather straightforward, I should think."

Adam read it, then glanced at his adversary. "I'll need a couple of days to put my affairs in order."

"Of course, of course," Appleby agreed with an expansive wave of his hand. He was feeling generous. After all, he'd gained what he'd planned all along.

"There's just one caveat," Adam said as the additional term of agreement appeared on the contract.

"Caveat!" The dandy's face lost its pleased expression. "Thought you were ready to sign, " he snapped accusingly.

"I am, but for one detail."

Appleby's eyes narrowed. "And that is . . . ?"

"I'm making Caitlin O'Brien my marchioness before I go . . ."

Ach, no! Even as she protested this in her heart, scrambling in her mind for ways to stop him, Caitlin noted Appleby eyeing Adam speculatively with this news. *He's up to something, and no mistake. Think, colleen, think!*

"And as I must do this in the forty-eight hours I've left," Adam was saying, "your assistance, Appleby, in securing a special license—"

"Done!" exclaimed the fiend, pleased the detail had been so trifling. "Now, if you'll just sign—"

"Not so fast," Adam told him. "What I also require with regard to Caitlin—to my future *wife*—is this: She is not to be touched by you and what you represent— in any way, whatsoever. Grant me that, and I'll sign now."

Caitlin could hold back no longer. "Adam—*no!*" she cried, rushing into the room.

Adam took but a split second to recover from the

shock of seeing her there. *"Caitlin!"* he screamed. "For the love of—get out of here, *now*. Run!"

When she didn't move, Appleby gave her a sinister smile. "Dear me, if it isn't the little Irish Angel! Do come in, my dear, and wel—"

"Don't listen to him, Caitlin!" Adam moved toward her, desperate to make her leave; he'd do it physically if he had to. "You know he can't be trust—"

Appleby silenced him by raising his hand, his meaning unmistakable: a threatened repeat of his "little lesson."

Adam would have braved the torture if it meant he could accomplish his goal. Anything, to remove Caitlin from Appleby's presence! Only one thing stopped him. He was terrified the fiend would turn the torture on Caitlin.

"I see we're making progress, Ravenskeep," Appleby said with a breezy smugness. He turned back to Caitlin. "As I was saying, my dear, welcome. Now, do have a seat, and tell us what it is that has brought you here."

Caitlin kept her eyes locked on the fiend as she took a chair opposite his, before the fireplace. Minutes ago, it had held dying embers; but the moment Appleby sat down, a fire had sprung up, and now it crackled in the grate. She forced herself not to look at Adam's bleak face. He stood, unmoving but close at hand, having refused to sit with them when Appleby invited him to do so, cheerily—*cheerily*, after all that had gone before!

She did everything she could to hide her terror. Innocuous as he appeared in his foppish attire, Appleby was past dangerous. He was Evil Incarnate, and he must not suspect she was afraid.

Still, she must be wary and vigilant. Despite her fear, she'd make herself concentrate on that terrible manifestation she'd seen when he first appeared. On the beast, the hellish figure her nightmares had always *meant* her to face. Aye, she would do this, to remind herself: 'Twas the devil with whom she was about to compound, and she must keep her wits about her. "I'm here, Mr. Appleby," she said, thinking quickly, gathering and sifting through the details of a plan that had begun to form in her mind, "t' propose a bargain o' me own."

"Splendid!" the fiend exclaimed. Menace in his eyes, he held up a warning finger when Adam started to object. "Do go on, my dear. I'm all ears, as it were."

Caitlin took a calming breath. "Andrew needs his father every bit as much as he needs the chance t' be made whole again. I am therefore offerin' me own soul, in place o'—"

"Nooo!" Adam's bone-chilling scream pierced the air. "Never, d'you hear?" he cried, pulling Caitlin from the chair. *"Never,* will I allow you to sacrifice yourself for me!" He had her by the arm, clearly bent on dragging her out of the room.

"Forgive me, *macushla, a stór,"* Caitlin murmured brokenly, tears blurring her vision. She shut her eyes and spoke the words rapidly, invoking Crionna's protective charm for the second time. Adam's hold went slack, and she stumbled from his grasp.

Chapter 13

Caitlin staggered away from Adam's frozen form. She felt all at once enervated, drained of her strength. Aye, weak as a kitten, and she needn't wonder at the cause. Crionna's cautionings regarding the charm sprang immediately to mind: At most, it should be employed only twice, the *bhean uasal* had warned; a third time would kill the one who used it. Ach, considering how she felt, she could well believe it!

Appleby eyed her with interest, then slowly circled Adam's eerily silent and unmoving figure. "Very nice," he said with grudging admiration. His gaze snapped back to Caitlin as she stumbled and fell into a chair. Amusement danced in his eyes, and he cocked a mocking eyebrow at her. "But you do realize, don't you, my clever young Druid witch, this was the last time that little gambit will be of use to you?"

Druid? Witch! *No, never mind him. He's after trying to shake your confidence. They're just sly, treacherous words.*

Remember, this is the glic diabhal *you're dealing with—the cunning devil who tricked your beloved. You'll pay no attention to him, Caitlin O'Brien!*

Despite this resolve, it was Appleby's word *gambit* that brought Caitlin back to her purpose. *I may be physically weak, but I've still my wits about me, thank the good Lord!* "Mr. Appleby," she said, determined not to let the frozen look of anguish in the eyes of the third person in the room distract her, "I do hereby challenge ye . . . to a game o' chess."

She had his immediate attention. "My dear Miss O'Brien, how very intriguing! You *are* full of surprises, aren't you?" He sauntered to the chair he'd occupied before and waved a manicured hand at her. "Do go on."

Caitlin struggled to voice a reply. The charm had so severely sapped her strength, speech itself had become an enormous chore. "As I . . . as I said earlier, Mr. Appleby . . . Andrew needs his da. If I . . . if I win, the lad's leg . . . is t' be made whole. And . . . and ye must . . . must agree t' take me . . . instead o' his father. I propose . . . playin' a single . . . a single game. The win . . . the win t' be determined . . . by a checkmate only. If . . . if a stalemate should occur—"

Appleby's snicker intervened: Clearly, he envisioned anything but. An outcome that implied their skills were so closely matched? He found the notion laughable. "And if you should lose . . . ?" he inquired unctuously.

"Ye must . . . ye must still heal the lad's leg . . . entirely." The hand she held up when he started to object felt leaden; it was all she could do to lift it. Nonetheless, her words drilled the air with surprising force. "That condition isn't subject t' hagglin', sorr! Don't even try."

Appleby sent her a disgruntled frown. "Cheeky baggage! Since when do losers come away with rewards?"

"When they make the winner's compensation worth his while!" she snapped. Anger lent her another spurt of energy, and she continued with increased vigor. "May I remind ye, sorr, 'tis me immortal *soul* I forfeit—even if I should win? I'm not so daft, I'd propose such a monumental loss without *some* compensation!"

He eyed her with visible annoyance. "Very well," he said sullenly. "But I've yet to hear what it is you offer if I should win. What of *my* compensation? After all, I've already the immediate prize of Ravenskeep's soul on offer. What have you to best that?"

"A double forfeit," she replied without missing a beat. She had thought it out carefully by now. Her proposal was a dangerous one, risky in the extreme. She had become fairly adept at chess since that night, months ago, when Adam had begun to instruct her in the fine points of the game. Still, no one knew better than she how far she was from being a master.

The devil, on the other hand, was an excellent gamesman, from all she'd heard. Yet she was willing to risk all for one important reason. Unlike her poor beloved, she could pray. And she would—with all her heart and mind. *And, Heaven help me, with all my soul . . . at least, while 'tis still mine to claim!*

She wasn't at all certain Heaven could approve of her single, terrible forfeit, of course. Or countenance her bargaining with the devil on any terms at all, for that matter. Still, perhaps there was a chance Heaven would look on what she was doing with compassion: Sure and the dear Lord would understand, far better than any mortal, a sacrifice that was made out of love?

Holy Mary, Mother of God, she prayed silently. *I ask that you pray for us all in this critical time. If I am foolish or arrogant in doing this thing, I pray you will ask God to forgive me. And if 'tis not asking too much, Blessed Virgin, perhaps you might put in a wee word, besides? 'Twould be grand if somehow Heaven could show this poor sinner a safe way out of the whole wicked business.*

Opening her eyes, she met the fiend's disapproving glare. *So he knows I was praying. Well, what did he expect from the "Irish Angel"—curses?* "If I should lose," she told him with a gaze that didn't falter, "ye must still heal the lad, but ye may have *both Adam's soul and mine* for all eternity."

There was but a split second's pause. "Done!" said the fiend with alacrity. With a flick of the wrist, a parchment suddenly materialized in his hand. "The terms, as you've just voiced them," he said, proffering the contract for her perusal. "Go ahead, look it over. You'll find everything in order."

Caitlin willed her hand not to shake as she took the paper.

"There, do you see?" he said when she'd finished reading. "It's all exactly as you put forth. Now, if you'll just sign—"

"Not so fast, sorr," Caitlin told him.

A small silver knife had materialized in Appleby's hand. "Now, what?" he snapped. Then, noting how she eyed the blade with distaste: "This is no time to be squeamish, miss! The contract must be signed in your own blood. A trifling matter, I do assure you. It will take but a moment to prick—"

"As a healer, I have tended many sick and injured, Mr. Appleby. I am not the least bit squeamish."

"Then, what in blazes can possibly be amiss?" he hissed. For a brief instant, Appleby's head with its human features wavered, taking on the aspect of a serpent. Its forked tongue darted out, as if to threaten Caitlin, before the image resolved once again into that

of the rouged dandy. "It's a perfectly good contract!"
he growled.

" 'Tisn't *this* contract concerns me," Caitlin told him.
" 'Tis what's written upon the ither one—the bargain
his lordship signed in April. I'll not sign any new
agreement till the auld one's cancelled. I must insist ye
produce it, sorr—that I may see it destroyed with me
own eyes. Without that, I'll sign naught."

"Presumptuous Irish chit!" he muttered irritably.
But, in truth, she had him. He could easily produce
Ravenskeep's contract, of course. But even hell had its
rules: He wasn't at liberty to alter or destroy a contract
without the consent of the undersigned. Appleby
slanted a glance at the immobilized marquis. Hell would
freeze over before *he* agreed! His gaze fell again on
Caitlin. "Er . . . I'm afraid I don't have his lordship's
contract with me," he hedged.

Caitlin suspected he was lying. *He who dines with the
devil must use a long spoon,* the old adage went. She'd do
well to remember it. She didn't trust Appleby as far as
she could spit, and perhaps not even that far. "Ye'll
forgive me, sorr, if I have trouble believin' ye. Why can't
ye produce it? After all, I saw ye conjure this one"—
she tapped the parchment in her hand—"out o' thin
air."

Appleby made a disgruntled sound in his throat, but
this wasn't what alerted Caitlin. Just before he did so,
she saw his glance flicker irritably to Adam.

She knew scarcely anything of formal contracts; what
little she had gleaned came from the village, back home.
She recalled a disagreement over a written contract
Father O'Malley had once been asked to settle. Drafted
by the priest—one of the few in the village who could
read and write—it had to do with the sale of some
chickens. A fox had stolen two of the fowl before the

transfer could be made, but the buyer had already sent payment. Yet the seller intended keeping the money, saying a bargain was a bargain. This outraged the buyer, who asked Father O'Malley to intervene: Could he cancel the old contract and set up a new one, based on a fair price, given the reduced livestock? The priest said he'd urge the seller to "do the right thing," of course. But, he pointed out, only with the consent of *both* parties could the old contract be torn up, a new one drafted, and then signed. (She recalled the seller caving in, under the priest's forbidding mien.)

"Mr. Appleby . . . ," she said, praying she was right in the conclusion she'd drawn. "Could it be ye're required t' have his lordship's consent in the matter?"

Appleby's penciled eyebrows shot to his hairline. The chit bore watching! But then, the Irish always had been a meddlesome lot, too clever for their own good. "Not at all," he lied, airily dismissing her interpretation with a mendacious wave of his hand. "The Ravenskeep contract's in our, er, archives. I shall require a deal of time to fetch it—that's all."

"Then, we have a problem," said Caitlin. She still felt he was lying, but given his insistence, she wasn't about to push it . . . for now. As for later . . . she must wait and see. She'd be wise to keep open any options she could come by. If he was as reluctant as she to call Adam into play, perhaps she could turn that reluctance to her advantage. She sorely needed all the weapons she could get!

On the other hand, unlikely as it seemed, he could be telling the truth. In which case, she might insist he fetch the paper from wherever it was his wretched contracts were stored. But that would take time, and she wasn't certain she had the luxury. She had no idea how long the effects of Crionna's charm would last. Or if prolonging them might do Adam irreparable harm. Not to mention the risk of having the charm wear off by itself, which would free Adam to interfere. She'd no doubt he would do all he could to stop her, given half a chance. "It won't answer," she told Appleby.

"Then, I suggest you come by a remedy, young woman—and soon," he grumbled, pointedly taking out his watch and glancing at it. "I'm a busy man, Miss O'Brien, with countless affairs to tend to. I have interests all over the world, and no time to waste."

With the ticking of the mantel clock reminding her how long Adam had already been enthralled, and her energy slipping away, Caitlin thought quickly. "I should like t' suggest a compromise," she said after a moment.

"Hmph." Appleby was obviously irritated but apparently willing to hear her out—which led Caitlin to suspect her surmise had been on target. "Well, don't just sit there gaping at me," he huffed. "Say your piece!"

"Well, t' begin," said Caitlin, "as evidence o' me good faith, Mr. Appleby, suppose I were t' swear, upon me honor—"

"Upon your soul," he corrected sharply.

She arched a brow at him.

"My dear Miss O'Brien, honor has no credit where I come from."

"Ach—silly me!" she replied with a flippancy she was far from feeling. And, unfortunately, with a strength she was far from owning. Speech still cost her dearly with each word she uttered. Nonetheless, suspecting it was unwise to let him see just how weak she was, she forced her words to come out smoothly. "Very well, then. I'll swear, upon me soul, t' sign this new contract—the one consigning me soul t' perdition instead o' his lordship's, should I win the game—but only after I've

218 *Veronica Sattler*

seen Andrew's leg made whole *and* his lordship's contract destroyed.''

Appleby eyed her appraisingly. Oral contracts such as she proposed were worthless in hell—he absolutely had to have a signature in blood. The Irishwoman didn't know the nicety of the rules, however; if she so swore, he made no doubt she'd deliver. Her offer made sense. "Clever chit, aren't you?" he said with reluctant admiration.

"I do me best."

"No doubt," he groused. He pondered the serpent's head of his walking stick for a moment, before meeting her gaze. "It's all highly irregular," he went on, "but I suppose it's acceptable. Swear to the double forfeit if you should lose, and we have a bargain."

Not daring to look at Adam's poor frozen face, Caitlin swore.

With a smug look, Appleby transported Adam's chess set from across the room. In an instant it, and the gaming table upon which it rested, sat between them, in front of the hearth. "Shall we toss a coin to see who goes first?" he inquired smoothly. A shiny copper materialized between his fingers.

Caitlin eyed the coin askance. She'd once seen a prestidigitator at a country fair cheat people with a cleverly weighted coin. And the devil, she was sure, had better tricks up his sleeve than any garden-variety charlatan. "We shall not," she said.

With a put-upon air, Appleby heaved a sigh. "My dear Miss O'Brien, it appears you don't trust me."

Caitlin ignored his much-aggrieved tone. "I do not, sorr.''

"Then, what do you propose we do about it?" he growled.

"I don't suppose 'twould do any good t' suggest a

true gentleman would automatically allow a lady t' take the white? No, I didn't think so. In that case, I suggest we 'shoot' for the right t' go first. 'Tis what the lad and I always do . . ."

Caitlin felt a stab of pain as it occurred to her she would never again share such things with Andrew. Once the bargains of this night came to pass, that part of her life, with all its simple pleasures, was over. Indeed, life as she knew it was over. *The lad needs his leg made right. He needs his da. Get on with it!*

"Each . . . puts a hand behind his back," she explained. She found herself laboring over the words. Speech continued to tax her strength, and it was becoming harder not to show it. "Then one opponent selects even . . . the ither, odd. Upon the count o' three, they—"

"I know how the bloody thing's done!" he snapped.

"Right." She dragged her hand behind her back with the strength of her will alone. *Mustn't collapse before I've seen this thing through!* "Now, on the count o' three . . ."

Against all expectation, Caitlin won white. This may have owed to sheer blind luck or, as she devoutly hoped, to the compassion of Heaven. Whichever, it gave her a measure of confidence she sorely needed. Because, while her mind may have been unaffected by that second use of the charm—it was sharp and clear as ever—her physical strength was nearly gone.

At one point she found herself wishing the game might be a short one—then cut off that foolish thought. If ever she needed to take her time, 'twas now. She must plan each move with painstaking care, no matter how weak she felt.

As it happened, the game was, indeed, a long one. On they played, into the night. Neither spoke, with Adam Lightfoot's mute witness underscoring a silence broken only by the ticking of the mantel clock. True to his nature, Appleby played with demonic brilliance. Gaming pieces fell, and all too many were white.

Yet black fell, too, though Caitlin's hands were leaden weights, barely able to remove them from the board. It didn't matter. The pleas to Heaven spoken in her head were strong and sure. With each humble prayer, she felt immeasurably empowered. She was playing better than she ever had before. She played so well, in fact, it came as no surprise to her—or to her scowling adversary—when she at last had cause to break the silence: "Checkm—"

"Scheming Celtic witch!" Outrage flared like living flame in the fiend's obsidian eyes. His hands slammed the table, and he rose half out of his chair, glaring at her with naked fury. "Pretending to be the neophyte!" he shrieked. "Hiding your powers under the guise of that pathetic milk-and-water innocence and—"

All at once, as if suddenly remembering something, Appleby eased back into his chair. The smile he sent her was so coldly avaricious and cruel, Caitlin shuddered. "Yet it hardly signifies, does it, my pretty new pet? You're mine now," he purred, "with all eternity to rue the day you tricked the Lord of Hell. Game's over, my dear. Time to pay—"

"I beg t' differ, sorr," said Caitlin, indicating the board with a weak wave of her hand. " 'Tis over"—*Holy Mother, help me! I've barely the strength to speak*—" 'tis over when . . . when the winner declares . . . declares the 'checkmate.' And . . . thanks t' yerself . . . I've not . . . I've not quite said it . . . yet."

"What nonsense is this?" Appleby leaned forward, black eyes narrowed and ugly with threat. "Don't think to gammon me, witch. You *swore on your immortal soul!*"

It cost her greatly, but Caitlin managed to produce

what she hoped was an insouciant shrug. "Accordin'
... accordin' t' the rules *I* learned, Mr. Appleby, the
game ... the game's not ended ... till the checkmate's
declared."

"Then, say it, damn you!"

"Not yet. Not before I—"

"What do you mean—*not yet?* Need I remind you that
you *swore*—"

"Aye, Mr. Appleby. I swore ... t' do certain things
... when I won ... and I shall ... do them. What I ...
what I require first, however ... is a wee bit o' time ...
t' set me affairs ... in order." She sent him a smile that
deepened his scowl. "Not t' mention ... sorr, time t'
see ... the lad's leg made whole ... and a certain ...
a certain agreement ... destroyed. Ye did say 'twould
... 'twould take time ... t' fetch ... his lordship's contract ... did ye not?"

"How much time?" he demanded in an ominous
voice.

"Three days should ... suffice."

"Three days! Three *hours,* perhaps, and even then,
I'm being generous!"

Crionna would have recognized the stubborn glint in
Caitlin's eyes. "Three days ... or it all ends here. I shall
refrain, sorr ... from declarin' the 'magic' word. The
word that ... that must be said ... t' bring ... t' bring
... a formal end ... t' the game."

"You impertinent Irish peasant! You swore—"

"Aye ... I swore." Sensing she had him now, Caitlin
summoned a last, desperate thread of energy, and her
words rang clearly in the room. "But there's nothin' in
what I swore said I had t' *finish* this game, Mr. Appleby!
And, until I do, it appears things must"—she glanced
at Adam's immobile figure for the first time in hours—
"remain as they are. And by the terms o' the one con-

tract ye do own, sorr, ye've no claim on his lordship for anither forty years.

"Now," she went on with a small smile, "about those three days . . . ?"

"Take them, then!" he snarled.

With a satisfied nod, Caitlin regarded the board, where her remaining knight and two bishops had his king trapped. "Checkmate," she declared.

"Three days," the fiend snarled, "and not a moment beyond! I shall come to collect you at . . ." With a sudden sly smile, he pointed a finger at the mantel clock. The clock's hands—Caitlin could have sworn, not a moment ago, they'd been telling half-five—both pointed straight up. To the *twelve.*

"At the final stroke of midnight," he finished with a gloating smile. Throwing a deprecating sneer at her, and another at his immobilized host, Appleby muttered a caustic invective—and vanished.

With a long, shuddering sigh, Caitlin struggled to rise out of her chair. Trembling visibly, thoroughly drained from the ordeal—and weaker than she ever let on to the fiend—she finally pushed herself upright. Only to find herself swaying with fatigue. Then her knees buckled, and she had to brace her hands on the table for support.

When at last she dragged her gaze to her beloved, Caitlin stared at him with bleak chagrin. She had no idea how the charm might be undone! "Adam . . . ," she whispered. Just before the room spun and she crumpled to the floor.

Released from the charm as Caitlin fell unconscious, Adam stirred and took a faltering step forward. With a groan, he ran his hand over his face and tried to think. He looked slowly about the chamber. It required but a moment to take in the scene before him and digest its

significance. He noted the gaming table before the fire
... his chess board upon it, with its telling arrangement
of pieces, both erect and fallen ... the mantel clock
with the hands pointing upward ....

Was it only just past midnight? He could have sworn—

Then he remembered ... Caitlin had done that Celtic
thing to him again, to keep him from—but where *was*
she? His eyes went again to the board, where white had
black's king hemmed in for the checkmate. Blood and
ashes, had the fiend won, then? Had he *taken* her?

His eyes darted wildly about the room. Then he
chanced to glance down. *Caitlin—ah, no!* Blood drained
from his face as he rushed to her side. "Caitlin! *Caitlin!*"
he cried, half out of his mind with dread. Fearing the
worst when she didn't respond, he bent an ear to her
chest. *Still alive, but breathing's shallow.*

Gathering her limp body in his arms, he rushed into
the hallway, yelling frantically for the lone footman that
was always on duty at night. "Jenkins," he barked as
the man came racing up the stairs. "Run and wake
Townsend—no, wait! You'd better rouse Mrs. Needham, too. Tell her to bring the hartshorn and vinaigrette. Then saddle my fastest hunter, ride to the village,
and fetch the physician—I forget his name."

"Dr. Mac Dougall, your lordsh—"

"Tell Mac Dougall it's a matter of life and death—
hurry, man!"

With a nervous glance at the limp body of the governess in the marquis's arms, the ashen-faced servant raced
to obey. Then Adam, his eyes haunted and brimming
with tears, turned and carried Caitlin to his chamber.
Carried his forever love—the impossible dream he'd
no sooner found than lost—to his chamber ... and its
cruelly mocking bed.

Chapter 14

"I've not seen the like of it before, m'lord." Angus Mac Dougall scratched perplexedly with his forefinger at the grizzled hair of a bushy side whisker. "Last night, as you know, there was simply no rousing her. Never saw a case of exhaustion so severe. Don't mind telling you now, m'lord, I feared for the lassie's life."

Adam cast a worried glance at the partially open door to his chambers. It was a few minutes after nine in the morning, and they were standing in the hallway outside. Mac Dougall had just finished examining his patient—for the second time since the frantic summons that had brought him to the marquis's home, at roughly a half hour after midnight. Mac Dougall wasn't the only one who'd feared for her life in those dark hours before dawn.

After Mac Dougall had left, with instructions to call him if there was any change, Adam held Caitlin in his arms for hours. She'd slept like the dead, he thought, suppressing a shudder. Yet it was a comparison he couldn't help making, though it filled him with terror and dread. She'd looked so pale and *lifeless*. Then, not an hour ago, she'd awakened. Just like that. Gave him a shaky smile and asked if she might have a cup of tea!

"And now?" he asked the physician. "Aside from being awake, how is she, sir?"

The physician smiled, showing large, even teeth stained yellow from years of smoking a pipe. The culprit could be seen sticking out of his waistcoat pocket. "Well, you can see for yourself, m'lord. Right as rain, as far as I could ascertain, and you may be sure I examined her quite thoroughly. A remarkable recovery, given the state she was in last night. Er, what was it exhausted her so? You never said, and I thought it best not to burden the lassie with questions."

Anxious to return to Caitlin, Adam gave a distracted shake of his head. "Working too hard, I expect."

"Working to the point of exhaustion, m'lord?" The physician looked incredulous. "As a governess?"

Would the man never leave? Adam tried to curb his impatience; Mac Dougall had come without complaint, in the middle of the night, after all. "Miss O'Brien takes her duties as governess quite seriously," he replied. "In addition, she's had training as a folk healer . . . herbs and simples, that sort of thing. Spends a deal of her free time ministering to my tenants and their families. And my son, sir, would never have gained the ability to maneuver on crutches without her tireless efforts . . . massages, therapeutic exercise and the like. Not to mention her positive encouragement."

"Ah," said the physician, satisfied with the explanation. Didn't he sometimes put in long, exhausting hours, himself, traveling great distances to see patients? "An admirable occupation, m'lord. Unlike many of my colleagues, I have great respect for these country healers. They fill a need, and, unlike some, I don't worry they'll put us physicians out of business. To tell the truth, there just might be a few things we can learn from them."

And some things you'd never wish to learn. With a sigh of relief, Adam saw his major domo rounding the top of the stairs. "Townsend, I'm sure Dr. Mac Dougall would appreciate some refreshment before he takes his leave." He turned to the physician. "I beg you will excuse me, sir. I'd like to look in on Miss O'Brien."

"Of course, m'lord, of course." Mac Dougall's eyebrows lifted as he watched the marquis hurry through the door to his chambers. *Uncommonly concerned over a mere governess . . . if, indeed, that's all she is to him. Well, none of my business. The gentry make their own rules. And this one, at least, has always paid my fees on time.* "Tell me, my good man," he said, turning to Townsend, "would you have a dram of good Scotch whiskey on hand? A wee early in the day for taking spirits, I own, but it's been a devilish long night."

When Adam came through the door, he found Caitlin sitting up, propped against a mound of pillows, in the big tester bed. She looked . . . lovely, heartbreakingly lovely. He couldn't bear to think of what would become of all that loveliness when . . . .but he wouldn't think about that now. Couldn't. He needed to fortify himself, put it off for a few more moments, at least, concentrate on her health. After that, they could address the future . . . her future . . . or what was left of it, he thought with a searing stab of agony.

She appeared a trifle pale, the dear freckles scattered across her nose more evident than usual. Yet she looked a deal healthier than when he'd left her with her tea and gone to summon the doctor. Her hair was neatly braided; her face had a freshly scrubbed look. Someone had replaced her plain cotton night shift. She wore a pretty batiste bed gown trimmed with ruffles and blue ribbons. He remembered Mrs. Needham had sent a pair of maids up to attend to her toilette while they waited for the physician to arrive.

"Adam," Caitlin murmured with a tender smile. Setting aside her dish of tea, she drank him in with her eyes as he hurried to her side.

"How are you feeling, love?" He slung a hip on the side of the bed and reached for her hand. "The doctor said you're 'right as rain,' but . . ."—he searched her face with troubled eyes—"I need to hear it from you. Are you all right, *macushla*?"

Swallowing hard, Caitlin lowered her gaze; when she raised her eyes to meet his, they were equally troubled. "I'm feelin' physically fit, *a stór*, but"—the rueful twist of her lips was meant to be a smile, but it fell far short— "as t' how I am . . ." She heaved a sigh. "I'll be better able t' tell ye that, once I learn whether ye can forgive me . . . or not."

He didn't need to ask what she meant. They both knew she'd arrested him with that wretched Gaelic charm to stop him cutting the new deal with Appleby. That she'd then gone on to cut her own deal with the cunning bastard was what loomed between them now. Adam lacked the details, but they hardly mattered; he'd learn them soon enough. It was the crux of what Caitlin had done—while he stood by, blank and helpless—that tore his heart and filled him with bitter remorse: She'd sacrificed herself for him, and he couldn't bear it.

"*Why*, Caitlin?" he asked, a world of pain and anguish in his eyes. "Why did you do it?"

"I think ye know the answer t' that, *macushla, a stór,*"

she whispered. Tears brimmed in her eyes, transformed them into shimmering emeralds. "All ye need do is ask why ye sacrificed yerself for yer son that April night. Ye did it—sacrificed yer immortal soul, t' save Andrew's life—because ye love him. So there it is. Ye gave away yer most valuable possession, Adam, for *love* . . . and so have I."

Fighting tears, Adam shook his head in furious denial. "Most valued possession?" he asked bitterly. "Caitlin, the night I summoned Appleby, I scarcely *had* a soul. What I bartered—gave away, as you say—was *next to worthless!* My life was meaningless. I was an empty shell, a sad travesty of a man, betraying all my parents raised me to value and hold dear. Don't you understand? I'd already damned myself—with nearly every execrable act you can imagine!"

He gave a mirthless laugh. "Perhaps the archfiend knew all along how little I had on offer. It wouldn't surprise me to learn he trimmed down his part of the exchange to fit, and my innocent son had to pay—"

"That is nonsense!" she cried. "Sheer nonsense, and ye know it. Haven't I heard ye say it, yerself, the divil's a cheat and a liar? So don't ye go makin' excuses for his foul deeds, Adam Lightfoot. And stop evadin' the truth. 'Twas *love* drove ye t' do what ye did—as it drove me! Deny that, and ye deny us both—*rob* us both—o' the only worthwhile reason for such a sacrifice."

Her voice softened, but her eyes were fierce. "The love I bear ye, Adam, just like the love we both bear the lad, has no limits or conditions. It doesn't say, 'I shall love ye, but only t' thus and such a point.' It doesn't say, when the goin' gets hard, 'I cannot follow!' Love, as I've come to understand it, t' *know* it, demands all— and *gives* all. And so we have, *macushla, a stór,* and so we have."

"I don't deserve such love," he murmured brokenly. Cupping her face, he smoothed away her tears with his thumbs. "I don't deserve *you.*"

"Ach! Is that the real reason ye were ready t' send me away? Not t' mention throwin' away forty years o' yer life, on top o' yer immortal soul—instead o' waitin' for me t' help ye find a way out o' yer terrible bargain? I told ye the dreams and visions have a purpose, Adam. That I believe I was sent here t' fulfill that purpose. Just as I believe ye were meant for the Light!"

Fresh tears sprang to her eyes, and her voice dropped to a watery whisper. "Could ye not trust me t' find the way?"

The sigh he heaved as he gathered her in his arms held bottomless sorrow and despair. "I was desperate to keep you safe from the fiend's clutches, my Caitlin. Only that. And, fool that I am, I drove you straight into his filthy hands! I'll never forgive myself—"

"But ye *must,*" she cried, pulling away to look at him. "Just as I must—as *we* must forgive each ither! 'Tis anither dimension o' love, d'ye see? Unconditional love, Adam. Its very nature is forgiveness . . . even o' the unforgivable."

He stared at her for a long moment. Marveling at the positive spirit she wore like a bright, shining banner. Then, with a weary sigh, he nodded. His beloved Irish Angel . . . so fierce in her defense of this love they had discovered in the midst of ruin and despair! She almost gave him hope that . . . .

He dropped the thought. No sense in hoping for the impossible. "Tell me the terms of your agreement," he said grimly. "How much time do you—do we have?"

Caitlin glanced at the all too familiar face of the mantel clock. "Three days from midnight last," she replied, tight-lipped with anger. She'd been too weak to address it last night, but she knew Appleby had cheated her of several hours. The devil, it appeared, in addition to everything else he represented, was a bad loser. Aye, petty and mean-spirited to the last!

Adam glanced at the chess set, returned to its proper place across the room by the servants. "I saw the board when I . . . regained my senses, Caitlin. Ah, love, surely, you must have realized he'd win," he added with a sorrowful shake of the head. "I cannot imagine why you ever thought—"

"But he *didn't* win, Adam. 'Twas I played white."

He looked at her as if she'd sprouted two heads. "But I distinctly saw . . . Caitlin, the black king was hemmed in!"

Belatedly realizing he'd missed critical details of what had gone on last night, including the specifics of the bargain she'd struck, Caitlin quickly filled him in. "Ye'd have been proud o' me, Adam," she finished moments later. "I managed t' play better than I iver dreamed I . . ."

She gave a quick shake of the head, as if to negate what she'd just said. "No, 'managed' is not the correct word, and I must be honest with ye, even if ye're not apt t' believe me in this. I've no means o' provin' it, d'ye see. But, Adam, there was a greater Power than mine—or Satan's—at work here last night."

When he merely stared at her, mute, she knew he was still unable to cross the great divide that separated them. The lack of faith that had left him vulnerable to Appleby, that lay at the root of his despair. With a sigh, she made another desperate attempt to reach him. "How else would ye explain a player with me level o' skill outplayin' the divil himself? I *beat* him, Adam— thereby gainin' not one concession from him, but two. Ach, he was furious when he lost! He—"

"Wait a minute!" Adam suddenly exclaimed. He

clasped her by the shoulders and looked at her, excitement on his face, hope dawning in his eyes. "Are you telling me you *signed nothing?* No contract? Is that where you left it?"

"A-aye, but—"

"Then, there *is* no contract between you! Caitlin, you're *free!* Without a contract, signed in his victim's blood . . ."

He paused, confused by the sorrow and regret in her eyes, the way she sadly shook her head. "What's wrong? Is there something I've failed to comprehend? You did say there was no contract?"

"I said there was no *written* contract, Adam," she explained. Hating the dying of that bright light of hope in his eyes. "But there's a contract nonetheless. Adam, I *swore.* Swore on me immortal soul, I'd sign the one we agreed upon, when he . . . when he comes for me."

"But . . . but"—he ran a hand through his hair in utter frustration, hardly able to believe they were having this conversation—"from what I've been able to collect, such an agreement isn't binding with him!"

"Perhaps not," Caitlin said with a rueful smile. "But 'tis with *me.* I spoke the bindin' words, Adam. I must honor them."

"Caitlin, that's patently absurd! This is the Lord of *Hell* we're talking about. He doesn't deal in *honor.*"

"Aye, he even said as much, but he does deal in *souls* . . . and I swore upon mine. Ach, niver think I'm ungrateful, or that I fail t' value yer efforts, *macushla.* No less, yer desperation t' save me. God in Heaven, it touches me t' the quick! But it won't answer," she added softly, caressing his face—his poor face, with its terrible disappointment—tenderly with her hand.

Adam searched her gaze one last time. Hoping against hope he'd misunderstood. Yet he knew he hadn't. Caitlin's honor was as much a part of her as breathing. She wouldn't be who she was if he were able to persuade her to disregard it. Defeated by the very things he loved in her, and held so dear, he caught the hand that caressed his face and brought it to his lips. "I love you so!"

Caitlin closed her eyes against a fresh onslaught of tears. "Adam," she whispered, "I knew ye'd understand. But . . . just think o' what's gained. Andrew's leg made whole, and the father he adores, t' *be* with him, and love him, through a lifetime!"

Bleakly, Adam eyed the clock, its steady *tick-tock, tick-tock* the only sound in the sudden stillness that fell between them. *But at what cost, my love? What terrible, unbearable cost?* "It . . . it was clever of you," he said when he could finally bring himself to comment, "demanding to see the old contract destroyed. I'm not sure I'd have thought of that. Though you may be sure, Appleby thought of it, which is why—"

There came a sudden, inordinately loud rapping on the outer door. Adam swung his head toward the antechamber in irritation. "What the devil—"

"Your lordship—I beg you will come quickly! Oh, come, *do.*"

"That's . . . Mrs. Needham," Adam muttered, uncertain what to think as he rose to investigate. Not only was it completely out of character for the staid housekeeper to pound on his door; but the woman's normally placid voice sounded on the verge of hysteria.

Caitlin was at his heels when he thrust the door open. "Madam," he said, "I trust you have a good explanation for—"

"Oh, begging your pardon, my lord, but it's"—tears poured down Mrs. Needham's plain, middle-aged face, and she gestured with unrestrained excitement in the direction of the stairs—"it's Lord Andrew! A *miracle's* happened, Lord Lightfoot. Your son's *walking.* Truly walking, my lord, on his own two strong and healthy legs!"

In the pregnant pause that followed, Adam looked at Caitlin; she, at him. Lasting but a heartbeat, the silent exchange contained a universe of comprehension. Steeped in emotions too raw for words, it told of ambivalence and pain, of bittersweet joy and unspeakable regret.

"Papa, Caitlin—you'll never guess what's happened!" Andrew's voice rang joyous, bubbling over with excitement as he hove into sight, dark curls bobbing above the newel post at the top of the stairs. Then he was running—*running*— toward them: infectious laughter on winged feet.

Blinking back tears, Caitlin watched Adam swoop Andrew into his arms, the child's giggles competing with the unabashed sobs of the father. Without further thought, she crossed herself. And poured out her heart to one she fervently hoped would understand. *Holy Mother,* she prayed silently, *how could I not? How?*

By then, a number of servants had gathered round. Others crowded at the periphery, trying to see over their fellows' shoulders. Still more poured into the hallway from the far reaches of the house. Some came running, some tiptoed shyly forth, but all wore grinning faces. Caitlin recalled Adam once saying bad news traveled quickly. Perhaps it did, but so, apparently, did good.

"Caitlin *told* me she believed my leg would grow stronger," Andrew was saying to his father. Which, given the crowd about him, meant he said it to them all. "She said it just last night, didn't you, Caitlin?"

Before she could reply, excited whispers stirred the air. Like the ringed circles a stone makes when it's dropped into a still pond, they rippled outward. Hushed voices, full of awe, reaching to the edges of the crowd:

"The Irish Angel's worked a miracle!"

"The work of the Irish Angel, and no mistake!"

"The Irish Angel's handiwork for sure!"

Caitlin and Adam exchanged wry glances. Neither had the heart to demur, nor would it have done any good. The voices of these humble folk held utter conviction. And then there was the larger truth that hovered in both their minds: The "miracle" done this day may have been "worked" by the Irish Angel, but its origins lay in Darkness and must forever remain their terrible, shameful secret.

With the clock ticking inexorably toward the fateful midnight, Adam wanted nothing more than to spend every minute alone with Caitlin. Yet, given what had happened to Andrew that morning, this wasn't possible. Helpless to avoid celebrating the event, Adam found himself declaring a holiday for the staff and everyone in the estate.

He recalled a custom practiced at Christmastime when he was a child. On the day before Christmas Eve, his parents had always ordered huge banquet tables set beneath the overhang in the courtyard. There, everyone, from the servants and tenants, to the folk in the village, to those on neighboring farms, was invited to the Hall for food and drink—the best the estate had to offer. With a pang of guilt, Adam realized the custom had fallen into disuse, because of his disinterest and neglect.

Now he had kegs of ale and small beer hauled from the cellars, and bottles of his finest wines, for he would stint on nothing. He asked the kitchens to lade the tables with food from the larder: cold roast fowl and great wheels of cheese; meat pies, succulent summer fruit; freshly baked breads and cakes meant for his own table; whatever would spare Cook and his people unnecessary labor.

People began arriving around noon. First came the tenant farmers and their families, and folk from the village soon followed. These were simple craftsmen and shopkeepers, most of whom had seen the lord's son from afar but had never spoken to the lad; for the late marchioness had never encouraged any mixing of the classes. Many bore simple homemade gifts to augment the lord's table: a jar of preserves, a bouquet of wildflowers set in a stoneware jug, a basket of just-picked berries. All cast shy, appraising glances at Caitlin that quickly became grins when they saw Andrew: Striding forward on two undamaged legs, the child joined his father in welcoming them and thanking them for coming.

Musicians arrived from a village across the downs, for word had quickly spread; they offered to play in honor of the "miracle," and Adam bade them welcome. The merry sounds of fiddle and hornpipe, pennywhistle, flute, and tambour echoed off the ancient stone walls. Folk from far and wide danced and laughed, far into the night.

It was toward evening that the vicar came, with Jeremy and Mrs. Wells. Wells gave short shrift to rumors of an Irish miracle worker, however; he asked instead if he might offer a prayer of thanksgiving for "God's handiwork." With an uncomfortable glance at Caitlin, who smiled and nodded, his host could only agree.

"The vicar's a good man, and I suppose he means well," Adam murmured when he joined Caitlin a short time later to watch the dancing. He didn't bother to tell her about pretending not to hear, when Wells archly mentioned his lordship's conspicuous and continued absence from church on Sundays.

"We can use all the prayers on offer," Caitlin told Adam. While she wished it were otherwise, she said nothing about his absenting himself from the vicinity while the vicar invoked Heaven. Adam, she'd begun to realize, never mentioned God or anything connected with God. Not at all. Not even in casual speech, the way some did, as when they said, "Thank God," or "Thank Heaven," and the like.

'Tis just as he said. He truly cannot bring himself to pray or acknowledge God in any way. 'Tis as if all mention of the Holy is locked inside him. Mother of God, in the wee time I have left, won't you help me find a way to lead him to the Light? "And have ye noticed, *macushla,*" she said to Adam aloud, "how Andrew's in transports, now Jeremy's come?"

"Noticed? I can scarcely tear my eyes off him." Adam caught her hand, gave it a squeeze as they watched Andrew run about with Jeremy and several lads from the village in a game of tag. "Except when I'm looking at you," he murmured, lifting her hand to his lips.

"Adam—someone might see!"

"Let them," he said, unspoken pain in his eyes as he lightly touched her hair, tenderly grazed her cheek with his knuckles. "They'll learn how I feel about you soon enough. Tonight I intend to announce our nuptials, which will take place day after tomorrow."

She looked at him aghast, only now recalling what he'd told her two nights ago . . . and told Appleby as well. *Was it only last night?* But of course it was, as she of all people had cause to know. Time was a ticking clock inside her head. A phantom hourglass whose sands would have run out a third of the way when this midnight came.

"I beg you will indulge me in this, love," Adam went on. "I said I meant to wed you, and last night changes . . ." He nearly said "nothing," thought better of it. "The events of last night haven't altered that. I sent word to Ravensford Hall this morning, asking the duke to procure a special license for us. He had to travel to London for it, which is why he's not here for the festiviti—"

"Adam," Caitlin said, hard put to keep her voice soft, "this is daft! All these arrangements, the fuss and bother of a weddin'? Why go through it, when we both know—"

"Because, in my heart, you are my wife, and I want the world to know. Because, in Andrew's heart, you have already become his new mother. And if you think he's in transports over Jeremy Wells—"

"And when he *loses* his mother for the second time in but a few months?" she asked. Over the pounding of her heart, over the ominous ticking in her head. "Loses her scarcely a day after she's taken the name, been made officially his? For God's sake, Adam—or if ye will not that, then for the child's sake—let it be!"

"Have you given up, then, Caitlin?" he asked fiercely. "Because *I* haven't! I intend to fight the hell-spawned scum, my darling. Fight him in any way I can devise, to the last stroke of the third midnight—and so must you!"

Chapter 15

Caitlin realized Adam meant every word he said when he told her he'd fight. As soon as the celebrations ended, he vowed, they would set about laying plans and strategies for outwitting the enemy. Caitlin didn't argue. An Adam armed with optimism, with the light of battle in his eye, was infinitely preferable to the Adam who looked so defeated that morning. But there was another reason, and it went to the heart of the matter.

Caitlin retained a firm and abiding faith in the dreams and visions that had brought her here. And while Crionna had warned her she'd be in great danger, there'd been nothing in the *bhean uasal's* warning that said Caitlin was hopelessly doomed. Indeed, hadn't she implied the very opposite?

As it happened, the celebrations didn't end nearly as soon as Adam might have wished, though he'd no one but himself to thank for it. The festivities only lengthened and intensified with the marquis's astonishing announcement, shortly after nine o'clock, that he and Miss O'Brien would wed. True, there was a moment of stunned silence when he finished speaking; but then Fergus—the carpenter who had made Andrew's crutches was a robust, uninhibited sort—let out a hearty cheer.

Hot on its heels came Andrew's excited "Hurrah!" His gladness and approval unmistakable, the child ran to Caitlin and his father, giving them each the fiercest of hugs. Then everyone—even the stately Townsend— joined in, their enthusiasm ringing over courtyard and lawns. Even the vicar, who, when asked to officiate, actually blushed. The poor man stammered he'd be "honored" and with good reason: The marriage of a peer was normally performed by a far loftier cleric than a humble country vicar; most often in a great London cathedral, such as St. Paul's. And if some ascribed this anomaly to the highly unusual circumstance of a marquis wedding a lowly governess, they were too polite to say so.

It was nearing midnight when the last guest finally departed. When a blissful, sleepy Andrew had been carried to his bed. Adam thanked the staff, accepted a final congratulatory word from Townsend and Mrs. Needham, and ushered his fiancée upstairs. Caitlin saw at once they were going to his rooms. "Perhaps we should be more circumspect," she whispered, darting a glance behind, to see if anyone saw where they were headed. "Now everyone knows, perhaps we ought t' sleep in our separate—"

"Who says we're going to sleep?" Adam asked with a wicked grin.

"I-I—" Caitlin blushed to the roots of her hair.

He chuckled and gave her hand a squeeze, then drew her inside his antechamber. But the moment he shut the door, Adam's face sobered. "Forgive me, love. For a moment there"—he gave his head a shake, as if to clear it—"I confess I found myself caught in a fantasy . . . of wishful thinking, you might say."

With a heavy sigh, he tucked an errant curl behind her ear, then ran a finger along her cheek in a gentle caress. "Odd, what the mind can do. I let myself imagine we were already wed and that those who bade us good night were our wedding guests. Imagined myself free to gently tease, as a prelude to making love to you"— he heaved a deprecating sigh—"like any other bride-groom."

"Aye," Caitlin said softly, nodding with understanding. "When I was a child, I often did the same. A favorite fantasy was that I had a family . . . a mother and father . . . brothers and sisters . . . all waitin' for me when I returned home from school. 'Tis a human thing, that wishful thinkin'. Especially when the world isn't all we long for it t' be. Ye needn't ask forgiveness for bein' human, *a stór.*"

"In this case, I do," he insisted, "because it wasn't fair. Not only are the things I'd wish away monstrous, and screaming for my full attention, but it was *my* fantasy, not yours—"

At that moment, the tall-case clock on the landing began to toll the hour. *Bong.* It echoed eerily over the silent house. *Bong.* Advancing immutably toward the stroke of twelve. *Bong.* Unmoving, they looked at each other. *Bong.* Caught in this palpable reminder. *Bong.* Of time running out. *Bong.* Eyes locked, wordlessly, they stood there. *Bong.* Until at last they heard the final chime. *Bong.* And felt it reverberate through the walls, and through their very bones.

Caitlin shivered. "I've a need o' yer fantasy t'night, Adam," she whispered, imploring him with her eyes.

"For a brief while, *macushla,* I need ye t' make me forget."

Adam read her need. It was identical to his own. Without a word, he pulled her into his arms. He made love to her then. Without preamble, there on the rug. Not the slow, achingly sensual lovemaking of before, no. This erupted with a force, like an apocalyptic thunder, which neither could control. Passions rose full-blown, impelled them toward a fierce and primitive mating. It was as if, by sharing the primal human act that created life, they could affirm it. Could banish doubt and demon and despair.

No, not a sweet and sensual joining at all. This roiled with emotions too keen for words, with passions released at full throttle. Caitlin tore feverishly at Adam's clothes. He never let her finish. Shoved her gown above her hips and thrust inside her liquid heat. Found her hot and ready. She climaxed at once, screaming his name in a storm of Gaelic. Only to pull his head toward her for a wet, open-mouthed tangling of tongues, dig her nails into his scalp, and come a second time. Her name boiled from his throat as Adam bared his teeth and found his own release. Sweat dampening their clothes and hair, still joined, they clung together, sated and spent.

And for a brief while, at least, time held them in the arms of oblivion.

When they could no longer ignore the hardness of the floor beneath the rug, when perspiration cooling on skin raised gooseflesh on arms and legs, Caitlin and Adam stirred. Assuring Adam he hadn't hurt her, Caitlin blushed only slightly and laughingly thanked him for sharing his "wishful thinking." Of course, she added with a wry grin, for the sake of their English brides, she hoped the local bridegrooms were possessed of milder fantasies!

Laughing, then murmuring his love as he caught her to him for one last kiss, Adam swept her in his arms and carried her inside. Not to sleep, though both were close to exhaustion, but to put their heads together and think. And think they did, far into the night. Till at length the dawn broke, found them gritty-eyed and bone-weary, drifting off in each other's arms.

And still without an answer.

Later that morning, after ordering the servants away from his chambers, Adam left Caitlin asleep in his bed and went in search of Andrew. He didn't mind if the staff guessed he and Caitlin were sharing a bed, but he knew she was sensitive about it. He therefore told everyone she was "in her rooms and not to be disturbed," left her a note to explain, and took Andrew for a ride in his gig.

His son deserved some uninterrupted time with his father, Adam told himself. But if the whole truth were known, he was close to despondent for not yet finding a plan to thwart their hellish adversary. Perhaps the fresh air would sharpen his faculties. As he'd told Caitlin just before dawn, there had to be a way—had to!

As it happened, the idea that gave Caitlin some hope didn't come from Adam. Indeed, he was still driving pell-mell over the downs, with Andrew laughing at his side, when the visitors arrived. Caitlin had just managed to slip into her rooms without being noticed when she heard a carriage on the drive. A peek out the window informed her it was a grand, important-looking conveyance. Perhaps, with Adam away, she ought to see to these guests? This might, after all, have something to do with last night's announcement. As his future marchioness, she'd be expected to . . . .

The words died in her mind, and she gave a brittle laugh. The mere thought of herself with that grand title was intimidating. Moreover, she felt like a fraud, thinking of herself as a *future* anything. Hurriedly shifting her clothes and running a brush through her hair, she made it to the front entrance hall just in time. Her eyes widened as Townsend admitted the duchess of Ravensford and sister Megan!

Megan and Ashleigh exchanged covert glances as Caitlin came forward to welcome them. They'd expected to find a radiantly happy bride-to-be. The woman who greeted them looked anything but. The tall redhead eyed her sister askance as Ashleigh congratulated Caitlin on her engagement. *The child has a drawn and haunted look about her, or I'm not Irish!*

When the duchess had kissed Caitlin's cheek and turned to meet her companion's gaze, Ashleigh's sapphire blue eyes said the same. Megan nodded, as if she'd made up her mind to something, and turned to her sister. "Forgive our manners for bargin' in on ye like this, darlin'. But, d'ye see, when Brett met Patrick in the city and gave him the news, I just couldn't wait. Drove me own carriage t' Ravensford Hall, whisked herself, here, inside, and here we are! Er . . . where's the lucky groom-t'-be?"

Caitlin explained as she led them into the drawing room and sent Townsend for tea. Megan and Ashleigh questioned Caitlin about Andrew's miraculous healing, and when she described it, but in an oddly diffident manner, the older women exchanged a solemn covert look. After that, they engaged Caitlin in small talk, about the weather and other trivia, until the tea tray arrived.

But the majordomo had barely shut the drawing room doors behind him when Megan fired the words she felt, as an older sister, she had a right to say. "All right, out with it, Caitlin. And, don't be givin' me that look! I know an O'Brien in trouble when I see one. Ach, it breaks me heart t' see ye so pale and dispirited! What's wrong, wee *macushla*?"

Perhaps it was the loving look in Megan's wide green eyes. Perhaps it was having a sister to share with, after a lifetime of having none. Perhaps the brave front she'd mustered, for Adam's sake more than her own, had withstood all it could bear. But whatever the cause, her bottom lip began to tremble. And then she was sobbing in Megan's arms.

Megan was a compassionate listener, and so, Caitlin quickly realized, was the little duchess. The whole story came pouring out. Between halting breaths, much of it told with heartrending sobs—and hiccups that had both women patting her shoulders and telling her to take her time—out it came, the dreams and visions that had sent her fleeing Ireland, the events that brought her to Adam Lightfoot's home and into his life, Appleby, the bargain resulting in that fatal game of chess, all of it.

There was a stunned silence when she'd finished. Over Caitlin's bowed head, the two older women exchanged incredulous stares. At length, Ashleigh sighed and reached for one of the hands Caitlin held in her lap; it clutched the monogrammed handkerchief the duchess had given her at some point during that terrible recitation. "My dear Caitlin, how very, very much you must love each other," she said softly.

"Aye," Megan added with a meaningful smile for her friend: Ashleigh and her Brett knew something of that kind of all-encompassing love; as did Megan and her beloved Patrick.

Caitlin managed a tremulous smile and nodded. She felt nearly as drained as when she'd last invoked Crionna's charm, but it was a good feeling this time. "I-I beg ye will both forgive me," she stammered. The duchess's handkerchief resembled a tortured knot as she twisted it in her hands. "I-I niver meant t' deny I had the Sight, but—"

"My dear," said Ashleigh, "if I'd been carrying such an egregious burden, you may be sure *I'd* have denied it, too. Think no more of it, and—here, have some tea. There's nothing like a bracing dish of tea to restore one's equilibrium. In fact, we'd all best have a splash." She shot Megan an arch look: *We must do something!* "Tea has also been known to sharpen the mind," she added pointedly

But Megan was well ahead of her friend. Prepared for something dire the moment Caitlin had brought up the Sight, she'd nonetheless been shocked, then incredulous as the grim story tumbled forth. Yet Megan was no stranger to adversity. There was a time the tall redhead had endured unspeakable hardship and degradation, then survived and prospered—by using her wits. Before her sister's final words left her lips, Megan was sifting through the details, her quick mind searching for a solution.

"Listen carefully," she said as Ashleigh waved Caitlin's trembling hands aside and did the honors with the tea. "I've an idea, and it may work, but it wants careful scrutiny. I need both o' ye bendin' yer minds to it, t' see if 'tis sound . . ."

The gist of Megan's plan hinged on something Caitlin hadn't known. "Since weddin' Patrick and becomin' a lady o' leisure, I've had time t' dip into all manner o' things that interest me,'' she told them. ''Now, one o' these interests is the Auld Tongue o' me homeland. And, strange as it may seem, I found meself fascinated one day with a passage in a dusty auld book about ancient Irish charms and curses.''

She paused a moment to let that sink in. ''Now, if I'm right—and I think I am—Crionna's charm is known in the ancient high Gaelic as the *Ard Cosaint* . . . the High Protection. But 'twas also sometimes called the *Ard Milleadh* . . . the High Destroyer.''

''It doesn't surprise me,'' Caitlin put in with a shiver. ''Remember, Crionna warned that its use more than twice would kill—''

''Aye, but that's not all!'' Megan said excitedly. ''The charm can be directed at *things,* as well as persons. If ye merely say it t' protect, ye can freeze a person in his tracks, as ye did with his lordship, two nights ago. But there's anither way t' use it, Caitlin. Ye can *destroy* a thing with it. As I understand it, all ye need do is concentrate on obliteratin' the object as ye speak the words, and—poof! It no longer exists.''

''That's . . . interestin','' said Caitlin. ''Odd that Crionna niver mentioned it.'' She heaved a sigh. ''Then again, she was terribly weak at the end. I suppose she simply hadn't the time nor the strength t' give me all the details. But, interestin' as it is, I still don't—''

''Don't ye see, *macushla?* 'Tis yer own contract ye must obliterate!''

''Why, of course!'' Ashleigh chimed in, equally excited. ''Having sworn upon her soul, she's committed to signing the wretched thing, but that's all. She must act quickly, of course, but when she does, she can *destroy* it in the next breath! The devil will be left empty-handed!''

And I shall be left dead. Caitlin's lips twisted wryly. The only detail she'd omitted in her recounting of events was that first use of the charm. When she'd feared Adam would rape her. She'd omitted it purposely, of course, wishing to protect her beloved from anything that would lead these two to think ill of him. So Megan and Ashleigh thought she's used it only once—the other night, to protect Adam from his own courageous folly. They believed she was therefore free to employ it again, with impunity.

Well, not with impunity, then, but I can still use it. Aye, I'll die from the ordeal, but with the contract destroyed, hell will have no claim on my soul—thank God and all the blessed saints! Holy Mother, I knew you would show me the way.

Caitlin turned to her sister and Ashleigh, a bright smile firmly in place. "Megan, I can't find a single objection t' yer plan. I think it'll work."

"It will—it's absolutely brilliant!" Ashleigh exclaimed.

"So 'tis settled, then," said Megan, giving Caitlin a hug. "Ye'll invoke the charm and send the bast—er, the rotter straight back t' hell!"

"Aye," said Caitlin. " 'Tis settled."

Chapter 16

As Megan and Ashleigh prepared to leave, Caitlin reviewed Megan's plan in her mind and knew she could say nothing of it to Adam. *He* certainly knew how many times she'd invoked the charm. And Adam, she felt certain, would accept nothing less than a scheme that saved her life, as well as her soul. Which wasn't in the offing.

Yet how was she to keep him from finding out? With the servants knowing she had visitors, she couldn't prevent him learning who'd come to call, though the visit itself was easily explained: The duchess and her sister had come to wish them happy on their engagement. The problem lay in preventing Megan and Ashleigh from spilling the beans. When he asked the duke to procure the special license, Adam had invited the Westmonts and the St. Clares to the wedding. They could be expected to return to the Hall for a wedding toast and some refreshments after the ceremony. And when they did, there'd be every opportunity for talk.

"You must relax, now your mind is relieved, my dear," Ashleigh was saying as Caitlin accompanied them to the entry hall—and frantically sought a plausible means of keeping them silent. "You're free to anticipate—to simply enjoy being a bride. Tell me, have you given any thought to what you'll wear?"

"W-wear?" Caitlin stammered. She was only half aware of what had been said. Her brain was furiously wrestling with her problem, rapidly discarding one solution after another.

"Why, yes," said the duchess as Townsend went to fetch their shawls, "considering you've had so little time to prepare. A pity this wedding couldn't have waited. I've a superb mantua maker in London, who'd have created a splendid wedding gown for you. Of course, I realize now why Ravenskeep arranged this marriage in such haste—"

Megan chuckled. "Ye may be sure there's waggin' tongues about who'll assume the worst, but don't fash yerself, *macushla.*" Her eyes twinkled as she eyed her sister's reddening face. "The scandal broth will cool. And even if a babe should appear in less than nine months—"

"Megan!" Ashleigh swatted the Irishwoman's arm with her fan.

"Merely pointin' out the obvious," Megan replied with an unrepentant grin.

"Nonetheless, I prefer to dwell on more seemly things," Ashleigh sniffed. She turned back to Caitlin. "Now, I do hope you won't think me presumptuous, my dear, but you and I are about the same size. Would you allow me to lend you a frock to wear for your wedding? I've a lovely ivory sarcenet that's quite tastefully accented with moss green furbelows. And with your skin and eyes, my dear . . . well, it would be perfect."

She chuckled, patting her rounded belly. "I dare say, I won't be fitting into it for a while. I'd be honored if you'd consent to wear it."

Caitlin was so touched, she forgot her pressing problem for a moment. "I—'tis I who's honored, Yer Gr—ach, I mean, Ashleigh. 'Tis kind o' ye."

"Then, it's settled," said Ashleigh. "I shall send it along with my ladies' maid this afternoon. In the event it requires a few adjustments. Betty's a wizard with needle and thread. She'll have you swearing it was made with none but you in mind."

"Er . . . speakin' o' swearin'," said Caitlin, seeing her opportunity. "May—may I swear ye both t' secrecy regardin' this plan o' Megan's? I-I'm not certain, but 'tis possible 'twould overset his lordship t' learn I've confided—"

"In us, without his leave?" Megan cut in with a grin. "Ach, these men!" she exclaimed with an arch glance at her sister-in-law.

"So sensitive!" said Ashleigh, rolling her eyes. "I vow, half of humanity goes about thinking the other half's too delicate to know what goes on in the world. Meanwhile, the 'delicate' half spends most of its time pretending it's so—and the rest of the time shielding the 'strong' half from learning we're on to them!"

"Ye've the right of it, there," said Megan with a chuckle. She patted Caitlin's hand. "Niver fear, darlin'. Just let his lordship assume ye thought it up yerself. Yer secret's safe with us."

"Safe as houses," said Ashleigh with a wink.

In a flurry of silk and lace, the two swept out the door to their carriage. Megan clucked to her team and tooled down the drive as adroitly as any young blade in town.

The duchess waved to Caitlin, and Caitlin waved back.
Watched until the vehicle rounded a curve in the drive.
The last thing she saw was her sister's bright hair catching fire in a shaft of sunlight before it vanished from
sight. Caitlin sagged with relief.

Adam and Andrew returned from their excursion
shortly after noon. Caitlin spied them in the distance
as she watched for them from her window. She'd found
herself missing them terribly after Megan and Ashleigh
left. Now she raced pell-mell down the stairs and out
the door, eager to greet them.

She was nearing the stables when she drew to a sudden
halt, seized by a stab of acute pain. *How very normal and
ordinary it seems, running to greet my menfolk as they return
from a jaunt over the downs. Yet there's nothing ordinary about
it. This is the last, the only time, we'll ever share such a precious
moment. Ah, Blessed Mother, how do I bear it?*

Hush, whispered a quiet voice inside her. *Every moment
we live is precious, though it may seem ordinary. Think of the
countless men and women who let the precious moments pass,
deeming them too ordinary to notice. You have been granted
this rare chance to see what others fail to see. To value the time
you have left, and through it, to appreciate the gift of life. To
know the preciousness of every ordinary minute.*

With this, Caitlin felt a curious calm descend. A still
serenity that settled deep inside her. Even the gentle
breeze ruffling her curls seemed to whisper of peace
and acceptance. Her heart brimming with love and gratitude, she smiled at Adam when he drew his team to a
halt. Grinned at Andrew as he climbed down from the
gig and ran to greet her. She could see the child was
beside himself with excitement.

"There you are, Caitlin!" he cried. "Papa and I had

a splendid ride in the phaeton, didn't we, Papa? We saw all manner of lovely things on our ride. Spotted cattle and haystacks and six ducks in a pond—I counted!—and folk who waved and wished us happy. And Papa let me take the ribbons! 'Course, we had to go very slowly for that part, but I did it without any ham-fisted fumbling—didn't I, Papa?"

"Not a ham fist in sight," his father agreed. Adam affectionately ruffled the dark, windblown curls so much like his own. His gaze, however, was on Caitlin, absorbing the sight of her like parched earth drinking in the rain. Caitlin's heart turned over as she saw the tortured look in his eyes: love held captive, imprisoned in helplessness and regret.

"Any news?" Adam whispered hopefully as he kissed her cheek. Caitlin looked so serene, he thought perhaps she might have discovered an answer to their plight. *He* certainly hadn't. As the morning passed without an inkling, he'd begun to sink into a dour and comfortless mood. Not even his son's exuberance could dispel it. It had been all he could do to maintain a tranquil, if not entirely happy, façade for Andrew's sake.

"I'm workin' on it," Caitlin whispered. She sounded confident and determined, which was deliberate. She'd thought long and hard about what to tell Adam when he asked, as she'd had no doubt he would. Megan had said to let him think Caitlin herself had found their solution . . . but of course, that was out of the question.

Instead, she'd decided to keep his spirits up as best she could. That meant letting him know she hadn't succumbed to doubt and despair. In the time they had left, she would savor what they had together, do all she could to help Adam savor and treasure it. They must make every second count. *Every moment we live is precious* . . . .

"We'll work on it together," he murmured. Caitlin was heartened to hear an echo of her own determination in his tone before Andrew claimed their attention.

"Caitlin, Papa says, now my leg's healed, I can begin riding my pony again! Would you like to meet him?" The child grabbed her hand, tugging her toward the stables. "His name is Toby, and he's been summering in the east pasture, but Papa asked the grooms to fetch him while we were gone riding, and he's just the bestest pony in the whole world, and . . ."

The three of them spent the day together, under a golden August sun whose heat was offset by the gently cooling breeze. As he introduced Caitlin to his pony, Andrew chattered away with all the ebullience of a healthy six-year-old. Next, they enjoyed a luncheon Cook had prepared; they dined al fresco, under the big elm shading the paddock where Toby munched a carrot, sent by Mrs. Needham in the picnic basket. Then it was a leisurely stroll through the formal gardens, with Andrew running—he rarely walked now, when he could run instead—ahead of the adults to investigate the maze at its center.

Afternoon found them inside the house, where they had an informal tea served in the smaller drawing room. There, Adam conferred briefly with the upper servants on preparations for the reception, which would take place immediately after the morning ceremony. This prompted all sorts of questions from Andrew:

Why was His Grace being called the best man? "Caitlin, shouldn't it be Papa?" Andrew asked with a frown. "I think *he's* the bestest man—and what's more, *he's* the one being married!" She and Adam explained the tradition and its nomenclature, and the child seemed satisfied. But it was the response he gained from the question he posed next that delighted him.

Why, Andrew asked, had Townsend muttered it was a pity there was no one to give the bride away? Again, the adults explained the tradition. "But there *is* someone," the child protested. "Caitlin's my governess *and* my bestest friend! Why can't *I* give her away?"

Adam and Caitlin looked at each other. "Are you thinking what I'm thinking?" Adam asked her.

"I am," she replied with a grin. The grin broadened as she turned to the disgruntled child. "Andrew, me boyo, ye've just found yerself a major role in the weddin'!"

After a quiet supper, again involving just the three of them, they tucked a blissful Andrew into bed. Then came the first difficult moment since Caitlin greeted Adam and Andrew at the stables. As he always did without fail, Adam tiptoed toward the door when his son prepared to say his prayers.

"Papa . . . ?" Andrew's voice sounded tentative . . . diffident.

His father halted, turned to face him. Caitlin noticed his face reflected the uncertainty in the child's. "What is it, son?"

"Papa, why do you always leave when I'm about to say my prayers? Don't . . . Don't you like them?"

Wordlessly, Adam looked at him, unable to form a reply.

Seconds ticked by, while Caitlin held her breath. She could feel the beating of her pulse beneath the skin. The agony of indecision on Adam's face was almost more than she could bear. *Oh, my love, stay! Hear the innocent prayers of your child, and let them open your heart!*

Adam gave no indication he'd heard her silent plea. "I'm sure I should like them very well," he told the child at last. "But I think Caitlin's a better listener than I am, and she's told me how you always include me in your prayers. Will you do that for me again tonight, Andrew? Will you say a prayer for me? I-I'm not half so good at it myself, do you see."

"Oh, I will, Papa! I shall say a special prayer, just for you."

Overcome with emotion, Caitlin had ducked her head through this exchange. Now she took a moment to blink away tears, then risked a look at Adam's face.

But he was already gone.

Caitlin searched for Adam when she left Andrew's room. He wasn't in the hallway where he always waited for her after they saw the child abed. He wasn't in his chambers. With growing concern, she made a swift tour of the downstairs, though she skirted the beehive of activity in the kitchens; the servants were busy preparing tomorrow's reception—a small one, but it did involve a duke and duchess—and she hardly thought Adam would be found there. Eventually, she questioned the footman on duty in the hall. He'd been at his post since his lordship escorted her and Lord Andrew upstairs, he informed her; and, no, his lordship had not come back down.

Trying not to give in to alarm, Caitlin all but flew up the stairs. Two dozen rooms and many anxious minutes later, she finally found Adam in the library. She breathed a sigh of relief—until she saw his face.

London gossip had been full of Lord Byron while she was there. Much had been made of the scandal, which Caitlin ignored; she did recall, however, someone mentioning the poet's face having a "brooding Underlook," a description that had puzzled her. She hadn't understood what it meant . . . until now. *The Darkness sits upon you like a shroud, Adam, a stór, and I've so little time left!*

"Ye must fight it, love," she said fiercely. "Fight the Dark and win the Light!"

"How, Caitlin?" he whispered brokenly. He stood by the unlighted hearth, a single taper burning on the mantel. His tall frame was swathed in shadow, scarcely discernible in the gloom. "In the name of all we hold dear, tell me *how*."

"I think ye know the answer t' that," she said softly. She went to him, until they stood but a hand's width apart. "Ye knew it when the lad fair broke yer heart with his askin'."

"Prayer?" he replied sardonically. His arm swept an arc that encompassed the poorly lit room. "What in the hell d'you think I've been trying to do here?" He gave a mirthless laugh that broke on a sob, his lips twisting in a bitter parody of a smile. "What in the *hell*, indeed!"

"Stop it!" She threw her arms about his waist, felt him resist—and clung like a burr till his arms closed about her. "I'll not let ye give in t' despair," she murmured against his chest. Beneath it, she could hear his heart pounding like a drum, and she took it for her mantra.

"Ye're here—and alive! Alive, when, not two nights past, 'twould have been easy for me t' give ye up for dead. Aye, dead, and soulless in the bargain! But I did not give ye up—no, I'll not hear a word about how I managed it, d'ye hear?

"Ach, would ye listen t' me?" she said with a muffled laugh. "Last night, 'twas yerself urgin' *me* not t' give up. Now, 'twould seem we've traded places. But, Adam, I'm after tryin' t' point out somethin' else as well."

She withdrew slightly, just enough to gaze up at him. "I've bought us time, Adam, and that's no small thing.

Time, and every second precious! Will ye spend it blatherin' o' hell and defeat, or will ye—"

"Enough!" he cried, and swept her up in his arms. Turned and carried her through the adjoining door . . . to his bed. To the only solace he could find: Caitlin's sweetly welcoming body—and her fierce, unflinching heart.

Their wedding day dawned clear and bright. With Caitlin still asleep in the bed behind him, Adam twitched the draperies aside and peered at the sky. His lips twisted in a bitter smile. For a bride and groom with a dark cloud hanging over their heads, that cloudless sky was a mockery. Then he turned from the window, saw Caitlin's tumble of burnished curls on the rumpled sheets, and quickly banished the thought.

Life is precious, she had murmured as they made love far into the night. *No matter what might happen, promise me ye'll remember that, Adam. That ye'll throw not a moment away!*

He had promised. Which meant he'd no business thinking those dark thoughts. Especially with the gift of a blue and cloudless sky staring him in the face. With the gift of Caitlin's love written indelibly in his mind and heart. Written, no matter what might happen, in his memory, forever.

"A penny for yer thoughts, *macushla.*" Caitlin's voice, low and throaty with sleep, poured over his senses like warm honey.

"Ah, but they're worth a deal more than that!" He pounced on the bed, braced his hands on either side of her bare shoulders, and grinned down at her. "If you want them, m'lady, you must pay me in proper coin."

"Oh?" she said, grinning back at him. He'd begun calling her "m'lady" during the night, "to accustom you to the lofty address," he'd told her with a playful twinkle. "And what is the proper coin, milord?"

"A kiss, m'lady."

"What, only one?" she teased. "Yer thoughts are cheaply purchased, then."

"Not so . . ."—he slowly lowered his head—"for I hold them dear"—his mouth hovered over hers—"but this"—he tugged at her lower lip with his teeth, lightly grazing the sensitive flesh—"is dearer yet . . ." And then he kissed her senseless.

Later—a long while later, with Adam checking to make certain she was unobserved—Caitlin slipped away to her rooms. While she waited for a pair of maids to ready her bath, she smiled dreamily to herself. When the heady aftermath of their lovemaking finally allowed speech, she'd reminded Adam he still hadn't revealed his "dearly purchased" thoughts. "I was thinking," he'd whispered, his breath warm against the damp curls at her ear, "of this glorious day—and a bride to match it."

She'd laughingly accused him of blathering the blarney. But as she gazed out her window now, she saw it was, indeed, a glorious day. A soft breeze ruffled the curtains. A shaft of sunlight slanted across the floor and over her bare toes. Her hands, as she pressed her palms to the sash, touched sun-warmed wood, and—there! A lark singing so sweetly, it brought tears to her eyes as she watched it soaring, soaring into the azure sky. Aye, a glorious day. Past glorious, she thought, for Adam had kept his promise.

Then there was no more time for thought. A parade

of footmen and maids carried in buckets of heated water and a great, shell pink enameled tub for her bath. Expert hands lowered Caitlin into scented water. Lathered and scrubbed and rinsed her to a fare-thee-well. Dried her gently with soft linen towels. And brushed her long hair dry before the fire, till it shone and glinted like a cascade of sun-kissed copper coins.

Next, one of the maids set about styling her hair. She wound Caitlin's yard-long tresses into an abundance of loops and coils that began at the crown of her head and fell artfully toward her nape. Pulling out wisps and tendrils about her face to soften the effect, she pronounced this "the Grecian mode," assuring Caitlin it was "all the crack." With this accomplished, the other maid brought forth the exquisite gown Ashleigh had sent the previous afternoon and laid it carefully on the bed.

Caitlin saw she'd already set out the articles contained in a surprise package the duchess had included with the gown. "Just a small prewedding gift for the bride," the accompanying note had read. Caitlin was still overwhelmed by Ashleigh's generosity.

The "small" gift consisted of a pair of silk hose, complete with embroidered garters; brand-new ivory kid slippers that fit her perfectly; elbow-length, moss green satin gloves to match the gown's furbelows; and the *pièce de résistance:* a set of lacey undergarments so fine, they looked to Caitlin as if they'd been spun from moonbeams.

At length, they drew her before the tall pier glass, bidding her to keep her eyes closed. "Till all's in place for the full effect, miss," the maid who had dressed her hair explained. She set upon Caitlin's head a coronet of moss green leaves and flowers: tiny, perfect gardenias with the dew still on them, cunningly interwoven with sprigs of baby's breath. With the marquis's approval, all had been plucked from Ravenskeep's conservatory that morning. The maids told Caitlin the flowers were gathered by none other than Townsend himself, and fashioned into a wreath by Mrs. Needham.

"Ohh," Caitlin breathed when she opened her eyes. "Sure and I scarcely recognize meself!" She met the pleased gazes of the maids in the glass. "I-I look like the faerie queen—like Queen Mabhe herself, and no mistake."

"Ye make a fine, loverly lady," the younger maid offered shyly.

"A right proper marchioness," the older said with a nod.

Just then, a knock resounded at the door.

One of the maids opened it, and there stood Andrew, who had come to collect her for the ride to the church. The bridegroom, it had been decided, would drive there ahead of them in his gig, leaving the coach for Caitlin and her proud young escort.

Dressed in formal attire—satin knee breeches and silver-buckled pumps, a white waistcoat and starched cravat setting off his cutaway tailcoat of dark blue kerseymere—Andrew reminded her of a young prince. On his dignity, he presented a solemn face as he made her a leg, wobbling only slightly. Then, as he straightened, he took his first real look at her; and dignity went by the boards.

"Caitlin, is that really you?" he cried, eyes like saucers. "You look like"—he bit his bottom lip, pondering for a second—"like Cinderella at the ball!"

"Milord is too kind," Caitlin murmured, sinking into a deep curtsy. "Or perhaps 'tis Prince Charmin' I'm seein'?" she amended, rising and smiling into his wide blue eyes. "Sure and ye must be royalty itself, rigged out in all the grand finery o' the world."

"Papa's valet did it," he mumbled, blushing. Then, on his dignity once more: "Allow me to escort you to the church, dear lady." He crooked his arm, offered it with solemn mien. "Our coach is waiting."

Chapter 17

They were wed in the small Norman church where the Lightfoot family had worshipped for generations. And if the vicar—who, after all, had his living from Ravenskeep—noticed that the marquis failed to participate in the prayers, he didn't say so. The bride noticed, of course, as did others. The best man was quick to note the lapse, being a man who rarely missed anything, but he did not remark upon it. His Grace had wrestled with his own demons upon a time and was not one to cast stones.

As for the remaining guests, Her Grace and Lady St. Clare nodded knowingly to each other upon the bridegroom's silence; then, with a glance at the bride, the pair shared conspiratorial smiles. Sir Patrick attributed the marquis's behavior to a clear-cut case of the wedding nerves; he silently cheered the poor fellow when Ravenskeep spoke his vows in a firm, clear voice.

What impressed everyone was the calm serenity—as

well as the fresh, unspoiled loveliness—of the bride. Caitlin moved through the ceremony with the grace and equanimity worthy of a queen. To some raised in the Roman church, the simple Anglican ceremony, conducted entirely in English, might well have proved offputting; but it was all one to her. She sailed through her vows with nary a misstep, a placid, benign expression on her face. The one exception occurred when the six-year-old at her side was asked, "Who giveth this woman?" The child replied with a ringing, *"I do!"*—at which point she smiled. Yet it was a gentle smile that in no way marred that collected, unruffled demeanor.

It was when the ceremony itself was over that something changed. They had all gathered in the small vestibule where the marriage lines were to be signed and witnessed. In that rather ordinary, unprepossessing room—and quite unexpectedly—Caitlin found it necessary to fortify herself in order to maintain her peaceful façade.

She wasn't entirely certain how it happened. One moment she was reaching for the quill the vicar handed her, ready to affix her signature below Adam's bold scrawl. The next, as she dipped the quill into the lovely little antique silver inkpot Mrs. Wells had provided, a clock somewhere—she was never sure where—began to toll the hour. Everyone heard it. The tiny chamber seemed to vibrate with the chimes: eleven of them. Eleven, not twelve. And even if there had been twelve, these would have signaled noon, not midnight. And yet, and yet . . . .

All at once, she was hearing another clock, in another time and place, and it was tolling the hour of midnight. Signaling the end of her last moments on earth. *'Tis but thirteen hours from now . . . .*

Clutching the quill tightly to keep it from trembling,

she made herself sign in a steady hand. *Thirteen is a number like any other number. 'Tis thought unlucky only by the ignorant and the superstitious. You will not cave in now, Caitlin O'Bri—ach, 'tis Caitlin Lightfoot now! Lady Caitlin Lightfoot, Marchioness of Ravenskeep, and you will not bring cowardice and dishonor t' the name!*

Willing her hand not to shake, she handed the quill to the duke for his witnessing, and things proceeded apace. Then it was over, everyone kissing her and wishing her happy, congratulating Adam and smiling at them both.

In the midst of all this, a small hand touched hers, and Caitlin looked down into Andrew's angelic face. "Caitlin . . . ?" he questioned shyly. "Would—would it be all right to call you Mama now?"

Touched to the quick, she felt the burn of tears behind her lids. She blinked them back and dropped to a crouch, so their eyes were level. " 'Twould be more than all right, Andrew. I've loved ye like me own since—ach, since I can't remember when! I'll adore ye callin' me Mama, wee *macushla*, and count me blessin's each and every time ye say it."

The child's radiant smile pierced her heart, even as the small arms flung joyously about her neck soothed it. "I love you, Mama."

"I love ye, child o' me heart," she murmured in an unsteady voice. And wondered, with a sickly panic, if there were any way to make it bearable for him: when the morrow came, and she was gone.

While she'd waited for them to return from their ride the day before, she composed a long letter to the child, which she'd leave with the one she'd written his father. In the latter, she'd asked Adam to give Andrew his when he judged the time was right. The thrust of both letters was the same: death could never undo the love they shared. She'd also written, she firmly believed her soul would win heaven—to soothe the lad; and more importantly in Adam's case, informing him she'd outwitted Appleby, with Megan's help. She ended the letters saying she expected them *both* to join her there. And until that far-off day, they must never doubt she was with them in spirit—and would be, for all time.

Cold comfort to the grieving? *Yet the child will have his da. Aye, they'll have each other, which is more than they would have had without your intervention. You must believe they'll be a comfort to each other—you must!*

But would that ever be enough? With a dismissing shake of her head, Caitlin swallowed her misgivings as Andrew trustingly clutched her hand and everyone filed out. It would have to be.

When they returned to the Hall, Caitlin was touched to see the staff lined up to greet them on the drive. Then she learned they were there not to greet the newlyweds, as she'd thought, but to greet her in particular! She was their new mistress, Adam whispered to her in an aside, and they expected it. It was also customary, he added with a sheepish grin, for the new mistress to say a few words to them at the end.

He introduced his marchioness with a formal speech, much as if she were meeting them for the first time. They stood all in a row, with Townsend at the head; then Mrs. Needham, proceeding through the ranks of maids, of footmen and underfootmen, of gardeners and undergardeners, to the meanest scullions and stable boys at the end. As the majordomo named each one in turn, the servants curtsied to her, or bowed, or simply tugged humbly at their forelocks, in the age-old sign of obeisance.

Caitlin found her tongue and thanked them, managing a few words of appreciation for their guidance and support since she'd first come to the Hall. "There may be some that feel I've risen above me station," she told them, "and so I have. 'Tis a long way from Ireland's bogs t' Ravenskeep Hall." She took a moment to smile at a young Irish maid named Bridget, who'd just been taken on a few days ago. "And longer still, t' the lord's table at the Hall. Yet I promise ye this: 'twill niver make me toplofty or foolishly proud. I want ye t' know I feel honored t' be yer mistress."

Led by Fergus, they gave her a rousing cheer—which even the stern glance of Townsend couldn't quell—and Caitlin had to swallow to dislodge the lump in her throat. But the majordomo had a surprise for her that was even more touching. At his quiet nod, the door opened—and through it walked Jepson and Mrs. Hodgkins!

Smiles wreathed the faces of the two London servants as they came forth to wish her happy. From the looks of Adam and Andrew—and the child's giggle—she knew this had been their well-guarded secret: a loving conspiracy between them. It wrung her heart.

The rest of the day passed in a blur. No matter how hard Caitlin tried to cling to what was happening, time flew. It seemed the guests had only just arrived when she and Adam were waving good-bye as their conveyances pulled away. The Westmonts and the St. Clares left first, with Ashleigh and Megan whispering encouragement with regard to "the plan" as they hugged her. Then the vicar and Mrs. Wells took their leave, though Jeremy remained behind to spend the afternoon with Andrew.

But this, too, seemed to pass in the blink of an eye. The boys began their play by rolling a ball of yarn for Athena the cat. She and Adam watched, sharing in the fun. Yet it seemed only minutes later that the vicar's manservant arrived to collect the child and drive him home for supper.

In fleeting moments, when she risked a glance at the clock, Caitlin began to hate the sight of it. It was becoming more and more impossible to forget what lay ahead. How could she savor every minute—as she'd enjoined Adam to do—when the hours raced by, like hounds on the chase!

Worse, she learned Adam hadn't been able to forget—though he'd been managing to hide it well. It happened during supper, with one of those surreptitious glances at the clock she hadn't been able to curtail. As she quickly tore her gaze away, she chanced to meet her husband's eyes across the table. He was quick to shutter them, but it was too late. She saw the wild grief and desperation burning there, like unholy blue fire in his own private hell. And for the first time, Caitlin had real doubt about what she'd done.

They spent a far longer time than usual putting Andrew to bed. Because they both knew this was more than likely the last time Caitlin would be there for the ritual, they'd tacitly agreed to make it memorable . . . and special. But what made this all so very hard was that the child must be shielded from their painful foreknowledge. For one thing, Andrew couldn't hope to understand the things they knew, or how they'd come to know them; and for another, there was always the hope, albeit a slim one, that what they feared wouldn't come to pass. Thus, they'd resolved to tuck him in with cheerful smiles, as if all were right with the world.

Adam's presence, while he was there, helped center Caitlin and gave her support in moments when she weakened. As when she wondered how the child would fare when there was no one to listen to his prayers, Adam's difficulty being what it was. *Will the lad continue in his simple child's faith, despite the absence of a loving parent beside him? Or will he, because he is alone, begin to doubt? God protect him from the loss of faith that's blinded his father to the Light!*

Another difficult moment arose when Andrew asked for the tale of the "Sleeping Beauty" as a bedtime story—Jeremy had recommended it—and they came to the place in which the princess falls into a deathlike slumber, through the enchantment of an evil witch. *My clever young Druid witch!* All at once plunged into the ugly recollection, Caitlin shivered. Andrew, of course, could know nothing of that, but he *was* given to comparing her to the heroines of the various fairy tales she'd read him . . . *You look like Cinderella at the ball!* Would he draw another, and much less benign, comparison when she was no longer among the living?

She envisioned the sleeping princess, lying on her bed, still as death. *Is that how he'll think of me when I'm gone? Will he imagine me in a tower room, all twined about with thorns, waiting for my hundred years to end? Will he grieve anew when he realizes he'll have died himself long before that magical awakening could ever come to pass?*

Still, with Adam in the room, Caitlin managed to carry on without faltering. Then came the moment when the child would say his prayers. When his father had slipped away—this time with a sweetly understanding nod from Andrew—she had all she could do to get through it without breaking down:

"God bless Caitlin—I mean, Mama—and thank You, God, for giving her to me . . ."

Holy Mother of God, help me find the strength to leave this child . . .

"God bless Papa . . ."

Help him to lead his father to the Light, to succeed where I could not . . .

"God bless Jeremy . . . God bless Jepson and Mrs. Hodgkins . . . God bless Townsend . . ."

Guide them as they fill his days with friendship and love . . . .

When the last prayer left his lips, when Caitlin had added hers and crossed herself, she had to believe her own had been heard. "G'night, Mama," Andrew murmured with a smile, and before she could respond, she saw he was asleep.

"Good-bye, wee son," she whispered, her eyes blurring with tears. Tears that had blessedly been held in abeyance till now. Sparing the child from asking why she cried, sparing her from answering him with a lie. And that, too, like so much else, had to be enough.

This time Adam had waited for her. He stood in the hallway, mere steps from Andrew's door. "Come," was all he said when he saw her face, and he opened his arms to her. Caitlin felt them close around her like a benediction. If this was the only kind of prayer he could manage, she might sorely lament what that limitation cost him, but she was passing glad of the human solace he offered tonight. To deny her need of it would require another lie she was loath to own. She craved those arms about her. Adam's solid presence was a comfort past telling. She needed it like all things green and growing needed the sun and the rain. She would savor what she could. 'Twas too late for regrets.

They made love for the last time in Adam's chamber. In the marriage bed of Catherine and Thomas Lightfoot, that was now theirs. As it happened, when he'd thought about their wedding night throughout the day, Adam hadn't intended to fall into bed at once. He'd wanted, above all, to delve through every corner of his mind, in the hours before midnight, to somehow find a way to save his wife. In his heart, however, he knew it would take a miracle to reverse the dark tide that swept them inexorably toward the abyss.

And Adam had long ago stopped believing in miracles.

In the end, the delving mind lacked conviction and surrendered to the passions of the heart. And of the flesh. He defied the fast-ticking minutes and swiftly fleeting hours by making love to his bride with slow, deliberate hands; with long and languidly arousing kisses; with whispered words of praise and adoration. It was much like the first time he'd made love to her . . . achingly slow and sensual . . . intoxicating and delicious in its anticipation . . . wildly fulfilling in its hectic, shattering climax. And yet it was not like the first at all, for never was joining so bittersweet.

And in those dwindling, bittersweet hours, Caitlin understood Adam's brave defiance. For years he'd been a military man, a fighter. And what was a fighter but a man of action? Yet now he found himself frustrated, unable to act. And so, true to his nature, he fought where he could. Caught in the net of helplessness that held him in thrall, he would recklessly—defiantly— thumb his nose at it. Caitlin knew exactly what he was doing. And in this, she became his willing accomplice.

"Ach, *macushla!*" she cried breathlessly, writhing on the bed as he covered her naked body with slow, burning kisses. "I've a need t' know the taste o' ye, as well." With this, she turned on her side to face him. It was a balmy night, and they'd opened the windows and pulled aside the draperies. A full moon rode high above the trees, bathing the chamber in silvery light; she could easily read the mild surprise on Adam's chiseled features. He said nothing, but the quirk of a brow pulled at the thin scar that slashed across his face.

Saying nothing more, Caitlin ran her tongue experimentally along his neck, and then across the muscular curve of his shoulder. "Ye taste salty," she whispered, moving slowly downward. And smiled to herself as she felt Adam suddenly go very still beneath the catlike laving of her tongue.

Proceeding to his pectorals, where the flat disc of a male nipple beckoned like an oasis amid the crisp whorls of chest hair, she encircled it with her lips. Sucking gently, she felt him shiver. And when she flicked the tightening center with her tongue, she heard him groan her name.

"D'ye like this, *a stór*?" she whispered, sending a breath of cooling air across the tiny, moist protrusion, causing it to pucker into a hard knot.

"Minx!" Adam accused—his turn to writhe now—as she grazed the turgid crest with her teeth. "You *know* I do."

"And this . . . ?" she questioned. Sheathing her teeth with her lips—as she'd often felt him do with her—she pinched the taut bud between them, then worried the captive flesh with her tongue. At the same instant, her hand slid across his flat abdomen. She grasped, at its base, the rigid length that had sprung against her belly. Gently, then more firmly, she squeezed the throbbing shaft and, with it thus in hand, began a slow, upward stroke toward the tip.

"Caitlin!" Adam rasped, stilling her hand by covering it with his. "Do you want this spent too soon—and upon the sheets?"

"Ach, niver! But, Adam, I—"

"Hush," he murmured, and pressed her gently back into the mattress. Now it was his turn again. And he played upon her quivering flesh like the master he was. First, he turned the tables on her, teasing her responsive nipples in exactly the same fashion she'd employed with him. He was not content with just one breast, however, but played upon each in turn. While his mouth worked its magical mischief, his deft fingers did wickedly arousing things to the one abandoned by tongue and teeth, for he was most reluctant to leave either unattended when he played upon its twin.

Next, his relentless mouth moved lower. Now gently nipping the soft, silken skin of her belly, now soothing each inch of sweetly abraded flesh with his lips and tongue. At length, cupping her buttocks with his hands, he lifted her toward him, and his questing mouth moved lower still.

Without thinking, Caitlin tangled her fingers in his dark curls as his head descended to her navel, and then below. Lower still, and her thighs were open to him. Ah, she couldn't think for the pleasure! Then, all at once, she knew his intent. Patrick and all the saints preserve her! He was after loving her on—

"Adam!" she gasped as his head moved unerringly between her thighs. And then words failed, and she sucked in a quavering breath. He'd found the sweet, hotly pulsing center of her longing. Pausing there, he dipped and delved with his tongue till she moaned in ecstasy and sobbed his name. Now he nuzzled the tight auburn curls above that slick, wet opening. Found, with clever lips and wicked tongue, the sensitive, pert little nub nestled within those curls. Teased it without mercy. And sent her spiraling over the edge.

* * *

"Sure and ye're the shameless man o' the world, *a stór,*" she whispered breathlessly. When power of speech at length returned. When she lay sprawled beneath him, on tangled sheets that bore the heady scent of passion.

"Quite," Adam agreed with a lazy, unrepentant grin.

A teasing light entered Caitlin's eyes, and a slow grin spread across her flushed face. "Yet turnabout's fair play, I'm thinkin'." Before he could respond, she slid from beneath him, turned, and quickly straddled his hips. Placing her hands on his chest, she pushed him firmly into the bed.

"Caitlin, what——?"

"Shh," she replied, stilling his lips with her fingers. And then it began. Murmuring words of wondering approval, she resumed that earlier exploration of his sleek, powerful body. "Ye've an uncommon strong and muscular neck, *a stór,*" she told him, trailing kisses along its corded length. "And a fine, broad pair o' shoulders, sure." Clasping those shoulders with both hands, she sank her teeth lightly into the curve where neck and shoulder joined, and grinned when she felt him shudder.

His chest, with those intriguing male nipples, lured her downward. Although Adam twisted restlessly beneath her touch, she nonetheless took her time. He'd taught her well, and she was unrelenting, as thorough as he'd been with her. But all the while, her ultimate objective stayed firmly fixed in her mind. Nibbling and laving, mercilessly teasing, she made her way steadily toward it. It was only when she nuzzled his navel, her breasts pressed wantonly against his thighs, that Adam realized what that objective was.

He was no stranger to such pleasuring, of course.

Over the years, a string of mistresses and other clever women in the dozens had sought to please him so. But . . . Caitlin? She was his wife now, the sweet, pure forever love of his heart. She was still an innocent, for all their recent sport. Never, would he have presumed to ask—

"Caitlin!" His voice sounded preternaturally loud in the quiet moonlit chamber, her name wrung from his throat like a prayer. Had Adam been able to think clearly, he'd have stopped to ponder: How was it her name on his lips resembled the very thing he found impossible to utter in any circumstance? But he was far from thinking clearly. His hands clenched the rumpled sheets as Caitlin took him into her mouth. Sweat beaded his brow as she kissed and tasted and sucked and plea-sured his engorged flesh. Driven to the brink with unbri-dled pleasure, he arched off the bed with a helpless cry.

And still, he managed to hold back. He was deter-mined now to give her free rein, sensing how greatly she relished the pleasure she gave him. Until he felt her small hand cup him. With a desperate clenching of teeth, he resisted—barely, just—the urge to spill himself inside that eager mouth. Twisting aside, he caught Cait-lin's lithe body and rolled with her, until she lay beneath.

Green eyes wide and luminous, she smiled up at him with unabashed delight: the cat that had got the cream.

"I love you more than life," he murmured thickly. *And more, a thousand times more, than all that lies beyond!*

"Aye, and so do I love ye, Adam, *a stór.*" Caitlin's eyes darkened as the import of the words came home to her. *I love you more than life.* The real and imminent proof of it was not far off. To keep him from guessing her thoughts, she closed her eyes and pulled his head down for a scorching, soul-searing kiss.

With a helpless groan, Adam buried himself inside her.

Chapter 18

Caitlin lay beside her husband in the bed, still as stone, listening carefully to his breathing. *Steady and deep, thank the dear God.* Adam appeared deep in slumber, yet she waited, for she had to be certain. While he was a soldier on campaign, she'd learned, he acquired the necessary habit of making do with catnaps; he'd trained himself to come awake from these on the instant, alert for danger. It had saved his life and those of his men, he'd told her, on countless occasions.

Tonight, however, Caitlin could ill afford such alertness on his part. Indeed, by encouraging him to make love repeatedly—not that it took any sort of persuading, for Adam had been all but insatiable this night—she'd done all she could to ensure he'd be too exhausted to awaken before she met Appleby—and her imminent fate. An encounter that must not take place here, but in her own chamber. *Not that I'm meant to have a chamber of my own any longer.*

She smiled sadly, recalling Mrs. Needham's kindly face when the housekeeper had asked if they might remove Caitlin's belongings to the marquis's chambers while she was at the church. "Her ladyship, Lord Andrew's mother," she had hastened to explain, "kept to the tradition of separate chambers, do you see, like most of the gentry. But his lordship's parents never held with that. They shared the rooms his lordship occupies now, Miss Caitlin. And . . . well, as nothing's been said of separate . . . er, chambers, upon your own marriage . . ." Her plain face had flushed a rosy red at that point. She'd looked so uncomfortable, Caitlin had rushed to assure her she'd never think of sleeping apart from her husband.

The smile turned wry as Caitlin was struck by the irony of it. How much easier it would be to steal away tonight if they had separate quarters. If Adam awoke, she stood a better chance of coaxing him back to sleep unaware by pretending she was merely going to fetch a night rail or some such trifle from her chambers. Implying she'd be right back.

A glance at the clock told her that was more than likely a foolish notion. Eleven minutes before twelve, and Adam knew what midnight would bring. Knew it in the marrow of his bones. If, in leaving, she chanced to wake him, she'd no doubt he'd immediately apprise himself of the hour. She'd be forced to meet the fiend in his presence, and that *must* not happen. No telling what recklessness Adam might attempt at the last minute, in his desperation to save her.

Indeed, she counted herself fortunate he'd fallen asleep at all. After all, despite the wild passion she herself had spent in their marriage bed, wasn't she lying here now, entirely awake? Not that she didn't ache with exhaustion. And feel sore in several new places, she mused with a rueful smile: Adam had been rather . . . inventive in their lovemaking tonight. She'd only kept herself awake out of her desperate need—and thank the good God she'd succeeded.

Another glance at the clock revealed a full minute had passed while she lay there ruminating. *Best get on with it, then.*

Taking a long, lingering look at her husband's beloved face, she fought an urge to drop a soft kiss on his brow. *Holy Virgin, this is a good man, despite his unfortunate—and, aye, tragic—loss of faith. Pray for him, Mother of God. In the name of your Son, have mercy on him, and help him to find it again.*

Not daring to move her hand to cross herself, Caitlin inched toward the edge of the bed. Now came the most difficult part. If Adam slept but lightly, he might well awaken when he sensed her weight leaving the mattress. Like all grand tester beds, this was a high one, its frame made to hold the mattress a good two feet from the floor. She glanced with regret at the portable stairs resting on their side several feet from the bed. Adam had kicked them aside when he carried her here in that first storm of passion. No help there.

Holding her breath, she maneuvered onto her belly and slowly . . . ever so slowly . . . began to slide over the side. It seemed forever till her feet would meet the carpet. At last she felt the fine Axminster wool beneath her toes. Now, if she could just—

At that moment, the mattress shifted. Adam had stirred, thrusting an arm across the pillow where her head had rested. Caitlin froze. On the other nights they shared this bed, they'd nearly always fallen asleep in each other's arms. In truth, she'd been fortunate in being able to prevent it happening tonight. Only twice, could she recall them lying apart after loving. And then not far apart, by any means. And on both occasions, hadn't he sought her out, even in his sleep? Turned and drawn her back into his arms? What if, upon finding her place empty now, he suddenly sprang awake?

Muscles tensed, Caitlin waited, the ticking of the clock matching the thudding of her heart. She clung to the edge of the bed without breathing. And was finally rewarded when his body relaxed again in slumber. Another glance at the clock told her she had nine minutes left. With one more silent prayer to the Virgin, she slid her weight to the floor. *Success.*

Yet she was still not ready to leave the chamber. Moving like a wraith, she went to gather up her bed gown, a fine, lovely thing Ashleigh and Megan had sent that morning. Plucking it from the carpet, where Adam had hastily discarded it in the heat of passion, she donned it quickly.

Next, she went to the clock on the mantel. Opening the case, she quickly moved the hands back until they read half-ten; if Adam should awaken, she thought perhaps he'd not panic if he believed they'd more time. She carefully closed the glass, winced at the *snick* of the tiny latch. A swift glance at the bed told her Adam hadn't moved, thank the dear God, and she made her way stealthily across the room.

Clouds had moved in, obscuring the moon, but she could still make out her bag of herbs and simples lying in the corner, beside Adam's huge armoire. She'd particularly asked Mrs. Needham to remove it here with the rest of her things, and for one important reason. The bag contained the letters she'd written Adam and the child. Bending down, she quietly withdrew them and carried them back to the mantel. The clock said another minute had passed. She forced herself not to panic while she propped the letters beside it, thought better of this, and placed them flat: Were Adam to awaken and spy them from the bed when he sought the time, he'd know something was afoot, sure.

Sparing precious seconds for a last glance at the bed, Caitlin swallowed hard. *Good-bye, my darling. Forgive me,* a stór, *for leaving you this way. Know, in your heart of hearts,* macushla, *that I'll always be with you. Know it, my love, and that I'll love you till the end of days.* With a swipe at the tears that had started, Caitlin turned and fled the room.

Candles guttered in the sconces hanging at intervals along the hallway, throwing ominous, flickering shadows on the walls. Caitlin tried to ignore them as she raced past on noiseless feet. Tried, but her imagination began to get the better of her. As she hurried by, the shadows appeared threatening and full of menace; they seemed to jump and recede, now beckoning to her, now luring her aside, for she knew not what. There, that one—it wore a demon's shape, sure! And there, the nameless form of some forgotten dread from childhood—now fully recalled and every bit as frightening. *They're shadows, nothing more! Pay them no heed, colleen. Ach, will this wretched hallway never end?*

The rooms she'd been given at Ravenskeep Hall were far grander than her single chamber in London, which had been in the servants' quarters on the third floor. These were closer, merely in another wing of the second; but as Caitlin raced against the clock ticking inside her head, they seemed impossibly far. If she failed to reach them in time, would the archfiend seize her here, in this endless, darkened hallway? Where some hapless servant, alerted by an untoward sound, might come upon them? And ask the cause?

Then again, Appleby seemed quite capable of mask-
ing what he was about. *He knows he must screen his dirty
business from decent folk—till he finds a way to lure them into
his filthy clutches!* On the other hand, she doubted the
fiend would scruple to forbear whisking her out of sight,
with one of those gestures that raised the hairs on the
back of her neck just thinking about it. *Aye, he's capable
of it well enough—and right before the poor servant's startled
eyes!*

At best, Adam would be left to explain the sorry business, if even he could! *Bad enough, he'll be left to deal with
a wife found dead. And in her old chambers, far from her
husband's bed—on their wedding night! Hurry then, colleen,
for haven't you burdened your dear love with enough, as it is?*

She was out of breath and tense as a harp string when
she at last reached her door. Her hand shook as she
tried the handle—*Locked! Sweet, merciful God . . . .* But,
no, it had merely stuck. With a grateful prayer of
thanks—she was all prayer inside, now—she thrust it
open, went inside. The small sitting room already
smelled close and stuffy from disuse; but that had to be
her imagination, for she had left it only that morning.
Sure and there was no denying her imagination ran
rampant tonight! The room, having no windows, was
also black as pitch.

By memory, she made her way to the bedchamber
beyond. She'd expected to find it moonlit, but was only
reminded of the gathering cloud cover she'd noted
earlier when she entered and found it inky dark. Chastis-
ing herself for forgetting to bring a candle, she waited
for her eyes to adjust to the gloom. There was really
only one reason she required light. She focused her
unseeing gaze on the mantel above the small marble
fireplace. Ach, what time was it? She needed to know
the time!

As if in answer, at that instant, a flash of lightning struck. As the draperies had been left undrawn, it illuminated the chamber, but briefly, gone before she could draw breath. No matter. Because her gaze had been directed toward the mantel clock, Caitlin had what she wanted:

It was three minutes to twelve.

Foolish, perhaps, to place such importance on knowing the time, but the knowledge helped her to focus and gather her wits. Releasing the breath she hadn't realized she'd been holding, she commanded herself to relax. Now, for the first time, she realized there was a ferocious wind blowing outside. 'Twas a late summer storm, coming in fast. She'd been too overwrought by her foolish fears and imaginings to notice.

Thunder rumbled ominously in the distance. Another bolt of lightning sundered the night sky, throwing the objects in the chamber into stark relief. Outside, the wind shrieked like a banshee. Or perhaps, she thought grimly, like all the souls of the damned. She could see the branches of trees through the windows, bending this way and that, whipped by the wind's force.

More thunder, nearer this time. When multiple flashes of lightning zigzagged across the sky, she used the sustained flare of brilliance to locate the tinderbox on the mantel. Succeeding in striking a spark, she coaxed a flame from the tinder, touched it to the candlestick she'd spied beside the tinderbox, and lifted the taper high. Mellow light illuminated the face of the clock:

Two minutes before twelve.

She had just enough time to go over Megan's plan in her mind. Refusing to be distracted by the earsplitting triple boom of thunder directly overhead, she remembered the rocking chair that stood near the bed. 'Twas as good a place as any to await her adversary. She turned toward it—and stifled a cry.

Appleby!

It was the triple boom of thunder that awakened Adam. Coming instantly alert, he knew his instinct for danger hadn't failed him. Something was terribly wrong. He jerked up in the bed, straining to see in the dark. Cursing himself for falling asleep—*how could he*, on this, of all nights!—he resolved not to panic. A flash of lightning, followed at once by a deafening crack of thunder, dashed his resolve to dust. His hands felt frantically about the place just beside him on the bed, and met only rumpled bedclothes. Caitlin! Where the devil was *Caitlin?*

The devil was smiling evilly at her—and sitting in *her* rocking chair. Tossed aside, upon the floor, was the pillow she'd sewn to cushion its seat. *How dare he throw it to the floor!* She recalled the tiny stitches she'd painstakingly worked, embroidering upon it for hours. It had been in those early days, when Andrew first began learning how to use the crutches. She recalled, too, matching her patience to the child's, until slowly, slowly, their persistence was rewarded. When Andrew had mastered the crutches, she had the image on her pillow completed. The pattern was the Tree of Life.

Appleby noted the direction of her glance and snickered when he saw her scowl. "Tut, tut, my dear. I should think that's scarcely worth your flying into the boughs," he said with a blithe gesture at the pillow. "Ah, you mortals and your tiresome little symbols! Take it from me, you'll hardly be wanting that one where you're going. Fact is, those who come to dwell in my realm soon loathe the slightest reminder of what they've lost."

Caitlin understood the significance of the symbol she'd embroidered, for she'd chosen it with a purpose. And she knew why the devil mocked it. The Tree of Life was meant to signify not the earthly existence, but God's gift of immortal life. Yet she was about to lose only the former. Thanks to dear Megan, her soul still had a chance of attaining the gift of God's Grace, though of course Appleby couldn't know that. To keep him from glimpsing any hint of that secret knowledge in her eyes, she turned and gestured impatiently at the clock. "Ye're a tad early, Mr. Appleby."

Lightning flickered, and the wind howled like a thing gone mad. Adam scanned the room in a panic while another peal of thunder rumbled angrily overhead. Leaping from the bed, he called Caitlin's name, hoping she was merely in the water closet, using the necessary. When no answer came, he used the flare of another bolt of lightning to scan the face of the clock. The hands said it was not long past half-ten, but ... something didn't feel right.

"Early ... am I?" Appleby said with a disingenuous lift of his penciled brows. "Dear me, you *are* quite the stickler. I was merely being accommodating, do you see." A sheet of parchment suddenly materialized in his hand. Caitlin knew at once this was the contract she'd sworn to sign.

"You'll require the typical moment or two, to peruse this, I'll warrant, to satisfy yourself it's accurate," he added with a snide certainty as he handed it over. "And it wants sufficient time for you to sign it properly, of course." Again, out of thin air, he produced the small silver blade she recognized all too well.

Caitlin forced herself to remain calm as she read over the contract. This was the paper she must destroy before he claimed her. It wanted careful timing. She must, *must* not get it wrong! In essence, the language stated what they'd agreed upon three nights before: Caitlin would forfeit her immortal soul in exchange for Andrew Lightfoot's leg made whole and Adam Lightfoot's freedom. Which brought her to the next step of her agenda: "My husband's auld contract, Mr. Appleby—where is it?"

"My dear marchioness," he replied with heavy sarcasm, "have you noted the time?" He used his walking stick to point at the clock. "It is nearly—"

"Ye know very well I cannot sign this contract without seein' the ither destroyed," she said sharply.

It was clear to Caitlin that Appleby had still hoped to trick her somehow. His face contorted and went instantly sour. The rouged and maquillaged features became the chilling travesty of a clown's face: a visage meant to amuse, but upon which someone had got the paint all horribly wrong. He muttered invective against her and all the Irish—he had always hated them, he informed her with an irate snarl. But Lord Appleby—alias Satan, alias Beelzebub, alias Lucifer, alias Old Harry, Old Scratch and countless other sobriquets, great and small—produced the contract. With a sullen, put-upon look, he held it up for her perusal.

Satisfied, Caitlin gave him a curt nod. "Destroy it."

With an aggravated glare, he produced a burst of flame that came out of nowhere. Thunder growled overhead as he incinerated it on the spot.

"Now, my clever little Druid pet," he said, handing over the small silver blade, "you will sign . . ."

Adam went to a window, hoping somehow to gain a better sense of the time from nature. He knew in an instant this was futile. The howling storm obliterated the moon and stars; indeed, made it impossible to see two feet beyond the sash. Sheets of wind-driven rain had soaked the draperies; they billowed wetly about the sash, and his bare feet squished on the carpet before the windows. Adam ignored it all, concentrating on the building sense of dread permeating every atom of his being.

He could well envision Caitlin slipping away to meet Appleby. It was just like her to do all she could to prevent him putting himself at risk trying to save her. And in that, she would not be off the mark. *He* had given the fiend no sworn promises! His ultimate plan, if all else failed, had been to offer himself in Caitlin's stead. After all, the little bastard had, as yet, no signed contract from her. If Caitlin were prevented from honoring her promise—even if it meant knocking her senseless, he'd do it in trice to save her—well, the fiend still had the one Adam himself had signed. He'd offer to forego the forty years clause, strike and initial it—after pricking his damned finger, of course—and go to hell, on the spot. He rather thought Appleby just might take him. *A bird in hand* . . . .

But all that was something he'd envisioned happening at the so-called witching hour. Yet here it was, not yet ten o'clock, and Caitlin . . . where the devil could she be? He couldn't begin to think where she'd go, in a raging storm, in the dead of night. Unless . . .

* * *

Caitlin took the proffered knife and pricked her finger. She stared stoically at the tiny drop of blood that welled scarlet at the tip. Wet and glistening like a crimson tear in the candlelight, it stood out starkly against her pale skin. She handed back the knife. The thunder overhead was deafening.

"Excellent," said Appleby, and the blade vanished. Though he never raised his voice to be heard above the storm, Caitlin noted with a shiver, he nonetheless made it possible for her to comprehend every syllable clearly. "Now," he added, "it wants a proper nib." He produced an elaborate quill, out of nowhere again, just as he'd done with all his other nefarious equipment. With a mocking flourish, he handed it to her and gestured at the little escritoire by the window. "Over there!" he snapped, all courtly behavior suddenly gone. "Quickly!"

Taking contract and quill with her, Caitlin crossed to the writing desk, keeping a careful eye on her adversary. He'd risen from the rocker and was standing before it, watching her intently. Laying the contract atop the desk's flat surface, she dipped the nib into the blood on her finger, began to sign . . .

The crash of the door against the wall was nearly obliterated by the latest crack of thunder. Adam burst into the room with a vengeance. "Appleby," he demanded, "take *me* instead! Now, this very instant! I'll make it worth your—"

His eyes found Caitlin at the escritoire, and they widened in terror. "Caitlin—stop it! I can't let you do this, d'you hear? It's got to be *me.*" He dashed across the small space that separated them, panic-stricken, for Caitlin's shoulders had squared, and she resolutely continued to scratch out her name.

Then several things seemed to happen all at once. *Ding.* The clock on the mantel, a delicate thing with a charming sound, began to chime the hour of midnight. *Ding.* As Adam tried to force her hand from the parchment, the fiercest bolt of lightning yet split the heavens. *Ding.* Caitlin caught a movement out of the corner of her eye. *Ding.* It was Appleby! *Ding.* He strode toward them. *Ding.* The fiend's hand was raised. *Ding.* 'Twas a gesture she recognized. *Ding.* He was after stopping Adam with one of his horrific *little lessons,* sure! *Ding.* Without thinking, Caitlin shut her eyes and invoked the charm toward her husband. *Ding.* The contract dropped to the floor, forgotten. *Ding.*

But she'd already signed it. *Ding.* And midnight was upon them! With her eyes closed, the Gaelic words still tumbling forth, it was only when the fiend's hand closed on her arm that Caitlin realized her mistake: She'd sacrificed her soul for nothing. He wasn't after harming Adam at all. Her contract was in his hand—and with the other, he was *claiming her.*

As the last syllables left her lips, she opened her eyes and squirmed in the archfiend's grasp, desperate for a last look at her beloved. As she did this, her hand involuntarily brushed against the parchment.

Appleby screamed. An inhuman sound, monstrous in its hatred and rage, it contained all the writhing agonies of the ages. The contract went up in flames, consuming an entire sleeve of his dandified coat, turning it and the fine linen shirtsleeve beneath to ash, the skin of his arm to a charred and blackened ruin. "Scheming Irish witch!" he shrieked. Venom and fury lanced each syllable, overpowering the storm that howled and raged overhead. "You *tricked* me—*me*, the Lord of Hell!"

"Thank God, oh, thank God!" Adam's hoarse cry rose above the storm.

Caitlin heard, and her eyes, fierce with triumph and joy, met the fiend's. "Ye'll not have either of us, now, Father o' Lies." She lifted her arm, pointed to her husband. "Adam Lightfoot just *prayed.*"

The look on Appleby's face said he knew she spoke the truth. Rage, primeval and terrible, distorted his dandy's mask. The storm outside shook the room as he swelled and grew. Gigantic, membranous wings crowded the walls and ceiling. Assuming his true shape, he towered over them, blood and gore dripping from inhuman jaws as he gnashed his razor teeth. With a last, bloodcurdling howl of rage, he vanished.

Caitlin slid lifelessly to the floor.

"Oh, my God—*Caitlin!*" Adam ran to her, dropped to his knees beside her prostrate body, and felt for a pulse. It was thready and weak. "Caitlin, please . . ." His mouth twisted in anguish as he closed his eyes and whispered brokenly, "Not now, oh, God, not now." Tears clogging his voice, he caught her to him. "Caitlin, I beg of you—don't *die.*"

He felt a slight movement. Hardly daring to believe, he pulled away to look at her face. Her eyes fluttered open, just briefly, but it gave him a thread of hope. Her voice was weak, the barest whisper. "We . . . won, *a stór* . . . we . . . beat him." She lost consciousness again.

The wind outside had died to nothing. Adam didn't notice. Grief and loss, terrible and all-consuming, washed over him in a gray tide of despair. Clutching his wife's lifeless body to his heart, he closed his eyes. Tears coursed down his face, unchecked. With the storm gone, his quavering voice echoed loudly in the still room:

"Our . . . Father . . . ," he began, groping for the words that had once been familiar, so many years ago, "Who art in Heaven . . . hallowed . . . hallowed be Thy name . . ."

Chapter 19

"Patrick . . . Patrick, wake up!" Megan St. Clare shook her husband's massive shoulder till he finally stirred. The bed creaked as the big man shifted his weight. Firelight bronzed his tousled black curls and glinted off the dark stubble on his chin. He blinked owlishly up at her, trying to gather his wits.

They'd had precious little sleep, what with the storm shaking the rafters when they'd prepared to turn in. They'd been sleepy enough, having made sweet and lazy love at length before the fire, but trying to sleep was futile with that hellish wind and thunder fit to wake the dead. And so, quipping that Mother Nature was as good an aphrodisiac as any he could think of, he'd taken his wife in his arms for another loving—as wild and as fierce as the storm itself. The storm finally quit, just as they'd climaxed and lay spent in each other's arms. With a chuckle, he'd told Megan it appeared both they *and* Mother Nature had won a well-earned rest.

Only, now it appeared his beautiful wife had other ideas.

"Wha . . . ?" he questioned groggily. He half raised himself on an elbow, although he'd have liked nothing better than to fall back asleep with Megan in his arms. But something about the way his wife held herself—poised and alert, like some graceful forest creature testing the wind—gave him pause.

"Patrick, somethin' odd's happened—I can feel it."

"Mother of God, Megan," he groaned. Bleary-eyed, he squinted at the tall-case clock that stood across the bedchamber. "We've had . . . what? Twenty minutes' sleep? And now you're waking me to tell me something's *odd*?"

She gave an impatient shake of her head, tossing the fire-bright mane of hair that tumbled about her bare shoulders. "Odd, as in *wrong*, me love. And ye know I'm niver mistaken about *that* sort o' feelin'."

Patrick rubbed a massive hand over his face, said good-bye to sleep, and sat up straight in the bed. Megan may not have had the Sight—an ability she still claimed her sister was born with, never mind all Caitlin's denials—but she did have these uncanny premonitions. He still recalled, with a shudder, the first time one of her "feelings" had struck—smack in the middle of Dolly Madison's dinner party. She'd made him drive her home at once. They were just in time to save their infant son from the fire sweeping the wing of their house that held the nursery. Brendan's nurse had stumbled and knocked herself senseless, overturning the lamp she'd been carrying on route to the kitchens, perhaps to fetch him a sugar teat, someone had surmised. The poor woman hadn't been as lucky as their son.

"A feeling about what, love?" He fervently hoped it had nothing to do with the lad. Brendan was miles away, staying with Megan's sister Bridie, in Ireland; while they were here in Kent, as guests of the Westmonts, because of Caitlin's wedding. He hoped it didn't mean trouble at home, either; their Virginia plantation was an ocean away.

Megan had already swung off the bed and begun searching for her clothes. Now she paused, looked at him gravely. " 'Tis Caitlin. I've a feelin' she's—ach, Patrick! The wee colleen made us promise not t' tell, but . . . well, now the time's come and gone, I suppose there's no longer any harm in it. She—"

"Whoa," he said, holding up his hand. "One thing at a time, love. Made *us* promise not to tell?"

"Ashleigh was there as well. We went t' see Caitlin the day before the—ach, will ye sit there, askin' questions all the night—or will ye don yer breeches and fetch the rig fer me? The lass is in trouble, Patrick, and I must go t' her!"

"We'll go to her, love." Patrick had rarely heard his wife this overwrought, and he climbed quickly from the bed. "Talk to me while we dress ourselves."

Megan heaved a sigh, then quickly resumed pulling clothes from a portmanteau that lay, half-packed, beside a tall chest of drawers. " 'Tis a long story, Patrick," she said, "and not a tame one. A tale as fearsome as an Irishman's soul when the fury's on him. I fear 'twill sorely try yer wits. At the very least, 'twill severely test yer grip on reality."

Patrick, who was only half Irish himself, grinned at her. "Megan, my love, since when has that stopped you?"

In another part of the house, Ashleigh Westmont paced the floor of her dressing room. She did this frequently of late, to spare Brett's sleep when the babe was restless and kept her awake nights. After all, she could always nap during the day. Her husband, however, was an aristocrat who took his duties seriously; he had obligations having to do with his vast holdings, and if he were to meet them, he needed his rest. Yet to say the babe was restless tonight was an understatement.

The storm explained why she and Brett had been unable to sleep for its duration—not that they hadn't put the time to good use, she mused with a wry smile. Only, now the storm had passed, and the child was still so fiercely active, one would think she harbored a cricket pitch inside her womb.

"Poor sweetheart, he's got you pacing again, has he?" Brett appeared at the doorway, bare-chested and disheveled—not so much from sleep as from their recent play abed, Ashleigh knew. He eyed her belly and gave her a lopsided grin. "One would think a future duke, even one yet unborn, might have better manners."

"What makes you think this one's a *he?*" she asked testily. Ashleigh's wasn't a high-strung temperament, even when she was increasing, but pregnancy *and* sleeplessness did nibble at her sunny disposition at times. Fortunately, Brett had been taking it all with the proverbial grain of salt, saying motherhood had its privileges.

"Call it paternal intuition," he replied, coming forward and taking her in his arms. "Or perhaps it's because I'd prefer to think that a daughter, like her sister, would be too much the lady to vex her mother so."

"You're supposed to be asleep, Your Grace," she said grumpily as he dropped a kiss on her brow. "While I nobly sacrifice myself for the future of the dukedom."

"The dukedom can go hang if it means distressing my wife." Turning her gently in his arms, Brett wrapped them about her from behind, resting his chin on her head. When he placed a hand on her swollen belly, however, he gave a startled grunt. "The lad has a powerful kick!"

"Do tell," said Ashleigh with a sigh. "Yet, in truth, it was never this bad until tonight. It's as if that wretched storm overset every—"

"I know," he said soothingly, kissing her ear. He adored his wife and was committed to doing everything possible to ease her discomfort during this pregnancy. Fact was, however, he'd been largely absent when she'd carried their first, and he was fascinated by everything about this one. At the moment, though, in deference to Ashleigh's sensibilities, he decided not to mention the interesting small bulge—he could swear he saw the shape of a tiny foot—briefly evident beneath her filmy bed gown.

"That bit of weather was a nasty piece of work," Ashleigh went on, but Brett thought she sounded a bit less grumpy as he continued to rub and soothe her distended belly.

"Oh, I agree," he told her. And he did, but of course, with Ashleigh in her present condition, he'd have agreed if she insisted the moon was a purple tennis ball. "Can't recall a storm hereabouts ever being that savage—not in tame old Kent. At sea, of course, now that's a different kettle of fish."

"Mm." She was smiling now. The babe had ceased its hijinks with Brett's soothing. "I seem to recall one particular storm at sea, however, that had precious little to do with the weather. The ocean was rather calm the night Marileigh was born."

"Don't remind me," he groaned. Their daughter had been born aboard one of his ships, on route from the Italian coast. Yet blessed as that event was, it had trig-

gered a storm of emotional turmoil for him. He'd been
forced to confront personal demons that had plagued
him nearly all his life. In the end, he came to realize he'd
held a host of unjust opinions, especially with regard to
women. And not least of those he'd judged unfairly—
and cruelly—had been Ashleigh. "I'm still amazed you
could love me, after I'd been such a damned witless—

"What the devil . . . ?" Someone in the hallway was
pounding on their door. "Wait here," Brett told her,
and went to investigate.

Ashleigh pulled a wrapper around her and followed
him through their bedchamber when she heard Patrick's voice coming from the anteroom beyond:

"Deeply sorry about the hour, Brett, but my damned
rig's sprung a wheel. Your cork-brained stableman
seems to think I need to ask your leave, so's it all right
if I borrow one of yours?"

Brett swore softly under his breath. "My apologies,
Patrick. Must be the new man we took on. Borrow anything you like, and tell the fool I'll have his head if he
ever again questions—wait a minute. Where the devil
are you haring off to at this ungodly—"

"Ravenskeep Hall. Megan's had one of her—look,
I'll explain later. Right now, I've a wife down at your
stables, threatening to horsewhip your mutton-
headed—"

"Patrick," Ashleigh put in anxiously, "does this have
anything to do with . . . uh, with Caitlin? A-and something that was supposed to happen at midnight?"

He gave her a measuring look. "It does," he said
tersely. "Megan's worried—"

"Then, I'm coming, too."

"Ashleigh, are you out of your mind?" Brett looked
at her as if she'd grown horns.

"I'll leave you two to sort it out between you," Patrick

muttered. Turning abruptly, he ran toward the head of the stairs.

"Ashleigh." Brett placed a staying hand on his wife's arm as she started for her dressing room. "Till now, I wasn't aware pregnancy affected a woman's wits."

"I'm as sane as a bishop, Brett Westmont! If it were *your* friend in trouble—"

"Then, prove it to me," he said gently. "Sweetheart, what's this all about?"

She heaved a sigh. "Will you at least allow me to dress while I explain? It will save time if I'm able to convince you I must go, and"—she shrugged—"well, no harm done if you still feel I'm mad to suggest it."

"Fair enough," he said, ushering her gently toward the dressing room with a pat on her bottom.

"There's really no need for you to dress as well," she told him as he followed her. Out of the corner of her eye, Ashleigh noted he was gathering up the apparel he'd discarded earlier—Brett had his own dressing room, but he was too impatient a lover to use it at bedtime. "I mean," she added, smiling to herself, "I could wake one of the grooms to drive me if—"

"Hammer the grooms," he growled. "If you go to Ravenskeep Hall—and I do mean *if*—no one's driving you there but me. Now tell me what the devil's happened to Ravenskeep's bride—and why it's got you and Megan the Bold in such a taking."

Ashleigh gestured at the upholstered divan in her dressing room. "Brett, darling, I think you had better sit down for this . . ."

The first thing Brett noticed when his barouche rounded the final bend in Ravenskeep Hall's long, winding drive was the lights. There were dozens of them, from the lanterns over the stables, to the torches borne by a pair of footmen hurrying across the lawn, to the candlelight gleaming from every window of the house itself. The damned place was lit up like a Vauxhall Gardens fireworks display! "Something's definitely afoot here," he muttered as he slowed his cattle to a trot and guided them round the curve of drive in front.

He hadn't known what to think when Ashleigh began her account in a hushed voice, her tone implying something ominous and dreadful in the offing. When at first she mentioned a "devil's bargain" that his neighbor in Kent had made while back in London, Brett had been perplexed, for the subject seemed utterly mundane. Knowing the reputation Ravenskeep had gained for himself since returning from the Peninsula, he had assumed she was referring to some ill-advised wager or the like. An unfortunate mistake on Ravenskeep's part, but hardly something to inspire dread.

Like himself, Adam Lightfoot had led a less than tame existence as a young buck on the town, but since his return he'd been nothing short of reckless. The man he'd known before the war was rakish and wild, true, but never imprudent or dishonorable; the returning war hero, on the other hand, had seemed determined to wipe out every shred of honor implicit in the military laurels that had been heaped upon him.

In short, Ravenskeep was, in Brett's estimation, eminently capable of having gotten himself in dun territory over gambling debts, or worse. Not that he'd be unique among the *haut ton* in suddenly finding himself with pockets to let, though Brett had felt it rather out of character for a man as intelligent and worldly wise as Ravenskeep.

Then again, there'd been the tragedy of that fatal carriage accident in the spring. Of course, word had it the Ravenskeep marriage had been loveless, the marquis and his marchioness all but strangers to each other; still, it was a common enough occurrence among the upper crust. His wife's demise might have been taken as regrettable, but it was surely nothing to inspire wild grief in her husband.

On the other hand, no one doubted Ravenskeep's love for his son, and the child had been left in a bad way. Not impossible to believe that aspect of the tragedy had unhinged his father, which might account for all manner of "devil's bargains." At that point in Ashleigh's recounting of Caitlin's story, Brett had hardly taken those words literally; rather, he'd left room for any number of interpretations, given the colorful metaphors he thought a callow young Irishwoman might be prone to employ.

At that point, but not after. His wife had soon disabused him of his initial—and quite rational—assumptions. Once Ashleigh began to explain how Caitlin came to be involved, he realized things had quickly passed the bounds of the rational.

God's blood, he could scarcely credit it! Hadn't, until he saw the fear and worry in Ashleigh's eyes. *She* certainly believed it, and Ashleigh was not a woman given to superstition or irrational fantasies. Moreover, there'd been that "miraculous" healing of Andrew Lightfoot's maimed leg to lend credence to what Caitlin had told her and Megan. There'd been nothing for it, then, but to follow the St. Clares here, he thought grimly, as he drew his team to a halt behind the gig Patrick had borrowed.

He was just alighting from the barouche when the front door opened. A middle-aged woman wearing a nightcap over an iron gray braid, and holding a shawl

clutched over her bed gown, stepped out. "Would you
be the physician, sir?" she inquired anxiously.

"Ah, welcome, Your Grace." Ravenskeep's majordomo appeared in the doorway, easing his way past the
woman before Brett could reply. "Sir Patrick said that
you and Her Grace might be coming."

"What's this about a physician?" Ashleigh asked worriedly as her husband helped her from the carriage.

"We've summoned the physician from the village,
Your Grace," said Townsend. "To attend to the marchioness, that is." Unlike the woman in the bed gown,
the majordomo was fully dressed, his manner impecca-
bly correct, but there was grave concern in his eyes.
"Her ladyship is lying abed, unconscious, do you see,
and—"

"Unconscious!" Ashleigh went pale.

The duke curled an arm about her shoulders to steady
her. "Easy, love," he murmured, taking his wife's hand
and giving it a reassuring squeeze. He still wasn't happy
with her being here. According to her physicians, Ashleigh was at least a fortnight away from delivering the
babe, but he had heard of women birthing early as a
result of something greatly oversetting. He had agreed
to bring her to the Hall only because he was certain
that keeping her at home—fretting over possible conse-
quences arising from that hair-raising "devil's bargain"—would have distressed her even more. "Is the
marquis with your mistress?" he asked the majordomo.

"He is, Your Grace. And now, I believe, Sir Patrick
and Lady St. Clare have joined them."

"And is his lordship . . . er, is the marquis well?" Brett
asked carefully. *Is he still alive and whole? Or has he perhaps
sprouted horns and a tail?*

"As to that, Your Grace, I cannot rightly say," Townsend replied as the duke led his wife up the steps. "It

was his lordship who roused the staff shortly after midnight and had me send for the physician." He paused a moment, as if considering whether he should say more; the commanding stare of the duke's intense turquoise eyes decided it, and he went on. "I, er, believe he found her ladyship lying unconscious in her former chambers. His lordship was still there with her when his shouts brought me running from the servants' wing, do you see. I saw him emerge from her door and start down the hallway. He held her ladyship, limp and clearly unconscious, in his arms, and I asked what he would have me do. He called instructions to me as he carried her. Said I was to send the physician to his chambers soon as he arrived. But since then, Your Grace, there has been . . . er, no further communication from his lordship. That is to say, none toward the staff. He—"

"No communication?" Brett questioned impatiently. "What the devil are you saying, man? Is he alive and conscious, or isn't he?"

"He won't speak to any of us, Your Grace, because he spends every minute on his knees!" The outburst came from the woman in the bed gown. "On his knees, praying over his poor lady wife!"

Brett and Ashleigh exchanged pointed glances. Brett couldn't help recalling the emphasis his wife had said Caitlin placed upon Ravenskeep's tragic loss of faith: in particular, his utter inability to pray. *Even if it meant saving his damned soul.* "And who might you be, madam?" he inquired briskly.

"Begging your pardon, Your Grace," she said, pausing to drop a curtsy to him, then another to the duchess. "I am Hodgkins, his lordship's London housekeeper. We were invited by the marquis to come down from town for the wedding, do you see. That is to say, he invited me along with Jepson, his lordship's butler. We had both grown very fond of the Irish Angel—er, I mean her ladyship, the marchioness—and she, of us, if I may say so, Your Grace."

"And do you say the marquis has been praying, Mrs. Hodgkins?" Ashleigh asked anxiously, as Townsend closed the door behind them.

"Indeed, Your Grace. Praying nonstop, poor man . . . er, that is, if I may be allowed to say so, Your Grace."

Brett gave his wife's hand another reassuring squeeze and regarded the servants' worried faces. "Perhaps you had better take us to them," he said.

By the time they approached Ravenskeep's chambers, Brett reconsidered the advisability of allowing Ashleigh to come. The scene in the hallway resembled a wake. A throng of servants—at least, he assumed they were servants, for most were still in their nightclothes—had gathered about the door. Each and every countenance was grave. Some of them were weeping softly, some were praying—he heard the click of rosary beads as a young maid with an Irish accent murmured over them, head bowed—while others simply stood there, wearing long Friday faces.

He turned to the major domo and was about to ask where the St. Clares were, when the crowd parted. A thin, unsmiling man approached from the opposite end of the hallway. He led young Lord Andrew by the hand, then paused and bent to whisper a word in the child's ear. Andrew nodded, thoughtfully but without a hint of the dour expressions of those ranged about him, and they drew near the door.

"Why, it's the duke and duchess!" the child exclaimed when he spied them. "Have you come to wake Mama up, too?" He glanced up at the man who still had him by the hand. "Jepson came to tell me about it, do you see, and we talked about how it was when *I* was the one couldn't wake up, after the bad accident. And I said it was Caitlin woke me—when no one else could, not even the Prince Regent's rude physician— and shouldn't I try to wake her, now she's the one needs help?"

"I see," said the duke, not troubling to hide a smile. *By God, the lad makes sense! It was obvious, first time I saw them together, the Irishwoman adores the child. And he, her, of course. Who better, to try penetrating that senseless state? Ravenskeep may be too irrational, too gripped by emotion, to reach her. I know I'd damned well be half-mad if it were Ashleigh lying there. The boy, on the other hand, seems . . . I don't believe I've ever seen a young child that collected and purposeful in the face of such a crisis. Could be just what's wanted.*

Brett met the eyes of the servant who held the child's hand. "Jepson, is it?"

"Yes, Your Grace," the butler replied, bowing. And after another bow, for Ashleigh: "I beg Your Graces will pardon me if I have overstepped my bounds, but—"

"Not at all," Ashleigh put in. "It's clear *someone* had to inform the child. As a mother, I can appreciate the care you've taken in the matter, Mr. Jepson. Indeed, from what I've heard"—she smiled at Andrew—"you appear to have made an admirable job of it."

"Thank you, Your Grace. I—"

Just then, the door opened, and Patrick St. Clare peered out. "There you are, lad. Come, your father's—" He spied Ashleigh and Brett. "You, too, Ashleigh. Megan's been asking for you." St. Clare flung the door wide, motioned the ducal pair forward, and, smiling, held out a hand for Andrew. The child gave him a quick smile, released the butler's hand, and took Patrick's.

Brett couldn't help smiling as well. His friend's enormous paw of a hand seemed to swallow Andrew's whole. The smile faded as they all started inside, and he threw Patrick a silent query over Ashleigh's head: *What's the story?*

The big man's uncertain shrug was less than satisfying. But the uneasiness in his eyes was worse.

The tableau at bedside drew Ashleigh up short. Since she was first to enter, when she paused to take it in, the other three were forced to halt behind her. She didn't notice. Megan's sister lay on the large tester bed, still as death. She couldn't help recalling Caitlin's rosy complexion, with its charming dusting of freckles across the nose. Now all she noticed was how very pale she was. So terribly pale, the freckles standing out against the unnatural whiteness of her skin like spatters of dried blood.

At the far side of the bed, Megan stood, tall and watchful, as poised and graceful as a cat. Indeed, almost regal in her bearing. With that fiery mane tumbling down her back, she resembled some pagan goddess out of Celtic lore. She was looking down at her sister. Her barely audible murmur—Ashleigh thought she recognized the words as Gaelic—was the only sound in the quiet room. A rosary dangled from Megan's hand— Ashleigh had never known her to carry a rosary—but she didn't appear to be using it. Or perhaps she was, in her own way. Megan had always had a penchant for making her own rules.

Half-kneeling, half-slumped beside his wife on the mattress, Ravenskeep bent over Caitlin's lifeless hand; he clutched it to him, his forehead nearly touching the limp fingers. The marquis's lips appeared to be moving, but Ashleigh was too far away to be sure. In any event, she couldn't apprehend any sounds.

The poor man looked half-dead himself. His hair was wildly disheveled, and a dark shadow of beard covered his jaw. The scar on his face stood out lividly against his tanned skin, which had taken on a grayish cast. He was barefoot and bare-torsoed, a pair of wrinkled, buff-colored breeches his only apparel. He reminded Ashleigh of someone who'd been in a physical fight, as if he'd been dealt several crippling blows. In a way, perhaps he had.

Brett's hands closed about Ashleigh's upper arms, and he urged her gently aside, making way for Ravenskeep's boy. Patrick stepped forward to join them but said nothing; his eyes, like theirs, were trained on the bed. The child went directly to it. There, he stopped for a moment, taking in the pair on the mattress. Then he reached out, and gently touched his father's arm. "Papa, don't be afraid," he said. Softly, but it stopped Megan's stream of Gaelic cold.

Ravensford's head came up with a start. "Andrew . . . ?" He looked at his son as if in a daze.

The boy nodded and again patted his arm. "I came to help Mama wake up."

When his father didn't answer, only stared at him numbly, the child patted his arm yet again. Then Andrew leaned over the mattress—the top of it met him at chest level—and stretched an arm out, until he was able to touch Caitlin's cheek. When he spoke, his child's voice piped loud and clear: "Mama, it's Andrew. I love you, Mama. We all do. We love you, ever so much, and we need you to be awake. Please, Mama . . . won't you wake up?"

Then, in a heartbeat, several things happened at once. A wrenching sob broke from Adam Lightfoot's throat.

Ashleigh gave a startled cry. Brett whipped his gaze from the bed to his wife. She was staring down at her feet. And plucking the skirt of her gown away from her legs. It was soaking wet, and so were the carpet and her shoes.

"Mother o' God, her water's broken!" cried Megan.

"By Heaven, she's *moving*," Patrick thundered. "There—her eyes just opened!"

"Look, Mama—we're all here!" This from Andrew, and he was laughing.

And from the bed, where Caitlin O'Brien Lightfoot used her husband's bare—and none too steady—shoulders to pull herself to a sitting position: "Ach, sure and someone had better fetch the doctor—right quick! Her Grace's wee son's that impatient t' be born!"

Epilogue

The tale of the extraordinary events that happened in Kent one night, in the second decade of the nineteenth century, became a legacy. And by the time the new millennium dawned, nearly two hundred years later, it had begun to take on the aspects of a legend. A story told and retold myriad times through the years. Yet it was passed down among only a select few. Beginning with those who had actually been there, it made its way through generations of their descendants. Some of them, that is, but not all.

Those who could be trusted to keep a secret heard it. The imprudent and loose-tongued did not. Neither did the faint-of-heart. Very young children and old, old grandmothers were spared certain details, lest they prove too unnerving, evoking bad dreams—or worse. In essence, it was only one story, but it varied in the telling. The version that came down depended upon what the original witness had seen, and of witnesses there were several.

Yet the most truncated version came from one who was not a true witness at all. Still, the vicar of Ravenskeep had a part to play in the saga of what had happened to the fifth marquis and his Irish bride. Not a large part, to be sure, since the facts had touched him only marginally. As a man of God, it fell to Mr. Wells to remind those who would listen of a transformation in his patron—a "before and after," as it were.

Wells was not an imaginative man, so perhaps this was a good thing. He could be relied upon to make much of a sinner who saw the light, without speculating too deeply upon the specifics. To Wells, the marquis was simply a man who had found God, perhaps through the inspiration of his young bride. He would begin by citing his patron as a man who had never attended church at all. Until he wed, Wells would go on, when the marquis's became the faith-inspiring voice that led the rest of the congregation in prayer—and continued to do so every Sunday, his wife and children beside him, for as long as he lived.

What that same man of God would have made of the *cause* of that transformation one can only surmise. The church, to be sure, made reference to the devil in its liturgy. In the rite of baptism, for instance, those who witnessed the baptism were asked to "renounce Satan." Suffice it to say that when Adam Lightfoot spoke those words, it never occurred to the good vicar to ask why his hand always reached for his wife's. Or why her voice would rise with his over the rest of the congregation's, until the rafters rung with their solemn renunciation.

* * *

The marquis's servants were marginal witnesses as well, but their impressions were the most far-reaching. The servants' grapevine worked with an efficiency that had no equal. That autumn and for many a season to come, tales of "some right peculiar doings" at Ravenskeep Hall spread well beyond Kent and throughout London as well. Some servants merely amplified what was already known and accepted as fact: The deserving Irish Angel who had healed the marquis's son rose to become his lady. But a few whispered of a passing strange malady that had left her near death on their wedding night, and of how her ladyship called upon those very same powers to heal herself.

Yet an Irish maid named Bridget told a somewhat different tale, though she related it strictly among her own. It was an Irish tale not meant for Sassenach ears, she said. Those who listened nodded sagely and did not doubt. There was a great evil lurking about the Hall the night her mistress nearly died, she told them. But, said Bridget, she could sense that someone had invoked the *Ard Milleadh,* and the High Destroyer had sent the thing on its dark and dirty way. Sure and that someone had to be the young mistress, she firmly attested. For wasn't Lady Ravenskeep the only one there, aside from Bridget herself, who was Irish and could know the words of the Old Tongue?

Bridget also told them she had heard the banshee wailing that night, but from a long way off, to be sure. And again, her listeners would nod. Every one of them knew the banshee only wailed when a life was about to end—an Irish life, sure. But the banshee, too, was banished that night, Bridget told them, though she insisted it was a close call.

* * *

Other versions of the tale belonged to family and close kin of those who had been there. They were never related without a shiver and a cautionary word. And while these accounts were far more accurate and closer to the truth, they were much darker as well. For a long time, Megan and Patrick St. Clare shared what they knew only with each other and then in hushed voices. Even then, it was not until they had reached their own shores, until they had put an ocean between them and the source, that they felt free to discuss the subject at length.

And when their offspring—five strapping sons and then a long-awaited daughter—were finally of an age to hear, they received the story as a sacred trust. "Ye're t' tell no one what we're about t' relate," their mother would begin, "unless ye're dead sure it won't go any further."

"It's a story best kept among ourselves," their father would add. "Among us St. Clares and those you'll wed when the time comes. You may pass it on to your children—but only when they're old enough to know."

" 'Tis a tale o' the divil walkin' among us," Megan always cautioned, "ready t' do his dirty work—and o' someone who had the God-given strength t' fight him. 'Tis a tale o' good and evil, as we should know, for we were there—not at the very start, perhaps, but at least for some of it."

"The part that ended well," Patrick would add, and Megan would make the sign of the cross. And then, only then, would they begin to recite the facts as they knew them.

* * *

Closer to home, the duke and duchess of Ravensford found themselves telling and retelling the story, too. But they almost always related it on the anniversary of its conclusion. A happy conclusion, not only for the principals, but for Ashleigh and Brett as well. For that same night their babe was born—a son, just as Caitlin had said. Yet because the event was so blessed with good fortune, their telling had a peculiar ambivalence to it. Neither the duke nor his wife ever related the strange circumstances surrounding the birth without a shiver. In the end, however, there was always a softening smile.

It wasn't that they made light of what had happened. No one who had seen Caitlin lying in that bed, pale and still as death, could recall it without a shudder. But newborn babes have a way of brightening the lives of those who bring them into being with love, and the infant John Westmont, the future duke, was no exception. True, many years went by before John or his sister Marileigh or the score of orphans who became their adopted siblings learned the truth. Till then, they could only wonder at those mysterious looks that passed between their parents on each occasion of the young heir's birthday.

In later years, when all of them were young adults, it was their friends that sensed something mysterious going on. As when his siblings teasingly called Lord John "the devil's own reject," and John would merrily reply, "Hah—better his reject than the alternative!" Unfortunately for these friends, the source of this banter was destined to remain a mystery. The young Westmonts might tease and joke about it, yet they, too, kept the truth among themselves.

* * *

The truest telling of all belonged, of course, to the principals themselves. No one had a more sober respect and appreciation for the circumstances than Adam and Caitlin Lightfoot. Yet they always shared their story with a measure of joy, even as they recalled the darkness that came before the Light. For them, not a day passed without remembering what had happened—and what had *nearly* happened. Or without some reference to it, beginning only hours after it all ended.

"I was nearly certain I'd lost you," Adam told Caitlin as they lay in each other's arms that night. The night after she had come back to him; after Ashleigh had been delivered of a son; after life at the Hall had slowly begun to return to normal. They were in their big tester bed, sated and replete after making love. *Making love for the first time,* Adam thought, *without a hellish shadow hanging over us. Thank God it's over.*

"Aye, *macushla,* nearly certain but not entirely, thank Heaven," Caitlin replied. "Else ye'd not have kept repeatin' The Lord's Prayer, sure."

"You *heard?*" he asked, rising on an elbow to stare at her. "I thought—"

"That I was senseless and deaf to it?" She reached up and touched his face, lovingly tracing the scar that cut across his high cheekbone. "I was, and then again, I was not. 'Twas like . . . like bein' wrapped in cotton wool . . . with sounds comin' at me through a great enormous barrier. Yet I knew one thing for certain: 'twas yer own dear voice I sensed, *a stór,* and the words were important."

"But it was Andrew's voice woke you," he reminded her.

"Aye, and the moment it did, all that went on before

I awoke fell in place. I could hear yer lovely recital o'
The Lord's Prayer, over and over, as if ye'd just spoken
the words. Sure and ye must have said them a hundred
times. Ach, for a man who niver prayed, ye seem passin'
fond o' that prayer," she teased.

He smiled sheepishly. "It was the only prayer I could
remember."

"Ach, don't ye know anythin', Adam Lightfoot?
Heaven doesn't require memorized words from us,
though the church has them in great supply, sure. But
even the humblest prayers will reach the dear Lord's
ears if they're heartfelt."

"Oh, I realize that now," he said, recalling his heartfelt *Thank God!* Even the archfiend had recognized
those words as true prayer. "But when I saw you lying
there like death itself, my love, I wasn't about to take
any chances. The only words that came to mind were
those I'd learned as a child. Perhaps because my childhood was the last time I'd known how to . . . Caitlin?
Sweetheart, what is it?"

Caitlin had suddenly gone very still. Adam's heart
climbed into his throat. She was staring straight ahead
as if frozen. Though her eyes were open, when he passed
a hand anxiously before her face, she didn't appear to
see it. "Caitlin!" He gave her shoulder a shake. "Caitlin,
for God's sake—talk to me!"

All of a sudden, she shook her head, blinked a couple
of times, and looked at him. Then she gave him a brilliant smile. Adam's relief was audible in the rush of air
expelled from his lungs. "God's my life, I beg of you—
don't *ever* frighten me that way again!" he cried, taking
her hand and giving it a squeeze. "I thought . . . I
thought . . ." He brought her fingers to his lips and
pressed a fervent kiss on them. "What, in God's name,
was that all about?"

Caitlin sighed, and this time her smile was wry. " 'Twas the Sight, *macushla*... I had a vision. And whilst I can try t' take the fright out o' them for ye, I cannot keep meself from havin' them. They just ... happen, *a stór,* and the dreams as well."

Recalling the history of her dreams that he was aware of, Adam shivered. "Sweetheart, if this is something dark and ominous—"

" 'Tis anythin' but," she said, grinning up at him *Thank you, God.* "Then, if it's not too much trouble, minx," he said, kissing her on the nose, "would the Irish Angel care to enlighten her poor ignorant husband?"

"Aye," she said softly. For a moment she gazed dreamily into space, recalling the vision. Or, rather, the stream of visions, for there had been several, one melding into the next, with vivid clarity. Returning her gaze to her husband, she took Adam's hand and placed it on her abdomen.

"I've yer babe growin' inside me, *a stór,*" she told him. "A wee son that'll look just like his da ... and like his brother, Andrew, o' course. A fine, healthy lad who'll pester his big brother no end. Though Andrew will adore him, make no mistake."

"I make no doubt we'll all adore him," Adam murmured, his head spinning.

Caitlin nodded. "We'll name the lad Thomas, after yer own da, and he and the Westmonts' son—John, they'll name him—will become fast friends. The pair o' them will follow Andrew about like a pair o' puppies, thinkin' he hung the moon. And all three will have their hands full when the girls arrive. They'll groan and complain iver so—"

"Wait a moment." Adam held up his hand while he tried to take it all in. He didn't doubt for a second that what she said would come to pass. Still, it was almost too much to absorb. "You were going on about the babe and then . . ." He shook his head as if to clear it. *"What* girls?"

Caitlin laughed. "Ours, *macushla*. Two years after this babe arrives, we'll be blessed with a pair o' twins, both female."

"Twins." Adam could only stare at her in wonder.

"Aye, twin girls, who'll look a great deal like me, and exactly like each ither, except . . ."

"What is it?" he asked, anxious when he saw her hesitate. "What's . . . have you seen something amiss with our daughters? Will they be sickly? Unfortunate? *Tell* me."

"Ach, don't fash yerself, *a stór!* They looked the picture o' health t' me, and happiness shone about them like an aura. 'Tis merely that . . ." Caitlin gave a small sigh. "The lasses will *look* identical, Adam, but there will be one significant distinction between the two. The older lass . . . Catherine, we'll name her . . . after yer ma, will be normal as rain in England. But the younger lass, the twin we'll call Rhianna . . ."

"Caitlin," Adam growled, "if you don't hurry up . . ."

She chuckled and shook her head. "I'm sorry, me love, but there's no help for it. Our younger daughter will have the Sight."

Adam looked as if he had been poleaxed. "Can't you *do* something?" he muttered. He thought of the complications his wife's gift had brought to their lives. True, it had also brought them together. Indeed, it had saved his immortal soul and given him back his life . . . and more, so very, very much more. Yet somehow it didn't seem cricket for a tiny, innocent babe—his own precious daughter—to be saddled with such a weighty thing.

Caitlin shook her head, but she was grinning. "Ye

should know by now, me darlin', that no amount o' human effort can wish the gift away. But not t' worry, *macushla*. 'Twill niver plague us in any way near what mine did. You and I, as well as her sister and their brothers . . . we'll all be free o' care where Rhianna's Sight is concerned.''

''Well, that's a relief,'' he said. Then he caught the twinkle in his wife's eye. ''All right, out with it. There's something you haven't told me.''

''Aye,'' she replied, chuckling. ''As I said, her family's safe enough from the portents in her visions and dreams, though she'll vex us with them a tad, on occasion. But 'tis our young neighbor she'll lead on a merry chase, and no mistake.''

''Our young neighbor?''

Caitlin nodded. ''Ashleigh and Brett's wee son, the babe just born. Our Rhianna, d'ye see, will drive the poor lad daft before he makes her his future duchess!''

Adam blinked and gazed at her in astonishment for several seconds. Then his shoulders shook, and he began to chuckle. The chuckles quickly mounted, soon breaking into all-out laughter. Caitlin's mirth merged with his. Their laughter rang out loud and clear, echoing throughout the house. Just as it would echo, again and again, through the long years of their lives.

That was the real portent of things to come, the truest one of all.